Mrs Gregg -

" ' SELL A THOUSAND MAY AT ONE-FIFTY,' VOCIFERATED THE
BEAR BROKER "

THE PIT: The Epic of the Wheat ✄ A DEAL IN WHEAT

AND OTHER STORIES OF THE NEW AND OLD WEST
BY
Frank Norris

NEW YORK P. F. COLLIER & SON *PUBLISHERS*

Published February, 1903

DEDICATED TO MY BROTHER

Charles Tilman Norris

IN MEMORY OF CERTAIN LAMENTABLE TALES OF THE
ROUND (DINING-ROOM) TABLE HEROES; OF THE EPIC
OF THE PEWTER PLATOONS, AND THE ROMANCE-CYCLE
OF "*GASTON LE FOX*," WHICH WE INVENTED, MAINTAINED,
AND FOUND MARVELOUS AT A TIME WHEN WE BOTH
WERE BOYS

PRINCIPAL CHARACTERS IN THE NOVEL

CURTIS JADWIN, capitalist and speculator
SHELDON CORTHELL, an artist
LANDRY COURT, broker's clerk
SAMUEL GRETRY, a broker
CHARLES CRESSLER, a dealer in grain
MRS. CRESSLER, his wife
LAURA DEARBORN, *protégée* of Mrs. Cressler
PAGE DEARBORN, her sister
MRS. EMILY WESSELS, aunt of Laura and Page

The Trilogy of The Epic of the Wheat includes the following novels:

THE OCTOPUS, *a Story of California.*
THE PIT, *A Story of Chicago.*
THE WOLF, *a Story of Europe.*

These novels, while forming a series, will be in no way connected with each other save only in their relation to (1) the production, (2) the distribution, (3) the consumption of American wheat. When complete, they will form the story of a crop of wheat from the time of its sowing as seed in California to the time of its consumption as bread in a village of Western Europe.

The first novel, "The Octopus," deals with the war between the wheat-grower and the Railroad Trust; the second, "The Pit," is the fictitious narrative of a "deal" in the Chicago wheat pit; while the third, "The Wolf," will probably have for its pivotal episode the relieving of a famine in an Old World community.

The author's most sincere thanks for assistance rendered in the preparation of the following novel are due to Mr. G. D. Moulson of New York, whose unwearied patience and untiring kindness helped him to the better understanding of the technical difficulties of a very complicated subject. And more especially he herewith acknowledges his unmeasured obligation and gratitude to Her Who Helped the Most of All.   F. N.

NEW YORK,
June 4, 1901.

CONTENTS

THE PIT

A STORY OF CHICAGO

A DEAL IN WHEAT

AND OTHER STORIES OF THE NEW AND OLD WEST

LIST OF ILLUSTRATIONS

THE PIT

I

AT eight o'clock, in the inner vestibule of the Auditorium Theatre by the window of the box office, Laura Dearborn, her younger sister Page, and their aunt—Aunt Wess'—were still waiting for the rest of the theatre-party to appear. A great, slow-moving press of men and women in evening dress filled the vestibule from one wall to another. A confused murmur of talk and the shuffling of many feet arose on all sides, while from time to time, when the outside and inside doors of the entrance chanced to be opened simultaneously, a sudden draught of air gushed in, damp, glacial, and edged with the penetrating keenness of a Chicago evening at the end of February.

The Italian Grand Opera Company gave one of the most popular pieces of its repertoire on that particular night, and the Cresslers had invited the two sisters and their aunt to share their box with them. It had been arranged that the party should assemble in the Auditorium vestibule at a quarter of eight, but by now the quarter was gone and the Cresslers still failed to arrive.

"I don't see," murmured Laura anxiously for the last time, "what can be keeping them. Are you sure, Page, that Mrs. Cressler meant here—inside?"

She was a tall young girl of about twenty-two or three, holding herself erect and with fine dignity. Even beneath the opera cloak it was easy to infer that her neck and shoulders were beautiful. Her almost extreme slenderness was, however, her characteristic; the curves of her figure, the contour of her shoulders, the swell of hip and breast were all low; from head to foot one could discover no pronounced salience. Yet there was no trace, no suggestion of angularity. She was slender as a willow shoot is slender—and equally graceful, equally erect.

Next to this charming tenuity, perhaps her paleness was her

most noticeable trait. But it was not a paleness of lack of color. Laura Dearborn's pallor was in itself a color. It was a tint rather than a shade like ivory; a warm white, blending into an exquisite, delicate brownness toward the throat. Set in the middle of this paleness of brow and cheek, her deep brown eyes glowed lambent and intense. They were not large, but in some indefinable way they were important. It was very natural to speak of her eyes, and in speaking to her, her friends always found that they must look squarely into their pupils. And all this beauty of pallid face and brown eyes was crowned by, and sharply contrasted with, the intense blackness of her hair, abundant, thick, extremely heavy, continually coruscating with sombre, murky reflections, tragic, in a sense vaguely portentous—the coiffure of a heroine of romance, doomed to dark crises.

On this occasion at the side of the topmost coil a white aigrette scintillated and trembled with her every movement. She was unquestionably beautiful. Her mouth was a little large, the lips firm set, and one would not have expected that she would smile easily; in fact, the general expression of her face was rather serious.

"Perhaps," continued Laura, "they would look for us outside." But Page shook her head. She was five years younger than Laura, just turned seventeen. Her hair, dressed high for the first time this night, was brown. But Page's beauty was no less marked than her sister's. The seriousness of her expression, however, was more noticeable. At times it amounted to undeniable gravity. She was straight, and her figure, all immature as yet, exhibited hardly any softer outlines than that of a boy.

"No, no," she said, in answer to Laura's question. "They would come in here; they wouldn't wait outside—not on such a cold night as this. Don't you think so, Aunt Wess'?"

But Mrs. Wessels, a lean, middle-aged little lady, with a flat pointed nose, had no suggestions to offer. She disengaged herself from any responsibility in the situation and, while waiting, found a vague amusement in counting the number of people who filtered in single file through the wicket where the tickets were presented. A great, stout gentleman in evening dress, perspiring, his cravat limp, stood here, tearing the checks from the tickets, and without ceasing, maintaining a continuous outcry that dominated the murmur of the throng:

"Have your tickets ready, please! Have your tickets ready."

"Such a crowd," murmured Page. "Did you ever see—and every one you ever knew or heard of. And such toilettes!"

With every instant the number of people increased; progress became impossible, except an inch at a time. The women were, almost without exception, in light-colored gowns, white, pale blue, Nile green, and pink, while over these costumes were thrown opera cloaks and capes of astonishing complexity and elaborateness. Nearly all were bare-headed, and nearly all wore aigrettes; a score of these, a hundred of them, nodded and vibrated with an incessant agitation over the heads of the crowd and flashed like mica flakes as the wearers moved. Everywhere the eye was arrested by the luxury of stuffs, the brilliance and delicacy of fabrics, laces as white and soft as froth, crisp, shining silks, suave satins, heavy gleaming velvets, and brocades and plushes, nearly all of them white—violently so—dazzling and splendid under the blaze of the electrics. The gentlemen, in long, black overcoats, and satin mufflers, and opera hats; their hands under the elbows of their womenfolk, urged or guided them forward, distressed, preoccupied, adjuring their parties to keep together; in their white-gloved fingers they held their tickets ready. For all the icy blasts that burst occasionally through the storm doors, the vestibule was uncomfortably warm, and into this steam-heated atmosphere a multitude of heavy odors exhaled—the scent of crushed flowers, of perfume, of sachet, and even—occasionally—the strong smell of damp sealskin.

Outside it was bitterly cold. All day a freezing wind had blown from off the Lake, and since five in the afternoon a fine powder of snow had been falling. The coachmen on the boxes of the carriages that succeeded one another in an interminable line before the entrance of the theatre, were swathed to the eyes in furs. The spume and froth froze on the bits of the horses, and the carriage wheels crunching through the dry, frozen snow gave off a shrill staccato whine. Yet for all this, a crowd had collected about the awning on the sidewalk, and even upon the opposite side of the street, peeping and peering from behind the broad shoulders of policemen—a crowd of miserables, shivering in rags and tattered comforters, who found, nevertheless, an unexplainable satisfaction in watching this prolonged defile of millionaires.

So great was the concourse of teams, that two blocks distant from the theatre they were obliged to fall into line, advancing only at intervals, and from door to door of the carriages thus immobilized ran a score of young men, their arms encumbered with pamphlets, shouting: "Score books, score books and librettos; score books with photographs of all the artists."

However, in the vestibule the press was thinning out. It was understood that the overture had begun. Other people who were waiting like Laura and her sister had been joined by their friends and had gone inside. Laura, for whom this opera night had been an event, a thing desired and anticipated with all the eagerness of a girl who had lived for twenty-two years in a second-class town of central Massachusetts, was in great distress. She had never seen grand opera, she would not have missed a note, and now she was in a fair way to lose the whole overture.

"Oh, dear," she cried. "Isn't it too bad. I can't imagine why they don't come."

Page, more metropolitan, her keenness of appreciation a little lost by two years of city life and fashionable schooling, tried to reassure her.

"You won't lose much," she said. "The air of the overture is repeated in the first act—I've heard it once before."

"If we even see the first act," moaned Laura. She scanned the faces of the late comers anxiously. Nobody seemed to mind being late. Even some of the other people who were waiting chatted calmly among themselves. Directly behind them two men, their faces close together, elaborated an interminable conversation, of which from time to time they could overhear a phrase or two.

"—and I guess he'll do well if he settles for thirty cents on the dollar. I tell you, dear boy, it was a *smash!*"

"—Never should have tried to swing a corner. The short interest was too small and the visible supply was too great."

Page nudged her sister and whispered: "That's the Helmick failure they're talking about, those men. Landry Court told me all about it. Mr. Helmick had a corner in corn, and he failed to-day, or will fail soon, or something."

But Laura, preoccupied with looking for the Cresslers, hardly listened. Aunt Wess', whose count was confused by all these figures murmured just behind her, began over again, her lips silently forming the words, "sixty-one, sixty-two, and two is sixty-four." Behind them the voice continued:

"They say Porteous will peg the market at twenty-six."

"Well, he ought to. Corn is worth that."

"—Never saw such a call for margins in my life. Some of the houses called eight cents."

Page turned to Mrs. Wessels: "By the way, Aunt Wess'; look at that man there by the box office window, the one with his back toward us, the one with his hands in his overcoat pockets. Isn't that Mr. Jadwin? The gentleman we are going to meet to-night. See who I mean?"

"Who? Mr. Jadwin? I don't know. I don't know, child. I never saw him, you know."

"Well, I think it is he," continued Page. "He was to be with our party to-night. I heard Mrs. Cressler say she would ask him. That's Mr. Jadwin, I'm sure. He's waiting for them, too."

"Oh, then ask him about it, Page," exclaimed Laura. "We're missing everything."

But Page shook her head:

"I only met him once, ages ago; he wouldn't know me. It was at the Cresslers', and we just said 'How do you do.' And then, maybe, it isn't Mr. Jadwin."

"Oh, I wouldn't bother, girls," said Mrs. Wessels. "It's all right. They'll be here in a minute. *I* don't believe the curtain has gone up yet."

But the man of whom they spoke turned around at the moment and cast a glance about the vestibule. They saw a gentleman of an indeterminate age—judged by his face he might as well have been forty as thirty-five. A heavy mustache touched with gray covered his lips. The eyes were twinkling and good-tempered. Between his teeth he held an unlighted cigar.

"It *is* Mr. Jadwin," murmured Page, looking quickly away. "But he don't recognize me."

Laura also averted her eyes.

"Well, why not go right up to him and introduce yourself, or recall yourself to him?" she hazarded.

"Oh, Laura, I *couldn't*," gasped Page. "I wouldn't for worlds."

"Couldn't she, Aunt Wess'?" appealed Laura. "Wouldn't it be all right?"

But Mrs. Wessels, ignoring forms and customs, was helpless. Again she withdrew from any responsibility in the matter.

"I don't know anything about it," she answered. "But Page oughtn't to be bold."

"Oh, bother; it isn't that," protested Page. "But it's just because—I don't know, I don't want to—Laura, I should just *die*," she exclaimed with abrupt irrelevance, "and besides, how would that help any?" she added.

"Well, we're just going to miss it *all*," declared Laura decisively. There were actual tears in her eyes. "And I had looked forward to it so."

"Well," hazarded Aunt Wess', "you girls can do just as you please. Only I wouldn't be bold."

"Well, would it be bold if Page, or if—if I were to speak to him. We're going to meet him anyways in just a few minutes."

"Better wait, hadn't you, Laura," said Aunt Wess', "and see. Maybe he'll come up and speak to us."

"Oh, as if!" contradicted Laura. "He don't know us—just as Page says. And if he did, he wouldn't. He wouldn't think it polite."

"Then I guess, girlie, it wouldn't be polite for you."

"I think it would," she answered. "I think it would be a woman's place. If he's a gentleman, he would feel that he just *couldn't* speak first. I'm going to do it," she announced suddenly.

"Just as you think best, Laura," said her aunt.

But, nevertheless, Laura did not move, and another five minutes went by.

Page took advantage of the interval to tell Laura about Jadwin. He was very rich, but a bachelor, and had made his money in Chicago real estate. Some of his holdings in the business quarter of the city were enormous; Landry Court had told her about him. Jadwin, unlike Mr. Cressler, was not opposed to speculation. Though not a member of the Board of Trade, he nevertheless at very long intervals took part in a "deal" in wheat, or corn, or provisions. He believed that all corners were doomed to failure, however, and had predicted Helmick's collapse six months ago. He had influence, was well known to all Chicago people, what he said carried weight, financiers consulted him, promoters sought his friendship, his name on the board of directors of a company was an all-sufficing indorsement; in a word, a "strong" man.

"I can't understand," exclaimed Laura, distrait, referring to the delay on the part of the Cresslers. "This was the night, and this was the place, and it is long past the time. We could telephone to the house, you know," she said, struck with an idea, "and see if they've started, or what has happened."

"I don't know—I don't know," murmured Mrs. Wessels vaguely. No one seemed ready to act upon Laura's suggestion, and again the minutes passed.

"I'm going," declared Laura again, looking at the other two, as if to demand what they had to say against the idea.

"I just couldn't," declared Page flatly.

"Well," continued Laura, "I'll wait just three minutes more, and then if the Cresslers are not here I will speak to him. It seems to me to be perfectly natural, and not at all bold."

She waited three minutes, and the Cresslers still failing to appear, temporized yet further, for the twentieth time repeating:

"I don't see—I can't understand."

Then, abruptly drawing her cape about her, she crossed the vestibule and came up to Jadwin.

As she approached, she saw him catch her eye. Then, as he appeared to understand that this young woman was about to speak to him, she noticed an expression of suspicion, almost of distrust, come into his face. No doubt he knew nothing of this other party who were to join the Cresslers in the vestibule. Why should this girl speak to him? Something had gone wrong, and the instinct of the man, no longer very young, to keep out of strange young women's troubles betrayed itself in the uneasy glance that he shot at her from under his heavy eyebrows. But the look faded as quickly as it had come. Laura guessed that he had decided that in such a place as this he need have no suspicions. He took the cigar from his mouth, and she, immensely relieved, realized that she had to do with a man who was a gentleman. Full of trepidation as she had been in crossing the vestibule, she was quite mistress of herself when the instant came for her to speak, and it was in a steady voice and without embarrassment that she said:

"I beg your pardon, but I believe this is Mr. Jadwin."

He took off his hat, evidently a little nonplussed that she should know his name, and by now she was ready even to browbeat him a little should it be necessary.

"Yes, yes," he answered, now much more confused than she, "my name is Jadwin."

"I believe," continued Laura steadily, "we were all to be in the same party to-night with the Cresslers. But they don't seem to come, and we—my sister and my aunt and I—don't know what to do."

She saw that he was embarrassed, convinced, and the knowledge that she controlled the little situation, that she could command him, restored her all her equanimity.

"My name is Miss Dearborn," she continued. "I believe you know my sister Page."

By some trick of manner she managed to convey to him the

impression that if he did not know her sister Page, that if for one instant he should deem her to be bold, he would offer a mortal affront. She had not yet forgiven him that stare of suspicion when first their eyes had met; he should pay her for that yet.

"Miss Page—your sister—Miss Page Dearborn? Certainly I know her," he answered. "And you have been waiting, too? What a pity!" And he permitted himself the awkwardness of adding: "I did not know that you were to be of our party."

"No," returned Laura upon the instant, "I did not know you were to be one of us to-night—until Page told me." She accented the pronouns a little, but it was enough for him to know that he had been rebuked. How, he could not just say; and for what it was impossible for him at the moment to determine; and she could see that he began to experience a certain distress, was beating a retreat, was ceding place to her. Who was she, then, this tall and pretty young woman, with the serious, unsmiling face, who was so perfectly at ease, and who hustled him about and made him feel as though he were to blame for the Cresslers' non-appearance; as though it was his fault that she must wait in the draughty vestibule. She had a great air with her; how had he offended her? If he had introduced himself to her, had forced himself upon her, she could not be more lofty, more reserved.

"I thought perhaps you might telephone," she observed.

"They haven't a telephone, unfortunately," he answered.

"Oh!"

This was quite the last slight, the Cresslers had not a telephone! He was to blame for that, too, it seemed. At his wits' end, he entertained for an instant the notion of dashing out into the street in a search for a messenger boy, who would take a note to Cressler and set him right again; and his agitation was not allayed when Laura, in frigid tones, declared:

"It seems to me that something might be done."

"I don't know," he replied helplessly. "I guess there's nothing to be done but just wait. They are sure to be along."

In the background, Page and Mrs. Wessels had watched the interview, and had guessed that Laura was none too gracious. Always anxious that her sister should make a good impression, the little girl was now in great distress.

"Laura is putting on her 'grand manner,'" she lamented. "I just know how she's talking. The man will hate the very sound of her name all the rest of his life." Then all at once, she uttered a joyful exclamation: "At last, at last," she cried, "and about time, too!"

The Cresslers and the rest of the party—two young men—had appeared, and Page and her aunt came up just in time to hear Mrs. Cressler—a fine old lady, in a wonderful ermine-trimmed cape, whose hair was powdered—exclaim at the top of her voice, as if the mere declaration of the fact was final, absolutely the last word upon the subject, "The bridge was turned!"

The Cresslers lived on the North Side. The incident seemed to be closed with the abruptness of a slammed door.

Page and Aunt Wess' were introduced to Jadwin, who was particular to announce that he remembered the young girl perfectly. The two young men were already acquainted with the Dearborn sisters and Mrs. Wessels. Page and Laura knew one of them well enough to address him familiarly by his Christian name.

This was Landry Court, a young fellow just turned twenty-three, who was "connected with" the staff of the great brokerage firm of Gretry, Converse & Co. He was astonishingly good-looking, small-made, wiry, alert, nervous, debonair, with blond hair and dark eyes that snapped like a terrier's. He made friends almost at first sight, and was one of those fortunate few who were favored equally of men and women. The healthiness of his eye and skin persuaded to a belief in the healthiness of his mind; and, in fact, Landry was as clean without as within. He was frank, open-hearted, full of fine sentiments and exaltations and enthusiasms. Until he was eighteen he had cherished an ambition to become the President of the United States.

"Yes, yes," he said to Laura, "the bridge was turned. It was an imposition. We had to wait while they let three tows through. I think two at a time is as much as is legal. And we had to wait for three. Yes, sir; three, think of that! I shall look into that to-morrow. Yes, sir; don't you be afraid of that. I'll look into it." He nodded his head with profound seriousness.

"Well," announced Mr. Cressler, marshaling the party, "shall we go in? I'm afraid, Laura, we've missed the overture."

Smiling, she shrugged her shoulders, while they moved to the wicket, as if to say that it could not be helped now.

Cressler, tall, lean, bearded, and stoop-shouldered, belonging to the same physical type that includes Lincoln—the type of the Middle West—was almost a second father to the parentless Dearborn girls. In Massachusetts, thirty years before this time, he had been a farmer, and the miller Dearborn used to grind his grain regularly. The two had been boys together, and had always remained fast friends, almost brothers. Then, in the years just before the War, had come the great movement westward, and Cressler had been one of those to leave an "abandoned" New England farm behind him, and with his family emigrate toward the Mississippi. He had come to Sangamon County in Illinois. For a time he tried wheat-raising, until the War, which skied the prices of all foodstuffs, had made him—for those days—a rich man. Giving up farming, he came to live in Chicago, bought a seat on the Board of Trade, and in a few years was a millionaire. At the time of the Turco-Russian War he and two Milwaukee men had succeeded in cornering all the visible supply of spring wheat. At the end of the thirtieth day of the corner the clique figured out its profits at close upon a million; a week later it looked like a million and a half. Then the three lost their heads; they held the corner just a fraction of a month too long, and when the time came that the three were forced to take profits, they found that they were unable to close out their immense holdings without breaking the price. In two days wheat that they had held at a dollar and ten cents collapsed to sixty. The two Milwaukee men were ruined, and two-thirds of Cressler's immense fortune vanished like a whiff of smoke.

But he had learned his lesson. Never since then had he speculated. Though keeping his seat on the Board, he had confined himself to commission trading, uninfluenced by fluctuations in the market. And he was never wearied of protesting against the evil and the danger of trading in margins. Speculation he abhorred as the small-pox, believing it to be impossible to corner grain by any means or under any circumstances. He was accustomed to say: "It can't be done; first, for the reason that there is a great harvest of wheat somewhere in the world for every month in the year; and, second, because the smart man who runs the corner has every other smart man in the world against him. And, besides, it's wrong; the world's food should not be at the mercy of the Chicago wheat pit."

As the party filed in through the wicket, the other young man who had come with Landry Court managed to place himself next to Laura. Meeting her eyes, he murmured:

"Ah, you did not wear them after all. My poor little flowers."

But she showed him a single American Beauty, pinned to the shoulder of her gown beneath her cape.

"Yes, Mr. Corthell," she answered, "one. I tried to select the prettiest, and I think I succeeded—don't you? It was hard to choose."

"Since you have worn it, it *is* the prettiest," he answered.

He was a slightly built man of about twenty-eight or thirty; dark, wearing a small, pointed beard, and a mustache that he brushed away from his lips like a Frenchman. By profession he was an artist, devoting himself more especially to the designing of stained windows. In this, his talent was indisputable. But he was by no means dependent upon his profession for a living, his parents—long since dead—having left him to the enjoyment of a very considerable fortune. He had a beautiful studio in the Fine Arts Building, where he held receptions once every two months, or whenever he had a fine piece of glass to expose. He had traveled, read, studied, occasionally written, and in matters pertaining to the coloring and fusing of glass was cited as an authority. He was one of the directors of the new Art Gallery that had taken the place of the old Exposition Building on the Lake Front.

Laura had known him for some little time. On the occasion of her two previous visits to Page he had found means to see her two or three times each week. Once, even, he had asked her to marry him, but she, deep in her studies at the time, consumed with vague ambitions to be a great actress of Shakespearian rôles, had told him she could care for nothing but her art. He had smiled and said that he could wait, and, strangely enough, their relations had resumed again upon the former footing. Even after she had gone away they had corresponded regularly, and he had made and sent her a tiny window—a veritable jewel—illustrative of a scene from "Twelfth Night."

In the foyer, as the gentlemen were checking their coats, Laura overheard Jadwin say to Mr. Cressler:

"Well, how about Helmick?"

The other made an impatient movement of his shoulders.

"Ask *me*, what was the fool thinking of—a corner! Pshaw!"

There were one or two other men about, making their over-coats and opera hats into neat bundles preparatory to checking them; and instantly there was a flash of a half-dozen eyes in the direction of the two men. Evidently the collapse of the Helmick deal was in the air. All the city seemed interested.

But from behind the heavy curtains that draped the entrance to the theatre proper came a muffled burst of music, followed by a long salvo of applause. Laura's cheeks flamed with impatience,

she hurried after Mrs. Cressler; Corthell drew the curtains for her
to pass, and she entered.

Inside it was dark, and a prolonged puff of hot air, thick with
the mingled odors of flowers, perfume, upholstery, and gas, envel-
oped her upon the instant. It was the unmistakable, unforgetable,
entrancing aroma of the theatre, that she had known only too seldom, but that in a second set her heart galloping.

Every available space seemed to be occupied. Men, even women,
were standing up, compacted into a suffocating pressure, and for the
moment everybody was applauding vigorously. On all sides Laura
heard:

"Bravo!"

"Good, good!"

"Very well done!"

"Encore! Encore!"

Between the people's heads and below the low dip of the overhanging balcony—a brilliant glare in the surrounding darkness—
she caught a glimpse of the stage. It was set for a garden; at the
back and in the distance a château; on the left a bower, and on the
right a pavilion. Before the footlights, a famous contralto, dressed
as a boy, was bowing to the audience, her arms full of flowers.

"Too bad," whispered Corthell to Laura, as they followed the
others down the side-aisle to the box. "Too bad, this is the second
act already; you've missed the whole first act—and this song. She'll
sing it over again, though, just for you, if I have to lead the applause
myself. I particularly wanted you to hear that."

Once in the box, the party found itself a little crowded, and
Jadwin and Cressler were obliged to stand, in order to see the
stage. Although they all spoke in whispers, their arrival was the
signal for certain murmurs of "Sh! Sh!" Mrs. Cressler made
Laura occupy the front seat. Jadwin took her cloak from her, and
she settled herself in her chair and looked about her. She could
see but little of the house or audience. All the lights were lowered; only through the gloom the swaying of a multitude of fans,
pale colored, like night-moths balancing in the twilight, defined
itself.

But soon she turned toward the stage. The applause died away,
and the contralto once more sang the aria. The melody was simple,
the tempo easily followed; it was not a very high order of music.
But to Laura it was nothing short of a revelation.

She sat spellbound, her hands clasped tight, her every faculty of attention at its highest pitch. It was wonderful, such music as that; wonderful, such a voice; wonderful, such orchestration; wonderful, such exaltation inspired by mere beauty of sound. Never, never was this night to be forgotten, this her first night of Grand Opera. All this excitement, this world of perfume, of flowers, of exquisite costumes, of beautiful women, of fine, brave men. She looked back with immense pity to the narrow little life of her native town she had just left forever, the restricted horizon, the petty round of petty duties, the rare and barren pleasures—the library, the festival, the few concerts, the trivial plays. How easy it was to be good and noble when music such as this had become a part of one's life; how desirable was wealth when it could make possible such exquisite happiness as hers of the moment. Nobility, purity, courage, sacrifice seemed much more worth while now than a few moments ago. All things not positively unworthy became heroic, all things and all men. Landry Court was a young chevalier, pure as Galahad. Corthell was a beautiful artist-priest of the early Renaissance. Even Jadwin was a merchant prince, a great financial captain. And she herself—ah, she did not know; she dreamed of another Laura, a better, gentler, more beautiful Laura, whom everybody loved dearly and tenderly, and who loved everybody, and who should die beautifully, gently, in some garden far away—die because of a great love—beautifully, gently in the midst of flowers, die of a broken heart, and all the world should be sorry for her, and would weep over her when they found her dead and beautiful in her garden, amid the flowers and the birds, in some far-off place, where it was always early morning and where there was soft music. And she was so sorry for herself, and so hurt with the sheer strength of her longing to be good and true, and noble and womanly, that as she sat in the front of the Cresslers' box on that marvelous evening, the tears ran down her cheeks again and again, and dropped upon her tight-shut, white-gloved fingers.

But the contralto had disappeared, and in her place the tenor held the stage—a stout, short young man in red plush doublet and gray silk tights. His chin advanced, an arm extended, one hand pressed to his breast, he apostrophized the pavilion that now and then swayed a little in the draught from the wings.

The aria was received with furor; thrice he was obliged to repeat it. Even Corthell, who was critical to extremes, approved, nodding his head. Laura and Page clapped their hands till the very last. But Landry Court, to create an impression, assumed a certain disaffection.

"He's not in voice to-night. Too bad. You should have heard him Friday in 'Aida.'"

The opera continued. The great soprano, the prima donna, appeared and delivered herself of a song for which she was famous with astonishing éclat. Then in a little while the stage grew dark, the orchestration lapsed to a murmur, and the tenor and the soprano re-entered. He clasped her in his arms and sang a half-dozen bars, then holding her hand, one arm still about her waist, withdrew from her gradually, till she occupied the front centre of the stage. He assumed an attitude of adoration and wonderment, his eyes uplifted as if entranced, and she, very softly, to the accompaniment of the sustained, dreamy chords of the orchestra, began her solo.

Laura shut her eyes. Never had she felt so soothed, so cradled and lulled and languid. Ah, to love like that! To love and be loved. There was no such love as that to-day. She wished that she could loose her clasp upon the sordid, material modern life that, perforce, she must hold to, she knew not why, and drift, drift off into the past, far away, through rose-colored mists and diaphanous veils, or resign herself, reclining in a silver skiff drawn by swans, to the gentle current of some smooth-flowing river that ran on forever and forever.

But a discordant element developed. Close by—the lights were so low she could not tell where—a conversation, kept up in low whispers, began by degrees to intrude itself upon her attention. Try as she would, she could not shut it out, and now, as the music died away fainter and fainter, till voice and orchestra blended together in a single, barely audible murmur, vibrating with emotion, with romance, and with sentiment, she heard, in a hoarse, masculine whisper, the words:

"The shortage is a million bushels at the very least. Two hundred carloads were to arrive from Milwaukee last night—"

She made a little gesture of despair, turning her head for an instant, searching the gloom about her. But she could see no one not interested in the stage. Why could not men leave their business outside, why must the jar of commerce spoil all the harmony of this moment?

However, all sounds were drowned suddenly in a long burst of applause. The tenor and soprano bowed and smiled across the footlights. The soprano vanished, only to reappear on the balcony of the pavilion, and while she declared that the stars and the night-bird together sang "He loves thee," the voices close at hand continued:

"—one hundred and six carloads—"

"—paralyzed the bulls—"

"—fifty thousand dollars—"

Then all at once the lights went up. The act was over.

Laura seemed only to come to herself some five minutes later. She and Corthell were out in the foyer behind the boxes. Everybody was promenading. The air was filled with the staccato chatter of a multitude of women. But she herself seemed far away —she and Sheldon Corthell. His face, dark, romantic, with the silky beard and eloquent eyes, appeared to be all she cared to see, while his low voice, that spoke close to her ear, was in a way a mere continuation of the melody of the duet just finished.

Instinctively she knew what he was about to say, for what he was trying to prepare her. She felt, too, that he had not expected to talk thus to her to-night. She knew that he loved her, that inevitably, sooner or later, they must return to a subject that for long had been excluded from their conversations, but it was to have been when they were alone, remote, secluded, not in the midst of a crowd, brilliant electrics dazzling their eyes, the humming of the talk of hundreds assaulting their ears. But it seemed as if these important things came of themselves, independent of time and place, like birth and death. There was nothing to do but to accept the situation, and it was without surprise that at last, from out the murmur of Corthell's talk, she was suddenly conscious of the words:

"So that it is hardly necessary, is it, to tell you once more that I love you?"

She drew a long breath.

"I know. I know you love me."

They had sat down on a divan, at one end of the promenade; and Corthell, skilful enough in the little arts of the drawing-room, made it appear as though they talked of commonplaces; as for Laura, exalted, all but hypnotized with this marvelous evening, she hardly cared; she would not even stoop to maintain appearances.

"Yes, yes," she said; "I know you love me."

"And is that all you can say?" he urged. "Does it mean nothing to you that you are everything to me?"

She was coming a little to herself again. Love was, after all,

sweeter in the actual—even in this crowded foyer, in this atmosphere of silk and jewels, in this show-place of a great city's society
—than in a mystic garden of some romantic dreamland. She felt
herself a woman again, modern, vital, and no longer a maiden of a
legend of chivalry.

"Nothing to me?" she answered. "I don't know. I should
rather have you love me than—not."

"Let me love you then for always," he went on. "You know
what I mean. We have understood each other from the very first.
Plainly, and very simply, I love you with all my heart. You know
now that I speak the truth, you know that you can trust me. I shall
not ask you to share your life with mine. I ask you for the great
happiness"—he raised his head sharply, suddenly proud—"the great
honor of the opportunity of giving you all that I have of good. God
give me humility, but that is much since I have known you. If I
were a better man because of myself, I would not presume to speak
of it, but if I am in anything less selfish, if I am more loyal, if I am
stronger, or braver, it is only something of you that has become a
part of me, and made me to be born again. So when I offer myself
to you, I am only bringing back to you the gift you gave me for a
little while. I have tried to keep it for you, to keep it bright and
sacred and unspotted. It is yours again now if you will have it."

There was a long pause; a group of men in opera hats and
white gloves came up the stairway close at hand. The tide of
promenaders set toward the entrances of the theatre. A little electric bell shrilled a note of warning.

Laura looked up at length, and as their glances met, he saw
that there were tears in her eyes. This declaration of his love for
her was the last touch to the greatest exhilaration of happiness she
had ever known. Ah, yes, she was loved, just as that young girl
of the opera had been loved. For this one evening, at least, the
beauty of life was unmarred, and no cruel word of hers should spoil
it. The world was beautiful. All people were good and noble and
true. To-morrow, with the material round of duties and petty responsibilities and cold, calm reason, was far, far away. Suddenly
she turned to him, surrendering to the impulse, forgetful of consequences.

"Oh, I am glad, glad," she cried, "glad that you love me!"

But before Corthell could say anything more Landry Court
and Page came up.

"We've been looking for you," said the young girl quietly. Page was displeased. She took herself and her sister—in fact, the whole scheme of existence—with extraordinary seriousness. She had no sense of humor. She was not tolerant; her ideas of propriety and the amenities were as immutable as the fixed stars. A fine way for Laura to act, getting off into corners with Sheldon Corthell. It would take less than that to make talk. If she had no sense of her obligations to Mrs. Cressler, at least she ought to think of the looks of things.

"They're beginning again," she said solemnly. "I should think you'd feel as though you had missed about enough of this opera."

They returned to the box. The rest of the party were reassembling.

"Well, Laura," said Mrs. Cressler, when they had sat down, "do you like it?"

"I don't want to leave it—ever," she answered. "I could stay here always."

"I like the young man best," observed Aunt Wess'. "The one who seems to be the friend of the tall fellow with a cloak. But why does he seem so sorry? Why don't he marry the young lady? Let's see, I don't remember his name."

"Beastly voice," declared Landry Court. "He almost broke there once. Too bad. He's not what he used to be. It seems he's terribly dissipated—drinks. Yes, sir, like a fish. He had delirium tremens once behind the scenes in Philadelphia, and stabbed a scene shifter with his stage dagger. A bad lot, to say the least."

"Now, Landry," protested Mrs. Cressler, "you're making it up as you go along." And in the laugh that followed Landry himself joined.

"After all," said Corthell, "this music seems to be just the right medium between the naïve melody of the Italian school and the elaborate complexity of Wagner. I can't help but be carried away with it at times—in spite of my better judgment."

Jadwin, who had been smoking a cigar in the vestibule during the *entr'acte*, rubbed his chin reflectively.

"Well," he said, "it's all very fine. I've no doubt of that, but I give you my word I would rather hear my old governor take his guitar and sing 'Father, oh father, come home with me now,' than all the fiddle-faddle, tweedle-deedle opera business in the whole world."

But the orchestra was returning, the musicians crawling out one by one from a little door beneath the stage hardly bigger than the

entrance of a rabbit hutch. They settled themselves in front of
their racks, adjusting their coat-tails, fingering their sheet music.
Soon they began to tune up, and a vague bourdon of many sounds—
the subdued snarl of the cornets, the dull mutter of the bass viols,
the liquid gurgling of the flageolets and wood-wind instruments,
now and then pierced by the strident chirps and cries of the violins,
rose into the air, dominating the incessant clamor of conversation
that came from all parts of the theatre.

Then suddenly the house lights sank and the footlights rose.
From all over the theatre came energetic whispers of "Sh! Sh!"
Three strokes, as of a great mallet, sepulchral, grave, came from behind the wings; the leader of the orchestra raised his baton, then
brought it slowly down, and while from all the instruments at once
issued a prolonged minor chord, emphasized by a muffled roll of the
kettledrum, the curtain rose upon a mediæval public square. The
soprano was seated languidly upon a bench. Her *grande scène* occurred in this act. Her hair was unbound; she wore a loose robe
of cream white, with flowing sleeves, which left the arms bare to
the shoulders. At the waist it was caught in by a girdle of silk
rope.

"This is the great act," whispered Mrs. Cressler, leaning over
Laura's shoulder. "She is superb later on. Superb."

"I wish those *men* would stop talking," murmured Laura,
searching the darkness distressfully, for between the strains of the
music she had heard the words:

"—Clearing House balance of three thousand dollars."

Meanwhile the prima donna, rising to her feet, delivered herself of a lengthy recitative, her chin upon her breast, her eyes looking out from under her brows, an arm stretched out over the footlights. The baritone entered, striding to the left of the footlights,
apostrophizing the prima donna in a rage. She clasped her hands
imploringly, supplicating him to leave her, exclaiming from time to
time:

"Va via, va via—
Vel chieco per pieta."

Then all at once, while the orchestra blared, they fell into each
other's arms.

"Why do they do that?" murmured Aunt Wess' perplexed. "I
thought the gentleman with the beard didn't like her at all."

"Why, that's the duke, don't you see, Aunt Wess'?" said Laura, trying to explain. "And he forgives her. I don't know exactly. Look at your libretto."

"—a conspiracy of the Bears . . . seventy cents . . . and naturally he busted."

The mezzo-soprano, the confidante of the prima donna, entered, and a trio developed that had but a mediocre success. At the end the baritone abruptly drew his sword, and the prima donna fell to her knees, chanting:

"Io tremo, ahimè !"

"And now he's mad again," whispered Aunt Wess', consulting her libretto, all at sea once more. "I can't understand. She says— the opera book *says* she says, 'I tremble.' I don't see why."

"Look now," said Page, "here comes the tenor. Now they're going to have it out."

The tenor, hatless, debouched suddenly upon the scene, and furious, addressed himself to the baritone, leaning forward, his hands upon his chest. Though the others sang in Italian, the tenor, a Parisian, used the French book continually, and now vilified the baritone, crying out:

"O traitre infâme
O lache et coupable."

"I don't see why he don't marry the young lady and be done with it," commented Aunt Wess'.

The act drew to its close. The prima donna went through her "great scene," wherein her voice climbed to C in alt, holding the note so long that Aunt Wess' became uneasy. As she finished, the house rocked with applause, and the soprano, who had gone out supported by her confidante, was recalled three times. A duel followed between the baritone and tenor, and the latter, mortally wounded, fell into the arms of his friends, uttering broken, vehement notes. The chorus—made up of the city watch and town's people— crowded in upon the back of the stage. The soprano and her confidante returned. The basso, a black-bearded, bull-necked man, sombre, mysterious, parted the chorus to right and left, and advanced to the footlights. The contralto, dressed as a boy, appeared. The soprano took the stage, and abruptly the closing scene of the act developed.

The violins raged and wailed in unison, all the bows moving together like parts of a well regulated machine. The kettledrums, marking the cadences, rolled at exact intervals. The director beat time furiously, as though dragging up the notes and chords with the end of his baton, while the horns and cornets blared, the bass viols growled, and the flageolets and piccolos lost themselves in an amazing complication of liquid gurgles and modulated roulades.

On the stage every one was singing. The soprano in the centre, vocalized in her highest register, bringing out the notes with vigorous twists of her entire body, and tossing them off into the air with sharp flirts of her head. On the right, the basso, scowling, could be heard in the intervals of the music repeating:

"Il perfido, l'ingrato,"

while to the left of the soprano the baritone intoned indistinguishable, sonorous phrases, striking his breast and pointing to the fallen tenor with his sword. At the extreme left of the stage the contralto, in tights and plush doublet, turned to the audience, extending her hands, or flinging back her arms. She raised her eyebrows with each high note, and sunk her chin into her ruff when her voice descended. At certain intervals her notes blended with those of the soprano's while she sang:

"Addio, felicità del ciel!"

The tenor, raised upon one hand, his shoulders supported by his friends, sustained the theme which the soprano led with the words:

> *"Je me meurs*
> *Ah malheur*
> *Ah je souffre*
> *Mon ame s'envole."*

The chorus formed a semicircle just behind him—the women on one side, the men on the other. They left much to be desired; apparently scraped hastily together from heaven knew what sources, after the manner of a management suddenly become economical. The women were fat, elderly, and painfully homely; the men lean, osseous, and distressed, in misfitting hose. But they had been conscientiously drilled. They made all their gestures together, moved in masses simultaneously, and, without ceasing, chanted over and over again:

"O terror, O blasfema."

The *finale* commenced. Everybody on the stage took a step forward, beginning all over again upon a higher key. The soprano's voice thrilled to the very chandelier. The orchestra redoubled its efforts, the director beating time with hands, head, and body.

"Il perfido, l'ingrato,"

thundered the basso.

"Ineffabil mistero,"

answered the baritone, striking his breast and pointing with his sword; while all at once the soprano's voice, thrilling out again, ran up an astonishing crescendo that evoked veritable gasps from all parts of the audience, then jumped once more to the famous C in alt, and held it long enough for the chorus to repeat

"O terror, O blasfema"

four times.

Then the director's baton descended with the violence of a blow. There was a prolonged crash of harmony, a final enormous chord, to which every voice and every instrument contributed. The singers struck tableau attitudes, the tenor fell back with a last wail:

"Je me meurs,"

and the soprano fainted into the arms of her confidante. The curtain fell.

The house roared with applause. The scene was recalled again and again. The tenor, scrambling to his feet, joined hands with the baritone, soprano, and other artists, and all bowed repeatedly. Then the curtain fell for the last time, the lights of the great chandelier clicked and blazed up, and from every quarter of the house came the cries of the programme sellers:

"Opera books. Books of the opera. Words and music of the opera."

During this, the last *entr'acte,* Laura remained in the box with Mrs. Cressler, Corthell, and Jadwin. The others went out to look down upon the foyer from a certain balcony.

In the box the conversation turned upon stage management, and Corthell told how, in "L'Africaine," at the Opéra, in Paris, the entire superstructure of the stage—wings, drops, and backs—turned

when Vasco de Gama put the ship about. Jadwin having criticised
the effect because none of the actors turned with it, was voted a
Philistine by Mrs. Cressler and Corthell. But as he was about to
answer, Mrs. Cressler turned to the artist, passing him her opera
glasses, and asking:

"Who are those people down there in the third row of the par-
quet—see, on the middle aisle—the woman is in red. Aren't those
the Gretrys?"

This left Jadwin and Laura out of the conversation, and the
capitalist was quick to seize the chance of talking to her. Soon she
was surprised to notice that he was trying hard to be agreeable, and
before they had exchanged a dozen sentences he had turned an
awkward compliment. She guessed by his manner that paying
attention to young girls was for him a thing altogether unusual.
Intuitively she divined that she, on this, the very first night of their
acquaintance, had suddenly interested him.

She had had neither opportunity nor inclination to observe him
closely during their interview in the vestibule, but now, as she sat
and listened to him talk, she could not help being a little attracted.
He was a heavy-built man, would have made two of Corthell, and
his hands were large and broad, the hands of a man of affairs, who
knew how to grip, and, above all, how to hang on. Those broad,
strong hands, and keen, calm eyes would enfold and envelop a Purpose with tremendous strength, and they would persist and persist
and persist, unswerving, unwavering, untiring, till the Purpose
was driven home. And the two long, lean, fibrous arms of him;
what a reach they could attain, and how wide and huge and even
formidable would be their embrace of affairs. One of those great
manœuvres of a fellow money-captain had that very day been concluded, the Helmick failure, and between the chords and bars of a
famous opera men talked in excited whispers, and one great leader
lay at that very moment, broken and spent, fighting with his last
breath for bare existence. Jadwin had seen it all. Uninvolved in
the crash, he had none the less been close to it, watching it, in touch
with it, foreseeing each successive collapse by which it reeled fatal-
ly to the final catastrophe. The voices of the two men that had so
annoyed her in the early part of the evening were suddenly raised
again:

"—It was terrific, there on the floor of the Board this morning.
By the Lord! they fought each other when the Bears began throwing the grain at 'em—in carload lots."

And abruptly, midway between two phases of that music-drama of passion and romance, there came to Laura the swift and vivid impression of that other drama that simultaneously—even at that very moment—was working itself out close at hand, equally pic- turesque, equally romantic, equally passionate; but more than that, real, actual, modern, a thing in the very heart of the very life in which she moved. And here he sat, this Jadwin, quiet, in evening dress, listening good-naturedly to this beautiful music, for which he did not care, to this rant and fustian, watching quietly all this posing and attitudinizing. How small and petty it must all seem to him!

Laura found time to be astonished. What! She had first met this man haughtily, in all the panoply of her "grand manner," and had promised herself that she would humble him, and pay him for that first mistrustful stare at her. And now, behold, she was study- ing him, and finding the study interesting. Out of harmony though she knew him to be with those fine emotions of hers of the early part of the evening, she nevertheless found much in him to admire. It was always just like that. She told herself that she was forever doing the unexpected thing, the inconsistent thing. Women were queer creatures, mysterious even to themselves.

"I am so pleased that you are enjoying it all," said Corthell's voice at her shoulder. "I knew you would. There is nothing like music such as this to appeal to the emotions, the heart—and with your temperament—"

Straightway he made her feel her sex. Now she was just a woman again, with all a woman's limitations, and her relations with Corthell could never be—so she realized—any other than sex-rela- tions. With Jadwin somehow it had been different. She had felt his manhood more than her womanhood, her sex side. And be- tween them it was more a give-and-take affair, more equality, more companionship. Corthell spoke only of her heart and to her heart. But Jadwin made her feel—or rather she made herself feel when he talked to her—that she had a head as well as a heart.

And the last act of the opera did not wholly absorb her attention. The artists came and went, the orchestra wailed and boomed, the audience applauded, and in the end the tenor, fired by a sudden sense of duty and of stern obligation, tore himself from the arms of the soprano, and calling out upon remorseless fate and upon heaven, and declaiming about the vanity of glory, and his heart that broke yet disdained tears, allowed himself to be dragged off the

scene by his friend the basso. For the fifth time during the piece
the soprano fainted into the arms of her long-suffering confidante.
The audience, suddenly remembering hats and wraps, bestirred
itself, and many parties were already upon their feet and filing out
at the time the curtain fell.

The Cresslers and their friends were among the last to regain
the vestibule. But as they came out from the foyer, where the
first draughts of outside air began to make themselves felt, there
were exclamations:

"It's raining."

"Why, it's raining right down."

It was true. Abruptly the weather had moderated, and the fine,
dry snow that had been falling since early evening had changed
to a lugubrious drizzle. A wave of consternation invaded the
vestibule for those who had not come in carriages, or whose carriages had not arrived. Tempers were lost; women, cloaked to the
ears, their heads protected only by fichus or mantillas, quarreled
with husbands or cousins or brothers over the question of umbrellas. The vestibules were crowded to suffocation, and the aigrettes
nodded and swayed again in alternate gusts, now of moist, chill
atmosphere from without, and now of stale, hot air that exhaled
in long puffs from the inside doors of the theatre itself. Here and
there in the press, footmen, their top hats in rubber cases, their
hands full of umbrellas, searched anxiously for their masters.

Outside upon the sidewalks and by the curbs, an apparently
inextricable confusion prevailed; policemen with drawn clubs labored and objurgated; anxious, preoccupied young men, their opera
hats and gloves beaded with rain, hurried to and fro, searching for
their carriages. At the edge of the awning the caller, a gigantic
fellow in gold-faced uniform, shouted the numbers in a roaring
sing-song that dominated every other sound. Coachmen, their wet
rubber coats reflecting the lamplight, called back and forth, furious
quarrels broke out between hansom drivers and the police officers,
steaming horses with jingling bits, their backs covered with dark
green cloths, plunged and pranced, carriage doors banged, and the
roll of wheels upon the pavement was as the reverberation of artillery caissons.

"Get your carriage, sir?" cried a ragged, half-grown arab at
Cressler's elbow.

"Hurry up, then," said Cressler. Then, raising his voice, for
the clamor was increasing with every second: "What's your num-

ber, Laura? You girls first. Ninety-three? Get that, boy? Ninety-three. Quick now."

The carriage appeared. Hastily they said good-by; hastily Laura expressed to Mrs. Cressler her appreciation and enjoyment. Corthell saw them to the carriage, and getting in after them shut the door behind him. They departed.

Laura sank back in the cool gloom of the carriage's interior redolent of damp leather and upholstery.

"What an evening! What an evening!" she murmured.

On the way home both she and Page appealed to the artist, who knew the opera well, to hum or whistle for them the arias that had pleased them most. Each time they were enthusiastic. Yes, yes, that was the air. Wasn't it pretty, wasn't it beautiful?

But Aunt Wess' was still unsatisfied.

"I don't see yet," she complained, "why the young man, the one with the pointed beard, didn't marry that lady and be done with it. Just as soon as they'd seem to have it all settled, he'd begin to take on again, and strike his breast and go away. I declare, I think it was all kind of foolish."

"Why, the duke—don't you see. The one who sang bass—" Page labored to explain.

"Oh, I didn't like him at all," said Aunt Wess'. "He stamped around so." But the audience itself had interested her, and the décolleté gowns had been particularly impressing.

"I never saw such dressing in all my life," she declared. "And that woman in the box next ours. Well! did you notice *that?*" She raised her eyebrows and set her lips together. "Well, I don't want to say anything."

The carriage rolled on through the darkened downtown streets, toward the North Side, where the Dearborns lived. They could hear the horses plashing through the layer of slush—mud, half-melted snow and rain—that encumbered the pavement. In the gloom the girls' wraps glowed pallid and diaphanous. The rain left long, slanting parallels on the carriage windows. They passed on down Wabash Avenue, and crossed over to State Street and Clarke Street, dark, deserted.

Laura, after a while, lost in thought, spoke but little. It had been a great evening—because of other things than mere music. Corthell had again asked her to marry him, and she, carried away by the excitement of the moment, had answered him encouragingly. On the heels of this she had had that little talk with the capitalist

Jadwin, and somehow since then she had been steadied, calmed.
The cold air and the rain in her face had cooled her flaming cheeks
and hot temples. She asked herself now if she did really, honestly
love the artist. No, she did not; really and honestly she did not;
and now as the carriage rolled on through the deserted streets of the
business districts, she knew very well that she did not want to
marry him. She had done him an injustice; but in the matter
of righting herself with him, correcting his false impression, she was
willing to procrastinate. She wanted him to love her, to pay her
all those innumerable little attentions which he managed with such
faultless delicacy. To say: "No, Mr. Corthell, I do not love you, I
will never be your wife," would—this time—be final. He would
go away, and she had no intention of allowing him to do that.

But abruptly her reflections were interrupted. While she
thought it all over she had been looking out of the carriage window through a little space where she had rubbed the steam from
the pane. Now, all at once, the strange appearance of the neighborhood as the carriage turned north from out Jackson Street into
La Salle, forced itself upon her attention. She uttered an exclamation.

The office buildings on both sides of the street were lighted
from basement to roof. Through the windows she could get
glimpses of clerks and bookkeepers in shirt sleeves bending over
desks. Every office was open, and every one of them full of a
feverish activity. The sidewalks were almost as crowded as though
at noontime. Messenger boys ran to and fro, and groups of men
stood on the corners in earnest conversation. The whole neighborhood was alive, and this, though it was close upon one o'clock
in the morning!

"Why, what is it all?" she murmured.

Corthell could not explain, but all at once Page cried:

"Oh, oh, I know. See, this is Jackson and La Salle Streets.
Landry was telling me. The 'commission district,' he called it.
And these are the brokers' offices working overtime—that Hel-
mick deal, you know."

Laura looked, suddenly stupefied. Here it was, then, that other
drama, that other tragedy, working on there furiously, fiercely
through the night, while she and all those others had sat there in
that atmosphere of flowers and perfume, listening to music. Suddenly it loomed portentous in the eye of her mind, terrible, tremendous. Ah, this drama of the "Provision Pits," where the rush

of millions of bushels of grain, and the clatter of millions of dollars, and the tramping and the wild shouting of thousands of men filled all the air with the noise of battle! Yes, here was drama in deadly earnest—drama and tragedy and death, and the jar of mortal fighting. And the echoes of it invaded the very sanctuary of art, and cut athwart the music of Italy and the cadence of polite conversation, and the shock of it endured when all the world should have slept, and galvanized into vivid life all these sombre piles of office buildings. It was dreadful, this labor through the night. It had all the significance of field hospitals after the battle—hospitals and the tents of commanding generals. The wounds of the day were being bound up, the dead were being counted, while, shut in their headquarters, the captains and the commanders drew the plans for the grapple of armies that was to recommence with daylight.

"Yes, yes, that's just what it is," continued Page. "See, there's the Rookery, and there's the Constable Building, where Mr. Helmick has his offices. Landry showed me it all one day. And, look back." She raised the flap that covered the little window at the back of the carriage. "See, down there, at the end of the street. There's the Board of Trade Building, where the grain speculating is done—where the wheat pits and corn pits are."

Laura turned and looked back. On either side of the vista in converging lines stretched the blazing office buildings. But over the end of the street the lead-colored sky was rifted a little. A long, faint bar of light stretched across the prospect, and silhouetted against this rose a sombre mass, unbroken by any lights, rearing a black and formidable façade against the blur of light behind it.

And this was her last impression of the evening. The lighted office buildings, the murk of rain, the haze of light in the heavens, and raised against it the pile of the Board of Trade Building, black, grave, monolithic, crouching on its foundations, like a monstrous sphinx with blind eyes, silent, grave—crouching there without a sound, without sign of life under the night and the drifting veil of rain.

II

LAURA DEARBORN'S native town was Barrington, in Worcester
County, Massachusetts. Both she and Page had been born there,
and there had lived until the death of their father, at a time when
Page was ready for the High School. The mother, a North Carolina girl, had died long before.

Laura's education had been unusual. After leaving the High
School her father had for four years allowed her a private tutor (an
impecunious graduate from the Harvard Theological School). She
was ambitious, a devoted student, and her instructor's task was
rather to guide than to enforce her application. She soon acquired
a reading knowledge of French, and knew her Racine in the original almost as well as her Shakespeare. Literature became for her
an actual passion. She delved into Tennyson and the Victorian
poets, and soon was on terms of intimacy with the poets and essay-
ists of New England. The novelists of the day she ignored almost
completely, and voluntarily. Only occasionally, and then as a con-
cession, she permitted herself a reading of Mr. Howells.

Moderately prosperous while he himself was conducting his
little mill, Dearborn had not been able to put by any money to speak
of, and when Laura and the local lawyer had come to close up the
business, to dispose of the mill, and to settle the claims against what
the lawyer grandiloquently termed "the estate," there was just
enough money left to pay for Page's tickets to Chicago and a
course of tuition for her at a seminary.

The Cresslers, on the event of Dearborn's death, had advised
both sisters to come West, and had pledged themselves to look
after Page during the period of her schooling. Laura had sent
the little girl on at once, but delayed taking the step herself.

Fortunately, the two sisters were not obliged to live upon their
inheritance. Dearborn himself had a sister—a twin of Aunt Wess'
—who had married a wealthy woollen merchant of Boston, and
this one, long since, had provided for the two girls. A large sum
had been set aside, which was to be made over to them when the
father died. For years now this sum had been accumulating interest. So that when Laura and Page faced the world, alone, upon

the steps of the Barrington cemetery, they had the assurance that, at least, they were independent.

For two years, in the solidly built colonial dwelling, with its low ceilings and ample fireplaces, where once the minute-men had swung their kettles, Laura, alone, thought it all over. Mother and father were dead; even the Boston aunt was dead. Of all her relations, Aunt Wess' alone remained. Page was at her finishing school at Geneva Lake, within two hours of Chicago. The Cresslers were the dearest friends of the orphan girls. Aunt Wess', herself a widow, also living in Chicago, added her entreaties to Mrs. Cressler's. All things seemed to point her westward, all things seemed to indicate that one phase of her life was ended.

Then, too, she had her ambitions. These hardly took definite shape in her mind; but vaguely she chose to see herself, at some far-distant day, an actress, a tragedienne, playing the rôles of Shakespeare's heroines. This idea of hers was more a desire than an ambition, but it could not be realized in Barrington, Massachusetts. For a year she temporized, procrastinated, loth to leave the old home, loth to leave the grave in the cemetery back of the Methodist-Episcopal chapel. Twice during this time she visited Page, and each time the great gray city threw the spell of its fascination about her. Each time she returned to Barrington the town dwindled in her estimation. It was picturesque, but lamentably narrow. The life was barren, the "New England spirit" prevailed in all its severity; and this spirit seemed to her a veritable cult, a sort of religion, wherein the Old Maid was the priestess, the Spinster the officiating devotee, the thing worshiped the Great Unbeautiful, and the ritual unremitting, unrelenting Housework. She detested it.

That she was an Episcopalian, and preferred to read her prayers rather than to listen to those written and memorized by the Presbyterian minister, seemed to be regarded as a relic of heathenish rites—a thing almost cannibalistic. When she elected to engage a woman and a "hired man" to manage her house, she felt the disapprobation of the entire village, as if she had sunk into some decadent and enervating Lower-Empire degeneracy.

The crisis came when Laura traveled alone to Boston to hear Modjeska in "Marie Stuart" and "Macbeth," and upon returning full of enthusiasm, allowed it to be understood that she had a half-formed desire of emulating such an example. A group of ladydeaconesses, headed by the Presbyterian minister, called upon her, with some intention of reasoning and laboring with her.

They got no further than the statement of the cause of this visit. The spirit and temper of the South, that she had from her mother, flamed up in Laura at last, and the members of the "committee," before they were well aware, came to themselves in the street outside the front gate, dazed and bewildered, staring at each other, all confounded and stunned by the violence of an outbreak of long-repressed emotion and long-restrained anger, that like an actual physical force had swept them out of the house.

At the same moment, Laura, thrown across her bed, wept with a vehemence that shook her from head to foot. But she had not the least compunction for what she had said, and before the month was out had said good-by to Barrington forever, and was on her way to Chicago, henceforth to be her home.

A house was bought on the North Side, and it was arranged that Aunt Wess' should live with her two nieces. Pending the installation, Laura and Page lived at a little family hotel in the same neighborhood. The Cresslers' invitation to join the theatre party at the Auditorium had fallen inopportunely enough, squarely in the midst of the ordeal of moving in. Indeed, the two girls had already passed one night in the new home, and they must dress for the affair by lamplight in their unfurnished quarters and under inconceivable difficulties. Only the lure of Italian opera, heard from a box, could have tempted them to have accepted the invitation at such a time and under such circumstances.

The morning after the opera, Laura woke in her bed—almost the only article of furniture that was in place in the whole house—with the depressing consciousness of a hard day's work at hand. Outside it was still raining, the room was cold, heated only by an inadequate oil stove, and through the slats of the inside shutters, which, pending the hanging of the curtains they had been obliged to close, was filtering a gloomy light of a wet Chicago morning.

It was all very mournful, and she regretted now that she had not abided by her original decision to remain at the hotel until the new house was ready for occupancy. But it had happened that their month at the hotel was just up, and rather than engage the rooms for another four weeks she had thought it easier as well as cheaper to come to the house. It was all a new experience for her, and she had imagined that everything could be moved in, put in place, and the household running smoothly in a week's time.

She sat up in bed, hugging her shoulders against the chill of the room and looking at her theatre gown, that—in default of a clean closet—she had hung from the gas fixture the night before. From the direction of the kitchen came the sounds of the newly engaged "girl" making the fire for breakfast, while through the register a thin wisp of blue smoke curled upward to prove that the "hired man" was tinkering with the unused furnace. The room itself was in lamentable confusion. Crates and packing boxes encumbered the uncarpeted floor; chairs wrapped in excelsior and jute were piled one upon another; a roll of carpet leaned in one corner and a pile of mattresses occupied another.

As Laura considered the prospect, she realized her blunder.

"Why, and oh, why," she murmured, "didn't we stay at the hotel till all this was straightened out?"

But in an adjoining room she heard Aunt Wess' stirring. She turned to Page, who upon the pillows beside her still slept, her stocking around her neck as a guarantee against draughts.

"Page, Page! Wake up, girlie. It's late, and there's worlds to do."

Page woke blinking.

"Oh, it's freezing cold, Laura. Let's light the oil stove and stay in bed till the room gets warm. Oh, dear, aren't you sleepy, and, oh, wasn't last night lovely? Which one of us will get up to light the stove? We'll count for it. Lie down, sissie, dear," she begged, "you're letting all the cold air in."

Laura complied, and the two sisters, their noses all but touching, the bedclothes up to their ears, put their arms about each other to keep the warmer.

Amused at the foolishness, they "counted" to decide as to who should get up to light the oil stove, Page beginning:

"Eeny—meeny—myny—mo—"

But before the "count" was decided Aunt Wess' came in, already dressed, and in a breath the two girls implored her to light the stove. While she did so, Aunt Wess' remarked, with the alacrity of a woman who observes the difficulties of a proceeding in which she has no faith:

"I don't believe that hired girl knows her business. She says now she can't light a fire in that stove. My word, Laura, I do believe you'll have enough of all this before you're done. You know I advised you from the very first to take a flat."

"Nonsense, Aunt Wess'," answered Laura, good-naturedly.

"We'll work it out all right. I know what's the matter with that
range. I'll be right down and see to it so soon as I'm dressed."

It was nearly ten o'clock before breakfast, such as it was, was
over. They ate it on the kitchen table, with the kitchen knives and
forks, and over the meal, Page having remarked: "Well, what will
we do first?" discussed the plan of campaign.

"Landry Court does not have to work to-day—he told me why,
but I've forgotten—and he said he was coming up to help," observed Laura, and at once Aunt Wess' smiled. Landry Court was
openly and strenuously in love with Laura, and no one of the new
household ignored the fact. Aunt Wess' chose to consider the affair
as ridiculous, and whenever the subject was mentioned, spoke of
Landry as "that boy."

Page, however, bridled with seriousness as often as the matter
came up. Yes, that was all very well, but Landry was a decent,
hard-working young fellow, with all his way to make and no time
to waste, and if Laura didn't mean that it should come to anything
it wasn't very fair to him to keep him dangling along like that.

"I guess," Laura was accustomed to reply, looking significantly
at Aunt Wess', "that our little girlie has a little bit of an eye on a
certain hard-working young fellow herself." And the answer invariably roused Page.

"Now, Laura," she would cry, her eyes snapping, her breath
coming fast. "Now, Laura, that isn't right at all, and you know I
don't like it, and you just say it because you know it makes me
cross. I won't have you insinuate that I would run after any man
or care in the least whether he's in love or not. I just guess I've
got some self-respect; and as for Landry Court, we're no more
nor less than just good friends, and I appreciate his business talents
and the way he rustles 'round, and he merely respects me as a
friend, and it don't go any further than that. 'An eye on him,' I
do declare! As if I hadn't yet to see the man I'd so much as look
at a second time."

And Laura, remembering her "Shakespeare," was ever ready
with the words:

"The lady doth protest too much, methinks."

Just after breakfast, in fact, Landry did appear.

"Now," he began, with a long breath, addressing Laura, who
was unwrapping the pieces of cut glass and bureau ornaments as

Page passed them to her from the depths of a crate. "Now, I've done a lot already. That's what made me late. I've ordered your newspaper sent here, and I've telephoned the hotel to forward any mail that comes for you to this address, and I sent word to the gas company to have your gas turned on—"

"Oh, that's good," said Laura.

"Yes, I thought of that; the man will be up right away to fix it, and I've ordered a cake of ice left here every day, and told the telephone company that you wanted a telephone put in. Oh, yes, and the bottled-milk man—I stopped in at a dairy on the way up. Now, what do we do first?"

He took off his coat, rolled up his shirt sleeves, and plunged into the confusion of crates and boxes that congested the rooms and hall-ways on the first floor of the house. The two sisters could hear him attacking his task with tremendous blows of the kitchen hammer. From time to time he called up the stairway:

"Hey, what do you want done with this jardinière thing? . . . Where does this hanging lamp go, Laura?"

Laura, having unpacked all the cut-glass ornaments, came down-stairs, and she and Landry set about hanging the parlor curtains.

Landry fixed the tops of the window moldings with a piercing eye, his arms folded.

"I see, I see," he answered to Laura's explanations. "I see. Now, where's a screwdriver, and a stepladder? Yes, and I'll have to have some brass nails, and your hired man must let me have that hammer again."

He sent the cook after the screwdriver, called the hired man from the furnace, shouted upstairs to Page to ask for the where-about of the brass nails, and delegated Laura to steady the step-ladder.

"Now, Landry," directed Laura, "those rods want to be about three inches from the top."

"Well," he said, climbing up, "I'll mark the place with the screw and you tell me if it is right."

She stepped back, her head to one side.

"No; higher, Landry. There, that's about it—or a *little* lower —so. That's *just* right. Come down now and help me put the hooks in."

They pulled a number of sofa cushions together and sat down on the floor side by side, Landry snapping the hooks in place where Laura had gathered the pleats. Inevitably his hands touched hers, and their heads drew close together. Page and Mrs. Wessels were unpacking linen in the upstairs hall. The cook and hired man raised a great noise of clanking stove lids and grates as they wrestled with the range in the kitchen.

"Well," said Landry, "you are going to have a pretty home." He was meditating a phrase of which he purposed delivering himself when opportunity afforded. It had to do with Laura's eyes, and her ability of understanding him. She understood him; she was to know that he thought so, that it was of immense importance to him. It was thus he conceived of the manner of love making. The evening before that palavering artist seemed to have managed to monopolize her about all of the time. Now it was his turn, and this day of household affairs, of little domestic commotions, appeared to him to be infinitely more desirous than the pomp and formality of evening dress and opera boxes. This morning the relations between himself and Laura seemed charming, intimate, unconventional, and full of opportunities. Never had she appeared prettier to him. She wore a little pink flannel dressing-sack with full sleeves, and her hair, carelessly twisted into great piles, was in a beautiful disarray, curling about her cheeks and ears. "I didn't see anything of you at all last night," he grumbled.

"Well, you didn't try."

"Oh, it was the Other Fellow's turn," he went on. "Say," he added, "how often are you going to let me come to see you when you get settled here? Twice a week—three times?"

"As if you wanted to see me as often as that. Why, Landry, I'm growing up to be an old maid. You can't want to lose your time calling on old maids."

He was voluble in protestations. He was tired of young girls. They were all very well to dance with, but when a man got too old for that sort of thing, he wanted some one with sense to talk to. Yes, he did. Some one with *sense*. Why, he would rather talk five minutes with her—

"Honestly, Landry?" she asked, as though he were telling a thing incredible.

He swore to her it was true. His eyes snapped. He struck his palm with his fist.

"An old maid like me?" repeated Laura.

"Old maid nothing!" he vociferated. "Ah," he cried, "you seem to understand me. When I look at you, straight into your eyes—"

From the doorway the cook announced that the man with the

last load of furnace coal had come, and handed Laura the voucher
to sign. Then needs must that Laura go with the cook to see if
the range was finally and properly adjusted, and while she was
gone the man from the gas company called to turn on the meter,
and Landry was obliged to look after him. It was half an hour
before he and Laura could once more settle themselves on the cushions in the parlor.

"Such a lot of things to do," she said; "and you are such a help,
Landry. It was so dear of you to want to come."

"I would do anything in the world for you, Laura," he exclaimed, encouraged by her words; "anything. You know I would.
It isn't so much that I want you to care for me—and I guess I
want *that* bad enough—but it's because I love to be with you, and
be helping you, and all that sort of thing. Now, all this," he
waved a hand at the confusion of furniture, "all this to-day—I just
feel," he declared with tremendous earnestness, "I just feel as
though I were entering into your life. And just sitting here beside
you and putting in these curtain hooks, I want you to know that
it's inspiring to me. Yes, it is inspiring; it's elevating. You don't
know how it makes a man feel to have the companionship of a good
and lovely woman."

"Landry, as though I were all that. Here, put another hook
in here."

She held the fold toward him. But he took her hand as their
fingers touched and raised it to his lips and kissed it. She did not
withdraw it, nor rebuke him, crying out instead, as though occupied with quite another matter:

"Landry, careful, my dear boy; you'll make me prick my fingers.
Ah—there, you did."

He was all commiseration and self-reproach at once, and turned
her hand palm upward, looking for the scratch.

"Um!" she breathed. "It hurts."

"Where now," he cried, "where was it? Ah, I was a beast; I'm
so ashamed." She indicated a spot on her wrist instead of her
fingers, and very naturally Landry kissed it again.

"How foolish!" she remonstrated. "The idea! As if I wasn't
old enough to be—"

"You're not so old but what you're going to marry me some
day," he declared.

"How perfectly silly, Landry!" she retorted. "Aren't you done
with my hand yet?"

"No, indeed," he cried, his clasp tightening over her fingers. "It's mine. You can't have it till I say—or till *you* say that—some day—you'll give it to me for good—for better or for worse."

"As if you really meant that," she said, willing to prolong the little situation. It was very sweet to have this clean, fine-fibred young boy so earnestly in love with her, very sweet that the lifting of her finger, the mere tremble of her eyelid should so perturb him.

"Mean it! Mean it!" he vociferated. "You don't know how much I do mean it. Why, Laura, why—why, I can't think of anything else."

"You!" she mocked. "As if I believed that. How many other girls have you said it to this year?"

Landry compressed his lips.

"Miss Dearborn, you insult me."

"Oh, my!" exclaimed Laura, at last withdrawing her hand.

"And now you're mocking me. It isn't kind. No, it isn't; it isn't *kind*."

"I never answered your question yet," she observed.

"What question?"

"About your coming to see me when we were settled. I *thought* you wanted to know."

"How about lunch?" said Page, from the doorway. "Do you know it's after twelve?"

"The girl has got something for us," said Laura. "I told her about it. Oh, just a pick-up lunch—coffee, chops. I thought we wouldn't bother to-day. We'll have to eat in the kitchen."

"Well, let's be about it," declared Landry, "and finish with these curtains afterward. Inwardly *I'm* a ravening wolf."

It was past one o'clock by the time that luncheon, "picked up" though it was, was over. By then everybody was very tired. Aunt Wess' exclaimed that she could not stand another minute, and retired to her room. Page, indefatigable, declaring they never would get settled if they let things dawdle along, set to work unpacking her trunk and putting her clothes away. Her fox terrier, whom the family, for obscure reasons, called the Pig, arrived in the middle of the afternoon in a crate, and shivering with the chill of the house, was tied up behind the kitchen range, where, for all the heat, he still trembled and shuddered at long intervals, his head down, his eyes rolled up, bewildered and discountenanced by so much confusion and so many new faces.

Outside the weather continued lamentable. The rain beat down steadily upon the heaps of snow on the grass-plats by the curb-stones, melting it, dirtying it, and reducing it to viscid slush. The sky was lead gray; the trees, bare and black as though built of iron and wire, dripped incessantly. The sparrows, huddling under the house-eaves or in interstices of the moldings, chirped feebly from time to time, sitting disconsolate, their feathers puffed out till their bodies assumed globular shapes. Delivery wagons trundled up and down the street at intervals, the horses and drivers housed in oilskins.

The neighborhood was quiet. There was no sound of voices in the streets. But occasionally, from far away in the direction of the river or the Lake Front, came the faint sounds of steamer and tug whistles. The sidewalks in either direction were deserted. Only a solitary policeman, his star pinned to the outside of his drip-ping rubber coat, his helmet shedding rivulets, stood on the corner absorbed in the contemplation of the brown torrent of the gutter plunging into a sewer vent.

Landry and Laura were in the library at the rear of the house, a small room, two sides of which were occupied with bookcases. They were busy putting the books in place. Laura stood half-way up the stepladder, taking volume after volume from Landry as he passed them to her.

"Do you wipe them carefully, Landry?" she asked.

He held a strip of cloth torn from an old sheet in his hand, and rubbed the dust from each book before he handed it to her.

"Yes, yes; very carefully," he assured her. "Say," he added, "where are all your modern novels? You've got Scott and Dickens and Thackeray, of course, and Eliot—yes, and here's Hawthorne and Poe. But I haven't struck anything later than Oliver Wendell Holmes."

Laura put up her chin. "Modern novels—no indeed. When I've yet to read 'Jane Eyre,' and have only read 'Ivanhoe' and 'The Newcomes' once."

She made a point of the fact that her taste was the extreme of conservatism, refusing to acknowledge hardly any fiction that was not almost classic. Even Stevenson aroused her suspicions.

"Well, here's 'The Wrecker,'" observed Landry, handing it up to her. "I read it last summer vacation at Waukesha. Just about took the top of my head off."

"I tried to read it," she answered. "Such an outlandish story, no love story in it, and so coarse, so brutal, and then so improbable. I couldn't get interested."

But abruptly Landry uttered an exclamation:

"Well, what do you call this? 'Wanda,' by Ouida. How is this for modern?"

She blushed to her hair, snatching the book from him.

"Page brought it home. It's hers."

But her confusion betrayed her, and Landry shouted derisively.

"Well, I *did* read it then," she suddenly declared defiantly. "No, I'm not ashamed. Yes, I read it from cover to cover. It made me cry like I haven't cried over a book since I was a little tot. You can say what you like, but it's beautiful—a beautiful love story—and it does tell about noble, unselfish people. I suppose it has its faults, but it makes you feel better for reading it, and that's what all your 'Wreckers' in the world would never do."

"Well," answered Landry, "I don't know much about that sort of thing. Corthell does. He can talk you blind about literature. I've heard him run on by the hour. He says the novel of the future is going to be the novel without a love story."

But Laura nodded her head incredulously.

"It will be long after I am dead—that's one consolation," she said.

"Corthell is full of crazy ideas anyhow," Landry went on, still continuing to pass the books up to her. "He's a good sort, and I like him well enough, but he's the kind of man that gets up a reputation for being clever and artistic by running down the very one particular thing that every one likes, and cracking up some book or picture or play that no one has ever heard of. Just let anything get popular once and Sheldon Corthell can't speak of it without shuddering. But he'll go over here to some Archer Avenue pawn shop, dig up an old brass stewpan, or coffeepot that some greasy old Russian Jew has chucked away, and he'll stick it up in his studio and regularly kow-tow to it, and talk about the 'decadence of American industrial arts.' I've heard him. I say it's pure affectation, that's what it is, pure affectation."

But the bookcase meanwhile had been filling up, and now Laura remarked:

"No more, Landry. That's all that will go here."

She prepared to descend from the ladder. In filling the higher shelves she had mounted almost to the topmost step.

"Careful now," said Landry, as he came forward. "Give me your hand."

She gave it to him, and then, as she descended, Landry had

the assurance to put his arm around her waist as if to steady her. He was surprised at his own audacity, for he had premeditated nothing, and his arm was about her before he was well aware. He yet found time to experience a qualm of apprehension. Just how would Laura take it? Had he gone too far?

But Laura did not even seem to notice, all her attention apparently fixed upon coming safely down to the floor. She descended and shook out her skirts.

"There," she said, "that's over with. Look, I'm all dusty."

There was a knock at the half-open door. It was the cook.

"What are you going to have for supper, Miss Dearborn?" she inquired. "There's nothing in the house."

"Oh, dear," said Laura with sudden blankness, "I never thought of supper. Isn't there anything?"

"Nothing but some eggs and coffee." The cook assumed an air of aloofness, as if the entire affair were totally foreign to any interest or concern of hers. Laura dismissed her, saying that she would see to it.

"We'll have to go out and get some things," she said. "We'll all go. I'm tired of staying in the house."

"No, I've a better scheme," announced Landry. "I'll invite you all out to dine with me. I know a place where you can get the best steak in America. It has stopped raining. See," he showed her the window.

"But, Landry, we are all so dirty and miserable."

"We'll go right now and get there early. There will be nobody there, and we can have a room to ourselves. Oh, it's all right," he declared. You just trust me."

"We'll see what Page and Aunt Wess' say. Of course, Aunt Wess' would have to come."

"Of course," he said. "I wouldn't think of asking you unless she could come."

A little later the two sisters, Mrs. Wessels, and Landry came out of the house, but before taking their car they crossed to the opposite side of the street, Laura having said that she wanted to note the effect of her parlor curtains from the outside.

"I think they are looped up just far enough," she declared. But Landry was observing the house itself.

"It is the best-looking house on the block," he answered.

In fact, the house was not without a certain attractiveness. It occupied a corner lot at the intersection of Huron and North State

streets. Directly opposite was St. James' Church, and at one time
the house had served as the rectory. For the matter of that, it had
been built for just that purpose. Its style of architecture was distinctly ecclesiastic, with a suggestion of Gothic to some of the doors
and windows. The material used was solid, massive, the walls
thick, the foundation heavy. It did not occupy the entire lot, the
original builder seeming to have preferred garden space to mere
amplitude of construction, and in addition to the inevitable "back
yard," a lawn bordered it on three sides. It gave the place a certain
air of distinction and exclusiveness. Vines grew thick upon the
southern walls; in the summer time fuchsias, geraniums, and pansies would flourish in the flower beds by the front stoop. The grass
plat by the curb boasted a couple of trees. The whole place was
distinctive, individual, and very homelike, and came as a grateful
relief to the endless lines of houses built of yellow Michigan limestone that pervaded the rest of the neighborhood in every direction.

"I love the place," exclaimed Laura. "I think it's as pretty a
house as I have seen in Chicago."

"Well, it isn't so spick and span," commented Page. "It gives
you the idea that we're not new-rich and showy and all."

But Aunt Wess' was not satisfied.

"*You* may see, Laura," she remarked, "how you are going to
heat all that house with that one furnace, but *I* don't."

Their car, or rather their train of cars, coupled together in
threes, in Chicago style, came, and Landry escorted them down
town. All the way Laura could not refrain from looking out of
the windows, absorbed in the contemplation of the life and aspects
of the streets.

"You give yourself away," said Page. "Everybody will know
you're from the country."

"I am," she retorted. "But there's a difference between just
mere 'country' and Massachusetts, and I'm not ashamed of it."

Chicago, the great gray city, interested her at every instant and
under every condition. As yet she was not sure that she liked it;
she could not forgive its dirty streets, the unspeakable squalor of
some of its poorer neighborhoods that sometimes developed, like
cancerous growths, in the very heart of fine residence districts. The
black murk that closed every vista of the business streets oppressed
her, and the soot that stained linen and gloves each time she stirred
abroad was a never-ending distress.

But the life was tremendous. All around, on every side, in

every direction the vast machinery of Commonwealth clashed and thundered from dawn to dark and from dark till dawn. Even now, as the car carried her further into the business quarter, she could hear it, see it, and feel in her every fibre the trepidation of its motion. The blackened waters of the river, seen an instant between stanchions as the car trundled across the State Street bridge, disappeared under fleets of tugs, of lake steamers, of lumber barges from Sheboygan and Mackinac, of grain boats from Duluth, of coal scows that filled the air with impalpable dust, of cumbersome schooners laden with produce, of grimy rowboats dodging the prows and paddles of the larger craft, while on all sides, blocking the horizon, red in color and designated by Brobdingnag letters, towered the hump-shouldered grain elevators.

Just before crossing the bridge on the north side of the river she had caught a glimpse of a great railway terminus. Down below there, rectilinear, scientifically paralleled and squared, the Yard disclosed itself. A system of gray rails beyond words complicated, opened out, and spread immeasurably. Switches, semaphores, and signal towers stood here and there. A dozen trains, freight and passenger, puffed and steamed, waiting the word to depart. Detached engines hurried in and out of sheds and roundhouses, seeking their trains, or bunted the ponderous freight cars into switches; trundling up and down, clanking, shrieking, their bells filling the air with the clangor of tocsins. Men in visored caps shouted hoarsely, waving their arms or red flags; drays, their big dappled horses, feeding in their nose bags, stood backed up to the open doors of freight cars and received their loads. A train departed roaring. Before midnight it would be leagues away boring through the Great Northwest, carrying Trade—the life blood of nations—into communities of which Laura had never heard. Another train, reeking with fatigue, the air brakes screaming, arrived and halted, debouching a flood of passengers, business men, bringing Trade—a galvanizing elixir—from the very ends and corners of the continent.

Or, again, it was South Water Street—a jam of delivery wagons and market carts backed to the curbs, leaving only a tortuous path between the endless files of horses, suggestive of an actual barrack of cavalry. Provisions, market produce, "garden truck" and fruits, in an infinite welter of crates and baskets, boxes, and sacks, crowded the sidewalks. The gutter was choked with an overflow of refuse cabbage leaves, soft oranges, decaying beet tops. The air was

thick with the heavy smell of vegetation. Food was trodden underfoot, food crammed the stores and warehouses to bursting. Food
mingled with the mud of the highway. The very dray horses were
gorged with an unending nourishment of snatched mouthfuls
picked from backboard, from barrel top, and from the edge of the
sidewalk. The entire locality reeked with the fatness of a hundred
thousand furrows. A land of plenty, the inordinate abundance of
the earth itself emptied itself upon the asphalt and cobbles of the
quarter. It was the Mouth of the City, and drawn from all directions, over a territory of immense area, this glut of crude subsistence was sucked in, as if into a rapacious gullet, to feed the sinews
and to nourish the fibres of an immeasurable colossus.

Suddenly the meaning and significance of it all dawned upon
Laura. The Great Gray City, brooking no rival, imposed its dominion upon a reach of country larger than many a kingdom of the
Old World. For thousands of miles beyond its confines was its
influence felt. Out, far out, far away in the snow and shadow of
Northern Wisconsin forests, axes and saws bit the bark of century-
old trees, stimulated by this city's energy. Just as far to the southward pick and drill leaped to the assault of veins of anthracite,
moved by her central power. Her force turned the wheels of har-
vester and seeder a thousand miles distant in Iowa and Kansas.
Her force spun the screws and propellers of innumerable squadrons
of lake steamers crowding the Sault Sainte Marie. For her and
because of her all the Central States, all the great Northwest
roared with traffic and industry; sawmills screamed; factories, their
smoke blackening the sky, clashed and flamed; wheels turned,
pistons leaped in their cylinders; cog gripped cog; beltings
clasped the drums of mammoth wheels; and converters of
forges belched into the clouded air their tempest breath of molten
steel.

It was Empire, the resistless subjugation of all this central world
of the lakes and prairies. Here, midmost in the land, beat the
Heart of the Nation, whence inevitably must come its immeasurable power, its infinite, inexhaustible vitality. Here, of all her
cities, throbbed the true life—the true power and spirit of America;
gigantic, crude with the crudity of youth, disdaining rivalry; sane
and healthy and vigorous; brutal in its ambition, arrogant in the
new-found knowledge of its giant strength, prodigal of its wealth,
infinite in its desires. In its capacity boundless, in its courage indomitable; subduing the wilderness in a single generation, defying

calamity, and through the flame and the débris of a commonwealth in ashes, rising suddenly renewed, formidable, and Titanic.

Laura, her eyes dizzied, her ears stunned, watched tirelessly.

"There is something terrible about it," she murmured, half to herself, "something insensate. In a way, it doesn't seem human. It's like a great tidal wave. It's all very well for the individual just so long as he can keep afloat, but once fallen how horribly quick it would crush him, annihilate him, how horribly quick, and with such horrible indifference! I suppose it's civilization in the making, the thing that isn't meant to be seen, as though it were too elemental, too—primordial; like the first verses of Genesis."

The impression remained long with her, and not even the gayety of their little supper could altogether disperse it. She was a little frightened—frightened of the vast, cruel machinery of the city's life, and of the men who could dare it, who conquered it. For a moment they seemed, in a sense, more terrible than the city itself—men for whom all this crash of conflict and commerce had no terrors. Those who could subdue it to their purposes, must they not be themselves more terrible, more pitiless, more brutal? She shrank a little. What could women ever know of the life of men, after all? Even Landry, extravagant as he was, so young, so exuberant, so seemingly innocent—she knew that he was spoken of as a good business man. He, too, then had his other side. For him the Battle of the Street was an exhilaration. Beneath that boyish exterior was the tough coarseness, the male hardness, the callousness that met the brunt and withstood the shock of onset.

Ah, these men of the city, what could women ever know of them, of their lives, of that other existence through which—freed from the influence of wife or mother or daughter or sister—they passed every day from nine o'clock till evening? It was a life in which women had no part, and in which, should they enter it, they would no longer recognize son or husband, or father or brother. The gentle-mannered fellow, clean-minded, clean-handed, of the breakfast or supper table was one man. The other, who and what was he? Down there in the murk and grime of the business district raged the Battle of the Street, and therein he was a being transformed, case-hardened, supremely selfish, asking no quarter; no, nor giving any. Fouled with the clutchings and grapplings of the attack, besmirched with the elbowing of low associates and obscure allies, he set his feet toward conquest, and mingled with the marchings of an army that surged forever forward and back; now in

merciless assault, beating the fallen enemy underfoot, now in repulse, equally merciless, trampling down the auxiliaries of the day
before, in a panic dash for safety; always cruel, always selfish,
always pitiless.

To contrast these men with such as Corthell was inevitable. She
remembered him, to whom the business district was an unexplored
country, who kept himself far from the fighting, his hands unstained, his feet unsullied.   He passed his life gently, in the calm,
still atmosphere of art, in the cult of the beautiful, unperturbed,
tranquil; painting, reading, or, piece by piece, developing his beautiful stained glass. Him women could know, with him they could
sympathize. And he could enter fully into their lives and help and
stimulate them. Of the two existences which did she prefer, that
of the business man or that of the artist?

Then suddenly Laura surprised herself. After all, she was a
daughter of the frontier, and the blood of those who had wrestled
with a new world flowed in her body. Yes, Corthell's was a beautiful life; the charm of dim painted windows, the attraction of darkened studios with their harmonies of color, their orientalisms, and
their arabesques was strong. No doubt, it all had its place. It fascinated her at times, in spite of herself. To relax the mind, to indulge the senses, to live in an environment of pervading beauty
was delightful. But the men to whom the woman in her turned
were not those of the studio. Terrible as the Battle of the Street
was, it was yet battle. Only the strong and the brave might dare
it, and the figure that held her imagination and her sympathy was
not the artist, soft of hand and of speech, elaborating graces of
sound and color and form, refined, sensitive, and temperamental;
but the fighter, unknown and unknowable to women as he was;
hard, rigorous, panoplied in the harness of the warrior, who strove
among the trumpets, and who, in the brunt of conflict, conspicuous,
formidable, set the battle in a rage around him, and exulted like a
champion in the shoutings of the captains.

They were not long at table, and by the time they were ready
to depart it was about half-past five. But when they emerged into
the street, it was discovered that once more the weather had
abruptly changed. It was snowing thickly. Again a bitter wind
from off the Lake tore through the streets. The slush and melted
snow was freezing, and the north side of every lamp-post and telegraph pole was sheeted with ice.

To add to their discomfort, the North State Street cars were blocked. When they gained the corner of Washington Street they could see where the congestion began, a few squares distant.

"There's nothing for it," declared Landry, "but to go over and get the Clarke Street cars—and at that you may have to stand up all the way home, at this time of day."

They paused, irresolute, a moment on the corner. It was the centre of the retail quarter. Close at hand a vast dry goods house, built in the old "iron-front" style, towered from the pavement, and through its hundreds of windows presented to view a world of stuffs and fabrics, upholsteries and textiles, kaleidoscopic, gleaming in the fierce brilliance of a multitude of lights. From each street doorway was pouring an army of "shoppers," women for the most part; and these—since the store catered to a rich clientèle—fashionably dressed. Many of them stood for a moment on the threshold of the storm-doorways, turning up the collars of their sealskins, settling their hands in their muffs, and searching the street for their coupés and carriages.

Among the number of those thus engaged, one, suddenly catching sight of Laura, waved a muff in her direction, then came quickly forward. It was Mrs. Cressler.

"Laura, my dearest girl! Of all the people. I *am* so glad to see you!" She kissed Laura on the cheek, shook hands all around, and asked about the sisters' new home. Did they want anything, or was there anything she could do to help? Then, interrupting herself, and laying a glove on Laura's arm:

"I've got more to *tell* you."

She compressed her lips and stood off from Laura, fixing her with a significant glance.

"Me? To tell me?"

"Where are you going now?"

"Home; but our cars are stopped. We must go over to—"

"Fiddlesticks! You and Page and Mrs. Wessels—all of you —are coming home to dine with me."

"But we've had dinner already," they all cried, speaking at once.

Page explained the situation, but Mrs. Cressler would not be denied.

"The carriage is right here," she said. "I don't have to call for Charlie. He's got a man from Cincinnati in tow, and they are going to dine at the Calumet Club."

It ended by the two sisters and Mrs. Wessels getting into Mrs. Cressler's carriage. Landry excused himself. He lived on the

South Side, on Michigan Avenue, and declaring that he knew they had had enough of him for one day, took himself off.

But whatever Mrs. Cressler had to tell Laura, she evidently was determined to save for her ears only. Arrived at the Dearborns' home, she sent her footman in to tell the "girl" that the family would not be home that night. The Cresslers lived hard by on the same street, and within ten minutes' walk of the Dearborns. The two sisters and their aunt would be back immediately after breakfast.

When they had got home with Mrs. Cressler, this latter suggested hot tea and sandwiches in the library, for the ride had been cold. But the others, worn out, declared for bed as soon as Mrs. Cressler herself had dined.

"Oh, bless you, Carrie," said Aunt Wess'; "I couldn't think of tea. My back is just about broken, and I'm going straight to my bed."

Mrs. Cressler showed them to their rooms. Page and Mrs. Wessels elected to sleep together, and once the door had closed upon them the little girl unburdened herself.

"I suppose Laura thinks it's all right, running off like this for the whole blessed night, and no one to look after the house but those two servants that nobody knows anything about. As though there weren't heaven knows what all to tend to there in the morning. I just don't see," she exclaimed, decisively, "how we're going to get settled at all. That Landry Court! My goodness, he's more hindrance than help. Did you ever *see!* He just dashes in as though he were doing it all, and messes everything up, and loses things, and gets things into the wrong place, and forgets this and that, and then he and Laura sit down and spoon. I never saw anything like it. First it's Corthell, and then Landry, and next it will be somebody else. Laura regularly mortifies me; a great, grown-up girl like that, flirting, and letting every man she meets think that he's just the one particular one of the whole earth. It's not good form. And Landry—as if he didn't know we've got more to do now than just to dawdle and dawdle. I could slap him. I like to see a man take life seriously and try to amount to something, and not waste the best years of his life trailing after women who are old enough to be his grandmother, and don't mean that it will ever come to anything."

In her room, in the front of the house, Laura was partly undressed when Mrs. Cressler knocked at her door. The latter had put on a wrapper of flowered silk, and her hair was bound in "invisible nets."

"I brought you a dressing-gown," she said. She hung it over the foot of the bed, and sat down on the bed itself, watching Laura, who stood before the glass of the bureau, her head bent upon her breast, her hands busy with the back of her hair. From time to time the hairpins clicked as she laid them down in the silver trays close at hand. Then putting her chin in the air, she shook her head, and the great braids, unlooped, fell to her waist.

"What pretty hair you have, child," murmured Mrs. Cressler. She was settling herself for a long talk with her protégé. She had much to tell, but now that they had the whole night before them, could afford to take her time.

Between the two women the conversation began slowly, with detached phrases and observations that did not call necessarily for answers—mere beginnings that they did not care to follow up.

"They tell me," said Mrs. Cressler, "that that Gretry girl smokes ten cigarettes every night before she goes to bed. You know the Gretrys—they were at the opera the other night."

Laura permitted herself an indefinite murmur of interest. Her head to one side, she drew the brush in slow, deliberate movements downward underneath the long, thick strands of her hair. Mrs. Cressler watched her attentively.

"Why don't you wear your hair that new way, Laura," she remarked, "further down on your neck? I see every one doing it now."

The house was very still. Outside the double windows they could hear the faint murmuring click of the frozen snow. A radiator in the hallway clanked and strangled for a moment, then fell quiet again.

"What a pretty room this is," said Laura. "I think I'll have to do our guest room something like this—a sort of white and gold effect. My hair? Oh, I don't know. Wearing it low that way makes it catch so on the hooks of your collar, and, besides, I was afraid it would make my head look so flat."

There was a silence. Laura braided a long strand, with quick, regular motions of both hands, and letting it fall over her shoulder, shook it into place with a twist of her head. She stepped out of her skirt, and Mrs. Cressler handed her her dressing-gown, and brought out a pair of quilted slippers of red satin from the wardrobe.

In the grate, the fire that had been lighted just before they had

come upstairs was crackling sharply. Laura drew up an armchair
and sat down in front of it, her chin in her hand. Mrs. Cressler
stretched herself upon the bed, an arm behind her head.

"Well, Laura," she began at length, "I have some real news
for you. My dear, I believe you've made a conquest."

"I!" murmured Laura, looking around. She feigned a surprise, though she guessed at once that Mrs. Cressler had Corthell
in mind.

"That Mr. Jadwin—the one you met at the opera."

Genuinely taken aback, Laura sat upright and stared wide-eyed.

"Mr. Jadwin!" she exclaimed. "Why, we didn't have five minutes' talk. Why, I hardly know the man. I only met him last
night."

But Mrs. Cressler shook her head, closing her eyes and putting
her lips together.

"That don't make any difference, Laura. Trust me to tell when
a man is taken with a girl. My dear, you can have him as easy as
that." She snapped her fingers.

"Oh, I'm sure you're mistaken, Mrs. Cressler."

"Not in the least. I've known Curtis Jadwin now for fifteen
years—nobody better. He's as old a family friend as Charlie and
I have. I know him like a book. And I tell you the man is in love
with you."

"Well, I hope he didn't tell you as much," cried Laura, promising herself to be royally angry if such was the case. But Mrs.
Cressler hastened to reassure her.

"Oh, my, no. But all the way home last night—he came home
with us, you know—he kept referring to you, and just so soon as
the conversation got on some other subject he would lose interest.
He wanted to know all about you—oh, you know how a man will
talk," she exclaimed. "And he said you had more sense and more
intelligence than any girl he had ever known."

"Oh, well," answered Laura deprecatingly, as if to say that that
did not count for much with her.

"And that you were simply beautiful. He said that he never
remembered to have seen a more beautiful woman."

Laura turned her head away, a hand shielding her cheek. She
did not answer immediately, then at length:

"Has he—this Mr. Jadwin—has he ever been married before?"

"No, no. He's a bachelor, and rich! He could buy and sell *us.*
And don't think, Laura, dear, that I'm jumping at conclusions. I

hope I'm woman of the world enough to know that a man who's
taken with a pretty face and smart talk isn't going to rush right
into matrimony because of that. It wasn't so much what Curtis
Jadwin said—though, dear me, *suz,* he talked enough about you—
as what he didn't say. I could tell. He was thinking hard. He
was *hit,* Laura. I know he was. And Charlie said he spoke about
you again this morning at breakfast. Charlie makes me tired sometimes," she added irrelevantly.

"Charlie?" repeated Laura.

"Well, of course I spoke to him about Jadwin, and how taken
he seemed with you, and the man roared at me."

"*He* didn't believe it, then."

"Yes, he did—when I could get him to talk seriously about it,
and when I made him remember how Mr. Jadwin had spoken in
the carriage coming home."

Laura curled her leg under her and sat nursing her foot and
looking into the fire. For a long time neither spoke. A little clock
of brass and black marble began to chime, very prettily, the half
hour of nine. Mrs. Cressler observed:

"That Sheldon Corthell seems to be a very agreeable kind of a
young man, doesn't he?"

"Yes," replied Laura thoughtfully, "he is agreeable."

"And a talented fellow, too," continued Mrs. Cressler. "But
somehow it never impressed me that there was very much *to* him."

"Oh," murmured Laura indifferently, "I don't know."

"I suppose," Mrs. Cressler went on, in a tone of resignation, "I
suppose he thinks the world and all of *you?*"

Laura raised a shoulder without answering.

"Charlie can't abide him," said Mrs. Cressler. "Funny, isn't
it, what prejudices men have? Charlie always speaks of him as
though he were a higher order of glazier. Curtis Jadwin seems to
like him. . . . What do you think of him, Laura—of Mr. Jadwin?"

"I don't know," she answered, looking vaguely into the fire. "I
thought he was a *strong* man—mentally I mean—and that he would
be kindly and—and—generous. Somehow," she said, musingly,
"I didn't think he would be the sort of man that women would take
to, at first—but then I don't know. I saw very little of him, as I
say. He didn't impress me as being a *woman's* man."

"All the better," said the other. "Who would want to marry a
woman's man? *I* wouldn't. Sheldon Corthell is that. I tell you
one thing, Laura, and when you are as old as I am you'll know it's

true: the kind of a man that *men* like—not women—is the kind of
a man that makes the best husband."

Laura nodded her head.

"Yes," she answered, listlessly, "I suppose that's true."

"You said Jadwin struck you as being a kindly man, a generous man. He's just that, and that charitable! You know he has
a Sunday-school over on the West Side, a Sunday-school for mission children, and I do believe he's more interested in that than
in his business. He wants to make it the biggest Sunday-school in
Chicago. It's an ambition of his. I don't want you to think that
he's good in a goody-goody way, because he's not. Laura," she
exclaimed, "he's a *fine man*. I didn't intend to brag him up to you,
because I wanted you to like him. But no one knows—as I say—
no one knows Curtis Jadwin better than Charlie and I, and we just
love him. The kindliest, biggest-hearted fellow—oh, well, you'll
know him for yourself, and then you'll see. He passes the plate in
our church."

"Dr. Wendell's church?" asked Laura.

"Yes, *you* know—the Second Presbyterian."

"I'm Episcopalian myself," observed Laura, still thoughtfully
gazing into the fire.

"I know, I know. But Jadwin isn't the blue-nosed sort. And
now see here, Laura, I want to tell you. J.—that's what Charlie
and I call Jadwin—J. was talking to us the other day about supporting a ward in the Children's Hospital for the children of his
Sunday-school that get hurt or sick. You see he has nearly eight
hundred boys and girls in his school, and there's not a week passes
that he don't hear of some one of them who has been hurt or taken
sick. And he wants to start a ward at the Children's Hospital that
can take care of them. He says he wants to get other people interested, too, and so he wants to start a contribution. He says he'll
double any amount that's raised in the next six months—that is, if
there's two thousand raised, he'll make it four thousand; understand? And so Charlie and I and the Gretrys are going to get up
an amateur play—a charity affair—and raise as much money as we
can. J. thinks it's a good idea, and—here's the point—we were
talking about it coming home in the carriage, and J. said he wondered if that Miss Dearborn wouldn't take part. And we are all
wild to have you. You know you do that sort of thing so well.
Now don't say yes or no to-night. You sleep over it. J. is crazy
to have you in it."

"I'd love to do it," answered Laura. "But I would have to see
—it takes so long to get settled, and there's so much to do about
a big house like ours, I might not have time. But I will let you
know."

Mrs. Cressler told her in detail about the proposed play.
Landry Court was to take part, and she enlisted Laura's influence
to get Sheldon Corthell to undertake a rôle. Page, it appeared, had
already promised to help. Laura remembered now that she had
heard her speak of it. However, the plan was so immature as
yet that it hardly admitted of very much discussion, and inevitably
the conversation came back to its starting-point."

"You know," Laura had remarked in answer to one of Mrs.
Cressler's observations upon the capabilities and business ability of
"J.," "you know I never heard of him before you spoke of our the-
atre party. I don't know anything about him."

But Mrs. Cressler promptly supplied the information. Curtis
Jadwin was a man about thirty-five, who had begun life without a
sou in his pockets. He was a native of Michigan. His people were
farmers, nothing more nor less than hardy, honest fellows, who
plowed and sowed for a living. Curtis had only a rudimentary
schooling, because he had given up the idea of finishing his studies
in the High School in Grand Rapids, on the chance of going into
business with a livery stable keeper. Then in time he had bought
out the business and had run it for himself. Some one in Chicago
owed him money, and in default of payment had offered him a
couple of lots on Wabash Avenue. That was how he happened
to come to Chicago. Naturally enough as the city grew the Wabash Avenue property—it was near Monroe Street—increased in
value. He sold the lots and bought other real estate, sold that and
bought somewhere else, and so on, till he owned some of the best
business sites in the city. Just his ground rent alone brought
him, heaven knew, how many thousands a year. He was one of
the largest real estate owners in Chicago. But he no longer bought
and sold. His property had grown so large that just the management of it alone took up most of his time. He had an office in the
Rookery, and perhaps being so close to the Board of Trade Building had given him a taste for trying a little deal in wheat now
and then. As a rule, he deplored speculation. He had no fixed
principles about it, like Charlie. Only he was conservative—occasionally he hazarded small operations. Somehow he had never married. There had been affairs. Oh, yes, one or two, of course.

Nothing very serious. He just didn't seem to have met the right girl, that was all. He lived on Michigan Avenue, near the corner of Twenty-first Street, in one of those discouraging eternal yellow limestone houses with a basement dining-room. His aunt kept house for him, and his nieces and nephews overran the place. There was always a raft of them there, either coming or going; and the way they exploited him! He supported them all; heaven knew how many there were; such drabs and gawks, all elbows and knees, who soaked themselves with cologne and made companions of the servants. They and the second girls were always squabbling about their things that they found in each other's rooms.

It was growing late. At length Mrs. Cressler rose.

"My goodness, Laura, look at the time; and I've been keeping you up when you must be killed for sleep."

She took herself away, pausing at the doorway long enough to say:

"Do try to manage to take part in the play. J. made me promise that I would get you."

"Well, I think I can," Laura answered. "Only I'll have to see first how our new régime is going to run—the house I mean."

When Mrs. Cressler had gone Laura lost no time in getting to bed. But after she turned out the gas she remembered that she had not "covered" the fire, a custom that she still retained from the daily round of her life at Barrington. She did not light the gas again, but guided by the firelight spread a shovelful of ashes over the top of the grate. Yet when she had done this, she still knelt there a moment, looking wide-eyed into the glow, thinking over the events of the last twenty-four hours. When all was said and done, she had, after all, found more in Chicago than the clash and trepidation of empire-making, more than the reverberation of the thunder of battle, more than the piping and choiring of sweet music.

First it had been Sheldon Corthell, quiet, persuasive, eloquent. Then Landry Court with his exuberance and extravagance and boyishness, and now—unexpectedly—behold, a new element had appeared—this other one, this man of the world, of affairs, mature, experienced, whom she hardly knew. It was charming, she told herself, exciting. Life never had seemed half so delightful. Romantic, she felt Romance, unseen, intangible, at work all about her. And love, which of all things knowable was dearest to her, came to her unsought.

Her first aversion to the Great Gray City was fast disappearing. She saw it now in a kindlier aspect.

"I think," she said at last, as she still knelt before the fire, looking deep into the coals, absorbed, abstracted, "I think that I am going to be very happy here."

III

ON a certain Monday morning, about a month later, Curtis Jadwin descended from his office in the Rookery Building, and turning southward, took his way toward the brokerage and commission office of Gretry, Converse and Co., on the ground floor of the Board of Trade Building, only a few steps away.

It was about nine o'clock; the weather was mild, the sun shone. La Salle Street swarmed with the multitudinous life that seethed about the doors of the innumerable offices of brokers and commission men of the neighborhood. To the right, in the peristyle of the Illinois Trust Building, groups of clerks, of messengers, of brokers, of clients, and of depositors formed and broke incessantly. To the left, where the façade of the Board of Trade blocked the street, the activity was astonishing, and in and out of the swing doors of its entrance streamed an incessant tide of coming and going. All the life of the neighborhood seemed to centre at this point—the entrance of the Board of Trade. Two currents that trended swiftly through La Salle and Jackson Streets, and that fed, or were fed by other tributaries that poured in through Fifth Avenue, and through Clark and Dearborn Streets, met at this point —one setting in, the other out. The nearer the currents the greater their speed. Men—mere flotsam in the flood—as they turned into La Salle Street from Adams or from Monroe, or even from as far as Madison, seemed to accelerate their pace as they approached. At the Illinois Trust the walk became a stride, at the Rookery the stride was also a trot. But at the corner of Jackson Street, the Board of Trade now merely the width of the street away, the trot became a run, and young men and boys, under the pretence of escaping the trucks and wagons of the cobbles, dashed across at a veritable gallop, flung themselves panting into the entrance of the Board, were ingulfed in the turmoil of the spot, and disappeared with a sudden fillip into the gloom of the interior.

Often Jadwin had noted the scene, and, unimaginative though

he was, had long since conceived the notion of some great, some resistless force within the Board of Trade Building that held the tide of the streets within its grip, alternately drawing it in and throwing it forth. Within there, a great whirlpool, a pit of roaring waters spun and thundered, sucking in the life tides of the city, sucking them in as into the mouth of some tremendous cloaca, the maw of some colossal sewer; then vomiting them forth again, spewing them up and out, only to catch them in the return eddy and suck them in afresh.

Thus it went, day after day. Endlessly, ceaselessly, the Pit, enormous, thundering, sucked in and spewed out, sending the swirl of its mighty central eddy far out through the city's channels. Terrible at the centre, it was, at the circumference, gentle, insidious, and persuasive, the send of the flowing so mild that to embark upon it, yielding to the influence, was a pleasure that seemed all devoid of risk. But the circumference was not bounded by the city. All through the Northwest, all through the central world of the Wheat the set and whirl of that innermost Pit made itself felt; and it spread and spread and spread till grain in the elevators of Western Iowa moved and stirred and answered to its centripetal force, and men upon the streets of New York felt the mysterious tugging of its undertow engage their feet, embrace their bodies, overwhelm them, and carry them bewildered and unresisting back and downward to the Pit itself.

Nor was the Pit's centrifugal power any less. Because of some sudden eddy spinning outward from the middle of its turmoil, a dozen bourses of continental Europe clamored with panic, a dozen Old-World banks, firm as the established hills, trembled and vibrated. Because of an unexpected caprice in the swirling of the inner current, some far-distant channel suddenly dried, and the pinch of famine made itself felt among the vine dressers of Northern Italy, the coal miners of Western Prussia. Or another channel filled, and the starved moujik of the steppes, and the hunger-shrunken coolie of the Ganges' watershed fed suddenly fat and made thank offerings before ikon and idol.

There in the centre of the Nation, midmost of that continent that lay between the oceans of the New World and the Old, in the heart's heart of the affairs of men, roared and rumbled the Pit. It was as if the Wheat, Nourisher of the Nations, as it rolled gigantic and majestic in a vast flood from West to East, here, like a Niagara, finding its flow impeded, burst suddenly into the appalling fury of the Maelstrom, into the chaotic spasm of a world-force, a primeval energy, blood-brother of the earthquake and the glacier, raging and wrathful that its power should be braved by some pinch of human spawn that dared raise barriers across its courses.

Small wonder that Cressler laughed at the thought of cornering wheat, and even now as Jadwin crossed Jackson Street, on his way to his broker's office on the lower floor of the Board of Trade Building, he noted the ebb and flow that issued from its doors, and remembered the huge river of wheat that rolled through this place from the farms of Iowa and ranches of Dakota to the mills and bakeshops of Europe.

"There's something, perhaps, in what Charlie says," he said to himself. "Corner this stuff—my God!"

Gretry, Converse & Co. was the name of the brokerage firm that always handled Jadwin's rare speculative ventures. Converse was dead long since, but the firm still retained its original name. The house was as old and as well established as any on the Board of Trade. It had a reputation for conservatism, and was known more as a Bear than a Bull concern. It was immensely wealthy and immensely important. It discouraged the growth of a clientèle of country customers, of small adventurers, knowing well that these were the first to go in a crash, unable to meet margin calls, and leaving to their brokers the responsibility of their disastrous trades. The large, powerful Bears were its friends, the Bears strong of grip, tenacious of jaw, capable of pulling down the strongest Bull. Thus the firm had no consideration for the "outsiders," the "public" —the Lambs. The Lambs! Such a herd, timid, innocent, feeble, as much out of place in La Salle Street as a puppy in a cage of panthers; the Lambs, whom Bull and Bear did not so much as condescend to notice, but who, in their mutual struggle of horn and claw, they crushed to death by the mere rolling of their bodies.

Jadwin did not go directly into Gretry's main office, but instead made his way in at the entrance of the Board of Trade Building, and going on past the stairways that on either hand led up to the "Floor" on the second story, entered the corridor beyond, and thence gained the customers' room of Gretry, Converse & Co. All the more important brokerage firms had offices on the ground floor of the building, offices that had two entrances, one giving upon the street, and one upon the corridor of the Board. Generally the corridor entrance admitted directly to the firm's customers' room. This was the case with the Gretry-Converse house.

Once in the customers' room, Jadwin paused, looking about him.

He could not tell why Gretry had so earnestly desired him to come to his office that morning, but he wanted to know how wheat was selling before talking to the broker. The room was large, and but for the lighted gas, burning crudely without globes, would have been dark. All one wall opposite the door was taken up by a great blackboard covered with chalked figures in columns, and illuminated by a row of overhead gas jets burning under a tin reflector. Before this board files of chairs were placed, and these were occupied by groups of nondescripts, shabbily dressed men, young and old, with tired eyes and unhealthy complexions, who smoked and expectorated, or engaged in interminable conversations.

In front of the blackboard, upon a platform, a young man in shirt-sleeves, his cuffs caught up by metal clamps, walked up and down. Screwed to the blackboard itself was a telegraph instrument, and from time to time, as this buzzed and ticked, the young man chalked up cabalistic and almost illegible figures under columns headed by initials of certain stocks and bonds, or by the words "Pork," "Oats," or, larger than all the others, "May Wheat." The air of the room was stale, close, and heavy with tobacco fumes. The only noises were the low hum of conversations, the unsteady click of the telegraph key, and the tapping of the chalk in the marker's fingers.

But no one in the room seemed to pay the least attention to the blackboard. One quotation replaced another, and the key and the chalk clicked and tapped incessantly. The occupants of the room, sunk in their chairs, seemed to give no heed; some even turned their backs; one, his handkerchief over his knee, adjusted his spectacles, and opening a newspaper two days old, began to read with peering deliberation, his lips forming each word. These nondescripts gathered there, they knew not why. Every day found them in the same place, always with the same fetid, unlighted cigars, always with the same frayed newspapers two days old. There they sat, inert, stupid, their decaying senses hypnotized and soothed by the sound of the distant rumble of the Pit, that came through the ceiling from the floor of the Board overhead.

One of these figures, that of a very old man, blear-eyed, decrepit, dirty, in a battered top hat and faded frock coat, discolored and weather-stained at the shoulders, seemed familiar to Jadwin. It recalled some ancient association, he could not say what. But he was unable to see the old man's face distinctly; the light was bad, and he sat with his face turned from him, eating a sandwich, which he held in a trembling hand.

Jadwin having noted that wheat was selling at 94, went away, glad to be out of the depressing atmosphere of the room.

Gretry was in his office, and Jadwin was admitted at once. He sat down in a chair by the broker's desk, and for the moment the two talked of trivialities. Gretry was a large, placid, smooth-faced man, stolid as an ox; inevitably dressed in blue serge, a quill tooth-pick behind his ear, a Grand Army button in his lapel. He and Jadwin were intimates. The two had come to Chicago almost simultaneously, and had risen together to become the wealthy men they were at the moment. They belonged to the same club, lunched together every day at Kinsley's, and took each other driving behind their respective trotters on alternate Saturday afternoons. In the middle of summer each stole a fortnight from his business, and went fishing at Geneva Lake in Wisconsin.

"I say," Jadwin observed, "I saw an old fellow outside in your customers' room just now that put me in mind of Hargus. You remember that deal of his, the one he tried to swing before he died. Oh—how long ago was that? Bless my soul, that must have been fifteen, yes twenty years ago."

The deal of which Jadwin spoke was the legendary operation of the Board of Trade—a mammoth corner in September wheat, manipulated by this same Hargus, a millionaire, who had tripled his fortune by the corner, and had lost it by some chicanery on the part of his associate before another year. He had run wheat up to nearly two dollars, had been in his day a king all-powerful. Since then all deals had been spoken of in terms of the Hargus affair. Speculators said, "It was almost as bad as the Hargus deal." "It was like the Hargus smash." "It was as big a thing as the Hargus corner." Hargus had become a sort of creature of legends, mythical, heroic, transfigured in the glory of his millions.

"Easily twenty years ago," continued Jadwin. "If Hargus could come to life now, he'd be surprised at the difference in the way we do business these days. Twenty years. Yes, it's all of that. I declare, Sam, we're getting old, aren't we?"

"I guess that *was* Hargus you saw out there," answered the broker. "He's not dead. Old fellow in a stove-pipe and greasy frock coat? Yes, that's Hargus."

"What!" exclaimed Jadwin. *"That* Hargus?"

"Of course it was. He comes round every day. The clerks give him a dollar every now and then."

"And he's not dead? And that was Hargus, that wretched, broken—whew! I don't want to think of it, Sam!" And Jadwin, taken all aback, sat for a moment speechless.

"Yes, sir," muttered the broker grimly, "that was Hargus."

There was a long slience. Then at last Gretry exclaimed briskly:

"Well, here's what I want to see you about."

He lowered his voice: "You know I've got a correspondent or two at Paris—all the brokers have—and we make no secret as to who they are. But I've had an extra man at work over there for the last six months, very much on the quiet. I don't mind telling you this much—that he's not the least important member of the United States Legation. Well, now and then he is supposed to send me what the reporters call "exclusive news"—that's what I feed him for, and I could run a private steam yacht on what it costs me. But news I get from him is a day or two in advance of everybody else. He hasn't sent me anything very important till this morning. This here just came in."

He picked up a despatch from his desk and read:

" 'Utica — headquarters — modification—organic—concomitant —within one month,' which means," he added, "this. I've just deciphered it," and he handed Jadwin a slip of paper on which was written:

"Bill providing for heavy import duties on foreign grains certain to be introduced in French Chamber of Deputies within one month."

"Have you got it?" he demanded of Jadwin, as he took the slip back. "Won't forget it?" He twisted the paper into a roll and burned it carefully in the office cuspidor.

"Now," he remarked, "do you come in? It's just the two of us, J., and I think we can make that Porteous clique look very sick."

"Hum!" murmured Jadwin surprised. "That *does* give you a twist on the situation. But to tell the truth, I had sort of made up my mind to keep out of speculation since my last little deal. A man gets into this game, and into it, and into it, and before you know he can't pull out—and he don't want to. Next he gets his nose scratched, and he hits back to make up for it, and just hits into the air and loses his balance—and down he goes. *I* don't want to make any more money, Sam. I've got my little pile, and before I get too old I want to have some fun out of it."

"But Lord love you, J.," objected the other, "this ain't speculation. You can see for yourself how sure it is. I'm not a baby at this business, am I? You'll let me know something of this game, won't you? And I tell you, J., it's found money. The man that sells wheat short on the strength of this has as good as got the money in his vest pocket already. Oh, nonsense, of course you'll come in. I've been laying for that Bull gang since long before the Helmick failure, and now I've got it right where I want it. Look here, J., you aren't the man to throw money away. You'd buy a business block if you knew you could sell it over again at a profit. Now here's the chance to make really a fine Bear deal. Why, as soon as this news gets on the floor there, the price will bust right down, and down, and down. Porteous and his crowd couldn't keep it up to save 'em from the receiver's hand one single minute."

"*I* know, Sam," answered Jadwin, "and the trouble is, not that I don't want to speculate, but that I *do*—too much. That's why I said I'd keep out of it. It isn't so much the money as the fun of playing the game. With half a show, I would get in a little more and a little more, till by and by I'd try to throw a big thing, and instead, the big thing would throw me. Why, Sam, when you told me that that wreck out there mumbling a sandwich was Hargus, it made me turn cold."

"Yes, in your feet," retorted Gretry. "I'm not asking you to risk all your money, am I, or a fifth of it, or a twentieth of it? Don't be an ass, J. Are we a conservative house, or aren't we? Do I talk like this when I'm not sure? Look here. Let me sell a million bushels for you. Yes, I know it's a bigger order than I've handled for you before. But *this* time I want to go *right into it,* head down and heels up, and get a twist on those Porteous buckoes, and raise 'em right out of their boots. We get a crop report this morning, and if the visible supply is as large as I think it is, the price will go off and unsettle the whole market. I'll sell short for you at the best figures we can get, and you can cover on the slump any time between now and the end of May."

Jadwin hesitated. In spite of himself he felt a Chance had come. Again that strange sixth sense of his, the inexplicable instinct, that only the born speculator knows, warned him. Every now and then during the course of his business career, this intuition came to him, this *flair,* this intangible, vague premonition, this presentiment that he must seize Opportunity or else Fortune, that so long had stayed at his elbow, would desert him. In the air about him he seemed to feel an influence, a sudden new element, the presence of a new force. It was Luck, the great power, the great goddess, and all at once it had stooped from out the invisible, and just over his head passed swiftly in a rush of glittering wings.

"The thing would have to be handled like glass," observed the broker thoughtfully, his eyes narrowing. "A tip like this is public property in twenty-four hours, and it don't give us any too much time. I don't want to break the price by unloading a million or more bushels on 'em all of a sudden. I'll scatter the orders pretty evenly. You see," he added, "here's a big point in our favor. We'll be able to sell on a strong market. The Pit traders have got some crazy war rumor going, and they're as flighty over it as a young ladies' seminary over a great big rat. And even without that, the market is top-heavy. Porteous makes me weary. He and his gang have been bucking it up till we've got an abnormal price. Ninety-four for May wheat! Why, it's ridiculous. Ought to be selling way down in the eighties. The least little jolt would tip her over. Well," he said abruptly, squaring himself at Jadwin, "do we come in? If that same luck of yours is still in working order, here's your chance, J., to make a killing. There's just that gilt-edged, full-morocco chance that a report of big 'visible' would give us."

Jadwin laughed. "Sam," he said, "I'll flip a coin for it."

"Oh, get out," protested the broker; then suddenly—the gambling instinct that a lifetime passed in that place had cultivated in him—exclaimed:

"All right. Flip a coin. But give me your word you'll stay by it. Heads you come in; tails you don't. Will you give me your word?"

"Oh, I don't know about that," replied Jadwin, amused at the foolishness of the whole proceeding. But as he balanced the half-dollar on his thumb-nail, he was all at once absolutely assured that it would fall heads. He flipped it in the air, and even as he watched it spin, said to himself, "It will come heads. It could not possibly be anything else. I *know* it will be heads."

And as a matter of course the coin fell heads.

"All right," he said, "I'll come in."

"For a million bushels?"

"Yes—for a million. How much in margins will you want?"

Gretry figured a moment on the back of an envelope.

"Fifty thousand dollars," he announced at length.

Jadwin wrote the check on a corner of the broker's desk, and held it a moment before him.

"Good-by," he said, apostrophizing the bit of paper. "Good-by. I ne'er shall look upon your like again."

Gretry did not laugh.

"Huh!" he grunted. "You'll look upon a hatful of them before the month is out."

That same morning Landry Court found himself in the corridor on the ground floor of the Board of Trade about nine o'clock. He had just come out of the office of Gretry, Converse & Co., where he and the other Pit traders for the house had been receiving their orders for the day.

As he was buying a couple of apples at the news stand at the end of the corridor, Semple and a young Jew named Hirsch, Pit traders for small firms in La Salle Street, joined him.

"Hello, Court, what do you know?"

"Hello, Barry Semple! Hello, Hirsch!" Landry offered the halves of his second apple, and the three stood there a moment, near the foot of the stairs, talking and eating their apples from the points of their penknives.

"I feel sort of seedy this morning," Semple observed between mouthfuls. "Was up late last night at a stag. A friend of mine just got back from Europe, and some of the boys were giving him a little dinner. He was all over the shop, this friend of mine; spent most of his time in Constantinople; had some kind of newspaper business there. It seems that it's a pretty crazy proposition, Turkey and the Sultan and all that. He said that there was nearly a row over the 'Higgins-Pasha' incident, and that the British agent put it pretty straight to the Sultan's secretary. My friend said Constantinople put him in mind of a lot of opera bouffe scenery that had got spilled out in the mud. Say, Court, he said the streets were dirtier than the Chicago streets."

"Oh, come now," said Hirsch.

"Fact! And the dogs! He told us he knows now where all the yellow dogs go to when they die."

"But, say," remarked Hirsch, "what is that about the Higgins-Pasha business? I thought that was over long ago."

"Oh, it is," answered Semple easily. He looked at his watch. "I guess it's about time to go up, pretty near half-past nine."

The three mounted the stairs, mingling with the groups of floor traders who, in steadily increasing numbers, had begun to move in the same direction. But on the way Hirsch was stopped by his brother.

"Hey, I got that box of cigars for you."

Hirsch paused. "Oh! All right," he said, then he added: "Say, how about that Higgins-Pasha affair? You remember that row between England and Turkey. They tell me the British agent in Constantinople put it pretty straight to the Sultan the other day."

The other was interested. "He did, hey?" he said. "The market hasn't felt it, though. Guess there's nothing to it. But there's Kelly yonder. He'd know. He's pretty thick with Porteous' men. Might ask him."

"*You* ask him and let me know. I got to go on the floor. It's nearly time for the gong."

Hirsch's brother found Kelly in the centre of a group of settlement clerks.

"Say, boy," he began, "*you* ought to know. They tell me there may be trouble between England and Turkey over the Higgins-Pasha incident, and that the British Foreign Office has threatened the Sultan with an ultimatum. I can see the market if that's so."

"Nothing in it," retorted Kelly. "But I'll find out—to make sure, by jingo."

Meanwhile, Landry had gained the top of the stairs, and turning to the right, passed through a great doorway, and came out upon the floor of the Board of Trade.

It was a vast inclosure, lighted on either side by great windows of colored glass, the roof supported by thin iron pillars elaborately decorated. To the left were the bulletin blackboards, and beyond these, in the northwest angle of the floor, a great railed-in space where the Western Union Telegraph was installed. To the right, on the other side of the room, a row of tables, laden with neatly arranged paper bags half full of samples of grains, stretched along the east wall from the doorway of the public room at one end to the telephone room at the other.

The centre of the floor was occupied by the pits. To the left and to the front of Landry the provision pit, to the right the corn pit, while further on at the north extremity of the floor, and nearly under the visitors' gallery, much larger than the other two, and flanked by the wicket of the official recorder, was the wheat pit itself.

Directly opposite the visitors' gallery, high upon the south wall,

a great dial was affixed, and on the dial a marking hand that indicated the current price of wheat, fluctuating with the changes
made in the Pit. Just now, it stood at ninety-three and three-
eighths, the closing quotation of the preceding day.

As yet, all the pits were empty. It was some fifteen minutes after
nine. Landry checked his hat and coat at the coat room near the
north entrance, and slipped into an old tennis jacket of striped blue
flannel. Then, hatless, his hands in his pockets, he leisurely crossed
the floor, and sat down in one of the chairs that were ranged in
files upon the floor in front of the telegraph inclosure. He scrutin-
ized again the despatches and orders that he held in his hands;
then, having fixed them in his memory, tore them into very small
bits, looking vaguely about the room, developing his plan of campaign for the morning.

In a sense, Landry Court had a double personality. Away from
the neighborhood and influence of La Salle Street, he was "rattle-
brained," absent-minded, impractical, and easily excited, the last
fellow in the world to be trusted with any business responsibility.
But the thunder of the streets around the Board of Trade, and,
above all, the movement and atmosphere of the floor itself awoke
within him a very different Landry Court; a whole new set of nerves
came into being with the tap of the nine-thirty gong, a whole new
system of brain machinery began to move with the first figure called
in the Pit. And from that instant until the close of the session, no
floor trader, no broker's clerk nor scalper was more alert, more
shrewd, or kept his head more surely than the same young fellow
who confused his social engagements for the evening of the same
day. The Landry Court the Dearborn girls knew was a far different
young man from him who now leaned his elbows on the arms of the
chair upon the floor of the Board, and, his eyes narrowing, his lips
tightening, began to speculate upon what was to be the temper of
the Pit that morning.

Meanwhile the floor was beginning to fill up. Over in the railed-
in space, where the hundreds of telegraph instruments were in
place, the operators were arriving in twos and threes. They hung
their hats and ulsters upon the pegs in the wall back of them, and
in linen coats, or in their shirt sleeves, went to their seats, or, sitting upon their tables, called back and forth to each other, joshing,
cracking jokes. Some few addressed themselves directly to work,
and here and there the intermittent clicking of a key began, like
a diligent cricket busking himself in advance of its mates.

From the corridors on the ground floor up through the south doors came the pit traders in increasing groups. The noise of footsteps began to echo from the high vaulting of the roof. A messenger boy crossed the floor chanting an unintelligible name.

The groups of traders gradually converged upon the corn and wheat pits, and on the steps of the latter, their arms crossed upon their knees, two men, one wearing a silk skull-cap all awry, conversed earnestly in low tones.

Winston, a great, broad-shouldered bass-voiced fellow of some thirty-five years, who was associated with Landry in executing the orders of the Gretry-Converse house, came up to him, and, omitting any salutation, remarked, deliberately, slowly:

"What's all this about this trouble between Turkey and England?"

But before Landry could reply, a third trader for the Gretry Company joined the two. This was a young fellow named Rusbridge, lean, black-haired, a constant excitement glinting in his deep-set eyes.

"Say," he exclaimed, "there's something in that, there's something in that!"

"Where did you hear it?" demanded Landry.

"Oh—everywhere." Rusbridge made a vague gesture with one arm. "Hirsch seemed to know all about it. It appears that there's talk of mobilizing the Mediterranean squadron. Darned if I know."

"Might ask that 'Inter-Ocean' reporter. He'd be likely to know. I've seen him 'round here this morning, or you might telephone the Associated Press," suggested Landry. "The office never said a word to *me*."

"Oh, the 'Associated.' They know a lot always, don't they?" jeered Winston. "Yes, I rung 'em up. They 'couldn't confirm the rumor.' That's always the way. You can spend half a million a year in leased wires and special service and subscriptions to news agencies, and you get the first smell of news like this right here on the floor. Remember that time when the Northwestern millers sold a hundred and fifty thousand barrels at one lick? The floor was talking of it three hours before the news slips were sent 'round, or a single wire was in. Suppose we had waited for the Associated people or the Commercial people then?"

"It's that Higgins-Pasha incident, I'll bet," observed Rusbridge, his eyes snapping.

"I heard something about that this morning," returned Landry. "But only that it was—"

"There! What did I tell you?" interrupted Rusbridge. "I said it was everywhere. There's no smoke without some fire. And I wouldn't be a bit surprised if we get cables before noon that the British War Office had sent an ultimatum."

And very naturally a few minutes later, Winston, at that time standing on the steps of the corn pit, heard from a certain broker, who had it from a friend who had just received a despatch from some one "in the know," that the British Secretary of State for War had forwarded an ultimatum to the Porte, and that diplomatic relations between Turkey and England were about to be suspended.

All in a moment, the entire Floor seemed to be talking of nothing else, and on the outskirts of every group one could overhear the words: "Seizure of custom house," "ultimatum," "Eastern question," "Higgins-Pasha incident." It was the rumor of the day, and before very long the pit traders began to receive a multitude of despatches countermanding selling orders, and directing them not to close out trades under certain very advanced quotations. The brokers began wiring their principals that the market promised to open strong and bullish.

But by now it was near to half-past nine. From the Western Union desks the clicking of the throng of instruments rose into the air in an incessant staccato stridulation. The messenger boys ran back and forth at top speed, dodging in and out among the knots of clerks and traders, colliding with one another, and without interruption intoning the names of those for whom they had despatches. The throng of traders concentrated upon the pits, and at every moment the deep-toned hum of the murmur of many voices swelled like the rising of a tide.

And at this moment, as Landry stood on the rim of the wheat pit, looking toward the telephone booth under the visitors' gallery, he saw the osseous, stoop-shouldered figure of Mr. Cressler—who, though he never speculated, appeared regularly upon the Board every morning—making his way toward one of the windows in the front of the building. His pocket was full of wheat, taken from a bag on one of the sample tables. Opening the window, he scattered the grain upon the sill, and stood for a long moment absorbed and interested in the dazzling flutter of the wings of innumerable pigeons who came to settle upon the ledge, pecking the grain with little, nervous, fastidious taps of their yellow beaks.

Landry cast a glance at the clock beneath the dial on the wall behind him. It was twenty-five minutes after nine. He stood in his accustomed place on the north side of the Wheat Pit, upon the topmost stair. The Pit was full. Below him and on either side of him were the brokers, scalpers, and traders—Hirsch, Semple, Kelly, Winston, and Rusbridge. The redoubtable Leaycraft, who, bidding for himself, was supposed to hold the longest line of May wheat of any one man in the Pit, the insignificant Grossmann, a Jew who wore a flannel shirt, and to whose outcries no one ever paid the least attention. Fairchild, Paterson, and Goodlock, the inseparable trio who represented the Porteous gang, silent men, middle-aged, who had but to speak in order to buy or sell a million bushels on the spot. And others, and still others, veterans of sixty-five, recruits just out of their teens, men who—some of them—in the past had for a moment dominated the entire Pit, but who now were content to play the part of "eighth-chasers," buying and selling on the same day, content with a profit of ten dollars. Others who might at that very moment be nursing plans which in a week's time would make them millionaires; still others who, under a mask of nonchalance, strove to hide the chagrin of yesterday's defeat. And they were there, ready, inordinately alert, ears turned to the faintest sound, eyes searching for the vaguest trace of meaning in those of their rivals, nervous, keyed to the highest tension, ready to thrust deep into the slightest opening, to spring, mercilessly, upon the smallest undefended spot. Grossmann, the little Jew of the grimy flannel shirt, perspired in the stress of the suspense, all but powerless to maintain silence till the signal should be given, drawing trembling fingers across his mouth. Winston, brawny, solid, unperturbed, his hands behind his back, waited immovably planted on his feet with all the gravity of a statue, his eyes preternaturally watchful, keeping Kelly—whom he had divined had some "funny business" on hand—perpetually in sight. The Porteous trio—Fairchild, Paterson, and Goodlock—as if unalarmed, unassailable, all but turned their backs to the Pit, laughing among themselves.

The official reporter climbed to his perch in the little cage on the edge of the Pit, shutting the door after him. By now the chanting of the messenger boys was an uninterrupted chorus. From all sides of the building, and in every direction, they crossed and recrossed each other, always running, their hands full of yellow envelopes. From the telephone alcoves came the prolonged, musical rasp of the call bells. In the Western Union booths the keys of the multitude of instruments raged incessantly. Bare-headed young men hurried up to one another, conferred an instant comparing despatches, then separated, darting away at top speed. Men called to each other half-way across the building. Over by the bulletin boards clerks and agents made careful memoranda of primary receipts, and noted down the amount of wheat on passage, the exports and the imports.

And all these sounds, the chatter of the telegraph, the intoning of the messenger boys, the shouts and cries of clerks and traders, the shuffle and trampling of hundreds of feet, the whirring of telephone signals rose into the troubled air, and mingled overhead to form a vast note, prolonged, sustained, that reverberated from vault to vault of the airy roof, and issued from every doorway, every opened window in one long roll of uninterrupted thunder. In the Wheat Pit the bids, no longer obedient of restraint, began one by one to burst out, like the first isolated shots of a skirmish line. Grossmann had flung out an arm, crying:

" 'Sell twenty-five May at ninety-five and an eighth," while Kelly and Semple had almost simultaneously shouted, "Give seven-eighths for May!"

The official reporter had been leaning far over to catch the first quotations, one eye upon the clock at the end of the room. The hour and minute hands were at right angles.

Then suddenly, cutting squarely athwart the vague crescendo of the floor came the single incisive stroke of a great gong. Instantly a tumult was unchained. Arms were flung upward in strenuous gestures, and from above the crowding heads in the Wheat Pit a multitude of hands, eager, the fingers extended, leaped into the air. All articulate expression was lost in the single explosion of sound as the traders surged downward to the centre of the Pit, grabbing each other, struggling toward each other, tramping, stamping, charging through with might and main. Promptly the hand on the great dial above the clock stirred and trembled, and as though driven by the tempest breath of the Pit moved upward through the degrees of its circle. It paused, wavered, stopped at length, and on the instant the hundreds of telegraph keys scattered throughout the building began clicking off the news to the whole country, from the Atlantic to the Pacific and from Mackinac to Mexico, that the Chicago market had made a slight advance and that May wheat, which had closed the day before at ninety-three and three-eighths, had opened that morning at ninety-four and a half.

But the advance brought out no profit-taking sales. The redoubtable Leaycraft and the Porteous trio, Fairchild, Paterson, and Goodlock, shook their heads when the Pit offered ninety-four for parts of their holdings. The price held firm. Goodlock even began to offer ninety-four. At every suspicion of a flurry Grossmann, always with the same gesture as though hurling a javelin, always with the same lamentable wail of distress, cried out:

" 'Sell twenty-five May at ninety-five and a fourth."

He held his five fingers spread to indicate the number of "contracts," or lots of five thousand bushels, which he wished to sell, each finger representing one "contract."

And it was at this moment that selling orders began suddenly to pour in upon the Gretry-Converse traders. Even other houses—Teller and West, Burbank & Co., Mattieson and Knight—received their share. The movement was inexplicable, puzzling. With a powerful Bull clique dominating the trading and every prospect of a strong market, who was it who ventured to sell short?

Landry among others found himself commissioned to sell. His orders were to unload three hundred thousand bushels on any advance over and above ninety-four. He kept his eye on Leaycraft, certain that he would force up the figure. But, as it happened, it was not Leaycraft but the Porteous trio who made the advance. Standing in the centre of the Pit, Paterson suddenly flung up his hand and drew it toward him, clutching the air—the conventional gesture of the buyer.

" 'Give an eighth for May."

Landry was at him in a second. Twenty voices shouted "sold," and as many traders sprang toward him with outstretched arms. Landry, however, was before them, and his rush carried Paterson half-way across the middle space of the Pit.

"Sold, sold."

Paterson nodded, and as Landry noted down the transaction the hand on the dial advanced again, and again held firm.

But after this the activity of the Pit fell away. The trading languished. By degrees the tension of the opening was relaxed. Landry, however, had refrained from selling more than ten "contracts" to Paterson. He had a feeling that another advance would come later on. Rapidly he made his plans. He would sell another fifty thousand bushels if the price went to ninety-four and a half, and would then "feel" the market, letting go small lots here and there, to test its strength, then, the instant he felt the market strong enough, throw a full hundred thousand upon it with a rush before it had time to break. He could feel—almost at his very finger-tips— how this market moved, how it strengthened, how it weakened. He knew just when to nurse it, to humor it, to let it settle, and when to crowd it, when to hustle it, when it would stand rough handling.

Grossmann still uttered his plaint⁻ from time to time, but no one so much as pretended to listen. The Porteous trio and Leaycraft kept the price steady at ninety-four and an eighth, but showed no inclination to force it higher. For a full five minutes not a trade was recorded. The Pit waited for the Report on the Visible Supply.

And it was during this lull in the morning's business that the idiocy of the English ultimatum to the Porte melted away. As inexplicably and as suddenly as the rumor had started, it now disappeared. Every one, simultaneously, seemed to ridicule it. England declare war on Turkey! Where was the joke? Who was the damn fool to have started that old, worn-out war scare? But, for all that, there was no reaction from the advance. It seemed to be understood that either Leaycraft or the Porteous crowd stood ready to support the market; and in place of the ultimatum story a feeling began to gain ground that the expected report would indicate a falling off in the "visible," and that it was quite on the cards that the market might even advance another point.

As the interest in the immediate situation declined, the crowd in the Pit grew less dense. Portions of it were deserted; even Grossmann, discouraged, retired to a bench under the visitors' gallery. And a spirit of horse-play, sheer foolishness, strangely inconsistent with the hot-eyed excitement of the few moments after the opening, invaded the remaining groups. Leaycraft, the formidable, as well as Paterson of the Porteous gang, and even the solemn Winston, found an apparently inexhaustible diversion in folding their telegrams into pointed javelins and sending them sailing across the room, watching the course of the missiles with profound gravity. A visitor in the gallery—no doubt a Western farmer on a holiday—having put his feet upon the rail, the entire Pit began to groan "boots, boots, boots."

A little later a certain broker came scurrying across the floor from the direction of the telephone room. Panting he flung himself up the steps of the Pit, forced his way among the traders with vigorous workings of his elbows, and shouted a bid.

"He's sick," shouted Hirsch. "Look out, he's sick. He's going

to have a fit." He grabbed the broker by both arms and hustled
him into the centre of the Pit. The others caught up the cry, a
score of hands pushed the newcomer from man to man. The Pit
traders clutched him, pulled his necktie loose, knocked off his hat,
vociferating all the while at top voice, "He's sick! He's sick!"

Other brokers and traders came up, and Grossmann, mistaking
the commotion for a flurry, ran into the Pit, his eyes wide, waving
his arm and wailing:

" 'Sell twenty-five May at ninety-five and a quarter."

But the victim, good-natured, readjusted his battered hat, and
again repeated his bid.

"Ah, go to bed," protested Hirsch.

"He's the man who struck Billy Paterson."

"Say, a horse bit him. Look out for him, he's going to have a
duck-fit."

The incident appeared to be the inspiration of a new "josh" that
had a great success, and a group of traders organized themselves
into an "anti-cravat committee," and made the rounds of the Pit,
twitching the carefully tied scarfs of the unwary out of place.
Grossmann, indignant at "t'ose monkey-doodle pizeness," withdrew
from the centre of the Pit. But while he stood in front of Leaycraft, his back turned, muttering his disgust, the latter, while carrying on a grave conversation with his neighbor, carefully stuck a
file of paper javelins all around the Jew's hat band, and then—still
without mirth and still continuing to talk—set them on fire.

Landry imagined by now that ninety-four and an eighth was
as high a figure as he could reasonably expect that morning, and
so began to "work off" his selling orders. Little by little he sold
the wheat "short," till all but one large lot was gone.

Then all at once, and for no discoverable immediate reason,
wheat, amid an explosion of shouts and vociferations, jumped to
ninety-four and a quarter, and before the Pit could take breath,
had advanced another eighth, broken to one-quarter, then jumped
to the five-eighths mark.

It was the Report on the Visible Supply beyond question, and
though it had not yet been posted, this sudden flurry was a sign
that it was not only near at hand, but would be bullish.

A few moments later it was bulletined in the gallery beneath
the dial and proved a tremendous surprise to nearly every man
upon the floor. No one had imagined the supply was so ample, so
all-sufficient to meet the demand. Promptly the Pit responded.

Wheat began to pour in heavily. Hirsch, Kelly, Grossmann, Leay-craft, the stolid Winston, and the excitable Rusbridge were hard at it. The price began to give. Suddenly it broke sharply. The hand on the great dial dropped to ninety-three and seven-eighths.

Landry was beside himself. He had not foreseen this break. There was no reckoning on that cursed "visible," and he still had 50,000 bushels to dispose of. There was no telling now how low the price might sink. He must act quickly, radically. He fought his way toward the Porteous crowd, reached over the shoulder of the little Jew Grossmann, who stood in his way, and thrust his hand almost into Paterson's face, shouting:

" 'Sell fifty May at seven-eighths."

It was the last one of his unaccountable selling orders of the early morning.

The other shook his head.

" 'Sell fifty May at three-quarters."

Suddenly some instinct warned Landry that another break was coming. It was in the very air around him. He could almost physically feel the pressure of renewed avalanches of wheat crowding down the price. Desperate, he grabbed Paterson by the shoulder.

" 'Sell fifty May at five-eighths."

"Take it," vociferated the other, as though answering a challenge.

And in the heart of this confusion, in this downward rush of the price, Luck, the golden goddess, passed with the flirt and flash of glittering wings, and hardly before the ticker in Gretry's office had signaled the decline, the memorandum of the trade was down upon Landry's card and Curtis Jadwin stood pledged to deliver, before noon on the last day of May, one million bushels of wheat into the hands of the representatives of the great Bulls of the Board of Trade.

But by now the real business of the morning was over. The Pit knew it. Grossmann, obstinate, hypnotized as it were by one idea, still stood in his accustomed place on the upper edge of the Pit, and from time to time, with the same despairing gesture, emitted his doleful outcry of " 'Sell twenty-five May at ninety-five and three-quarters."

Nobody listened. The traders stood around in expectant attitudes, looking into one another's faces, waiting for what they could not exactly say; loth to leave the Pit lest something should "turn up" the moment their backs were turned.

By degrees the clamor died away, ceased, began again irregularly, then abruptly stilled. Here and there a bid was called, an offer made, like the intermittent crack of small arms after the stopping of the cannonade.

" 'Sell five May at one-eighth."

" 'Sell twenty at one-quarter."

" 'Give one-eighth for May."

For an instant the shoutings were renewed. Then suddenly the gong struck. The traders began slowly to leave the Pit. One of the floor officers, an old fellow in uniform and vizored cap, appeared, gently shouldering toward the door the groups wherein the bidding and offering were still languidly going on. His voice full of remonstration, he repeated continually:

"Time's up, gentlemen. Go on now and get your lunch. Lunch time now. Go on now, or I'll have to report you. Time's up."

The tide set toward the doorways. In the gallery the few visitors rose, putting on coats and wraps. Over by the check counter, to the right of the south entrance to the floor, a throng of brokers and traders jostled each other, reaching over one another's shoulders for hats and ulsters. In steadily increasing numbers they poured out of the north and south entrances, on their way to turn in their trading cards to the offices.

Little by little the floor emptied. The provision and grain pits were deserted, and as the clamor of the place lapsed away the telegraph instruments began to make themselves heard once more, together with the chanting of the messenger boys.

Swept clean in the morning, the floor itself, seen now through the thinning groups, was littered from end to end with scattered grain—oats, wheat, corn, and barley, with wisps of hay, peanut shells, apple parings, and orange peel, with torn newspapers, odds and ends of memoranda, crushed paper darts, and above all with a countless multitude of yellow telegraph forms, thousands upon thousands, crumpled and muddied under the trampling of innumerable feet. It was the débris of the battle-field, the abandoned impedimenta and broken weapons of contending armies, the detritus of conflict, torn, broken, and rent, that at the end of each day's combat incumbered the field.

At last even the tick of the last of telegraph keys died down. Shouldering themselves into their overcoats, the operators departed, calling back and forth to one another, making "dates," and cracking jokes. Washerwomen appeared with steaming pails, porters pushing great brooms before them began gathering the refuse of the floor into heaps.

Between the wheat and corn pits a band of young fellows, some of them absolute boys, appeared. These were the settlement clerks. They carried long account books. It was their duty to get the trades of the day into a "ring"—to trace the course of a lot of wheat which had changed hands perhaps a score of times during the trading—and their calls of "Wheat sold to Teller and West," "May wheat sold to Burbank & Co.," "May oats sold to Matthewson and Knight," "Wheat sold to Gretry, Converse & Co.," began to echo from wall to wall of the almost deserted room.

A cat, gray and striped, and wearing a dog collar of nickel and red leather, issued from the coat-room and picked her way across the floor. Evidently she was in a mood of the most ingratiating friend-liness, and as one after another of the departing traders spoke to her, raised her tail in the air and arched her back against the legs of the empty chairs. The janitor put in an appearance, lowering the tall colored windows with a long rod. A noise of hammering and the scrape of saws began to issue from a corner where a couple of carpenters tinkered about one of the sample tables.

Then at last even the settlement clerks took themselves off. At once there was a great silence, broken only by the harsh rasp of the carpenters' saws and the voice of the janitor exchanging jokes with the washerwomen. The sound of footsteps in distant quarters re-echoed as if in a church.

The washerwomen invaded the floor, spreading soapy and steaming water before them. Over by the sample tables a negro porter in shirt-sleeves swept entire bushels of spilled wheat, crushed, broken, and sodden, into his dust pans.

The day's campaign was over. It was past two o'clock. On the great dial against the eastern wall the indicator stood—sentinel fashion—at ninety-three. Not till the following morning would the whirlpool, the great central force that spun the Niagara of wheat in its grip, thunder and bellow again.

Later on even the washerwomen, even the porter and janitor, departed. An unbroken silence, the peacefulness of an untroubled calm, settled over the place. The rays of the afternoon sun flooded through the west windows in long parallel shafts full of floating golden motes. There was no sound; nothing stirred. The floor of the Board of Trade was deserted. Alone, on the edge of the aban-doned Wheat Pit, in a spot where the sunlight fell warmest—an atom of life, lost in the immensity of the empty floor—the gray cat made her toilet, diligently licking the fur on the inside of her thigh, one leg, as if dislocated, thrust into the air above her head.

IV

In the front parlor of the Cresslers' house a little company was gathered—Laura Dearborn and Page, Mrs. Wessels, Mrs. Cressler, and young Miss Gretry, an awkward, plain-faced girl of about nineteen, dressed extravagantly in a décolleté gown of blue silk. Curtis Jadwin and Cressler himself stood by the open fireplace smoking. Landry Court fidgeted on the sofa, pretending to listen to the Gretry girl, who told an interminable story of a visit to some wealthy relative who had a country seat in Wisconsin and who raised fancy poultry. She possessed, it appeared, three thousand hens, Brahma, Faverolles, Houdans, Dorkings, even peacocks and tame quails.

Sheldon Corthell, in a dinner coat, an unlighted cigarette between his fingers, discussed the spring exhibit of water-colors with Laura and Mrs. Cressler, Page listening with languid interest. Aunt Wess' turned the leaves of a family album, counting the number of photographs of Mrs. Cressler which it contained.

Black coffee had just been served. It was the occasion of the third rehearsal for the play which was to be given for the benefit of the hospital ward for Jadwin's mission children, and Mrs. Cressler had invited the members of the company for dinner. Just now every one awaited the arrival of the "coach," Monsieur Gerardy, who was always late.

"To my notion," observed Corthell, "the water-color that pretends to be anything more than a sketch oversteps its intended limits. The elaborated water-color, I contend, must be judged by the same standards as an oil painting. And if that is so, why not have the oil painting at once?"

"And with all that, if you please, not an egg on the place for breakfast," declared the Gretry girl in her thin voice. She was constrained, embarrassed. Of all those present she was the only one to mistake the character of the gathering and appear in formal costume. But one forgave Isabel Gretry such lapses as these. Invariably she did the wrong thing; invariably she was out of place in the matter of inadvertent speech, an awkward accident, the wrong toilette. For all her nineteen years, she yet remained the hoyden, young, undeveloped and clumsy.

"Never an egg, and three thousand hens in the runs," she continued. "Think of that! The Plymouth Rocks had the pip. And the others, my lands! I don't know. They just didn't lay."

"Ought to tickle the soles of their feet," declared Landry with profound gravity.

"Tickle their feet!"

"Best thing in the world for hens that don't lay. It sort of stirs them up. Oh, every one knows that."

"Fancy now! I'll write to Aunt Alice to-morrow."

Cressler clipped the tip of a fresh cigar, and, turning to Curtis Jadwin, remarked:

"I understand that Leaycraft alone lost nearly fifteen thousand."

He referred to Jadwin's deal in May wheat, the consummation of which had been effected the previous week. Squarely in the midst of the morning session, on the day following the "short" sale of Jadwin's million of bushels, had exploded the news of the intended action of the French chamber. Amid a tremendous clamor the price fell. The Bulls were panic-stricken. Leaycraft the redoubtable was overwhelmed at the very start. The Porteous trio heroically attempted to shoulder the wheat, but the load was too much. They as well gave ground, and, bereft of their support, May wheat, which had opened at ninety-three and five-eighths to ninety-two and a half, broke with the very first attack to ninety-two, hung there a moment, then dropped again to ninety-one and a half, then to ninety-one. Then, in a prolonged shudder of weakness, sank steadily down by quarters to ninety, to eighty-nine, and at last— a final collapse—touched eighty-eight cents. At that figure Jadwin began to cover. There was danger that the buying of so large a lot might bring about a rally in the price. But Gretry, a consummate master of Pit tactics, kept his orders scattered and bought gradually, taking some two or three days to accumulate the grain. Jadwin's luck—the never-failing guardian of the golden wings— seemed to have the affair under immediate supervision, and reports of timely rains in the wheat belt kept the price inert while the trade was being closed. In the end the "deal" was brilliantly successful, and Gretry was still chuckling over the setback to the Porteous gang. Exactly the amount of his friend's profits Jadwin did not know. As for himself, he had received from Gretry a check for fifty thousand dollars, every cent of which was net profit.

"I'm not going to congratulate you," continued Cressler. "As far as that's concerned, I would rather you had lost than won—if it would have kept you out of the Pit for good. You're cocky now. I know—Good Lord, don't I know. I had my share of it. I know how a man gets drawn into this speculating game—"

"Charlie, this wasn't speculating," interrupted Jadwin. "It was a certainty. It was found money. If I had known a certain piece of real estate was going to appreciate in value I would have bought it, wouldn't I?"

"All the worse, if it made it seem easy and sure to you. Do you know," he added suddenly. "Do you know that Leaycraft has gone to keep books for a manufacturing concern out in Dubuque?"

Jadwin pulled his mustache. He was looking at Laura Dearborn over the heads of Landry and the Gretry girl.

"I didn't suppose he'd be getting measured for a private yacht," he murmured. Then he continued, pulling his mustache vigorously: "Charlie, upon my word, what a beautiful—what beautiful *hair* that girl has!"

Laura was wearing it very high that evening, the shining black coils transfixed by a strange hand-cut ivory comb that had been her grandmother's. She was dressed in black taffeta, with a single great cabbage-rose pinned to her shoulder. She sat very straight in her chair, one hand upon her slender hip, her head a little to one side, listening attentively to Corthell.

By this time the household of the former rectory was running smoothly; everything was in place, the Dearborns were "settled," and a routine had begun. Her first month in her new surroundings had been to Laura an unbroken series of little delights. For formal social distractions she had but little taste. She left those to Page, who, as soon as Lent was over, promptly became involved in a bewildering round of teas, "dancing clubs," dinners, and theatre parties. Mrs. Wessels was her chaperon, and the little middle-aged lady found the satisfaction of a belated youth in conveying her pretty niece to the various functions that occupied her time. Each Friday night saw her in the gallery of a certain smart dancing school of the south side, where she watched Page dance her way from the "first waltz" to the last figure of the german. She counted the couples carefully, and on the way home was always able to say how the attendance of that particular evening compared with that of the former occasion, and also to inform Laura how many times Page had danced with the same young man.

Laura herself was more serious. She had begun a course of reading; no novels, but solemn works full of allusions to "Man" and "Destiny," which she underlined and annotated. Twice a week —on Mondays and Thursdays—she took a French lesson. Corthell managed to enlist the good services of Mrs. Wessels and escorted her to numerous piano and 'cello recitals, to lectures, to concerts. He even succeeded in achieving the consecration of a specified afternoon once a week, spent in his studio in the Fine Arts Building on the Lake Front, where he read to them "Saint Agnes Eve," "Sordello," "The Light of Asia"—poems which, with their inversions, obscurities, and astonishing arabesques of rhetoric, left Aunt Wess' bewildered, breathless, all but stupefied.

Laura found these readings charming. The studio was beautiful, lofty, the light dim; the sound of Corthell's voice returned from the thick hangings of velvet and tapestry in a subdued murmur. The air was full of the odor of pastilles.

Laura could not fail to be impressed with the artist's tact, his delicacy. In words he never referred to their conversation in the foyer of the Auditorium; only by some unexplained subtlety of attitude he managed to convey to her the distinct impression that he loved her always—that he was patient, waiting for some indefinite, unexpressed development.

Landry Court called upon her as often as she would allow. Once he had prevailed upon her and Page to accompany him to the matinee to see a comic opera. He had pronounced it "bully," unable to see that Laura evinced only a mild interest in the performance. On each propitious occasion he had made love to her extravagantly. He continually protested his profound respect with a volubility and earnestness that was quite uncalled for.

But, meanwhile, the situation had speedily become more complicated by the entrance upon the scene of an unexpected personage. This was Curtis Jadwin. It was impossible to deny the fact that "J." was in love with Mrs. Cressler's *protégée*. The business man had none of Corthell's talent for significant reticence, none of his tact, and older than she, a man-of-the-world, accustomed to deal with situations with unswerving directness, he, unlike Landry Court, was not in the least afraid of her. From the very first she found herself upon the defensive. Jadwin was aggressive, assertive, and his addresses had all the persistence and vehemence of veritable attack. Landry she could manage with the lifting of a finger, Corthell disturbed her only upon those rare occasions when he made love to her. But Jadwin gave her no time to so much as think of *finesse*. She was not even allowed to choose her own time and place for fencing, and to parry his invasion upon those intimate personal grounds which she pleased herself to keep secluded called upon her every feminine art of procrastination and strategy.

He contrived to meet her everywhere. He impressed Mrs. Cressler as auxiliary into his campaign, and a series of *rencontres* followed one another with astonishing rapidity. Now it was another opera party, now a box at McVicker's, now a dinner, or more often a drive through Lincoln Park behind Jadwin's trotters. He even had the Cresslers and Laura over to his mission Sunday-school for the Easter festival, an occasion of which Laura carried away a confused recollection of enormous canvas mottoes, that looked more like campaign banners than texts from the Scriptures, sheaves of calla lilies, imitation bells of tinfoil, revival hymns vociferated with deafening vehemence from seven hundred distended mouths, and through it all the disagreeable smell of poverty, the odor of uncleanliness that mingled strangely with the perfume of the lilies and the aromatic whiffs from the festoons of evergreen.

Thus the first month of her new life had passed. Laura did not trouble herself to look very far into the future. She was too much amused with her emancipation from the narrow horizon of her New England environment. She did not concern herself about consequences. Things would go on for themselves, and consequences develop without effort on her part. She never asked herself whether or not she was in love with any of the three men who strove for her favor. She was quite sure she was not ready—yet —to be married. There was even something distasteful in the idea of marriage. She liked Landry Court immensely; she found the afternoons in Corthell's studio delightful; she loved the rides in the park behind Jadwin's horses. She had no desire that any one of these affairs should exclude the other two. She wished nothing to be consummated. As for love, she never let slip an occasion to shock Aunt Wess' by declaring:

"I love—nobody. I shall never marry."

Page, prim, with great parade of her ideas of "good form," declared between her pursed lips that her sister was a flirt. But this was not so. Laura never manœuvred with her lovers, nor intrigued to keep from any one of them knowledge of her companionship with the other two. So upon such occasions as this, when all three found themselves face to face, she remained unperturbed.

At last, toward half-past eight, Monsieur Gerardy arrived. All through the winter amateur plays had been in great favor, and Gerardy had become, in a sense, a fad. He was in great demand. Consequently, he gave himself airs. His method was that of severity; he posed as a taskmaster, relentless, never pleased, hustling the amateur actors about without ceremony, scolding and browbeating. He was a small, excitable man who wore a frock coat much too small for him, a flowing purple cravat drawn through a finger ring, and enormous cuffs set off with huge buttons of Mexican onyx. In his lapel was an inevitable carnation, dried, shrunken, and lamentable. He was redolent of perfume and spoke of himself as an artist. He caused it to be understood that in the intervals of "coaching society plays" he gave his attention to the painting of landscapes. Corthell feigned to ignore his very existence.

The play-book in his hand, Monsieur Gerardy clicked his heels in the middle of the floor and punctiliously saluted every one present, bowing only from his shoulders, his head dropping forward as if propelled by successive dislocations of the vertebræ of his neck.

He explained the cause of his delay. His English was without accent, but at times suddenly entangled itself in curious Gallic constructions.

"Then I propose we begin at once," he announced. "The second act to-night, then, if we have time, the third act—from the book. And I expect the second act to be letter-perfect—let-ter-per-fect. There is nothing there but that." He held up his hand, as if to refuse to consider the least dissension. "There is nothing but that—no other thing."

All but Corthell listened attentively. The artist, however, turning his back, had continued to talk to Laura without lowering his tone, and all through Monsieur Gerardy's exhortation his voice had made itself heard. "Management of light and shade" . . . "color scheme" . . . "effects of composition."

Monsieur Gerardy's eye glinted in his direction. He struck his play-book sharply into the palm of his hand.

"Come, come!" he cried. "No more nonsense. Now we leave the girls alone and get to work. Here is the scene. Mademoiselle Gretry, if I derange you!" He cleared a space at the end of the parlor, pulling the chairs about. "Be attentive now. Here"—he placed a chair at his right with a flourish, as though planting a banner—"is the porch of Lord Glendale's country house."

"Ah," murmured Landry, winking solemnly at Page, "the chair is the porch of the house."

"And here," shouted Monsieur Gerardy, glaring at him and slamming down another chair, "is a rustic bench and practicable table set for breakfast."

Page began to giggle behind her play-book. Gerardy, his nostrils expanded, gave her his back. The older people, who were not to take part—Jadwin, the Cresslers, and Aunt Wess'—retired to a far corner, Mrs. Cressler declaring that they would constitute the audience.

"On stage," vociferated Monsieur Gerardy, perspiring from his exertions with the furniture. " 'Marion enters, timid and hesitating, L. C.' Come, who's Marion? Mademoiselle Gretry, if you please, and for the love of God remember your crossings. Sh! sh!" he cried, waving his arms at the others. "A little silence, if you please. Now, Marion."

Isabel Gretry, holding her play-book at her side, one finger marking the place, essayed an entrance with the words:

" 'Ah, the old home once more. See the clambering roses have—' "

But Monsieur Gerardy, suddenly compressing his lips as if in a heroic effort to repress his emotion, flung himself into a chair, turning his back and crossing his legs violently. Miss Gretry stopped, very much disturbed, gazing perplexedly at the coach's heaving shoulders.

There was a strained silence, then:

"Isn't—isn't that right?"

As if with the words she had touched a spring, Monsieur Gerardy bounded to his feet.

"Grand God! Is that left-centre where you have made the entrance? In fine, I ask you a little—*is* that left-centre? You have come in by the rustic bench and practicable table set for breakfast. A fine sight on the night of the performance that. Marion climbs over the rustic breakfast and practicable—over the rustic bench and practicable table, ha, ha, to make the entrance." Still holding the play-book, he clapped hands with elaborate sarcasm. "Ah, yes, good business that. That will bring down the house."

Meanwhile the Gretry girl turned again from left-centre.

" 'Ah, the old home again. See—' "

"Stop!" thundered Monsieur Gerardy. "Is that what you call timid and hesitating? Once more, those lines. . . . No, no.

It it not it at all. More of slowness, more of— Here, watch me."

He made the entrance with laborious exaggeration of effect, dragging one foot after another, clutching at the palings of an imaginary fence, while pitching his voice at a feeble falsetto, he quavered:

" 'Ah! The old home—ah . . . once more. See—' like that," he cried, straightening up. "Now then. We try that entrance again. Don't come on too quick after the curtain. Attention. I clap my hands for the curtain, and count three." He backed away, and, tucking the play-book under his arm, struck his palms together. "Now, one—two—*three*."

But this time, Isabel Gretry, in remembering her "business," confused her stage directions once more.

" 'Ah, the old home—' "

"Left-centre," interrupted the coach, in a tone of long-suffering patience.

She paused bewildered, and believing that she had spoken her lines too abruptly, began again:

" 'See, the clambering—' "

"*Left*-centre."

" 'Ah, the old home—' "

Monsieur Gerardy settled himself deliberately in his chair and, resting his head upon one hand, closed his eyes. His manner was that of Galileo under torture declaring "still it moves."

"*Left*-centre."

"Oh—oh, yes. I forgot."

Monsieur Gerardy apostrophized the chandelier with mirthless humor.

"Oh, ha, ha! She forgot."

Still another time Marion tried the entrance, and, as she came on, Monsieur Gerardy made vigorous signals to Page, exclaiming in a hoarse whisper:

"Lady Mary, ready. In a minute you come on. Remember the cue."

Meanwhile Marion had continued:

" 'See the clambering vines—' "

"Roses."

" 'The clambering rose vines—' "

"Roses, pure and simple."

" 'See! The clambering roses, pure and—' "

"Mademoiselle Gretry, will you do me the extreme obligation to bound yourself by the lines of the book?"

"I thought you said—"

"Go on, go on, go on! Is it God-possible to be thus stupid? Lady Mary, ready."

" 'See, the clambering roses have wrapped the old stones in a loving embrace. The birds build in the same old nests—' "

"Well, well, Lady Mary, where are you? You enter from the porch."

"I'm waiting for my cue," protested Page. "My cue is: 'Are there none that will remember me.' "

"Say," whispered Landry, coming up behind Page, "it would look bully if you could come out leading a greyhound."

"Ah, so, Mademoiselle Gretry," cried Monsieur Gerardy, "you left out the cue." He became painfully polite. "Give the speech once more, if you please."

"A dog would look bully on the stage," whispered Landry. "And I know where I could get one."

"Where?"

"A friend of mine. He's got a beauty, blue-gray—"

They become suddenly aware of a portentous silence. The coach, his arms folded, was gazing at Page with tightened lips.

" 'None who will remember me,' " he burst out at last. "Three times she gave it."

Page hurried upon the scene with the words:

" 'Ah, another glorious morning. The vines are drenched in dew.' " Then, raising her voice and turning toward the "house," " 'Arthur.' "

" 'Arthur,' " warned the coach. "That's you, Mr. Corthell. Ready. Well, then, Mademoiselle Gretry, you have something to say there."

"I can't say it," murmured the Gretry girl, her handkerchief to her face.

"What now? Continue. Your lines are 'I must not be seen here. It would betray all,' then conceal yourself in the arbor. Continue. Speak the line. It is the cue of Arthur."

"I can't," mumbled the girl behind her handkerchief.

"Can't. Why, then?"

"I—I have the nose-bleed."

Upon the instant Monsieur Gerardy quite lost his temper. He turned away, one hand to his head, rolling his eyes as if in mute appeal to heaven, then, whirling about, shook his play-book at the unfortunate Marion, crying out furiously:

"Ah, it lacked but that. You ought to understand at last, that when one rehearses for a play one does not have the nose-bleed. It is not decent."

Miss Gretry retired precipitately, and Laura came forward to say that she would read Marion's lines.

"No, no!" cried Monsieur Gerardy. "You—ah, if they were all like you! You are obliging, but it does not suffice. I am insulted."

The others, astonished, gathered about the "coach." They labored to explain. Miss Gretry had intended no slight. In fact, she was often taken that way; she was excited, nervous. But Monsieur Gerardy was not to be placated. Ah, no! He knew what was due a gentleman. He closed his eyes and raised his eyebrows to his very hair, murmuring superbly that he was offended. He had but one phrase in answer to all their explanations:

"One does not permit one's self to bleed at the nose during rehearsal."

Laura began to feel a certain resentment. The unfortunate Gretry girl had gone away in tears. What with the embarrassment of the wrong gown, the browbeating, and the nose-bleed, she was not far from hysterics. She had retired to the dining-room with Mrs. Cressler, and from time to time the sounds of her distress made themselves heard. Laura believed it quite time to interfere. After all, who was this Gerardy person, to give himself such airs? Poor Miss Gretry was to blame for nothing. She fixed the little Frenchman with a direct glance, and Page, who caught a glimpse of her face, recognized "the grand manner," and whispered to Landry.

"He'd better look out; he's gone just about as far as Laura will allow."

"It is not convenient," vociferated the "coach." "It is not permissible. I am offended."

"Monsieur Gerardy," said Laura, "we will say nothing more about it, if you please."

There was a silence. Monsieur Gerardy had pretended not to hear. He breathed loud through his nose, and Page hastened to observe that anyhow Marion was not on in the next scenes. Then abruptly, and resuming his normal expression, Monsieur Gerardy said:

"Let us proceed. It advances nothing to lose time. Come. Lady Mary and Arthur, ready."

The rehearsal continued. Laura, who did not come on during the act, went back to her chair in the corner of the room.

But the original group had been broken up. Mrs. Cressler was in the dining-room with the Gretry girl, while Jadwin, Aunt Wess', and Cressler himself were deep in a discussion of mind-reading and spiritualism.

As Laura came up, Jadwin detached himself from the others and met her.

"Poor Miss Gretry!" he observed. "Always the square peg in the round hole. I've sent out for some smelling salts."

It seemed to Laura that the capitalist was especially well-looking on this particular evening. He never dressed with the "smartness" of Sheldon Corthell or Landry Court, but in some way she did not expect that he should. His clothes were not what she was aware were called "stylish," but she had had enough experience with her own tailor-made gowns to know that the material was the very best that money could buy. The apparent absence of any padding in the broad shoulders of the frock coat he wore, to her mind, more than compensated for the "ready-made" scarf, and if the white waistcoat was not fashionably cut, she knew that *she* had never been able to afford a piqué skirt of just that particular grade.

"Suppose we go into the reception room," he observed abruptly. "Charlie bought a new clock last week that's a marvel. You ought to see it."

"No," she answered. "I am quite comfortable here, and I want to see how Page does in this act."

"I am afraid, Miss Dearborn," he continued, as they found their places, "that you did not have a very good time Sunday afternoon."

He referred to the Easter festival at his mission school. Laura had left rather early, alleging neuralgia and a dinner engagement.

"Why, yes, I did," she replied. "Only, to tell the truth, my head ached a little." She was ashamed that she did not altogether delight in her remembrance of Jadwin on that afternoon. He had "addressed" the school, with earnestness it was true, but in a strain decidedly conventional. And the picture he made leading the singing, beating time with the hymn-book, and between the verses declaring that "he wanted to hear every one's voice in the next verse," did not appeal very forcibly to her imagination. She fancied Sheldon Corthell doing these things, and could not forbear to smile. She had to admit, despite the protests of conscience, that she did prefer the studio to the Sunday-school.

"Oh," remarked Jadwin, "I'm sorry to hear you had a headache. I suppose my little Micks" (he invariably spoke of his mission children thus) "do make more noise than music."

"I found them very interesting."

"No, excuse me, but I'm afraid you didn't. My little Micks are not interesting—to look at nor to listen to. But I kind of—well, I don't know," he began pulling his mustache. "It seems to *suit* me to get down there and get hold of these people. You know Moody put me up to it. He was here about five years ago, and I went to one of his big meetings, and then to all of them. And I met the fellow, too, and I tell you, Miss Dearborn, he stirred me all up. I didn't "get religion." No, nothing like that. But I got a notion it was time to be up and doing, and I figured it out that business principles were as good in religion as they are—well, in La Salle Street, and that if the church people—the men, I mean—put as much energy, and shrewdness, and competitive spirit into the saving of souls as they did into the saving of dollars that we might get somewhere. And so I took hold of a half-dozen broken-down, bankrupt Sunday-school concerns over here on Archer Avenue that were fighting each other all the time, and amalgamated them all— a regular trust, just as if they were iron foundries—and turned the incompetents out and put my subordinates in, and put the thing on a business basis, and by now, I'll venture to say, there's not a better *organized* Sunday-school in all Chicago, and I'll bet if D. L. Moody were here to-day he'd say, 'Jadwin, well done, thou good and faithful servant.'"

"I haven't a doubt of it, Mr. Jadwin," Laura hastened to exclaim. "And you must not think that I don't believe you are doing a splendid work."

"Well, it *suits* me," he repeated. "I like my little Micks, and now and then I have a chance to get hold of the kind that it pays to push along. About four months ago I came across a boy in the Bible class; I guess he's about sixteen; name is Bradley—Billy Bradley, father a confirmed drunk, mother takes in washing, sister—we won't speak about; and he seemed to be bright and willing to work, and I gave him a job in my agent's office, just directing envelopes. Well, Miss Dearborn, that boy has a desk of his own now, and the agent tells me he's one of the very best men he's got. He does his work so well that I've been able to discharge two other fellows who

sat around and watched the clock for lunch hour, and Bradley does
their work now better and quicker than they did, and saves me
twenty dollars a week; that's a thousand a year. So much for a
business-like Sunday-school; so much for taking a good aim when
you cast your bread upon the waters. The last time I saw Moody
I said, 'Moody, my motto is "Not slothful in business, fervent in
spirit, praising the Lord." ' I remember we were out driving at
the time, I took him out behind Lizella—she's almost straight Wilkes'
blood and can trot in two-ten, but you can believe *he* didn't know
that—and, as I say, I told him what my motto was, and he said, 'J.,
good for you; you keep to that. There's no better motto in the world
for the American man of business.' He shook my hand when he
said it, and I haven't ever forgotten it."

Not a little embarrassed, Laura was at a loss just what to say,
and in the end remarked lamely enough:

"I am sure it is the right spirit—the best motto."

"Miss Dearborn," Jadwin began again suddenly, "why don't
you take a class down there? The little 'Micks aren't so dreadful
when you get to know them."

"I !" exclaimed Laura, rather blankly. She shook her head.
"Oh, no, Mr. Jadwin. I should be only an incumbrance. Don't
misunderstand me. I approve of the work with all my heart, but I
am not fitted—I feel no call. I should be so inapt that I know I
should do no good. My training has been so different, you know,"
she said, smiling. "I am an Episcopalian—'of the straightest sect
of the Pharisees.' I should be teaching your little Micks all about
the meaning of candles, and 'Eastings,' and the absolution and
remission of sins."

"I wouldn't care if you did," he answered. "It's the indirect
influence I'm thinking of—the indirect influence that a beautiful,
pure-hearted, noble-minded woman spreads around her wherever
she goes. I know what it has done for me, and I know
that not only my little Micks, but every teacher and every
superintendent in that school would be inspired, and stimulated, and born again so soon as ever you set foot in the building. Men need good women, Miss Dearborn. Men who are doing
the work of the world. I believe in women as I believe in Christ.
But I don't believe they were made—any more than Christ was—
to cultivate—beyond a certain point—their own souls, and refine
their own minds, and live in a sort of warmed-over, dilettante,
stained-glass world of seclusion and *ex*clusion. No, sir, that won't

do for the United States and the men who are making them the greatest nation of the world. The men have got all the get-up-and-get they want, but they need the women to point them straight, and to show them how to lead that other kind of life that isn't all grind. Since I've known you, Miss Dearborn, I've just begun to wake up to the fact that there *is* that other kind, but I can't lead that life without you. There's *no* kind of life that's worth anything to me now that don't include you. I don't need to tell you that I want you to marry me. You know that by now, I guess, without any words from me. I love you, and I love you as a man, not as a boy, seriously and earnestly. I can give you no idea *how* seriously, *how* earnestly. I want you to be my wife. Laura, my dear girl, I *know* I could make you happy."

"It isn't," answered Laura slowly, perceiving as he paused that he expected her to say something, "so much a question of that."

"What is it, then? I won't make a scene. Don't you love me? Don't you think, my girl, you could ever love me?"

Laura hesitated a long moment. She had taken the rose from her shoulder, and plucking the petals one by one, put them delicately between her teeth. From the other end of the room came the clamorous exhortations of Monsieur Gerardy. Mrs. Cressler and the Gretry girl watched the progress of the rehearsal attentively from the doorway of the dining-room. Aunt Wess' and Mr. Cressler were discussing psychic research and séances, on the sofa on the other side of the room. After a while Laura spoke.

"It isn't that either," she said, choosing her words carefully.

"What is it, then?"

"I don't know—exactly. For one thing, I don't think I *want* to be married, Mr. Jadwin—to anybody."

"I would wait for you."

"Or to be engaged."

"But the day must come, sooner or later, when you must be both engaged and married. You *must* ask yourself *some time* if you love the man who wishes to be your husband. Why not ask yourself now?"

"I do," she answered. "I do ask myself. I have asked myself."

"Well, what do you decide?"

"That I don't know."

"Don't you think you would love me in time? Laura, I am sure you would. I would *make* you."

"I don't know. I suppose that is a stupid answer. But it is, if

I am to be honest, and I am trying very hard to be honest—with you and with myself—the only one I have. I am happy just as I am. I like you and Mr. Cressler and Mr. Corthell—everybody. But, Mr. Jadwin"—she looked him full in the face, her dark eyes full of gravity—"with a woman it is so serious—to be married. More so than any man ever understood. And, oh, one must be so sure, so sure. And I am not sure now. I am not sure now. Now and then I tell myself, and even poor, dear Aunt Wess', that I shall never love anybody, that I shall never marry. But I should be bitterly sorry if I thought that was true. It is one of the greatest happinesses to which I look forward, that some day I shall love some one with all my heart and soul, and shall be a true wife, and find my husband's love for me the sweetest thing in my life. But I am sure that that day has not come yet."

"And when it does come," he urged, "may I be the first to know?"

She smiled a little gravely.

"Ah," she answered, "I would not know myself that that day had come until I woke to the fact that I loved the man who had asked me to be his wife, and then it might be too late—for you."

"But now, at least," he persisted, "you love no one."

"Now," she repeated, "I love—no one." .

"And I may take such encouragement in that as I can?"

And then, suddenly, capriciously even, Laura, an inexplicable spirit of inconsistency besetting her, was a very different woman from the one who an instant before had spoken so gravely of the seriousness of marriage. She hesitated a moment before answering Jadwin, her head on one side, looking at the rose leaf between her fingers. In a low voice she said at last:

"If you like."

But before Jadwin could reply, Cressler and Aunt Wess', who had been telling each other of their "experiences," of their "premonitions," of the unaccountable things that had happened to them, at length included the others in their conversation.

" 'J.,' " remarked Cressler, "did anything funny ever happen to *you*—warnings, presentiments, that sort of thing? Mrs. Wessels and I have been talking spiritualism. Laura, have *you* ever had any 'experiences'?"

She shook her head.

"No, no. I am too material, I am afraid."

"How about you, 'J.'?"

"Nothing much, except that I believe in 'luck'—a little. The other day I flipped a coin in Gretry's office. If it fell heads I was to sell wheat short, and somehow I knew all the time that the coin would fall heads—and so it did."

"And you made a great deal of money," said Laura. "I know. Mr. Court was telling me. That was splendid."

"That was deplorable, Laura," said Cressler, gravely. "I hope some day," he continued, "we can all of us get hold of this man and make him solemnly promise never to gamble in wheat again."

Laura stared. To her mind the word "gambling" had always been suspect. It had a bad sound. It seemed to be associated with depravity of the baser sort.

"Gambling!" she murmured.

"They call it buying and selling," he went on, "down there in La Salle Street. But it is simply betting. Betting on the condition of the market weeks, even months, in advance. You bet wheat goes up. I bet it goes down. Those fellows in the Pit don't own the wheat; never even see it. Wouldn't know what to do with it if they had it. They don't care in the least about the grain. But there are thousands upon thousands of farmers out here in Iowa and Kansas or Dakota who do, and hundreds of thousands of poor devils in Europe who care even more than the farmer. I mean the fellows who raise the grain and the other fellows who eat it. It's life or death for either of them. And right between these two comes the Chicago speculator, who raises or lowers the price out of all reason, for the benefit of his pocket. You see, Laura, here is what I mean." Cressler had suddenly become very earnest. Absorbed, interested, Laura listened intently. "Here is what I mean," pursued Cressler. "It's like this: If we send the price of wheat down too far, the farmer suffers, the fellow who raises it; if we send it up too far, the poor man in Europe suffers, the fellow who eats it. And food to the peasant on the continent is bread—not meat or potatoes, as it is with us. The only way to do so that neither the American farmer nor the European peasant suffers is to keep wheat at an average, legitimate value. The moment you inflate or depress that, somebody suffers right away. And that is just what these gamblers are doing all the time, booming it up or booming it down. Think of it, the food of hundreds and hundreds of thousands of people just at the mercy of a few men down there on the Board of Trade. They make the price. They say just how much the peasant shall pay for his loaf of bread. If he can't pay the price he simply starves. And as for the farmer, why it's ludicrous. If I build a house and offer it for sale, I put my own price on it, and if the price offered don't suit me I don't sell. But if I go out here in Iowa and raise a crop of wheat, I've got to sell it, whether I want to or not, at the figure named by some fellows in Chicago. And to make themselves rich, they may make me sell it at a price that bankrupts me."

Laura nodded. She was intensely interested. A whole new order of things was being disclosed, and for the first time in her life she looked into the workings of political economy.

"Oh, that's only one side of it," Cressler went on, heedless of Jadwin's good-humored protests. "Yes, I know I am a crank on speculating. I'm going to preach a little if you'll let me. I've been a speculator myself, and a ruined one at that, and I know what I am talking about. Here is what I was going to say. These fellows themselves, the gamblers—well, call them speculators, if you like. Oh, the fine, promising, manly young men I've seen wrecked—absolutely and hopelessly wrecked and ruined by speculation! It's as easy to get into as going across the street. They make three hundred, five hundred, yes, even a thousand dollars sometimes in a couple of hours, without so much as raising a finger. Think what that means to a boy of twenty-five who's doing clerk work at seventy-five a month. Why, it would take him maybe ten years to save a thousand, and here he's made it in a single morning. Think you can keep him out of speculation then? First thing you know he's thrown up his honest, humdrum position—oh, I've seen it hundreds of times—and takes to hanging round the customers' rooms down there on La Salle Street, and he makes a little, and makes a little more, and finally he is so far in that he can't pull out, and then some billionaire fellow, who has the market in the palm of his hand, tightens one finger, and our young man is ruined, body and mind. He's lost the taste, the very capacity for legitimate business, and he stays on hanging round the Board till he gets to be—all of a sudden—an old man. And then some day some one says, 'Why, where's So-and-so?' and you wake up to the fact that the young fellow has simply disappeared—lost. I tell you, the fascination of this Pit gambling is something no one who hasn't experienced it can have the faintest conception of. I believe it's worse than liquor, worse than morphine. Once you get into it, it grips you and draws you and draws you, and the nearer you get to the end the easier it seems to win, till all of a sudden, ah! there's the whirlpool. . . . 'J.,' keep away from it, my boy."

Jadwin laughed, and leaning over, put his fingers upon Cressler's breast, as though turning off a switch.

"Now, Miss Dearborn," he announced, "we've shut him off. Charlie means all right, but now and then some one brushes against him and opens that switch."

Cressler good-humoredly laughed with the others, but Laura's smile was perfunctory and her eyes were grave. But there was a diversion. While the others had been talking the rehearsal had proceeded, and now Page beckoned to Laura from the far end of the parlor, calling out:

"Laura—'Beatrice,' it's the third act. You are wanted."

"Oh, I must run," exclaimed Laura, catching up her play-book. "Poor Monsieur Gerardy—we must be a trial to him."

She hurried across the room, where the coach was disposing the furniture for the scene, consulting the stage directions in his book:

"Here the kitchen table, here the old-fashioned writing-desk, here the *armoire* with practicable doors, here the window. Soh! Who is on? Ah, the young lady of the sick nose, 'Marion.' She is discovered—knitting. And then the duchess—later. That's you, Mademoiselle Dearborn. You interrupt—you remember. But then you, ah, you always are right. If they were all like you. Very well, we begin."

Creditably enough the Gretry girl read her part, Monsieur Gerardy interrupting to indicate the crossings and business. Then at her cue, Laura, who was to play the rôle of the duchess, entered with the words:

"I beg your pardon, but the door stood open. May I come in?" Monsieur Gerardy murmured:

"Elle est vraiment superbe."

Laura to the very life, to every little trick of carriage and manner, was the high-born gentlewoman visiting the home of a dependant. Nothing could have been more dignified, more gracious, more gracefully condescending than her poise. She dramatized not only her rôle, but the whole of her surroundings. The interior of the little cottage seemed to define itself with almost visible distinctness the moment she set foot upon the scene.

Gerardy tiptoed from group to group, whispering:

"Eh? Very fine, our duchess. She would do well professionally."

But Mrs. Wessels was not altogether **convinced.** Her eyes following her niece, she said to Corthell:

"It's Laura's 'grand manner.' My word, I know her in *that* part. That's the way she is when she comes down to the parlor of an evening, and Page introduces her to one of her young men."

"I nearly die," protested Page, beginning to laugh. "Of course it's very natural I should want my friends to like my sister. And Laura comes in as though she were walking on eggs, and gets their names wrong, as though it didn't much matter, and calls them Pinky when their name is Pinckney, and don't listen to what they say, till I want to sink right through the floor with mortification."

In haphazard fashion the rehearsal wore to a close. Monsieur Gerardy stormed and fretted and insisted upon repeating certain scenes over and over again. By ten o'clock the actors were quite worn out. A little supper was served, and very soon afterward Laura made a move toward departing. She was wondering who would see her home, Landry, Jadwin, or Sheldon Corthell.

The day had been sunshiny, warm even, but since nine o'clock the weather had changed for the worse, and by now a heavy rain was falling. Mrs. Cressler begged the two sisters and Mrs. Wessels to stay at her house overnight, but Laura refused. Jadwin was suggesting to Cressler the appropriateness of having the coupé brought around to take the sisters home, when Corthell came up to Laura.

"I sent for a couple of hansoms long since," he said. "They are waiting outside now." And that seemed to settle the question. For all Jadwin's perseverance, the artist seemed—for this time at least—to have the better of the situation.

As the good-bys were being said at the front door Page remarked to Landry:

"You had better go with us as far as the house, so that you can take one of our umbrellas. You can get in with Aunt Wess' and me. There's plenty of room. You can't go home in this storm without an umbrella."

Landry at first refused haughtily. He might be too poor to parade a lot of hansom cabs around, but he was too proud, to say the least, to ride in 'em when some one else paid.

Page scolded him roundly. What next? The idea. He was not to be so completely silly. She didn't propose to have the responsibility of his catching pneumonia just for the sake of a quibble.

"Some people," she declared, "never seemed to be able to find out that they are grown up."

"Very well," he announced, "I'll go if I can tip the driver a dollar."

Page compressed her lips.

"The man that can afford dollar tips," she said, "can afford to hire the cab in the first place."

"Seventy-five cents, then," he declared resolutely. "Not a cent less. I should feel humiliated with any less."

"Will you please take me down to the cab, Landry Court?" she cried. And without further comment Landry obeyed.

"Now, Miss Dearborn, if you are ready," exclaimed Corthell, as he came up. He held the umbrella over her head, allowing his shoulders to get the drippings.

They cried good-by again all around, and the artist guided her down the slippery steps. He handed her carefully into the hansom, and following, drew down the glasses.

Laura settled herself comfortably far back in her corner, adjusting her skirts and murmuring:

"Such a wet night. Who would have thought it was going to rain? I was afraid you were not coming at first," she added. "At dinner Mrs. Cressler said you had an important committee meeting —something to do with the Art Institute, the award of prizes; was that it?"

"Oh, yes," he answered, indifferently, "something of the sort was on. I suppose it was important—for the Institute. But for me there is only one thing of importance nowadays," he spoke with a studied carelessness, as though announcing a fact that Laura must know already, "and that is, to be near you. It is astonishing. You have no idea of it, how I have ordered my whole life according to that idea."

"As though you expected me to believe that," she answered.

In her other lovers she knew her words would have provoked vehement protestation. But for her it was part of the charm of Corthell's attitude that he never did or said the expected, the ordinary. Just now he seemed more interested in the effect of his love for Laura upon himself than in the manner of her reception of it.

"It is curious," he continued. "I am no longer a boy. I have no enthusiasms. I have known many women, and I have seen enough of what the crowd calls love to know how futile it is, how empty, a vanity of vanities. I had imagined that the poets were wrong, were idealists, seeing the things that should be rather than the things that were. And then," suddenly he drew a deep breath:

"*this* happiness; and to *me*. And the miracle, the wonderful is there—all at once—in my heart, in my very hand, like a mysterious, beautiful exotic. The poets *are* wrong," he added. "They have not been idealists enough. I wish—ah, well, never mind."

"What is it that you wish?" she asked, as he broke off suddenly. Laura knew even before she spoke that it would have been better not to have prompted him to continue. Intuitively she had something more than a suspicion that he had led her on to say these very words. And in admitting that she cared to have the conversation proceed upon this footing, she realized that she was sheering toward unequivocal coquetry. She saw the false move now, knew that she had lowered her guard. On all accounts it would have been more dignified to have shown only a mild interest in what Corthell wished. She realized that once more she had acted upon impulse, and she even found time to wonder again how it was that when with this man her impulses and not her reason prevailed so often. With Landry or with Curtis Jadwin she was always calm, tranquilly self-possessed. But Corthell seemed able to reach all that was impetuous, all that was unreasoned in her nature. To Landry she was more than anything else, an older sister, indulgent, kindhearted. With Jadwin she found that all the serious, all the sincere, earnest side of her character was apt to come to the front. But Corthell stirred troublous, unknown deeps in her, certain undefined trends of recklessness; and for so long as he held her within his influence she could not forget her sex a single instant.

It dismayed her to have this strange personality of hers, this other headstrong, impetuous self, discovered to her. She hardly recognized it. It made her a little afraid; and yet, wonder of wonders, she could not altogether dislike it. There was a certain fascination in resigning herself for little instants to the dominion of this daring stranger that was yet herself.

Meanwhile Corthell had answered her:

"I wish," he said, "I *wish* you could say something—I hardly know what—something to me. So little would be so much."

"But what *can* I say?" she protested. "I don't know—I—what *can* I say?"

"It must be yes or no for me," he broke out. "I can't go on this way."

"But why not? Why not?" exclaimed Laura. "Why must we —terminate anything? Why not let things go on just as they are? We are quite happy as we are. There's never been a time of my life when I've been happier than this last three or four months. I don't want to change anything. Ah, here we are."

The hansom drew up in front of the house. Aunt Wess' and Page were already inside. The maid stood in the vestibule in the light that streamed from the half-open front door, an umbrella in her hand. And as Laura alighted, she heard Page's voice calling from the front hall that the others had umbrellas, that the maid was not to wait.

The hansom splashed away, and Corthell and Laura mounted the steps of the house.

"Won't you come in?" she said. "There is a fire in the library."

But he said no, and for a few seconds they stood under the vestibule light, talking. Then Corthell, drawing off his right-hand glove, said:

"I suppose that I have my answer. You do not wish for a change. I understand. You wish to say by that, that you do not love me. If you did love me as I love you, you would wish for just that—a change. You would be as eager as I for that wonderful, wonderful change that makes a new heaven and a new earth."

This time Laura did not answer. There was a moment's silence. Then Corthell said:

"Do you know, I think I shall go away."

"Go away?"

"Yes, to New York. Possibly to Paris. There is a new method of fusing glass that I've promised myself long ago I would look into. I don't know that it interests me much—now. But I think I had better go. At once, within the week. I've not much heart in it; but it seems—under the circumstances—to be appropriate." He held out his bared hand. Laura saw that he was smiling.

"Well, Miss Dearborn—good-by."

"But *why* should you go?" she cried, distressfully. "How perfectly—ah, don't go," she exclaimed, then in desperate haste added: "It would be absolutely foolish."

"*Shall* I stay?" he urged. Do *you* tell me to stay?"

"Of course I do," she answered. "It would break up the play —your going. It would spoil my part. You play opposite me, you know. Please stay."

"Shall I stay," he asked, "for the sake of your part? There is no one else you would rather have?" He was smiling straight into her eyes, and she guessed what he meant.

She smiled back at him, and, the spirit of daring never more awake in her, replied, as she caught his eye:

"There is no one else I would rather have."

Corthell caught her hand of a sudden.

"Laura," he cried, "let us end this fencing and quibbling once and for all. Dear, dear girl, I *love* you with all the strength of all the good in me. Let me be the best a man can be to the woman he loves."

Laura flashed a smile at him.

"If you can make me love you enough," she answered.

"And you think I can?" he exclaimed.

"You have my permission to try," she said.

She hoped fervently that now, without further words, he would leave her. It seemed to her that it would be the most delicate chivalry on his part—having won this much—to push his advantage no further. Se waited anxiously for his next words. She began to fear that she had trusted too much upon her assurance of his tact.

Corthell held out his hand again.

"It is good-night, then, not good-by?"

"It is good-night," said Laura.

With the words he was gone, and Laura, entering the house, shut the door behind her with a long breath of satisfaction.

Page and Landry were still in the library. Laura joined them, and for a few moments the three stood before the fireplace talking about the play. Page at length, at the first opportunity, excused herself and went to bed. She made a great show of leaving Landry and Laura alone, and managed to convey the impression that she understood they were anxious to be rid of her.

"Only remember," she remarked to Laura severely, "to lock up and turn out the hall gas. Annie has gone to bed *long* ago."

"I must dash along, too," declared Landry when Page was gone.

He buttoned his coat about his neck, and Laura followed him out into the hall and found an umbrella for him.

"You were beautiful to-night," he said, as he stood with his hand on the door knob. "Beautiful. I could not keep my eyes off of you, and I could not listen to anybody but you. And now," he declared, solemnly, "I will see your eyes and hear your voice all the rest of the night. I want to explain," he added, "about those hansoms—about coming home with Miss Page and Mrs. Wessels. Mr. Corthell—those were *his* hansoms, of course. But I wanted an umbrella, and I gave the driver seventy-five cents."

"Why, of course, of course," said Laura, not quite divining what he was driving at.

"I don't want you to think that I would be willing to put myself under obligations to anybody."

"Of course, Landry; I understand."

He thrilled at once.

"Ah," he cried, "you don't know what it *means* to me to look into the eyes of a woman who really understands."

Laura stared, wondering just what she had said.

"Will you turn this hall light out for me, Landry?" she asked. "I never can reach."

He left the front door open and extinguished the jet in its dull red globe. Promptly they were involved in darkness.

"Good-night," she said. "Isn't it dark?"

He stretched out his hand to take hers, but instead his groping fingers touched her waist. Suddenly Laura felt his arm clasp her. Then all at once, before she had time to so much as think of resistance, he had put both arms about her and kissed her squarely on her cheeks. Then the front door closed, and she was left abruptly alone, breathless, stunned, staring wide-eyed into the darkness.

Her first sensation was one merely of amazement. She put her hand quickly to her cheek, first the palm and then the back, murmuring confusedly:

"What? Why?—why?"

Then she whirled about and ran up the stairs, her silks clashing and fluttering about her as she fled, gained her own room, and swung the door violently shut behind her. She turned up the lowered gas and, without knowing why, faced her mirror at once, studying her reflection and watching her hand as it all but scoured the offended cheek.

Then, suddenly, with an upward, uplifting rush, her anger surged within her. She, Laura, Miss Dearborn, who loved no man, who never conceded, never capitulated, whose "grand manner" was a thing proverbial, in all her pitch of pride, in her own home, her own fortress, had been kissed, like a schoolgirl, like a chambermaid, in the dark, in a corner.

And by—great heavens!—*Landry Court*. The boy whom she fancied she held in such subjection, such profound respect. Landry Court had dared, had dared to kiss her, to offer her this wretchedly commonplace and petty affront, degrading her to the level of a pretty waitress, making her ridiculous.

She stood rigid, drawn to her full height, in the centre of her bedroom, her fists tense at her sides, her breath short, her eyes flashing, her face aflame. From time to time her words, half smothered, burst from her.

"What does he *think* I *am?* How dared he? How dared he?"

All that she could say, any condemnation she could formulate only made her position the more absurd, the more humiliating. It had all been said before by generations of shopgirls, schoolgirls, and servants, in whose company the affront had ranged her. Landry was to be told in effect that he was never to presume to seek her acquaintance again. Just as the enraged hussy of the street corners and Sunday picnics shouted that the offender should "never dare speak to her again as long as he lived." Never before had she been subjected to this kind of indignity. And simultaneously with the assurance she could hear the shrill voice of the drab of the public balls proclaiming that she had "never been kissed in all her life before."

Of all slights, of all insults, it was the one that robbed her of the very dignity she should assume to rebuke it. The more vehemently she resented it, the more laughable became the whole affair.

But she would resent it, she would resent it, and Landry Court should be driven to acknowledge that the sorriest day of his life was the one on which he had forgotten the respect in which he had pretended to hold her. He had deceived her, then, all along. Because she had—foolishly—relaxed a little toward him, permitted a certain intimacy, this was how he abused it. Ah, well, it would teach her a lesson. Men were like that. She might have known it would come to this. Wilfully they chose to misunderstand, to take advantage of her frankness, her good nature, her good comradeship.

She had been foolish all along, flirting—yes, that was the word for it—flirting with Landry and Corthell and Jadwin. No doubt they all compared notes about her. Perhaps they had bet who first should kiss her. Or, at least, there was not one of them who would not kiss her if she gave him a chance.

But if she, in any way, had been to blame for what Landry had done, she would atone for it. She had made herself too cheap, she had found amusement in encouraging these men, in equivocating, in coquetting with them. Now it was time to end the whole business, to send each one of them to the right-about with an *un*equivocal definite word. She was a good girl, she told herself. She was, in her heart, sincere; she was above the inexpensive diversion of flirting. She had started wrong in her new life, and it was time, high time, to begin over again—with a clean page—to show these men that they dared not presume to take liberties with so much as the tip of her little finger.

So great was her agitation, so eager her desire to act upon her resolve, that she could not wait till morning. It was a physical impossibility for her to remain under what she chose to believe suspicion another hour. If there was any remotest chance that her three lovers had permitted themselves to misunderstand her, they were to be corrected at once, were to be shown their place, and that without mercy.

She called for the maid, Annie, whose husband was the janitor of the house, and who slept in the top story.

"If Henry hasn't gone to bed," said Laura, "tell him to wait up till I call him, or to sleep with his clothes on. There is something I want him to do for me—something important."

It was close upon midnight. Laura turned back into her room, removed her hat and veil, and tossed them, with her coat, upon the bed. She lighted another burner of the chandelier, and drew a chair to her writing-desk between the windows.

Her first note was to Landry Court. She wrote it almost with a single spurt of the pen, and dated it carefully, so that he might know it had been written immediately after he had left. Thus it ran:

"Please do not try to see me again at any time or under any circumstances. I want you to understand, very clearly, that I do not wish to continue our acquaintance."

Her letter to Corthell was more difficult, and it was not until she had rewritten it two or three times that it read to her satisfaction.

"My dear Mr. Corthell," so it was worded, "you asked me to-night that our fencing and quibbling be brought to an end. I quite agree with you that it is desirable. I spoke as I did before you left upon an impulse that I shall never cease to regret. I do not wish you to misunderstand me, nor to misinterpret my attitude in any way. You asked me to be your wife, and, very foolishly and wrongly, I gave you—intentionally—an answer which might easily be construed into an encouragement. Understand now that I do

not wish you to try to make me love you. I would find it extremely
distasteful. And, believe me, it would be quite hopeless. I do not
now, and never shall care for you as I should care if I were to be
your wife. I beseech you that you will not, in any manner, refer
again to this subject. It would only distress and pain me.

"Cordially yours,

"LAURA DEARBORN."

The letter to Curtis Jadwin was almost to the same effect. But
she found the writing of it easier than the others. In addressing
him she felt herself grow a little more serious, a little more dignified
and calm. It ran as follows:

"MY DEAR MR. JADWIN:

"When you asked me to become your wife this evening, you
deserved a straightforward answer, and, instead, I replied in a spirit
of capriciousness and disingenuousness, which I now earnestly regret, and which I ask you to pardon and to ignore.

"I allowed myself to tell you that you might find encouragement
in my foolishly spoken words. I am deeply sorry that I should have
so forgotten what was due to my own self-respect and to your
sincerity.

"If I have permitted myself to convey to you the impression
that I would ever be willing to be your wife, let me hasten to correct it. Whatever I said to you this evening, I must answer now—
as I should have answered then—truthfully and unhesitatingly, no.

"This, I insist, must be the last word between us upon this
unfortunate subject, if we are to continue, as I hope, very good
friends.

"Cordially yours,

"LAURA DEARBORN."

She sealed, stamped, and directed the three envelopes, and
glanced at the little leather-cased traveling clock that stood on the
top of her desk. It was nearly two.

"I could not sleep, I could not sleep," she murmured, "if I did
not know they were on the way."

In answer to the bell, Henry appeared, and Laura gave him the
letters, with orders to mail them at once in the nearest box.

When it was all over she sat down again at her desk, and leaning an elbow upon it, covered her eyes with her hand for a long

moment. She felt suddenly very tired, and when at last she lowered her hand, her fingers were wet. But in the end she grew calmer. She felt that, at all events, she had vindicated herself, that her life would begin again to-morrow with a clean page; and when at length she fell asleep, it was to the dreamless unconsciousness of an almost tranquil mind.

She slept late the next morning and breakfasted in bed between ten and eleven. Then, as the last vibrations of last night's commotion died away, a very natural curiosity began to assert itself. She wondered how each of the three men "would take it." In spite of herself she could not keep from wishing that she could be by when they read their dismissals.

Toward the early part of the afternoon, while Laura was in the library reading "Queen's Gardens," the special delivery brought Landry Court's reply. It was one *roulade* of incoherence, even in places blistered with tears. Landry protested, implored, debased himself to the very dust. His letter bristled with exclamation points, and ended with a prolonged wail of distress and despair.

Quietly, and with a certain merciless sense of pacification, Laura deliberately reduced the letter to strips, burned it upon the hearth, and went back to her Ruskin.

A little later, the afternoon being fine, she determined to ride out to Lincoln Park, not fifteen minutes from her home, to take a little walk there, and to see how many new buds were out.

As she was leaving, Annie gave into her hands a pasteboard box, just brought to the house by a messenger boy.

The box was full of Jacqueminot roses, to the stems of which a note from Corthell was tied. He wrote but a single line:

"So it should have been 'good-by' after all."

Laura had Annie put the roses in Page's room.

"Tell Page she can have them; I don't want them. She can wear them to her dance to-night," she said.

While to herself she added:

"The little buds in the park will be prettier."

She was gone from the house over two hours, for she had elected to walk all the way home. She came back flushed and buoyant from her exercise, her cheeks cool with the Lake breeze, a young maple leaf in one of the revers of her coat. Annie let her in, murmuring:

"A gentleman called just after you went out. I told him you

were not at home, but he said he would wait. He is in the library now."

"Who is he? Did he give his name?" demanded Laura.

The maid handed her Curtis Jadwin's card.

V

THAT year the spring burst over Chicago in a prolonged scintillation of pallid green. For weeks continually the sun shone. The Lake, after persistently cherishing the grays and bitter greens of the winter months, and the rugged white-caps of the northeast gales, mellowed at length, turned to a softened azure blue, and lapsed by degrees to an unruffled calmness, incrusted with innumerable coruscations.

In the parks, first of all, the buds and earliest shoots asserted themselves. The horse-chestnut bourgeons burst their sheaths to spread into trefoils and flame-shaped leaves. The elms, maples, and cottonwoods followed. The sooty, blackened snow upon the grass plats, in the residence quarters, had long since subsided, softening the turf, filling the gutters with rivulets. On all sides one saw men at work laying down the new sod in rectangular patches.

There was a delicious smell of ripening in the air, a smell of sap once more on the move, of humid earths disintegrating from the winter rigidity, of twigs and slender branches stretching themselves under the returning warmth, elastic once more, straining in their bark.

On the North Side, in Washington Square, along the Lakeshore Drive, all up and down the Lincoln Park Boulevard, and all through Erie, Huron, and Superior Streets, through North State Street, North Clarke Street, and La Salle Avenue, the minute sparkling of green flashed from tree top to tree top, like the first kindling of dry twigs. One could almost fancy that the click of igniting branch tips was audible as whole beds of yellow-green sparks defined themselves within certain elms and cottonwoods.

Every morning the sun invaded earlier the east windows of Laura Dearborn's bedroom. Every day at noon it stood more nearly overhead above her home. Every afternoon the checkered shadows of the leaves thickened upon the drawn curtains of the library. Within doors the bottle-green flies came out of their lethargy and droned and bumped on the panes. The double windows were removed, screens and awnings took their places; the summer pieces were put into the fireplaces.

All of a sudden vans invaded the streets, piled high with mattresses, rocking-chairs, and bird cages; the inevitable "spring moving" took place. And these furniture vans alternated with great trucks laden with huge elm trees on their way from nursery to lawn. Families and trees alike submitted to the impulse of transplanting, abandoning the winter quarters, migrating with the spring to newer environments, taking root in other soils. Sparrows wrangled on the sidewalks and built ragged nests in the interstices of cornice and coping. In the parks one heard the liquid modulations of robins. The florists' wagons appeared, and from house to house, from lawn to lawn, iron urns and window boxes filled up with pansies, geraniums, fuchsias, and trailing vines. The flower beds, stripped of straw and manure, bloomed again, and at length the great cottonwoods shed their berries, like clusters of tiny grapes, over street and sidewalk.

At length came three days of steady rain, followed by cloudless sunshine and full-bodied, vigorous winds straight from out the south.

Instantly the living embers in tree top and grass plat were fanned to flame. Like veritable fire, the leaves blazed up. Branch after branch caught and crackled; even the driest, the deadest, were infolded in the resistless swirl of green. Tree top ignited tree top; the parks and boulevards were one smother of radiance. From end to end and from side to side of the city, fed by the rains, urged by the south winds, spread billowing and surging the superb conflagration of the coming summer.

Then, abruptly, everything hung poised; the leaves, the flowers, the grass, all at fullest stretch, stood motionless, arrested, while the heat, distilled, as it were, from all this seething green, rose like a vast pillar over the city, and stood balanced there in the iridescence of the sky, moveless and immeasurable.

From time to time it appeared as if this pillar broke in the guise of summer storms, and came toppling down upon the city in tremendous detonations of thunder and weltering avalanches of rain. But it broke only to re-form, and no sooner had the thunder ceased, the rain intermitted, and the sun again come forth, than one received the vague impression of the swift rebuilding of the vast, invisible column that smothered the city under its bases, towering higher and higher into the rain-washed, crystal-clear atmosphere.

Then the aroma of wet dust, of drenched pavements, musty, acute—the unforgettable exhalation of the city's streets after a shower—pervaded all the air, and the little outdoor activities resumed again under the dripping elms and upon the steaming sidewalks.

The evenings were delicious. It was yet too early for the exodus northward to the Wisconsin lakes, but to stay indoors after nightfall was not to be thought of. After six o'clock, all through the streets in the neighborhood of the Dearborns' home, one could see the family groups "sitting out" upon the front "stoop." Chairs were brought forth, carpets and rugs unrolled upon the steps. From within, through the opened windows of drawing-room and parlor, came the brisk gayety of pianos. The sidewalks were filled with children clamoring at "tag," "I-spy," or "run-sheep-run." Girls in shirt-waists and young men in flannel suits promenaded to and fro. Visits were exchanged from "stoop" to "stoop," lemonade was served, and claret punch. In their armchairs on the top step, elderly men, householders, capitalists, well-to-do, their large stomachs covered with white waistcoats, their straw hats upon their knees, smoked very fragrant cigars in silent enjoyment, digesting their dinners, taking the air after the grime and hurry of the business districts.

It was on such an evening as this, well on toward the last days of the spring, that Laura Dearborn and Page joined the Cresslers and their party, sitting out like other residents of the neighborhood on the front steps of their house. Almost every evening nowadays the Dearborn girls came thus to visit with the Cresslers. Sometimes Page brought her mandolin.

Every day of the warm weather seemed only to increase the beauty of the two sisters. Page's brown hair was never more luxuriant, the exquisite coloring of her cheeks never more charming, the boyish outlines of her small, straight figure—immature and a little angular as yet—never more delightful. The seriousness of her straight-browed, grave, gray-blue eyes was still present, but the eyes themselves were, in some indefinable way, deepening, and all the maturity that as yet was withheld from her undeveloped little form looked out from beneath her long lashes.

But Laura was veritably regal. Very slender as yet, no trace of fulness to be seen over hip or breast, the curves all low and flat, she yet carried her extreme height with tranquil confidence, the unperturbed assurance of a *chatelaine* of the days of feudalism.

Her coal-black hair, high-piled, she wore as if it were a coronet. The warmth of the exuberant spring days had just perceptibly mellowed the even paleness of her face, but to compensate for this all the splendor of coming midsummer nights flashed from her deep-brown eyes.

On this occasion she had put on her coat over her shirt-waist, and a great bunch of violets was tucked into her belt. But no sooner had she exchanged greetings with the others and settled herself in her place than she slipped her coat from her shoulders.

It was while she was doing this that she noted, for the first time, Landry Court standing half in and half out of the shadow of the vestibule behind Mr. Cressler's chair.

"This is the first time he has been here since—since that night," Mrs. Cressler hastened to whisper in Laura's ear. "He told me about—well, he told me what occurred, you know. He came to dinner to-night, and afterward the poor boy nearly wept in my arms. You never saw such penitence."

Laura put her chin in the air with a little movement of incredulity. But her anger had long since been a thing of the past. Good-tempered, she could not cherish resentment very long. But as yet she had greeted Landry only by the briefest of nods.

"Such a warm night!" she murmured, fanning herself with part of Mr. Cressler's evening paper. "And I never was so thirsty."

"Why, of course," exclaimed Mrs. Cressler. "Isabel," she called, addressing Miss Gretry, who sat on the opposite side of the steps, "isn't the lemonade near you? Fill a couple of glasses for Laura and Page."

Page murmured her thanks, but Laura declined.

"No; just plain water for me," she said. "Isn't there some inside? Mr. Court can get it for me, can't he?"

Landry brought the pitcher back, running at top speed and spilling half of it in his eagerness. Laura thanked him with a smile, addressing him, however, by his last name. She somehow managed to convey to him in her manner the information that though his offence was forgotten, their old-time relations were not, for one instant, to be resumed.

Later on, while Page was thrumming her mandolin, Landry whistling a "second," Mrs. Cressler took occasion to remark to Laura:

"I was reading the Paris letter in the 'Inter-Ocean' to-day, and I saw Mr. Corthell's name on the list of American arrivals at the

Continental. I guess," she added, "he's going to be gone a long
time. I wonder sometimes if he will *ever* come back. A fellow
with his talent, I should imagine, would find Chicago—well, less
congenial, anyhow, than Paris. But, just the same, I do think it
was mean of him to break up our play by going. I'll bet a cookie
that he wouldn't take part any more just because you wouldn't. He
was just crazy to do that love scene in the fourth act with you.
And when *you* wouldn't play, of course, *he* wouldn't; and then
everybody seemed to lose interest with you two out. 'J.' took it all
very decently though, don't you think?"

Laura made a murmur of mild assent.

"He was disappointed, too," continued Mrs. Cressler. "I could
see that. He thought the play was going to interest a lot of our
church people in his Sunday-school. But he never said a word
when it fizzled out. Is he coming to-night?"

"Well, I declare," said Laura. "How should I know, if you
don't?"

Jadwin was an almost regular visitor at the Cresslers' during the
first warm evenings. He lived on the South Side, and the distance
between his home and that of the Cresslers was very considerable.
It was seldom, however, that Jadwin did not drive over. He came
in his double-seated buggy, his negro coachman beside him, the
two coach dogs, "Rex" and "Rox," trotting under the rear axle.
His horses were not showy, nor were they made conspicuous by
elaborate boots, bandages, and all the other solemn paraphernalia
of the stable, yet men upon the sidewalks, amateurs, breeders, and
the like—men who understood good stock—never failed to stop to
watch the team go by, heads up, the check rein swinging loose,
ears all alert, eyes all alight, the breath deep, strong, and slow, and
the stride, machine-like, even as the swing of a metronome, thrown
out from the shoulder to knee, snapped on from knee to fetlock,
from fetlock to pastern, finishing squarely, beautifully, with the
thrust of the hoof, planted an instant, then, as it were, flinging the
roadway behind it, snatched up again, and again cast forward.

On these occasions Jadwin himself inevitably wore a black
"slouch" hat, suggestive of the general of the Civil War, a gray
"dust overcoat" with a black velvet collar, and tan gloves, discolored with the moisture of his palms and all twisted and crumpled
with the strain of holding the thoroughbreds to their work.

He always called the time of the trip from the buggy at the
Cresslers' horse block, his stop watch in his hand, and, as he joined

the groups upon the steps, he was almost sure to remark: "Tugs were loose all the way from the river. They pulled the whole rig by the reins. My hands are about dislocated."

"Page plays very well," murmured Mrs. Cressler as the young girl laid down her mandolin. "I hope 'J.' does come to-night," she added. "I love to have him 'round. He's so hearty and whole-souled."

Laura did not reply. She seemed a little preoccupied this evening, and conversation in the group died away. The night was very beautiful, serene, quiet and, at this particular hour of the end of the twilight, no one cared to talk much. Cressler lighted another cigar, and the filaments of delicate blue smoke hung suspended about his head in the moveless air. Far off, from the direction of the mouth of the river, a lake steamer whistled a prolonged tenor note. Somewhere from an open window in one of the neighboring houses a violin, accompanied by a piano, began to elaborate the sustained phrases of "Schubert's Serenade." Theatrical as was the theme, the twilight and the muffled hum of the city, lapsing to quiet after the fibrile activities of the day, combined to lend it a dignity, a persuasiveness. The children were still playing along the sidewalks, and their staccato gayety was part of the quiet note to which all sounds of the moment seemed chorded.

After a while Mrs. Cressler began to talk to Laura in a low voice. She and Charlie were going to spend a part of June at Oconomowoc, in Wisconsin. Why could not Laura make up her mind to come with them? She had asked Laura a dozen times already, but couldn't get a yes or no answer from her. What was the reason she could not decide? Didn't she think she would have a good time?

"Page can go," said Laura. "I would like to have you take her. But as for me, I don't know. My plans are so unsettled this summer." She broke off suddenly. "Oh, now, that I think of it, I want to borrow your 'Idylls of the King.' May I take it for a day or two? I'll run in and get it now," she added as she rose. "I know just where to find it. No, please sit still, Mr. Cressler. I'll go."

And with the words she disappeared indoors, leaving Mrs. Cressler to murmur to her husband:

"Strange girl. Sometimes I think I don't know Laura at all. She's so inconsistent. How funny she acts about going to Oconomowoc with us!"

Mr. Cressler permitted himself an amiable grunt of protest.

"Pshaw! Laura's all right. The handsomest girl in Cook County."

"Well, that's not much to do with it, Charlie," sighed Mrs. Cressler. "Oh, dear," she added vaguely. "I don't know."

"Don't know what?"

"I hope Laura's life will be happy."

"Oh, for God's sake, Carrie!"

"There's something about that girl," continued Mrs. Cressler, "that makes my heart bleed for her."

Cressler frowned, puzzled and astonished.

"Hey—what!" he exclaimed. "You're crazy, Carrie!"

"Just the same," persisted Mrs. Cressler, "I just yearn toward her sometimes like a mother. Some people are born to trouble, Charlie; born to trouble, as the sparks fly upward. And you mark my words, Charlie Cressler, Laura is that sort. There's all the pathos in the world in just the way she looks at you from under all that black, black hair, and out of her eyes—the saddest eyes sometimes, great, sad, mournful eyes."

"Fiddlesticks!" said Mr. Cressler, resuming his paper.

"I'm positive that Sheldon Corthell asked her to marry him," mused Mrs. Cressler after a moment's silence. "I'm sure that's why he left so suddenly."

Her husband grunted grimly as he turned his paper so as to catch the reflection of the vestibule light.

"Don't you think so, Charlie?"

"Uh! *I* don't know. I never had much use for that fellow, anyhow."

"He's wonderfully talented," she commented, "and so refined. He always had the most beautiful manners. Did you ever notice his hands?"

"I thought they were like a barber's. Put him in 'J.'s' rig there, behind those horses of his, and how long do you suppose he'd hold those trotters with that pair of hands? Why," he blustered, suddenly, "they'd pull him right over the dashboard."

"Poor little Landry Court!" murmured his wife, lowering her voice. "He's just about heart-broken. He wanted to marry her too. My goodness, she must have brought him up with a round turn. I can see Laura when she is really angry. Poor fellow!"

"If you *women* would let that boy alone, he might amount to something."

"He told me his life was ruined."

Cressler threw his cigar from him with vast impatience.

"Oh, *rot!*" he muttered.

"He took it terribly, seriously, Charlie, just the same."

"I'd like to take that young boy in hand and shake some of the nonsense out of him that you women have filled him with. He's got a level head. On the floor every day, and never yet bought a hatful of wheat on his own account. Don't know the meaning of speculation and don't want to. There's a boy with some sense."

"It's just as well," persisted Mrs. Cressler reflectively, "that Laura wouldn't have him. Of course they're not made for each other. But I thought that Corthell would have made her happy. But she won't ever marry 'J.' He asked her to; she didn't tell me, but I know he did. And she's refused him flatly. She won't marry anybody, she says. Said she didn't love anybody, and never would. I'd have loved to have seen her married to 'J.,' but I can see now that they wouldn't have been congenial; and if Laura wouldn't have Sheldon Corthell, who was just made for her, I guess it was no use to expect she'd have 'J.' Laura's got a temperament, and she's artistic, and loves paintings, and poetry, and Shakespeare, and all that, and Curtis don't care for those things at all. They wouldn't have had anything in common. But Corthell—that was different. And Laura did care for him, in a way. He interested her immensely. When he'd get started on art subjects Laura would just hang on every word. My lands, I wouldn't have gone away if I'd been in his boots. You mark my words, Charlie, there was the man for Laura Dearborn, and she'll marry him yet, or I'll miss my guess."

"That's just like you, Carrie—you and the rest of the women," exclaimed Cressler, "always scheming to marry each other off. Why don't you let the girl alone? Laura's all right. She minds her own business, and she's perfectly happy. But you'd go to work and get up a sensation about her, and say that your 'heart bleeds for her,' and that she's born to trouble, and has sad eyes. If she gets into trouble it'll be because some one else makes it for her. You take my advice, and let her paddle her own canoe. She's got the head to do it; don't you worry about that. By the way—" Cressler interrupted himself, seizing the opportunity to change the subject. "By the way, Carrie, Curtis has been speculating again. I'm sure of it."

"Too bad," she murmured.

"So it is," Cressler went on. "He and Gretry are thick as thieves these days. Gretry, I understand, has been selling September wheat for him all last week, and only this morning they closed out another scheme—some corn game. It was all over the Floor just about closing time. They tell me that Curtis landed between eight and ten thousand. Always seems to win. I'd give a lot to keep him out of it; but since his deal in May wheat he's been getting into it more and more."

"Did he sell that property on Washington Street?" she inquired.

"Oh," exclaimed her husband, "I'd forgot. I meant to tell you. No, he didn't sell it. But he did better. He wouldn't sell, and those department store people took a lease. Guess what they pay him. Three hundred thousand a year. 'J.' is getting rich all the time, and why he can't be satisfied with his own business instead of monkeying 'round La Salle Street is a mystery to me."

But, as Mrs. Cressler was about to reply, Laura came to the open window of the parlor.

"Oh, Mrs. Cressler," she called, "I don't seem to find your 'Idylls' after all. I thought they were in the little bookcase."

"Wait. I'll find them for you," exclaimed Mrs. Cressler.

"Would you mind?" answered Laura, as Mrs. Cressler rose.

Inside, the gas had not been lighted. The library was dark and cool, and when Mrs. Cressler had found the book for Laura the girl pleaded a headache as an excuse for remaining within. The two sat down by the raised sash of a window at the side of the house that overlooked the "side yard," where the morning-glories and nasturtiums were in full bloom.

"The house *is* cooler, isn't it?" observed Mrs. Cressler.

Laura settled herself in her wicker chair, and with a gesture that of late had become habitual with her pushed her heavy coils of hair to one side and patted them softly to place.

"It is getting warmer, I do believe," she said, rather listlessly. "I understand it is to be a very hot summer." Then she added, "I'm to be married in July, Mrs. Cressler."

Mrs. Cressler gasped, and, sitting bolt upright, stared for one breathless instant at Laura's face, dimly visible in the darkness. Then, stupefied, she managed to vociferate:

"What! Laura! Married? My darling girl!"

"Yes," answered Laura calmly. "In July—or maybe sooner."

"Why, I thought you had rejected Mr. Corthell. I thought that's why he went away."

"Went away? He never went away. I mean it's not Mr. Corthell. It's Mr. Jadwin."

"Thank God!" declared 'Mrs. Cressler fervently, and with the words kissed Laura on both cheeks. "My dear, dear child, you can't tell how glad I am. From the very first I've said you were made for one another. And I thought all the time that you'd told him you wouldn't have him."

"I did," said Laura. Her manner was quiet. She seemed a little grave. "I told him I did not love him. Only last week I told him so."

"Well, then why did you promise?"

"My goodness!" exclaimed Laura, with a show of animation. "You don't realize what it's been. Do you suppose you can say 'no' to that man?"

"Of course not, of course not," declared Mrs. Cressler joyfully. "That's 'J.' all over. I might have known he'd have you if he set out to do it."

"Morning, noon, and night," Laura continued. "He seemed willing to wait as long as I wasn't definite; but one day I wrote to him and gave him a square 'No,' so as he couldn't mistake, and just as soon as I'd said that he—he—began. I didn't have any peace until I'd promised him, and the moment I had promised he had a ring on my finger. He'd had it ready in his pocket for weeks, it seems. No," she explained, as Mrs. Cressler laid her fingers upon her left hand, "that I would not have—yet."

"Oh, it was like 'J.' to be persistent," repeated Mrs. Cressler.

"Persistent!" murmured Laura. "He simply wouldn't talk of anything else. It was making him sick, he said. And he did have a fever—often. But he would come out to see me just the same. One night, when it was pouring rain— Well, I'll tell you. He had been to dinner with us, and afterward, in the drawing-room, I told him 'no' for the hundredth time just as plainly as I could, and he went away early—it wasn't eight. I thought that now at last he had given up. But he was back again before ten the same evening. He said he had come back to return a copy of a book I had loaned him—'Jane Eyre' it was. Raining! I never saw it rain as it did that night. He was drenched, and even at dinner he had had a low fever. And then I was sorry for him. I told him he could come to see me again. I didn't propose to have him come down with pneumonia, or typhoid, or something. And so it all began over again."

"But you loved him, Laura?" demanded Mrs. Cressler. "You love him now?"

Laura was silent. Then at length:

"I don't know," she answered.

"Why, of course you love him, Laura," insisted Mrs. Cressler. "You wouldn't have promised him if you hadn't. Of course you love him, don't you?"

"Yes, I—I suppose I must love him, or—as you say—I wouldn't have promised to marry him. He does everything, every little thing I say. He just seems to think of nothing else but to please me from morning until night. And when I finally said I would marry him, why, Mrs. Cressler, he choked all up, and the tears ran down his face, and all he could say was, 'May God bless you! May God bless you!' over and over again, and his hand shook so that— Oh, well," she broke off abruptly. Then added, "Somehow it makes tears come to my eyes to think of it."

"But, Laura," urged Mrs. Cressler, "you love Curtis, don't you? You—you're such a strange girl sometimes. Dear child, talk to me as though I were your mother. There's no one in the world loves you more than I do. You love Curtis, don't you?"

Laura hesitated a long moment.

"Yes," she said, slowly, at length. "I think I love him very much—sometimes. And then sometimes I think I don't. I can't tell. There are days when I'm sure of it, and there are others when I wonder if I want to be married, after all. I thought when love came it was to be—oh, uplifting, something glorious like Juliet's love or Marguerite's. Something that would—" Suddenly she struck her hand to her breast, her fingers shut tight, closing to a fist. "Oh, something that would shake me all to pieces. I thought that was the only kind of love there was."

"Oh, that's what you read about in trashy novels," Mrs. Cressler assured her, "or the kind you see at the matinées. I wouldn't let that bother me, Laura. There's no doubt that 'J.' loves *you*."

Laura brightened a little. "Oh, no," she answered, "there's no doubt about that. It's splendid, that part of it. He seems to think there's nothing in the world too good for me. Just imagine, only yesterday I was saying something about my gloves, I really forget what—something about how hard it was for me to get the kind of gloves I liked. Would you believe it, he got me to give him my measure, and when I saw him in the evening he told me he had

cabled to Brussels to some famous glovemaker and had ordered I
don't know how many pairs."

"Just like him, just like him!" cried Mrs. Cressler. "I know you
will be happy, Laura, dear. You can't help but be with a man who
loves you as 'J.' does."

"I think I shall be happy," answered Laura, suddenly grave.
"Oh, Mrs. Cressler, I want to be. I hope that I won't come to
myself some day, after it is too late, and find that it was all a mistake." Her voice shook a little. "You don't know how nervous I
am these days. One minute I am one kind of girl, and the next
another kind. I'm so nervous and—oh, I don't know. Oh, I guess
it will be all right." She wiped her eyes, and laughed a note. "I
don't see why I should cry about it," she murmured.

"Well, Laura," answered Mrs. Cressler, "if you don't love Curtis, don't marry him. That's very simple."

"It's like this, Mrs. Cressler," Laura explained. "I suppose I
am very uncharitable and unchristian, but I like the people that like
me, and I hate those that don't like me. I can't help it. I know
it's wrong, but that's the way I am. And I love to be loved. The
man that would love me the most would make me love him. And
when Mr. Jadwin seems to care so much, and do so much, and—
you know how I mean; it does make a difference of course. I suppose I care as much for Mr. Jadwin as I ever will care for any
man. I suppose I must be cold and unemotional."

Mrs. Cressler could not restrain a movement of surprise.

"You unemotional? Why, I thought you just said, Laura, that
you had imagined love would be like Juliet and like that girl in
'Faust'—that it was going to shake you all to pieces."

"Did I say that? Well, I told you I was one girl one minute
and another another. I don't know myself these days. Oh, hark,"
she said, abruptly, as the cadence of hoofs began to make itself
audible from the end of the side street. "That's the team now. I
could recognize those horses' trot as far as I could hear it. Let's
go out. I know he would like to have me there when he drives up.
And you know"—she put her hand on Mrs. Cressler's arm as the
two moved toward the front door—"this is all absolutely a secret
as yet."

"Why, of course, Laura, dear. But tell me just one thing more,"
Mrs. Cressler asked in a whisper, "are you going to have a church
wedding?"

"Hey, Carrie," called Mr. Cressler from the stoop, "here's J."

Laura shook her head.

"No, I want it to be very quiet—at our house. We'll go to Geneva Lake for the summer. That's why, you see, I couldn't promise to go to Oconomowoc with you."

They came out upon the front steps, Mrs. Cressler's arm around Laura's waist. It was dark by now, and the air was perceptibly warmer.

The team was swinging down the street close at hand, the hoof beats exactly timed, as if there were but one instead of two horses.

"Well, what's the record to-night, J.?" cried Cressler, as Jadwin brought the bays to a stand at the horse block. Jadwin did not respond until he had passed the reins to the coachman, and taking the stop watch from the latter's hand, he drew on his cigar, and held the glowing tip to the dial.

"Eleven minutes and a quarter," he announced, "and we had to wait for the bridge at that."

He came up the steps, fanning himself with his slouch hat, and dropped into the chair that Landry had brought for him.

"Upon my word," he exclaimed, gingerly drawing off his driving gloves, "I've no feeling in my fingers at all. Those fellows will pull my hands clean off some day."

But he was hardly settled in his place before he proposed to send the coachman home, and to take Laura for a drive toward Lincoln Park, and even a little way into the park itself. He promised to have her back within an hour.

"I haven't any hat," objected Laura. "I should love to go, but I ran over here to-night without any hat."

"Well, I wouldn't let that stand in my way, Laura," protested Mrs. Cressler. "It will be simply heavenly in the Park on such a night as this."

In the end Laura borrowed Page's hat, and Jadwin took her away. In the light of the street lamps Mrs. Cressler and the others watched them drive off, sitting side by side behind the fine horses. Jadwin, broad-shouldered, a fresh cigar between his teeth, each rein in a double turn about his large, hard hands; Laura, slim, erect, pale, her black, thick hair throwing a tragic shadow low upon her forehead.

"A fine-looking couple," commented Mr. Cressler as they disappeared.

The hoof beats died away, the team vanished. Landry Court,

who stood behind the others, watching, turned to Mrs. Cressler. She thought she detected a little unsteadiness in his voice, but he repeated bravely:

"Yes, yes, that's right. They are a fine, a—a fine-looking couple together, aren't they? A fine-looking couple, to say the least."

A week went by, then two, soon May had passed. On the fifteenth of that month Laura's engagement to Curtis Jadwin was formally announced. The day of the wedding was set for the first week in June.

During this time Laura was never more changeable, more puzzling. Her vivacity seemed suddenly to have been trebled, but it was invaded frequently by strange reactions and perversities that drove her friends and family to distraction.

About a week after her talk with Mrs. Cressler, Laura broke the news to Page. It was a Monday morning. She had spent the time since breakfast in putting her bureau drawers to rights, scattering sachet powders in them, then leaving them open so as to perfume the room. At last she came into the front "upstairs sitting-room," a heap of gloves, stockings, collarettes—the odds and ends of a wildly disordered wardrobe—in her lap. She tumbled all these upon the hearth rug, and sat down upon the floor to sort them carefully. At her little desk nearby, Page, in a blue and white shirt-waist and golf skirt, her slim little ankles demurely crossed, a cone of foolscap over her forearm to guard against ink spots, was writing in her journal. This was an interminable affair, voluminous, complex, that the young girl had kept ever since she was fifteen. She wrote in it—she hardly knew what—the small doings of the previous day, her comings and goings, accounts of dances, estimates of new acquaintances. But besides this she filled page after page with "impressions," "outpourings," queer little speculations about her soul, quotations from poets, solemn criticisms of new novels, or as often as not mere purposeless meanderings of words, exclamatory, rhapsodic—involved lucubrations quite meaningless and futile, but which at times she re-read with vague thrills of emotion and mystery.

On this occasion Page wrote rapidly and steadily for a few moments after Laura's entrance into the room. Then she paused, her eyes growing wide and thoughtful. She wrote another line and paused again. Seated on the floor, her hands full of gloves, Laura was murmuring to herself.

"Those are good . . . and those, and the black suèdes make

eight. . . . And if I could only find the mate to this white one.
. . . Ah, here it is. That makes nine, nine pair."

She put the gloves aside, and turning to the stockings drew one
of the silk ones over her arm, and spread out her fingers in the
foot.

"Oh, dear," she whispered, "there's a thread started, and now
it will simply run the whole length. . . ."

Page's scratching paused again.

"Laura," she asked dreamily, "Laura, how do you spell 'abys-
mal'?"

"With a y, honey," answered Laura, careful not to smile.

"Oh, Laura," asked Page, "do you ever get very, very sad without knowing why?"

"No, indeed," answered her sister, as she peeled the stocking
from her arm. "When I'm sad I know just the reason, you may
be sure."

Page sighed again.

"Oh, I don't know," she murmured indefinitely. "I lie awake
at night sometimes and wish I were dead."

"You mustn't get morbid, honey," answered her older sister
calmly. "It isn't natural for a young healthy little body like you
to have such gloomy notions."

"Last night," continued Page, "I got up out of bed and sat by
the window a long time. And everything was so still and beautiful,
and the moonlight and all—and I said right out loud to myself,

"My breath to heaven in vapor goes—

You know those lines from Tennyson:

"My breath to heaven in vapor goes:
    May my soul follow soon."

I said it right out loud just like that, and it was just as though something in me had spoken. I got my journal and wrote down, 'Yet
in a few days, and thee, the all-beholding sun shall see no more.'
It's from Thanatopsis, you know, and I thought how beautiful it
would be to leave all this world, and soar and soar, right up to
higher planes and be at peace. Laura, dearest, do you think I ever
ought to marry?"

"Why not, girlie? Why shouldn't you marry? Of course
you'll marry some day, if you find—"

"I should like to be a nun," Page interrupted, shaking her head, mournfully.

"—if you find the man who loves you," continued Laura, "and whom you—you admire and respect—whom you love. What would you say, honey, if—if your sister, if I should be married some of these days?"

Page wheeled about in her chair.

"Oh, Laura, tell me," she cried, "are you joking? Are you going to be married? Who to? I hadn't an idea, but I thought— I suspected—"

"Well," observed Laura, slowly, "I might as well tell you— some one will if I don't—Mr. Jadwin *wants* me to marry him."

"And what did you say? What did you say? Oh, I'll never tell. Oh, Laura, tell me all about it."

"Well, why shouldn't I marry him? Yes—I promised. I said yes. Why shouldn't I? He loves me, and he is rich. Isn't that enough?"

"Oh, no, it isn't. You must love—you do love him?"

"I? Love? Pooh!" cried Laura. "Indeed not. I love nobody."

"Oh, Laura," protested Page earnestly. "Don't, don't talk that way. You mustn't. It's wicked."

Laura put her head in the air.

"I wouldn't give any man that much satisfaction. I think that is the way it ought to be. A man ought to love a woman more than she loves him. It ought to be enough for him if she lets him give her everything she wants in the world. He ought to serve her like the old knights—give up his whole life to satisfy some whim of hers; and it's her part, if she likes, to be cold and distant. That's my idea of love."

"Yes, but they weren't cold and proud to their knights after they'd promised to marry them," urged Page. "They loved them in the end, and married them for love."

"Oh, 'love'!" mocked Laura. "I don't believe in love. You only get your ideas of it from trashy novels and matinées. Girlie," cried Laura, "I am going to have the most beautiful gowns. They're the last things that Miss Dearborn shall buy for herself, and"—she fetched a long breath—"I tell you they are going to be creations."

When at length the lunch bell rang, Laura jumped to her feet, adjusting her coiffure with thrusts of her long, white hands, the fingers extended, and ran from the room exclaiming that the whole morning had gone and that half her bureau drawers were still in disarray.

Page, left alone, sat for a long time lost in thought, sighing deeply at intervals, then at last she wrote in her journal:

"A world without Love—oh, what an awful thing that would be. Oh, love is so beautiful—so beautiful, that it makes me sad. When I think of love in all its beauty I am sad, sad like Romola in George Eliot's well-known novel of the same name."

She locked up her journal in the desk drawer, and wiped her pen point until it shone, upon a little square of chamois skin. Her writing-desk was a miracle of neatness, everything in its precise place, the writing-paper in geometrical parallelograms, the pen tray neatly polished.

On the hearth rug, where Laura had sat, Page's searching eye discovered traces of her occupancy—a glove button, a white thread, a hairpin. Page was at great pains to gather them up carefully and drop them into the waste basket.

"Laura is so fly-away," she observed, soberly.

When Laura told the news to Aunt Wess' the little old lady showed no surprise.

"I've been expecting it of late," she remarked. "Well, Laura, Mr. Jadwin is a man of parts. Though, to tell the truth, I thought at first it was to be that Mr. Corthell. He always seemed so distinguished-looking and elegant. I suppose now that that young Mr. Court will have a regular conniption fit."

"Oh, Landry," murmured Laura.

"Where are you going to live, Laura? Here? My word, child, don't be afraid to tell me I must pack. Why, bless you—"

"No, no," exclaimed Laura, energetically, "you are to stay right here. We'll talk it all over just as soon as I know more decidedly what our plans are to be. No, we won't live here. Mr. Jadwin is going to buy a new house—on the corner of North Avenue and State Street. It faces Lincoln Park—you know it, the Farnsworth place."

"Why, my word, Laura," cried Aunt Wess' amazed, "why, it's a palace! Of course I know it. Why, it takes in the whole block, child, and there's a conservatory pretty near as big as this house. *Well!*"

"Yes, I know," answered Laura, shaking her head. "It takes my breath away sometimes. Mr. Jadwin tells me there's an art

gallery, too, with an organ in it—a full-sized church organ. Think
of it. Isn't it beautiful, beautiful? Isn't it a happiness? And I'll
have my own carriage and coupé, and oh, Aunt Wess', a saddle
horse if I want to, and a box at the opera, and a country place—
that is to be bought day after to-morrow. It's at Geneva Lake.
We're to go there after we are married, and Mr. Jadwin has bought
the dearest, loveliest, daintiest little steam yacht. He showed the
photograph of her yesterday. Oh, honey, honey! It all comes over
me sometimes. Think, only a year ago, less than that, I was vege-
tating there at Barrington, among those wretched old blue-noses,
helping Martha with the preserves and all and all; and now"—
she threw her arms wide—"I'm just going to live. Think of it,
that beautiful house, and servants, and carriages, and paintings,
and, oh, honey, how I will dress the part!"

"But I wouldn't think of those things so much, Laura," answered Aunt Wess', rather seriously. "Child, you are not marrying him for carriages and organs and saddle horses and such.
You're marrying this Mr. Jadwin because you love him. Aren't
you?"

"Oh," cried Laura, "I would marry a ragamuffin if he gave me
all these things—gave them to me because he loved me."

Aunt Wess' stared. "I wouldn't talk that way, Laura," she
remarked. "Even in fun. At least not before Page."

That same evening Jadwin came to dinner with the two sisters
and their aunt. The usual evening drive with Laura was foregone
for this occasion. Jadwin had stayed very late at his office, and
from there was to come direct to the Dearborns. Besides that, Nip
—the trotters were named Nip and Tuck—was lame.

As early as four o'clock in the afternoon Laura, suddenly moved
by an unreasoning caprice, began to prepare an elaborate toilet.
Not since the opera night had she given so much attention to her
appearance. She sent out for an extraordinary quantity of flowers;
flowers for the table, flowers for Page and Aunt Wess', great
"American beauties" for her corsage, and a huge bunch of violets
for the bowl in the library. She insisted that Page should wear her
smartest frock, and Mrs. Wessels her grenadine of great occasions.
As for herself, she decided upon a dinner gown of black, décolleté,
with sleeves of lace. Her hair she dressed higher than ever. She
resolved upon wearing all her jewelry, and to that end put on all
her rings, secured the roses in place with an amethyst brooch, caught
up the little locks at the back of her head with a heart-shaped pin

of tiny diamonds, and even fastened the ribbon of satin that girdled her waist with a clasp of flawed turquoises.

Until five in the afternoon she was in the gayest spirits, and went down to the dining-room to supervise the setting of the table, singing to herself.

Then, almost at the very last, when Jadwin might be expected at any moment, her humor changed again, and again, for no discoverable reason.

Page, who came into her sister's room after dressing, to ask how she looked, found her harassed and out of sorts. She was moody, spoke in monosyllables, and suddenly declared that the wearing anxiety of housekeeping was driving her to distraction. Of all days in the week, why had Jadwin chosen this particular one to come to dinner. Men had no sense, could not appreciate a woman's difficulties. Oh, she would be glad when the evening was over.

Then, as an ultimate disaster, she declared that she herself looked "Dutchy." There was no style, no smartness to her dress; her hair was arranged unbecomingly; she was growing thin, peaked. In a word, she looked "Dutchy."

All at once she flung off her roses and dropped into a chair.

"I will not go down to-night," she cried. "You and Aunt Wess' must make out to receive Mr. Jadwin. I simply will not see any one to-night, Mr. Jadwin least of all. Tell him I'm gone to bed sick—which is the truth, I am going to bed, my head is splitting."

All persuasion, entreaty, or cajolery availing nothing. Neither Page nor Aunt Wess' could shake her decision. At last Page hazarded a remonstrance to the effect that if she had known that Laura was not going to be at dinner she would not have taken such pains with her own toilet.

Promptly thereat Laura lost her temper.

"I do declare, Page," she exclaimed, "it seems to me that I get very little thanks for ever taking any interest in your personal appearance. There is not a girl in Chicago—no millionaire's daughter—has any prettier gowns than you. I plan and plan, and go to the most expensive dressmakers so that you will be well dressed, and just as soon as I dare to express the desire to see you appear like a gentlewoman, I get it thrown in my face. And why do I do it? I'm sure I don't know. It's because I'm a poor, weak, foolish, indulgent sister. I've given up the idea of ever being loved by you; but I do insist on being respected." Laura rose, stately, severe. It was the "grand manner" now, unequivocally, unmistakably. "I do insist upon being respected," she repeated. "It would be wrong and wicked of me to allow you to ignore and neglect my every wish. I'll not have it, I'll not tolerate it."

Page, aroused, indignant, disdained an answer, but drew in her breath and held it hard, her lips tight pressed.

"It's all very well for you to pose, miss," Laura went on; "to pose as injured innocence. But you understand very well what I mean. If you don't love me, at least I shall not allow you to flout me—deliberately, defiantly. And it does seem strange," she added, her voice beginning to break, "that when we two are all alone in the world, when there's no father or mother—and you are all I have, and when I love you as I do, that there might be on your part— a little consideration—when I only want to be loved for my own sake, and not—and not—when I want to be, oh, loved—loved— loved—"

The two sisters were in each other's arms by now, and Page was crying no less than Laura.

"Oh, little sister," exclaimed Laura, "I know you love me. I know you do. I didn't mean to say that. You must forgive me and be very kind to me these days. I know I'm cross, but sometimes these days I'm so excited and nervous I can't help it, and you must try to bear with me. Hark, there's the bell."

Listening, they heard the servant open the door, and then the sound of Jadwin's voice and the clank of his cane in the porcelain cane rack. But still Laura could not be persuaded to go down. No, she was going to bed; she had neuralgia; she was too nervous to so much as think. Her gown was "Dutchy." And in the end, so unshakable was her resolve that Page and her aunt had to sit through the dinner with Jadwin and entertain him as best they could.

But as the coffee was being served the three received a genuine surprise. Laura appeared. All her finery was laid off. She wore the simplest, the most veritably monastic, of her dresses, plain to the point of severity. Her hands were bare of rings. Not a single jewel, not even the most modest ornament relieved her sober appearance. She was very quiet, spoke in a low voice, and declared she had come down only to drink a glass of mineral water and then to return at once to her room.

As a matter of fact, she did nothing of the kind. The others prevailed upon her to take a cup of coffee. Then the dessert was recalled, and, forgetting herself in an animated discussion with Jadwin as to the name of their steam yacht, she ate two plates of wine jelly before she was aware. She expressed a doubt as to whether a little salad would do her good, and after a vehement exhortation from Jadwin, allowed herself to be persuaded into accepting a sufficiently generous amount.

"I think a classical name would be best for the boat," she declared. "Something like 'Arethusa' or 'The Nereid.'"

They rose from the table and passed into the library. The evening was sultry, threatening a rainstorm, and they preferred not to sit on the "stoop." Jadwin lighted a cigar; he still wore his business clothes—the inevitable "cutaway," white waistcoat, and gray trousers of the middle-aged man of affairs.

"Oh, call her the 'Artemis,'" suggested Page.

"Well, now, to tell the truth," observed Jadwin, "those names look pretty in print; but somehow I don't fancy them. They're hard to read, and they sound somehow frilled up and fancy. But if you're satisfied, Laura—"

"I knew a young man once," began Aunt Wess', "who had a boat—that was when we lived at Kenwood and Mr. Wessels belonged to the 'Farragut'—and this young man had a boat he called 'Fanchon.' He got tipped over in her one day, he and the three daughters of a lady I knew well, and two days afterward they found them at the bottom of the lake, all holding on to each other; and they fetched them up just like that in one piece. The mother of those girls never smiled once since that day, and her hair turned snow white. That was in 'seventy-nine. I remember it perfectly. The boat's name was 'Fanchon.'"

"But that was a sail boat, Aunt Wess'," objected Laura. "Ours is a steam yacht. There's all the difference in the world."

"I guess they're all pretty risky, those pleasure boats," answered Aunt Wess'. "My word, you couldn't get me to set foot on one."

Jadwin nodded his head at Laura, his eyes twinkling.

"Well, we'll leave 'em all at home, Laura, when we go," he said.

A little later one of Page's "young men" called to see her, and Page took him off into the drawing-room across the hall. Mrs. Wessels seized upon the occasion to slip away unobserved, and Laura and Jadwin were left alone.

"Well, my girl," began Jadwin, "how's the day gone with you?"

She had been seated at the centre table, by the drop light—the only light in the room—turning over the leaves of "The Age of Fable," looking for graceful and appropriate names for the yacht. Jadwin leaned over her and put his hand upon her shoulder.

"Oh, about the same as usual," she answered. "I told Page and Aunt Wess' this morning."

"What did they have to say?" Jadwin laid a soft but clumsy hand upon Laura's head, adding, "Laura, you have the most wonderful hair I ever saw."

"Oh, they were not surprised. Curtis, don't, you are mussing me." She moved her head impatiently; but then smiling, as if to mitigate her abruptness, said, "It always makes me nervous to have my hair touched. No, they were not surprised; unless it was that we were to be married so soon. They were surprised at that. You know I always said it was too soon. Why not put it off, Curtis—until the winter?"

But he scouted this, and then, as she returned to the subject again, interrupted her, drawing some papers from his pocket.

"Oh, by the way," he said, "here are the sketch plans for the alterations of the house at Geneva. The contractor brought them to the office to-day. He's made that change about the dining-room."

"Oh," exclaimed Laura, interested at once, "you mean about building on the conservatory?"

"Hum—no," answered Jadwin a little slowly. "You see, Laura, the difficulty is in getting the thing done this summer. When we go up there we want everything finished, don't we? We don't want a lot of workmen clattering around. I thought maybe we could wait about that conservatory till next year, if you didn't mind."

Laura acquiesced readily enough, but Jadwin could see that she was a little disappointed. Thoughtful, he tugged his mustache in silence for a moment. Perhaps, after all, it could be arranged. Then an idea presented itself to him. Smiling a little awkwardly, he said:

"Laura, I tell you what. I'll make a bargain with you."

She looked up as he hesitated. Jadwin sat down at the table opposite her and leaned forward upon his folded arms.

"Do you know," he began, "I happened to think— Well, here's what I mean," he suddenly declared decisively. "Do you know, Laura, that ever since we've been engaged you've never— Well, you've never—never kissed me of your own accord. It's foolish to talk that way now, isn't it? But, by George! That

would be—would be such a wonderful thing for me. I know," he
hastened to add, "I know, Laura, you aren't demonstrative. I ought
not to expect, maybe, that you— Well, maybe it isn't much. But
I was thinking a while ago that there wouldn't be a sweeter thing
imaginable for me than if my own girl would come up to me some
time—when I wasn't thinking—and of her own accord put her two
arms around me and kiss me. And—well, I was thinking about it,
and—" He hesitated again, then finished abruptly with, "And it
occurred to me that you never had."

Laura made no answer, but smiled rather indefinitely, as she continued to search the pages of the book, her head to one side.

Jadwin continued:

"We'll call it a bargain. Some day—before very long, mind
you—you are going to kiss me—that way, understand, of your own
accord, when I'm not thinking of it; and I'll get that conservatory
in for you. I'll manage it somehow. I'll start those fellows at it
to-morrow—twenty of 'em if it's necessary. How about it? Is it
a bargain? Some day before long. What do you say?"

Laura hesitated, singularly embarrassed, unable to find the right
words.

"Is it a bargain?" persisted Jadwin.

"Oh, if you put it that way," she murmured, "I suppose so—
yes."

"You won't forget, because I shan't speak about it again. Promise you won't forget."

"No, I won't forget. Why not call her the 'Thetis'?"

"I was going to suggest the 'Dart,' or the 'Swallow,' or the
'Arrow.' Something like that—to give a notion of speed."

"No. I like the 'Thetis' best."

"That settles it then. She's your steam yacht, Laura."

Later on, when Jadwin was preparing to depart, they stood for
a moment in the hallway, while he drew on his gloves and took a
fresh cigar from his case.

"I'll call for you here at about ten," he said. "Will that do?"

He spoke of the following morning. He had planned to take
Page, Mrs. Wessels, and Laura on a day's excursion to Geneva
Lake to see how work was progressing on the country house. Jadwin had set his mind upon passing the summer months after the
marriage at the lake, and as the early date of the ceremony made it
impossible to erect a new building, he had bought, and was now
causing to be remodeled, an old but very well constructed house just

outside of the town and once occupied by a local magistrate. The grounds were ample, filled with shade and fruit trees, and fronted upon the lake. Laura had never seen her future country home. But for the past month Jadwin had had a small army of workmen and mechanics busy about the place, and had managed to galvanize the contractors with some of his own energy and persistence. There was every probability that the house and grounds would be finished in time.

"Very well," said Laura, in answer to his question, "at ten we'll be ready. Good-night." She held out her hand. But Jadwin put it quickly aside, and took her swiftly and strongly into his arms, and turning her face to his, kissed her cheek again and again.

Laura submitted, protesting:

"Curtis! Such foolishness. Oh, dear; can't you love me without crumpling me so? Curtis! Please. You are so rough with me, dear."

She pulled away from him, and looked up into his face, surprised to find it suddenly flushed; his eyes were flashing.

"My God," he murmured, with a quick intake of breath, "my God, how I love you, my girl! Just the touch of your hand, the smell of your hair. Oh, sweetheart. It is wonderful! Wonderful!" Then abruptly he was master of himself again.

"Good-night," he said. "Good-night. God bless you," and with the words was gone.

They were married on the last day of June of that summer at eleven o'clock in the morning in the church opposite Laura's house —the Episcopalian church of which she was a member. The wedding was very quiet. Only the Cresslers, Miss Gretry, Page, and Aunt Wess' were present. Immediately afterward the couple were to take the train for Geneva Lake—Jadwin having chartered a car for the occasion.

But the weather on the wedding day was abominable. A warm drizzle, which had set in early in the morning, developed by eleven o'clock into a steady downpour, accompanied by sullen grumblings of very distant thunder.

About an hour before the appointed time Laura insisted that her aunt and sister should leave her. She would allow only Mrs. Cressler to help her. The time passed. The rain continued to fall. At last it wanted but fifteen minutes to eleven.

Page and Aunt Wess', who presented themselves at the church in advance of the others, found the interior cool, dark, and damp.

They sat down in a front pew, talking in whispers, looking about them. Druggeting shrouded the reader's stand, the baptismal font, and bishop's chair. Every footfall and every minute sound echoed noisily from the dark vaulting of the nave and chancel. The janitor or sexton, a severe old fellow, who wore a skull-cap and loose slippers, was making a great to-do with a pile of pew cushions in a remote corner. The rain drummed with incessant monotony upon the slates overhead, and upon the stained windows on either hand. Page, who attended the church regularly every Sunday morning, now found it all strangely unfamiliar. The saints in the windows looked odd and unecclesiastical; the whole suggestion of the place was uncanonical. In the organ loft a tuner was at work upon the organ, and from time to time the distant mumbling of the thunder was mingled with a sonorous, prolonged note from the pipes.

"My word, how it is raining," whispered Aunt Wess', as the pour upon the roof suddenly swelled in volume.

But Page had taken a prayer-book from the rack, and kneeling upon a hassock was repeating the Litany to herself.

It annoyed Aunt Wess'. Excited, aroused, the little old lady was never more in need of a listener. Would Page never be through?

"And Laura's new frock," she whispered, vaguely. "It's going to be ruined."

Page, her lips forming the words, "Good Lord deliver us," fixed her aunt with a reproving glance. To pass the time Aunt Wess' began counting the pews, missing a number here and there, confusing herself, always obliged to begin over again. From the direction of the vestry room came the sound of a closing door. Then all fell silent again. Even the shuffling of the janitor ceased for an instant.

"Isn't it still?" murmured Aunt Wess', her head in the air. "I wonder if that was them. I heard a door slam. They tell me that the rector has been married three times." Page, unheeding and demure, turned a leaf, and began with "All those who travel by land or water." Mr. Cressler and young Miss Gretry appeared. They took their seats behind Page and Aunt Wess', and the party exchanged greetings in low voices. Page reluctantly laid down her prayer-book.

"Laura will be over soon," whispered Mr. Cressler. "Carrie is with her. I'm going into the vestry room. J. has just come." He took himself off, walking upon his tiptoes.

Aunt Wess' turned to Page, repeating:

"Do you know they say this rector has been married three times?"

But Page was once more deep in her prayer-book, so the little old lady addressed her remark to the Gretry girl.

This other, however, her lips tightly compressed, made a despairing gesture with her hand, and at length managed to say: "Can't talk."

"Why, heavens, child, whatever is the matter?"

"Makes them worse—when I open my mouth—I've got the hiccoughs."

Aunt Wess' flounced back in her seat, exasperated, out of sorts.

"Well, my word," she murmured to herself, "I never saw such girls."

"Preserve to our use the kindly fruits of the earth," continued Page.

Isabel Gretry's hiccoughs drove Aunt Wess' into "the fidgets." They "got on her nerves." What with them and Page's uninterrupted murmur, she was at length obliged to sit in the far end of the pew, and just as she had settled herself a second time the door of the vestry room opened and the wedding party came out; first Mrs. Cressler, then Laura, then Jadwin and Cressler, and then, robed in billowing white, venerable, his prayer book in his hand, the bishop of the diocese himself. Last of all came the clerk, osseous, perfumed, a gardenia in the lapel of his frock coat, terribly excited, and hurrying about on tiptoe, saying "Sh! Sh!" as a matter of principle.

Jadwin wore a new frock coat and a resplendent Ascot scarf, which Mr. Cressler had bought for him, and Page knew at a glance that he was agitated beyond all measure, and was keeping himself in hand only by a tremendous effort. She could guess that his teeth were clinched. He stood by Cressler's side, his head bent forward, his hands—the fingers incessantly twisting and untwisting —clasped behind his back. Never for once did his eyes leave Laura's face.

She herself was absolutely calm, only a little paler perhaps than usual; but never more beautiful, never more charming. Abandoning for this once her accustomed black, she wore a tan traveling dress, tailor-made, very smart, a picture hat with heavy plumes set off with a clasp of rhinestones, while into her belt was thrust a great bunch of violets. She drew off her gloves and handed them to Mrs. Cressler. At the same moment Page began to cry softly to herself.

"There's the last of Laura," she whimpered. "There's the last of my dear sister for me."

Aunt Wess' fixed her with a distressful gaze. She sniffed once or twice, and then began fumbling in her reticule for her handkerchief.

"If only her dear father were here," she whispered huskily. "And to think that's the same little girl I used to rap on the head with my thimble for annoying the cat! Oh, if Jonas could be here this day."

"She'll never be the same to me after now," sobbed Page, and as she spoke the Gretry girl, hypnotized with emotion and taken all unawares, gave vent to a shrill hiccough, a veritable yelp, that woke an explosive echo in every corner of the building.

Page could not restrain a giggle, and the giggle strangled with the sobs in her throat, so that the little girl was not far from hysterics.

And just then a sonorous voice, magnificent, orotund, began suddenly from the chancel with the words:

"Dearly beloved, we are gathered together here in the sight of God, and in the face of this company to join together this Man and this Woman in holy matrimony."

Promptly a spirit of reverence, not to say solemnity, pervaded the entire surroundings. The building no longer appeared secular, unecclesiastical. Not in the midst of all the pomp and ceremonial of the Easter service had the chancel and high altar disengaged a more compelling influence. All other intrusive noises died away; the organ was hushed; the fussy janitor was nowhere in sight; the outside clamor of the city seemed dwindling to the faintest, most distant vibration; the whole world was suddenly removed, while the great moment in the lives of the Man and Woman began.

Page held her breath; the intensity of the situation seemed to her, almost physically, straining tighter and tighter with every passing instant. She was awed, stricken; and Laura appeared to her to be all at once a woman transfigured, semi-angelic, unknowable, exalted. The solemnity of those prolonged, canorous syllables: "I require and charge you both, as ye shall answer at the dreadful day of judgment, when the secrets of all hearts shall be disclosed," weighed down upon her spirits with an almost intolerable majesty. Oh, it was all very well to speak lightly of marriage, to consider it in a vein of mirth. It was a pretty solemn affair, after all; and she herself, Page Dearborn, was a wicked, wicked girl, full of sins, full of deceits and frivolities, meriting of punishment—on "that dreadful day of judgment." Only last week she had deceived Aunt Wess' in the matter of one of her "young men." It was time she stopped. To-day would mark a change. Henceforward, she resolved, she would lead a new life.

"God the Father, God the Son, and God the Holy Ghost . . ."

To Page's mind the venerable bishop's voice was filling all the church; as on the day of Pentecost, when the apostles received the Holy Ghost, the building was filled with a "mighty rushing wind."

She knelt down again, but could not bring herself to close her eyes completely. From under her lids she still watched her sister and Jadwin. How Laura must be feeling now! She was, in fact, very pale. There was emotion in Jadwin's eyes. Page could see them plainly. It seemed beautiful that even he, the strong, modern man-of-affairs, should be so moved. How he must love Laura. He was fine, he was noble; and all at once this fineness and nobility of his so affected her that she began to cry again. Then suddenly came the words:

" . . . That in the world to come ye may have life everlasting. Amen."

There was a moment's silence, then the group about the altar rail broke up.

"Come," said Aunt Wess', getting to her feet, "it's all over, Page. Come, and kiss your sister—Mrs. Jadwin."

In the vestry room Laura stood for a moment, while one after another of the wedding party—even Mr. Cressler—kissed her. When Page's turn came, the two sisters held each other in a close embrace a long moment, but Laura's eyes were always dry. Of all present she was the least excited.

"Here's something," vociferated the ubiquitous clerk, pushing his way forward. "It was on the table when we came out just now. The sexton says a messenger boy brought it. It's for Mrs. Jadwin."

He handed her a large box. Laura opened it. Inside was a great sheaf of Jacqueminot roses and a card, on which was written:

"May that same happiness which you have always inspired in the lives and memories of all who know you be with you always.
"Yrs.   S. C."

The party, emerging from the church, hurried across the street to the Dearborns' home, where Laura and Jadwin were to get their valises and hand-bags. Jadwin's carriage was already at the door.

They all assembled in the parlor, every one talking at once, while the servants, bare-headed, carried the baggage down to the carriage.

"Oh, wait—wait a minute, I'd forgotten something," cried Laura.

"What is it? Here, I'll get it for you," cried Jadwin and Cressler as she started toward the door. But she waved them off, crying:

"No, no. It's nothing. You wouldn't know where to look."

Alone she ran up the stairs, and gained the second story; then paused a moment on the landing to get her breath and to listen. The rooms near by were quiet, deserted. From below she could hear the voices of the others—their laughter and gayety. She turned about, and went from room to room, looking long into each; first Aunt Wess's bedroom, then Page's, then the "front sitting-room," then, lastly, her own room. It was still in the disorder caused by that eventful morning; many of the ornaments—her own cherished knick-knacks—were gone, packed and shipped to her new home the day before. Her writing-desk and bureau were bare. On the backs of chairs, and across the footboard of the bed, were the odds and ends of dress she was never to wear again.

For a long time Laura stood looking silently at the empty room. Here she had lived the happiest period of her life; not an object there, however small, that was not hallowed by association. Now she was leaving it forever. Now the new life, the Untried, was to begin. Forever the old days, the old life were gone. Girlhood was gone; the Laura Dearborn that only last night had pressed the pillows of that bed, where was she now? Where was the little black-haired girl of Barrington.

And what was this new life to which she was going forth, under these leaden skies, under this warm mist of rain? The tears—at last—were in her eyes, and the sob in her throat, and she found herself, as she leaned an arm upon the lintel of the door, whispering:

"Good-by. Good-by. Good-by."

Then suddenly Laura, reckless of her wedding finery, forgetful of trivialities, crossed the room and knelt down at the side of the bed. Her head in her folded arms, she prayed—prayed in the little unstudied words of her childhood, prayed that God would take care of her and make her a good girl; prayed that she might be happy;

prayed God to help her in the new life, and that she should be a good and loyal wife.

And then, as she knelt there, all at once she felt an arm, strong, heavy even, laid upon her. She raised her head and looked—for the first time—direct into her husband's eyes.

"I knew—" began Jadwin. "I thought— Dear, I understand, I understand."

He said no more than that. But suddenly Laura knew that he, Jadwin, her husband, did "understand," and she discovered, too, in that moment just what it meant to be completely, thoroughly understood—understood without chance of misapprehension, without shadow of doubt; understood to her heart's heart. And with the knowledge a new feeling was born within her. No woman, not her dearest friend, not even Page, had ever seemed so close to her as did her husband now. How could she be unhappy henceforward? The future was already brightening.

Suddenly she threw both arms around his neck, and drawing his face down to her, kissed him again and again, and pressed her wet cheek to his—tear-stained like her own.

"It's going to be all right, dear," he said, as she stood from him, though still holding his hand. "It's going to be all right."

"Yes, yes, all right, all right," she assented. "I never seemed to realize it till this minute. From the first I must have loved you without knowing it. And I've been cold and hard to you, and now I'm sorry, sorry. You were wrong, remember that time in the library, when you said I was undemonstrative. I'm not. I love you dearly, dearly, and never for once, for one little moment, am I ever going to allow you to forget it."

Suddenly, as Jadwin recalled the incident of which she spoke, an idea occurred to him.

"Oh, our bargain—remember? You didn't forget, after all."

"I did. I did," she cried. "I did forget it. That's the very sweetest thing about it."

VI

THE months passed. Soon three years had gone by, and the third winter since the ceremony in St. James' Church drew to its close.

Since that day when—acting upon the foreknowledge of the French import duty—Jadwin had sold his million of bushels short, the price of wheat had been steadily going down. From ninety-three and ninety-four it had dropped to the eighties. Heavy crops the world over had helped the decline. No one was willing to buy wheat. The bear leaders were strong, unassailable. Lower and lower sagged the price; now it was seventy-five, now seventy-two. From all parts of the country in solid, waveless tides wheat—the mass of it incessantly crushing down the price—came rolling in upon Chicago and the Board of Trade Pit. All over the world the farmers saw season after season of good crops. They were good in the Argentine Republic, and on the Russian steppes. In India, on the little farms of Burmah, of Mysore, and of Sind the grain, year after year, headed out fat, heavy and well-favored. In the great San Joaquin valley of California the ranches were one welter of fertility. All over the United States, from the Dakotas, from Nebraska, Iowa, Kansas, and Illinois, from all the wheat belt came steadily the reports of good crops.

But at the same time the low price of grain kept the farmers poor. New mortgages were added to farms already heavily "papered"; even the crops were mortgaged in advance. No new farm implements were bought. Throughout the farming communities of the "Middle West" there were no longer purchases of buggies and parlor organs. Somewhere in other remoter corners of the world the cheap wheat, that meant cheap bread, made living easy and induced prosperity, but in the United States the poverty of the farmer worked upward through the cogs and wheels of the whole great machine of business. It was as though a lubricant had dried up. The cogs and wheels worked slowly and with dislocations. Things were a little out of joint. Wall Street stocks were down. In a word, "times were bad." Thus for three years. It became a proverb on the Chicago Board of Trade that the quickest way to make money was to sell wheat short. One could with almost absolute certainty be sure of buying cheaper than one had sold. And that peculiar, indefinite thing known—among the most unsentimental men in the world—as "sentiment" prevailed more and more strongly in favor of low prices. "The 'sentiment,'" said the market reports, "was bearish"; and the traders, speculators, eighth-chasers, scalpers, brokers, bucket-shop men, and the like— all the world of La Salle Street—had become so accustomed to these "Bear conditions" that it was hard to believe that they would not continue indefinitely.

Jadwin, inevitably, had been again drawn into the troubled

waters of the Pit. Always, as from the very first, a Bear, he had once more raided the market, and had once more been successful. Two months after this raid he and Gretry planned still another coup, a deal of greater magnitude than any they had previously hazarded. Laura, who knew very little of her husband's affairs—to which he seldom alluded—saw by the daily papers that at one stage of the affair the "deal" trembled to its base.

But Jadwin was now "blooded to the game." He no longer needed Gretry's urging to spur him. He had developed into a strategist, bold, of inconceivable effrontery, delighting in the shock of battle, never more jovial, more daring than when under stress of the most merciless attack. On this occasion, when the "other side" resorted to the usual tactics to drive him from the Pit, he led on his enemies to make one single false step. Instantly—disregarding Gretry's entreaties as to caution—Jadwin had brought the vast bulk of his entire fortune to bear, in the manner of a general concentrating his heavy artillery, and crushed the opposition with appalling swiftness.

He issued from the grapple triumphantly, and it was not till long afterward that Laura knew how near, for a few hours, he had been to defeat.

And again the price of wheat declined. In the first week in April, at the end of the third winter of Jadwin's married life, May wheat was selling on the floor of the Chicago Board of Trade at sixty-four, the July option at sixty-five, the September at sixty-six and an eighth. During February of the same year Jadwin had sold short five hundred thousand bushels of May. He believed with Gretry and the majority of the professional traders that the price would go to sixty.

March passed without any further decline. All through this month and through the first days of April Jadwin was unusually thoughtful. His short wheat gave him no concern. He was now so rich that a mere half-million bushels was not a matter for anxiety. It was the "situation" that arrested his attention.

In some indefinable way, warned by that blessed sixth sense that had made him the successful speculator he was, he felt that somewhere, at some time during the course of the winter, a change had quietly, gradually come about, that it was even then operating. The conditions that had prevailed so consistently for three years, were they now to be shifted a little? He did not know, he could not say.

But in the plexus of financial affairs in which he moved and lived he felt—a difference.

For one thing "times" were better, business was better. He could not fail to see that trade was picking up. In dry goods, in hardware, in manufactures, there seemed to be a different spirit, and he could imagine that it was a spirit of optimism. There, in that great city where the Heart of the Nation beat, where the diseases of the times or the times' healthful activities were instantly reflected, Jadwin sensed a more rapid, an easier, more untroubled run of life blood. All through the Body of Things, money, the vital fluid, seemed to be flowing more easily. People seemed richer, the banks were lending more, securities seemed stable, solid. In New York, stocks were booming. Men were making money—were making it, spending it, lending it, exchanging it. Instead of being congested in vaults, safes and cash boxes, tight, hard, congealed, it was loosening, and, as it were, liquefying, so that it spread and spread and permeated the entire community. The People had money. They were willing to take chances.

So much for the financial conditions.

The spring had been backward, cold, bitter, inhospitable, and Jadwin began to suspect that the wheat crop of his native country, that for so long had been generous, and of excellent quality, was now to prove—it seemed quite possible—scant and of poor condition. He began to watch the weather, and to keep an eye upon the reports from the little county seats and "centres" in the winter wheat States. These, in part, seemed to confirm his suspicions.

From Keokuk, in Iowa, came the news that winter wheat was suffering from want of moisture. Benedict, Yates' Centre, and Douglass, in southeastern Kansas, sent in reports of dry, windy weather that was killing the young grain in every direction, and the same conditions seemed to prevail in the central counties. In Illinois, from Quincy and Waterloo in the west, and from Ridgway in the south, reports came steadily to hand of freezing weather and bitter winds. All through the lower portions of the State the snowfall during the winter had not been heavy enough to protect the seeded grain. But the Ohio crop, it would appear, was promising enough, as was also that of Missouri. In Indiana, however, Jadwin could guess that the hopes of even a moderate yield were fated to be disappointed; persistent cold weather, winter continuing almost up to the first of April, seemed to have definitely settled the question.

But more especially Jadwin watched Nebraska, that State which is one single vast wheat field. How would Nebraska do, Nebraska, which alone might feed an entire nation? County seat after county seat began to send in its reports. All over the State the grip of winter held firm even yet. The wheat had been battered by incessant gales, had been nipped and harried by frost; everywhere the young half-grown grain seemed to be perishing. It was a massacre, a veritable slaughter.

But, for all this, nothing could be decided as yet. Other winter wheat States, from which returns were as yet only partial, might easily compensate for the failures elsewhere, and besides all that, the Bears of the Board of Trade might keep the price inert even in the face of the news of short yields. As a matter of fact, the more important and stronger Bear traders were already piping their usual strain. Prices were bound to decline, the three years' sagging was not over yet. They, the Bears, were too strong; no Bull news could frighten them. Somehow there was bound to be plenty of wheat. In face of the rumors of a short crop they kept the price inert, weak.

On the tenth of April came the Government report on the condition of winter wheat. It announced an average far below any known for ten years past. On March tenth the same bulletin had shown a moderate supply in farmers' hands, less than one hundred million bushels, in fact, and a visible supply of less than forty millions.

The Bear leaders promptly set to work to discount this news. They showed how certain foreign conditions would more than offset the effect of a poor American harvest. They pointed out the fact that the Government report on condition was brought up only to the first of April, and that since that time the weather in the wheat belt had been favorable beyond the wildest hopes.

The April report was made public on the afternoon of the tenth of the month. That same evening Jadwin invited Gretry and his wife to dine at the new house on North Avenue; and after dinner, leaving Mrs. Gretry and Laura in the drawing-room, he brought the broker up to the billiard-room for a game of pool.

But when Gretry had put the balls in the triangle, the two men did not begin to play at once. Jadwin had asked the question that had been uppermost in the minds of each during dinner.

"Well, Sam," he had said, by way of a beginning, "what do you think of this Government report?"

The broker chalked his cue placidly.

"I expect there'll be a bit of reaction on the strength of it, but the market will go off again. I said wheat would go to sixty, and I still say it. It's a long time between now and May."

"I wasn't thinking of crop conditions only," observed Jadwin. "Sam, we're going to have better times and higher prices this summer."

Gretry shook his head and entered into a long argument to show that Jadwin was wrong.

But Jadwin refused to be convinced. All at once he laid the flat of his hand upon the table.

"Sam, we've touched bottom," he declared, "touched bottom all along the line. It's a paper dime to the Sub-Treasury."

"I don't care about the rest of the line," said the broker doggedly, sitting on the edge of the table, "wheat will go to sixty." He indicated the nest of balls with a movement of his chin. "Will you break?"

Jadwin broke and scored, leaving one ball three inches in front or a corner pocket. He called the shot, and as he drew back his cue he said, deliberately:

"Just as sure as I make this pocket wheat will—not go—off—another—*cent.*"

With the last word he drove the ball home and straightened up. Gretry laid down his cue and looked at him quickly. But he did not speak. Jadwin sat down on one of the straight-backed chairs upon the raised platform against the wall and rested his elbows upon his knees.

"Sam," he said, "the time is come for a great big change." He emphasized the word with a tap of his cue upon the floor. "We can't play our game the way we've been playing it the last three years. We've been hammering wheat down and down and down, till we've got it below the cost of production; and now she won't go any further with all the hammering in the world. The other fellows, the rest of this Bear crowd, don't seem to see it, but I see it. Before fall we're going to have higher prices. Wheat is going up, and when it does I mean to be right there."

"We're going to have a dull market right up to the beginning of winter," protested the other.

"Come and say that to me at the beginning of winter, then," Jadwin retorted. "Look here, Sam, I'm short of May five hundred thousand bushels, and to-morrow morning you are going to send your boys on the floor for me and close that trade."

"You're crazy, J.," protested the broker. "Hold on another month, and I promise you, you'll thank me."

"Not another day, not another hour. This Bear campaign of ours has come to an end. That's said and signed."

"Why, it's just in its prime," protested the broker. "Great heavens, you mustn't get out of the game now, after hanging on for three years."

"I'm not going to get out of it."

"Why, good Lord!" said Gretry, "you don't mean to say that—"

"That I'm going over. That's exactly what I do mean. I'm going to change over so quick to the other side that I'll be there before you can take off your hat. I'm done with a Bear game. It was good while it lasted, but we've worked it for all there was in it. I'm not only going to cover my May shorts and get out of that trade, but"—Jadwin leaned forward and struck his hand upon his knee—"but I'm going to *buy*. I'm going to buy September wheat, and I'm going to buy it to-morrow, five hundred thousand bushels of it, and if the market goes as I think it will later on, I'm going to buy more. I'm no Bear any longer. I'm going to boost this market right through till the last bell rings; and from now on Curtis Jadwin spells B-u- double l—Bull."

"They'll slaughter you," said Gretry, "slaughter you in cold blood. You're just one man against a gang—a gang of cutthroats. Those Bears have got millions and millions back of them. You don't suppose, do you, that old man Crookes, or Kenniston, or little Sweeny, or all that lot would give you one little bit of a chance for your life if they got a grip on you. Cover your shorts if you want to, but, for God's sake, don't begin to buy in the same breath. You wait a while. If this market has touched bottom, we'll be able to tell in a few days. I'll admit, for the sake of argument, that just now there's a pause. But nobody can tell whether it will turn up or down yet. Now's the time to be conservative, to play it cautious."

"If I was conservative and cautious," answered Jadwin, "I wouldn't be in this game at all. I'd be buying U. S. four per cents. That's the big mistake so many of these fellows down here make. They go into a game where the only ones who can possibly win are the ones who take big chances, and then they try to play the thing cautiously. If I wait a while till the market turns up and everybody is buying, how am I any the better off? No, sir, you buy the Sep-

tember option for me to-morrow—five hundred thousand bushels.
I deposited the margin to your credit in the Illinois Trust this
afternoon."

There was a long silence. Gretry spun a ball between his
fingers, top-fashion.

"Well," he said at last, hesitatingly, "well—I don't know, J.—
you are either Napoleonic—or—or a colossal idiot."

"Neither one nor the other, Samuel. I'm just using a little
common-sense. . . . Is it your shot?"

"I'm blessed if I know."

"Well, we'll start a new game. Sam, I'll give you six balls and
beat you in"—he looked at his watch—"beat you before half-past
nine."

"For a dollar?"

"I never bet, Sam, and you know it."

Half an hour later Jadwin said:

"Shall we go down and join the ladies? Don't put out your
cigar. That's one bargain I made with Laura before we moved in
here—that smoking was allowable everywhere."

"Room enough, I guess," observed the broker, as the two
stepped into the elevator. "How many rooms have you got here,
by the way?"

"Upon my word, I don't know," answered Jadwin. "I discov-
ered a new one yesterday. Fact. I was having a look around, and
I came out into a little kind of smoking-room or other that, I swear,
I'd never seen before. I had to get Laura to tell me about it."

The elevator sank to the lower floor, and Jadwin and the broker
stepped out into the main hallway. From the drawing-room near
by came the sound of women's voices.

"Before we go in," said Jadwin, "I want you to see our art
gallery and the organ. Last time you were up, remember, the men
were still at work in here."

They passed down a broad corridor, and at the end, just before
parting the heavy, sombre curtains, Jadwin pressed a couple of
electric buttons, and in the open space above the curtain sprang up
a lambent, steady glow.

The broker, as he entered, gave a long whistle. The art gallery
took in the height of two of the stories of the house. It was shaped
like a rotunda, and topped with a vast airy dome of colored glass.
Here and there about the room were glass cabinets full of bibelots,
ivory statuettes, old snuff boxes, fans of the sixteenth and seven-

teenth centuries. The walls themselves were covered with a multitude of pictures, oils, water-colors, with one or two pastels.

But to the left of the entrance, let into the frame of the building, stood a great organ, large enough for a cathedral, and giving to view, in the dulled incandescence of the electrics, its sheaves of mighty pipes.

"Well, this is something like," exclaimed the broker.

"I don't know much about 'em myself," hazarded Jadwin, looking at the pictures, "but Laura can tell you. We bought most of 'em while we were abroad, year before last. Laura says this is the best." He indicated a large "Bougereau" that represented a group of nymphs bathing in a woodland pool.

"H'm!" said the broker, "you wouldn't want some of your Sunday-school superintendents to see this now. This is what the boys down on the Board would call a bar-room picture."

But Jadwin did not laugh.

"It never struck me in just that way," he said, gravely.

"It's a fine piece of work, though," Gretry hastened to add. "Fine, great coloring."

"I like this one pretty well," continued Jadwin, moving to a canvas by Detaille. It was one of the inevitable studies of a cuirassier; in this case a trumpeter, one arm high in the air, the hand clutching the trumpet, the horse, foam-flecked, at a furious gallop. In the rear, through clouds of dust, the rest of the squadron was indicated by a few points of color.

"Yes, that's pretty neat," concurred Gretry. "He's sure got a gait on. Lord, what a lot of accoutrements those French fellows stick on. Now our boys would chuck about three-fourths of that truck before going into action. . . . Queer way these artists work," he went on, peering close to the canvas. "Look at it close up and it's just a lot of little daubs, but you get off a distance"—he drew back, cocking his head to one side—"and you see now. Hey—see how the thing bunches up. Pretty neat, isn't it?" He turned from the picture and rolled his eyes about the room.

"Well, well," he murmured. "This certainly is the real thing, J. I suppose, now, it all represents a pretty big pot of money."

"I'm not quite used to it yet myself," said Jadwin. "I was in here last Sunday, thinking it all over, the new house, and the money and all. And it struck me as kind of queer the way things have turned out for me. . . . Sam, do you know, I can remember the time, up there in Ottawa County, Michigan, on my old dad's farm, when I used to have to get up before daybreak to tend the stock, and my sister and I used to run out quick into the stable and stand in the warm cow fodder in the stalls to warm our bare feet. . . . She up and died when she was about eighteen —galloping consumption. Yes, sir. By George, how I loved that little sister of mine! *You* remember her, Sam. Remember how you used to come out from Grand Rapids every now and then to go squirrel shooting with me?"

"Sure, sure. Oh, I haven't forgot."

"Well, I was wishing the other day that I could bring Sadie down here, and—oh, I don't know—give her a good time. She never had a good time when she was alive. Work, work, work; morning, noon, and night. I'd like to have made it up to her. I believe in making people happy, Sam. That's the way I take my fun. But it's too late to do it now for my little sister."

"Well," hazarded Gretry, "you got a good wife in yonder to—"

Jadwin interrupted him. He half turned away, thrusting his hands suddenly into his pockets. Partly to himself, partly to his friend, he murmured:

"You bet I have, you bet I have. Sam," he exclaimed, then turned away again. ". . . Oh, well, never mind," he murmured.

Gretry, embarrassed, constrained, put his chin in the air, shutting his eyes in a knowing fashion.

"I understand," he answered. "I understand, J."

"Say, look at this organ here," said Jadwin briskly. "Here's the thing I like to play with."

They crossed to the other side of the room.

"Oh, you've got one of those attachment things," observed the broker.

"Listen now," said Jadwin. He took a perforated roll from the case near at hand and adjusted it, Gretry looking on with the solemn interest that all American business men have in mechanical inventions. Jadwin sat down before it, pulled out a stop or two, and placed his feet on the pedals. A vast preliminary roaring breath soughed through the pipes, with a vibratory rush of power. Then there came a canorous snarl of bass, and then, abruptly, with resistless charm, and with full-bodied, satisfying amplitude of volume the opening movement of the overture of "Carmen."

"Great, great!" shouted Gretry, his voice raised to make himself heard. "That's immense."

The great-lunged harmony was filling the entire gallery, clear cut, each note clearly, sharply treated with a precision that, if mechanical, was yet effective. Jadwin, his eyes now on the stops, now on the sliding strip of paper, played on. Through the sonorous clamor of the pipes Gretry could hear him speaking, but he caught only a word or two.

"Toréador . . . horse-power . . . Madame Calvé . . . electric motor . . . fine song . . . storage battery."

The "movement" thinned out, and dwindled to a strain of delicate lightness, sustained by the smallest pipes and developing a new motive; this was twice repeated, and then ran down to a series of chords and bars that prepared for and prefigured some great effect close at hand. There was a short pause, then with the sudden releasing of a tremendous rush of sound, back surged the melody, with redoubled volume and power, to the original movement.

"That's bully, bully!" shouted Gretry, clapping his hands, and his eye, caught by a movement on the other side of the room, he turned about to see Laura Jadwin standing between the opened curtains at the entrance.

Seen thus unexpectedly, the broker was again overwhelmed with a sense of the beauty of Jadwin's wife. Laura was in evening dress of black lace; her arms and neck were bare. Her black hair was piled high upon her head, a single American Beauty rose nodded against her bare shoulder. She was even yet slim and very tall, her face pale with that unusual paleness of hers that was yet a color. Around her slender neck was a marvelous collar of pearls many strands deep, set off and held in place by diamond clasps.

With Laura came Mrs. Gretry and Page. The broker's wife was a vivacious, small, rather pretty blond woman, a little angular, a little faded. She was garrulous, witty, slangy. She wore turquoises in her ears morning, noon, and night.

But three years had made a vast difference in Page Dearborn. All at once she was a young woman. Her straight, hard, little figure had developed, her arms were rounded, her eyes were calmer. She had grown taller, broader. Her former exquisite beauty was perhaps not quite so delicate, so fine, so virginal, so charmingly angular and boyish. There was infinitely more of the woman in it; and perhaps because of this she looked more like Laura than at any time of her life before. But even yet her expression was one of gravity, of seriousness. There was always a certain aloofness about Page. She looked out at the world solemnly, and as if sepa-

rated from its lighter side. Things humorous interested her only
as inexplicable vagaries of the human animal.

"We heard the organ," said Laura, "so we came in. I wanted
Mrs. Gretry to listen to it."

.   .   .   .

The three years that had just passed had been the most important years of Laura Jadwin's life. Since her marriage she had
grown intellectually and morally with amazing rapidity. Indeed,
so swift had been the change that it was not so much a growth as a
transformation. She was no longer the same half-formed, impulsive girl who had found a delight in the addresses of her three
lovers, and who had sat on the floor in the old home on State
Street and allowed Landry Court to hold her hand. She looked
back upon the Miss Dearborn of those days as though she were
another person. How she had grown since then! How she had
changed! How different, how infinitely more serious and sweet
her life since then had become!

A great fact had entered her world, a great new element, that
dwarfed all other thoughts, all other considerations. This was her
love for her husband. It was as though until the time of her
marriage she had walked in darkness, a darkness that she fancied
was day; walked perversely, carelessly, and with a frivolity that
was almost wicked. Then, suddenly, she had seen a great light.
Love had entered her world. In her new heaven a new light was
fixed, and all other things were seen only because of this light; all
other things were touched by it, tempered by it, warmed and vivi-
fied by it.

It had seemed to date from a certain evening at their country
house at Geneva Lake in Wisconsin, where she had spent her honey-
moon with her husband. They had been married about ten days.
It was a July evening, and they were quite alone on board the little
steam yacht the "Thetis." She remembered it all very plainly. It
had been so warm that she had not changed her dress after dinner
—she recalled that it was of Honiton lace over old-rose silk, and
that Curtis had said it was the prettiest he had ever seen. It was
an hour before midnight, and the lake was so still as to appear
veritably solid. The moon was reflected upon the surface with never
a ripple to blur its image. The sky was gray with starlight, and
only a vague bar of black between the star shimmer and the pale
shield of the water marked the shore line. Never since that night
could she hear the call of whip-poor-wills or the piping of night

frogs that the scene did not come back to her. The little "Thetis" had throbbed and panted steadily. At the door of the engine room, the engineer—the gray MacKenny, his back discreetly turned—sat smoking a pipe and taking the air. From time to time he would swing himself into the engine room, and the clink and scrape of his shovel made itself heard as he stoked the fire vigorously.

Stretched out in a long wicker deck chair, hatless, a drab coat thrown around her shoulders, Laura had sat near her husband, who had placed himself upon a camp stool where he could reach the wheel with one hand.

"Well," he had said at last, "are you glad you married me, Miss Dearborn?" And she had caught him about the neck and drawn his face down to hers, and, her head thrown back, their lips all but touching, had whispered over and over again:

"I love you—love you—love you!"

That night was final. The marriage ceremony, even that moment in her room, when her husband had taken her in his arms and she had felt the first stirring of love in her heart, all the first week of their married life had been for Laura a whirl, a blur. She had not been able to find herself. Her affection for her husband came and went capriciously. There were moments when she believed herself to be really unhappy. Then, all at once, she seemed to awake. Not the ceremony at St. James' Church, but that awakening had been her marriage. Now it was irrevocable; she was her husband's; she belonged to him indissolubly, forever and forever, and the surrender was a glory. Laura in that moment knew that love, the supreme triumph of a woman's life, was less a victory than a capitulation.

Since then her happiness had been perfect. Literally and truly there was not a cloud, not a mote in her sunshine. She had everything—the love of her husband, great wealth, extraordinary beauty, perfect health, an untroubled mind, friends, position—everything. God had been good to her, beyond all dreams and all deserving. For her had been reserved all the prizes, all the guerdons; for her who had done nothing to merit them.

Her husband she knew was no less happy. In those first three years after their marriage life was one unending pageant; and their happiness became for them some marvelous, bewildering thing, dazzling, resplendent, a strange, glittering, jeweled Wonder-worker that suddenly had been put into their hands.

As one of the first results of this awakening, Laura reproached herself with having done but little for Page. She told herself that she had not been a good sister, that often she had been unjust, quick-tempered, and had made the little girl to suffer because of her caprices. She had not sympathized sufficiently with her small troubles—so she made herself believe—and had found too many occasions to ridicule Page's intenseness and queer little solemnities. True, she had given her a good home, good clothes, and a good education, but she should have given more—more than mere duty-gifts. She should have been more of a companion to the little girl, more of a help; in fine, more of a mother. Laura felt all at once the responsibilities of the elder sister in a family bereft of parents. Page was growing fast, and growing astonishingly beautiful; in a little while she would be a young woman, and over the near horizon, very soon now, must inevitably loom the grave question of her marriage.

But it was only this realization of certain responsibilities that during the first years of her married life at any time drew away Laura's consideration of her husband. She began to get acquainted with the real man-within-the-man that she knew now revealed himself only after marriage. Jadwin her husband was so different from, so infinitely better than, Jadwin her lover, that Laura sometimes found herself looking back with a kind of retrospective apprehension on the old days and the time when she was simply Miss Dearborn. How little she had known him after all! And how, in the face of this ignorance, this innocence, this absence of any insight into his real character, had she dared to take the irretrievable step that bound her to him for life? The Curtis Jadwin of those early days was so much another man. He might have been a rascal; she could not have known it. As it was, her husband had promptly come to be, for her, the best, the finest man she had ever known. But it might easily have been different.

His attitude toward her was thoughtfulness itself. Hardly ever was he absent from her, even for a day, that he did not bring her some little present, some little keepsake—or even a bunch of flowers—when he returned in the evening. The anniversaries—Christmas, their wedding day, her birthday—he always observed with great éclat. He took a holiday from his business, surprised her with presents under her pillow, or her dinner-plate, and never failed to take her to the theatre in the evening.

However, it was not only Jadwin's virtues that endeared him to his wife. He was no impeccable hero in her eyes. He was tremendously human. He had his faults, his certain lovable weaknesses, and it was precisely these traits that Laura found so adorable.

For one thing, Jadwin could be magnificently inconsistent. Let him set his mind and heart upon a given pursuit, pleasure, or line of conduct not altogether advisable at the moment, and the ingenuity of the excuses by which he justified himself were monuments of elaborate sophistry. Yet, if later he lost interest, he reversed his arguments with supreme disregard for his former words.

Then, too, he developed a boyish pleasure in certain unessential though cherished objects and occupations, that he indulged extravagantly and to the neglect of things, not to say duties, incontestably of more importance.

One of these objects was the "Thetis." In every conceivable particular the little steam yacht was complete down to the last bolt, the last coat of varnish; but at times during their summer vacations, when Jadwin, in all reason, should have been supervising the laying out of certain unfinished portions of the "grounds"—supervision which could be trusted to no subordinate—he would be found aboard the "Thetis," hatless, in his shirt sleeves, in solemn debate with the gray MacKenny and—a cleaning rag, or monkey-wrench, or paint brush in his hand—tinkering and pottering about the boat, over and over again. Wealthy as he was, he could have maintained an entire crew on board whose whole duty should have been to screw, and scrub, and scour. But Jadwin would have none of it. "Costs too much," he would declare, with profound gravity. He had the self-made American's handiness with implements and paint brushes, and he would, at high noon and under a murderous sun, make the trip from the house to the dock where the "Thetis" was moored, for the trivial pleasure of tightening a bolt—which did not need tightening; or wake up in the night to tell Laura of some wonderful new idea he had conceived as to the equipment or decoration of the yacht. He had blustered about the extravagance of a "crew," but the sums of money that went to the brightening, refitting, overhauling, repainting, and reballasting of the boat—all absolutely uncalled-for—made even Laura gasp, and would have maintained a dozen sailors an entire year.

This same inconsistency prevailed also in other directions. In the matter of business Jadwin's economy was unimpeachable. He would cavil on a half-dollar's overcharge; he would put himself to downright inconvenience to save the useless expenditure of a dime—

and boast of it. But no extravagance was ever too great, no time ever too valuable, when bass were to be caught.

For Jadwin was a fisherman unregenerate. Laura, though an early riser when in the city, was apt to sleep late in the country, and never omitted a two-hours' nap in the heat of the afternoon. Her husband improved these occasions, when he was deprived of her society, to indulge in his pastime. Never a morning so forbidding that his lines were not in the water by five o'clock; never a sun so scorching that he was not coaxing a "strike" in the stumps and reeds in the shade under the shores.

It was the one pleasure he could not share with his wife. Laura was unable to bear the monotony of the slow-moving boat, the hours spent without results, the enforced idleness, the cramped positions. Only occasionally could Jadwin prevail upon her to accompany him. And then what preparations! Queen Elizabeth approaching her barge was attended with no less solicitude. MacKenny (who sometimes acted as guide and oarsman) and her husband exhausted their ingenuity to make her comfortable. They held anxious debates: "Do you think she'll like that?" "Wouldn't this make it easier for her?" "Is that the way she liked it last time?" Jadwin himself arranged the cushions, spread the carpet over the bottom of the boat, handed her in, found her old gloves for her, baited her hook, disentangled her line, saw to it that the mineral water in the icebox was sufficiently cold, and performed an endless series of little attentions looking to her comfort and enjoyment. It was all to no purpose, and at length Laura declared:

"Curtis, dear, it is no use. You just sacrifice every bit of your pleasure to make me comfortable—to make me enjoy it; and I just don't. I'm sorry, I want to share every pleasure with you, but I don't like to fish, and never will. You go alone. I'm just a hindrance to you." And though he blustered at first, Laura had her way.

Once in the period of these three years Laura and her husband had gone abroad. But her experience in England—they did not get to the Continent—had been a disappointment to her. The museums, art galleries, and cathedrals were not of the least interest to Jadwin, and though he followed her from one to another with uncomplaining stoicism, she felt his distress, and had contrived to return home three months ahead of time.

It was during this trip that they had bought so many of the pictures and appointments for the North Avenue house, and Laura's

disappointment over her curtailed European travels was mitigated
by the anticipation of her pleasure in settling in the new home.
This had not been possible immediately after their marriage. For
nearly two years the great place had been given over to contractors,
architects, decorators, and gardeners, and Laura and her husband
had lived, while in Chicago, at a hotel, giving up the one-time
rectory on Cass Street to Page and to Aunt Wess'.

But when at last Laura entered upon possession of the North
Avenue house, she was not—after the first enthusiasm and excitement over its magnificence had died down—altogether pleased with
it, though she told herself the contrary. Outwardly, it was all that
she could desire. It fronted Lincoln Park, and from all the windows
upon that side the most delightful outlooks were obtainable—green
woods, open lawns, the parade ground, the Lincoln monument, dells,
bushes, smooth drives, flower beds, and fountains. From the great
bay window of Laura's own sitting-room she could see far out over
Lake Michigan, and watch the procession of great lake steamers,
from Milwaukee, far-distant Duluth, and the Sault Sainte Marie—
the famous "Soo"—defiling majestically past, making for the mouth
of the river, laden to the water's edge with whole harvests of wheat.
At night, when the windows were open in the warm weather, she
could hear the mournful wash and lapping of the water on the embankments.

The grounds about her home were beautiful. The stable itself
was half again as large as her old home opposite St. James's, and
the conservatory, in which she took the keenest delight, was a wonderful affair—a vast bubble-like structure of green panes, whence,
winter and summer, came a multitude of flowers for the house—
violets, lilies of the valley, jonquils, hyacinths, tulips, and her own
loved roses.

But the interior of the house was, in parts, less satisfactory.
Jadwin, so soon as his marriage was a certainty, had bought the
house, and had given over its internal furnishings to a firm of
decorators. Innocently enough, he had intended to surprise his
wife, had told himself that she should not be burdened with the
responsibility of selection and planning. Fortunately, however, the
decorators were men of taste. There was nothing to offend, and
much to delight in the results they obtained in the dining-room,
breakfast-room, parlors, drawing-rooms, and suites of bedrooms.
But Laura, though the beauty of it all enchanted her, could never
rid herself of a feeling that it was not hers. It impressed her with

its splendor of natural woods and dull "color effects," its cunning electrical devices, its mechanical contrivances for comfort, like the ready-made luxury and "convenience" of a Pullman.

However, she had intervened in time to reserve certain of the rooms to herself, and these—the library, her bedroom, and more especially that apartment from whose bay windows she looked out upon the Lake, and which, as if she were still in her old home, she called the "upstairs sitting-room"—she furnished to suit herself.

For very long she found it difficult, even with all her resolution, with all her pleasure in her new-gained wealth, to adapt herself to a manner of living upon so vast a scale. She found herself continually planning the marketing for the next day, forgetting that this now was part of the housekeeper's duties. For months she persisted in "doing her room" after breakfast, just as she had been taught to do in the old days when she was a little girl at Barrington. She was afraid of the elevator, and never really learned how to use the neat little system of telephones that connected the various parts of the house with the servants' quarters. For months her chiefest concern in her wonderful surroundings took the form of a dread of burglars.

Her keenest delights were her stable and the great organ in the art gallery; and these alone more than compensated for her uneasiness in other particulars.

Horses Laura adored—black ones with flowing tails and manes, like certain pictures she had seen. Nowadays, except on the rarest occasions, she never set foot out of doors, except to take her carriage, her coupé, her phaeton, or her dog-cart. Best of all she loved her saddle horses. She had learned to ride, and the morning was inclement indeed that she did not take a long and solitary excursion through the Park, followed by the groom and Jadwin's two spotted coach dogs.

The great organ terrified her at first. But on closer acquaintance she came to regard it as a vast-hearted, sympathetic friend. She already played the piano very well, and she scorned Jadwin's self-playing "attachment." A teacher was engaged to instruct her in the intricacies of stops and of pedals, and in the difficulties of the "echo" organ, "great" organ, "choir," and "swell." So soon as she had mastered these, Laura entered upon a new world of delight. Her taste in music was as yet a little immature—Gounod, and even Verdi, were its limitations. But to hear, responsive to the lightest pressures of her finger-tips, the mighty instrument go

thundering through the cadences of the "Anvil Chorus" gave her
a thrilling sense of power that was superb.

The untrained, unguided instinct of the actress in Laura had
fostered in her a curious penchant toward melodrama. She had a
taste for the magnificent. She reveled in these great musical
"effects" upon her organ, the grandiose easily appealed to her,
while as for herself, the rôle of the *grande dame,* with this wonderful house for background and environment, came to be for her,
quite unconsciously, a sort of game in which she delighted.

It was by this means that, in the end, she succeeded in fitting
herself to her new surroundings. Innocently enough, and with
a harmless, almost childlike, affectation, she posed a little, and by
so doing found the solution of the incongruity between herself—
the Laura of moderate means and quiet life—and the massive luxury
with which she was now surrounded. Without knowing it, she
began to act the part of a great lady—and she acted it well. She
assumed the existence of her numerous servants as she assumed
the fact of the trees in the park; she gave herself into the hands of
her maid, not as Laura Jadwin of herself would have done it,
clumsily and with the constraint of inexperience, but as she would
have done it if she had been acting the part on the stage, with an
air, with all the nonchalance of a marquise, with—in fine—all the
superb condescension of her "grand manner."

She knew very well that if she relaxed this hauteur her servants
would impose on her, would run over her, and in this matter she
found new cause for wonder in her husband.

The servants, from the frigid butler to the under groom, adored
Jadwin. A half-expressed wish upon his part produced a more
immediate effect than Laura's most explicit orders. He never descended to familiarity with them, and, as a matter of fact, ignored
them to such an extent that he forgot or confused their names.
But where Laura was obeyed with precise formality and chilly
deference, Jadwin was served with obsequious alacrity, and with a
good humor that even livery and "correct form" could not altogether conceal.

Laura's eyes were first opened to this genuine affection which
Jadwin inspired in his servants by an incident which occurred in
the first months of their occupancy of the new establishment. One
of the gardeners discovered the fact that Jadwin affected gardenias
in the lapel of his coat, and thereat was at immense pains to supply
him with a fresh bloom from the conservatory each morning. The

flower was to be placed at Jadwin's plate, and it was quite the event of the day for the old fellow when the master appeared on the front steps with the flower in his coat. But a feud promptly developed over this matter between the gardener and the maid who took the butler's place at breakfast every morning. Sometimes Jadwin did not get the flower, and the gardener charged the maid with remissness in forgetting to place it at his plate after he had given it into her hands. In the end the affair became so clamorous that Jadwin himself had to intervene. The gardener was summoned and found to have been in fault only in his eagerness to please

"Billy," said Jadwin, to the old man at the conclusion of the whole matter, "you're an old fool."

And the gardener thereupon had bridled and stammered as though Jadwin had conferred a gift.

"Now, if I had called him 'an old fool,'" observed Laura, "he would have sulked the rest of the week."

The happiest time of the day for Laura was the evening. In the daytime she was variously occupied, but her thoughts continually ran forward to the end of the day, when her husband would be with her. Jadwin breakfasted early, and Laura bore him company no matter how late she had stayed up the night before. By half-past eight he was out of the house, driving down to his office in his buggy behind Nip and Tuck. By nine Laura's own saddle horse was brought to the carriage porch, and until eleven she rode in the park. At twelve she lunched with Page, and in the afternoon—in the "upstairs sitting-room"—read her Browning or her Meredith, the latter one of her newest discoveries, till three or four. Sometimes after that she went out in her carriage. If it was to "shop" she drove to the "Rookery," in La Salle Street, after her purchases were made, and sent the footman up to her husband's office to say that she would take him home. Or as often as not she called for Mrs. Cressler or Aunt Wess' or Mrs. Gretry, and carried them off to some exhibit of paintings, or flowers, or more rarely—for she had not the least interest in social affairs—to teas or receptions.

But in the evenings, after dinner, she had her husband to herself. Page was almost invariably occupied by one or more of her young men in the drawing-room, but Laura and Jadwin shut themselves in the library, a lofty paneled room—a place of deep leather chairs, tall bookcases, etchings, and sombre brasses—and there, while Jadwin lay stretched out upon the broad sofa, smoking cigars, one hand behind his head, Laura read aloud to him.

His tastes in fiction were very positive. Laura at first had tried to introduce him to her beloved Meredith. But after three chapters, when he had exclaimed, "What's the fool talking about?" she had given over and begun again from another starting-point. Left to himself, his wife sorrowfully admitted that he would have gravitated to the "Mysterious Island" and "Michael Strogoff," or even to "Mr. Potter of Texas" and "Mr. Barnes of New York." But she had set herself to accomplish his literary education, so, Meredith failing, she took up "Treasure Island" and "The Wrecker." Much of these he made her skip.

"Oh, let's get on with the 'story,'" he urged. But Pinkerton for long remained for him an ideal, because he was "smart" and "alive."

"I'm not long very many on art," he announced. "But I believe that any art that don't make the world better and happier is no art at all, and is only fit for the dump heap."

But at last Laura found his abiding affinity in Howells.

"Nothing much happens," he said. "But I *know* all those people." He never could rid himself of a surreptitious admiration for Bartley Hubbard. He, too, was "smart" and "alive." He had the "get there" to him. "Why," he would say, "I know fifty boys just like him down there in La Salle Street." Lapham he loved as a brother. Never a point in the development of his character that he missed or failed to chuckle over. Bromfield Cory was poohed and boshed quite out of consideration as a "loafer," a "dilletanty," but Lapham had all his sympathy.

"Yes, sir," he would exclaim, interrupting the narrative, "that's just it. That's just what I would have done if I had been in his place. Come, this chap knows what he's writing about—not like that Middleton ass, with his 'Dianas' and 'Amazing Marriages.'"

Occasionally the Jadwins entertained. Laura's husband was proud of his house, and never tired of showing his friends about it. Laura gave Page a "coming-out" dance, and nearly every Sunday the Cresslers came to dinner. But Aunt Wess' could, at first, rarely be induced to pay the household a visit. So much grandeur made the little widow uneasy, even a little suspicious. She would shake her head at Laura, murmuring:

"My word, it's all very fine, but, dear me, Laura, I hope you do pay for everything on the nail, and don't run up any bills. I

don't know what your dear father would say to it all, no, I don't."
And she would spend hours in counting the electric bulbs, which
she insisted were only devices for some new-fangled gas.

"Thirty-three in this one room alone," she would say. "I'd like
to see your dear husband's face when he gets his gas bill. And a
dressmaker that *lives* in the house. . . . Well—I don't want
to say anything."

Thus three years had gone by. The new household settled to a
régime. Continually Jadwin grew richer. His real estate appre-
ciated in value, rents went up. Every time he speculated in wheat,
it was upon a larger scale, and every time he won. He was a Bear
always, and, on those rare occasions when he referred to his ventures in Laura's hearing, it was invariably to say that prices were
going down. Till at last had come that spring when he believed
that the bottom had been touched, had had the talk with Gretry,
and had, in secret, "turned Bull," with the suddenness of a
strategist.

The matter was yet in Gretry's mind while the party remained
in the art gallery; and as they were returning to the drawing-room
he detained Jadwin an instant.

"If you are set upon breaking your neck," he said, "you might
tell me at what figure you want me to buy for you to-morrow."

"At the market," returned Jadwin. "I want to get into the
thing quick."

A little later, when they had all reassembled in the drawing-
room, and while Mrs. Gretry was telling an interminable story of
how Isabel had all but asphyxiated herself the night before, a servant announced Landry Court, and the young man entered, spruce
and debonair, a bouquet in one hand and a box of candy in the
other.

Some days before this Page had lectured him solemnly on the
fact that he was over-absorbed in business, and was starving his
soul. He should read more, she told him, and she had said that if
he would call upon her on this particular night, she would indicate
a course of reading for him.

So it came about that, after a few moments' conversation with
the older people in the drawing-room, the two adjourned to the
library.

There, by way of a beginning, Page asked him what was his
favorite character in fiction. She spoke of the beauty of Ruskin's
thoughts, of the gracefulness of Charles Lamb's style. The con-

versation lagged a little. Landry, not to be behind her, declared for the modern novel, and spoke of the "newest book." But Page never read new books; she was not interested, and their talk, unable to establish itself upon a common ground, halted, and was in a fair way to end, until at last, and by insensible degrees, they began to speak of themselves and of each other. Promptly they were all aroused. They listened to one another's words with studious attention, answered with ever-ready promptness, discussed, argued, agreed, and disagreed over and over again.

Landry had said:

"When I was a boy, I always had an ambition to excel all the other boys. I wanted to be the best baseball player on the block—and I was, too. I could pitch three curves when I was fifteen, and I find I am the same now that I am a man grown. When I do a thing, I want to do it better than any one else. From the very first I have always been ambitious. It is my strongest trait. Now," he went on, turning to Page, "your strongest trait is your thoughtfulness. You are what they call introspective."

"Yes, yes," she answered. "Yes, I think so, too."

"You don't need the stimulation of competition. You are at your best when you are with just one person. A crowd doesn't interest you."

"I hate it," she exclaimed.

"Now with me, with a man of my temperament, a crowd is a real inspiration. When every one is talking and shouting around me, or to me, even my mind works at its best. But," he added, solemnly, "it must be a crowd of men. I can't abide a crowd of women."

"They chatter so," she assented. "I can't either."

"But I find that the companionship of one intelligent, sympathetic woman is as much of a stimulus as a lot of men. It's funny, isn't it, that I should be like that?"

"Yes," she said, "it is funny—strange. But I believe in companionship. I believe that between man and woman that is the great thing—companionship. Love," she added, abruptly, and then broke off with a deep sigh. "Oh, I don't know," she murmured. Do you remember those lines:

> " 'Man's love is of his life a thing apart,
>   'Tis woman's whole existence.'

Do you believe that?"

"Well," he asserted, gravely, choosing his words with deliberation, "it might be so, but all depends upon the man and woman. Love," he added, with tremendous gravity, "is the greatest power in the universe."

"I have never been in love," said Page. "Yes, love is a wonderful power."

"I've never been in love, either."

"Never, never been in love?"

"Oh, I've thought I was in love," he said, with a wave of his hand.

"I've never even thought I was," she answered, musing.

"Do you believe in early marriages?" demanded Landry.

"A man should never marry," she said, deliberately, "till he can give his wife a good home, and good clothes and—and that sort of thing. I do not think I shall ever marry."

"You! Why, of course you will. Why not?"

"No, no. It is my disposition. I am morose and taciturn. Laura says so."

Landry protested with vehemence.

"And," she went on, "I have long, brooding fits of melancholy."

"Well, so have I," he threw out recklessly. "At night, sometimes—when I wake up. Then I'm all down in the mouth, and I say, 'What's the use, by jingo!'"

"Do you believe in pessimism? I do. They say Carlyle was a terrible pessimist."

"Well—talking about love. I understand that you can't believe in pessimism and love at the same time. Wouldn't you feel unhappy if you lost your faith in love?"

"Oh, yes, terribly."

There was a moment's silence, and then Landry remarked:

"Now you are the kind of woman that would only love once, but love for that once mighty deep and strong."

Page's eyes grew wide. She murmured:

"'Tis a woman's whole existence—whole existence. Yes, I think I am like that."

"Do you think Enoch Arden did right in going away after he found them married?"

"Oh, have you read that? Oh, isn't that a beautiful poem? Wasn't he noble? Wasn't he grand? Oh, yes, yes, he did right."

"By George, I wouldn't have gone away. I'd have gone right into that house, and I would have made things hum. I'd have thrown the other fellow out, lock, stock and barrel."

"That's just like a man, so selfish, only thinking of himself. You don't know the meaning of love—great, true, unselfish love."

"I know the meaning of what's mine. Think I'd give up the woman I loved to another man?"

"Even if she loved the other man best?"

"I'd have my girl first, and find out how she felt about the other man afterward."

"Oh, but think if you gave her up, how noble it would be. You would have sacrificed all that you held the dearest to an ideal. Oh, if I were in Enoch Arden's place, and my husband thought I was dead, and I knew he was happy with another woman, it would just be a joy to deny myself, sacrifice myself to spare him unhappiness. That would be my idea of love. Then I'd go into a convent."

"Not much. I'd let the other fellow go to the convent. If I loved a woman, I wouldn't let anything in the world stop me from winning her."

"You have so much determination, haven't you?" she said, looking at him.

Landry enlarged his shoulders a little and wagged his head.

"Well," he said, "I don't know, but I'd try pretty hard to get what I wanted, I guess."

"I love to see that characteristic in men," she observed. "Strength, determination."

"Just as a man loves to see a woman womanly," he answered. "Don't you hate strong-minded women?"

"Utterly."

"Now, you are what I would call womanly—the womanliest woman I've ever known."

"Oh, I don't know," she protested, a little confused.

"Yes, you are. You are beautifully womanly—and so high-minded and well read. It's been inspiring to me. I want you should know that. Yes, sir, a real inspiration. It's been inspiring, elevating, to say the least."

"I like to read, if that's what you mean," she hastened to say.

"By Jove, I've got to do some reading, too. It's so hard to find time. But I'll make time. I'll get that 'Stones of Venice' I've heard you speak of, and I'll sit up nights—and keep awake with black coffee—but I'll read that book from cover to cover."

"That's your determination again," Page exclaimed. "Your eyes just flashed when you said it. I believe if you once made up your mind to do a thing, you would do it, no matter how hard it was, wouldn't you?"

"Well, I'd—I'd make things hum, I guess," he admitted.

The next day was Easter Sunday, and Page came down to nine o'clock breakfast a little late, to find Jadwin already finished and deep in the pages of the morning paper. Laura, still at table, was pouring her last cup of coffee.

They were in the breakfast room, a small, charming apartment, light and airy, and with many windows, one end opening upon the house conservatory. Jadwin was in his frock coat, which later he would wear to church. The famous gardenia was in his lapel. He was freshly shaven, and his fine cigar made a blue haze over his head. Laura was radiant in a white morning gown. A newly cut bunch of violets, large as a cabbage, lay on the table before her.

The whole scene impressed itself sharply upon Page's mind— the fine sunlit room, with its gay open spaces and the glimpse of green leaves from the conservatory, the view of the smooth, trim lawn through the many windows, where an early robin, strayed from the park, was chirruping and feeding; her beautiful sister Laura, with her splendid, overshadowing coiffure, her pale, clear skin, her slender figure; Jadwin, the large, solid man of affairs, with his fine cigar, his gardenia, his well-groomed air. And then the little accessories that meant so much—the smell of violets, of good tobacco, of fragrant coffee; the gleaming damasks, china and silver of the breakfast table; the trim, fresh-looking maid, with her white cap, apron, and cuffs, who came and went; the thoroughbred setter dozing in the sun, and the parrot dozing and chuckling to himself on his perch upon the terrace outside the window.

At the bottom of the lawn was the stable, and upon the concrete in front of its wide-open door the groom was currying one of the carriage horses. While Page addressed herself to her fruit and coffee, Jadwin put down his paper, and, his elbows on the arms of his rattan chair, sat for a long time looking out at the horse. By and by he got up and said:

"That new feed has filled 'em out in good shape. Think I'll go out and tell Jarvis to try it on the buggy team." He pushed open the French windows and went out, the setter sedately following.

Page dug her spoon into her grape-fruit, then suddenly laid it down and turned to Laura, her chin upon her palm.

"Laura," she said, "do you think I ought to marry—a girl of my temperament?"

"Marry?" echoed Laura.

"Sh-h!" whispered Page. "Laura, don't talk so loud. Yes, do you?"

"Well, why not marry, dearie? Why shouldn't you marry when the time comes? Girls as young as you are not supposed to have temperaments."

But instead of answering Page put another question:

"Laura, do you think I am womanly?"

"I think sometimes, Page, that you take your books and your reading too seriously. You've not been out of the house for three days, and I never see you without your note-books and text-books in your hand. You are at it, dear, from morning till night. Studies are all very well—"

"Oh, studies!" exclaimed Page. "I hate them. Laura, what is it to be womanly?"

"To be womanly?" repeated Laura. "Why, I don't know, honey. It's to be kind and well-bred and gentle mostly, and never to be bold or conspicuous—and to love one's home and to take care of it, and to love and believe in one's husband, or parents, or children—or even one's sister—above any one else in the world."

"I think that being womanly is better than being well read," hazarded Page.

"We can be both, Page," Laura told her. "But, honey, I think you had better hurry through your breakfast. If we are going to church this Easter, we want to get an early start. Curtis ordered the carriage half an hour earlier."

"Breakfast!" echoed Page. "I don't want a thing." She drew a deep breath and her eyes grew large. "Laura," she began again presently, "Laura . . . Landry Court was here last night, and —oh, I don't know, he's so silly. But he said—well, he said this— well, I said that I understood how he felt about certain things, about 'getting on,' and being clean and fine and all that sort of thing, you know; and then he said, 'Oh, you don't know what it means to me to look into the eyes of a woman who really understands.' "

"*Did* he?" said Laura, lifting her eyebrows.

"Yes, and he seemed so fine and earnest. Laura, wh—" Page adjusted a hairpin at the back of her head, and moved closer to Laura, her eyes on the floor. "Laura—what do you suppose it did mean to him—don't you think it was foolish of him to talk like that?"

"Not at all," Laura said decisively. "If he said that he meant it—meant that he cared a great deal for you."

"Oh, I didn't mean that!" shrieked Page. "But there's a great deal more to Landry than I think we've suspected. He wants to be more than a mere money-getting machine, he says, and he wants to cultivate his mind and understand art and literature and that. And he wants me to help him, and I said I would. So if you don't mind, he's coming up here certain nights every week, and we're going to—I'm going to read to him. We're going to begin with the 'Ring and the Book.' "

In the latter part of May, the weather being unusually hot, the Jadwins, taking Page with them, went up to Geneva Lake for the summer, and the great house fronting Lincoln Park was deserted.

Laura had hoped that now her husband would be able to spend his entire time with her, but in this she was disappointed. At first Jadwin went down to the city but two days a week, but soon this was increased to alternate days. Gretry was a frequent visitor at the country house, and often he and Jadwin, their rocking-chairs side by side in a remote corner of the porch, talked "business" in low tones till far into the night.

"Dear," said Laura, finally, "I'm seeing less and less of you every day, and I had so looked forward to this summer, when we were to be together all the time."

"I hate it as much as you do, Laura," said her husband. "But I do feel as though I ought to be on the spot just for now. I can't get it out of my head that we're going to have livelier times in a few months."

"But even Mr. Gretry says that you don't need to be right in your office every minute of the time. He says you can manage your Board of Trade business from out here just as well, and that you only go into town because you can't keep away from La Salle Street and the sound of the Wheat Pit."

Was this true? Jadwin himself had found it difficult to answer. There had been a time when Gretry had been obliged to urge and coax to get his friend to so much as notice the swirl of the great maelstrom in the Board of Trade Building. But of late Jadwin's eye and ear were forever turned thitherward, and it was he, and no longer Gretry, who took initiatives.

Meanwhile he was making money. As he had predicted, the price of wheat had advanced. May had been a fair-weather month

with easy prices, the monthly Government report showing no loss
in the condition of the crop. Wheat had gone up from sixty to
sixty-six cents, and at a small profit Jadwin had sold some two
hundred and fifty thousand bushels. Then had come the hot
weather at the end of May. On the floor of the Board of Trade
the Pit traders had begun to peel off their coats. It began to look
like a hot June, and when cash wheat touched sixty-eight, Jadwin,
now more than ever convinced of a coming Bull market, bought
another five hundred thousand bushels.

This line he added to in June. Unfavorable weather—excessive heat, followed by flooding rains—had hurt the spring wheat,
and in every direction there were complaints of weevils and chinch-
bugs. Later on other deluges had discolored and damaged the
winter crop. Jadwin was now, by virtue of his recent purchases,
"long" one million bushels, and the market held firm at seventy-two
cents—a twelve-cent advance in two months.

"She'll react," warned Gretry, "sure. Crookes and Sweeny
haven't taken a hand yet. Look out for a heavy French crop.
We'll get reports on it soon now. You're playing with a gun, J.,
that kicks further than it shoots."

"We've not shot her yet," Jadwin said. "We're only just load-
ing her—for Bears," he added, with a wink.

In July came the harvesting returns from all over the country,
proving conclusively that for the first time in six years the United
States crop was to be small and poor. The yield was moderate.
Only part of it could be graded as "contract." Good wheat would
be valuable from now on. Jadwin bought again, and again it was
a "lot" of half a million bushels.

Then came the first manifestation of that marvelous golden luck
that was to follow Curtis Jadwin through all the coming months.
The French wheat crop was announced as poor. In Germany the
yield was to be far below the normal. All through Hungary the
potato and rye crops were light.

About the middle of the month Jadwin again called the broker
to his country house, and took him for a long evening's trip around
the lake, aboard the "Thetis." They were alone. MacKenny was
at the wheel, and seated on camp stools in the stern of the little boat,
Jadwin outlined his plans for the next few months.

"Sam," he said, "I thought back in April there that we were
to touch top prices about the first of this month, but this French
and German news has colored the cat different. I've been figuring

that I would get out of this market around the seventies, but she's going higher. I'm going to hold on yet a while."

"You do it on your own responsibility, then," said the broker. "I warn you the price is top-heavy."

"Not much. Seventy-two cents is too cheap. Now I'm going into this hard; and I want to have my own lines out—to be independent of the trade papers that Crookes could buy up any time he wants to. I want you to get me some good, reliable correspondents in Europe; smart, bright fellows that we can depend on. I want one in Liverpool, one in Paris, and one in Odessa, and I want them to cable us about the situation every day."

Gretry thought a while.

"Well," he said, at length, " . . . yes. I guess I can arrange it. I can get you a good man in Liverpool—Traynard is his name—and there's two or three in Paris we can pick up. Odessa—I don't know. I couldn't say just this minute. But I'll fix it."

These correspondents began to report at the end of July. All over Europe the demand for wheat was active. Grain handlers were not only buying freely, but were contracting for future delivery. In August came the first demands for American wheat, scattered and sporadic at first, then later, a little, a very little more insistent.

Thus the summer wore to its end. The fall "situation" began slowly to define itself, with eastern Europe—densely populated, overcrowded—commencing to show uneasiness as to its supply of food for the winter; and with but a moderate crop in America to meet foreign demands. Russia, the United States, and Argentine would have to feed the world during the next twelve months.

Over the Chicago Wheat Pit the hand of the great indicator stood at seventy-five cents. Jadwin sold out his September wheat at this figure, and then in a single vast clutch bought three million bushels of the December option.

Never before had he ventured so deeply into the Pit. Never before had he committed himself so irrevocably to the scend of the current. But something was preparing. Something indefinite and huge. He guessed it, felt it, knew it. On all sides of him he felt a quickening movement. Lethargy, inertia were breaking up. There was buoyancy to the current. In its ever-increasing swiftness there was exhilaration and exuberance.

And he was upon the crest of the wave. Now the forethought, the shrewdness, and the prompt action of those early spring days were beginning to tell. Confident, secure, unassailable, Jadwin plunged in. Every week the swirl of the Pit increased in speed, every week the demands of Europe for American wheat grew more frequent; and at the end of the month the price—which had fluctuated between seventy-five and seventy-eight—in a sudden flurry rushed to seventy-nine, to seventy-nine and a half, and closed, strong, at the even eighty cents.

On the day when the latter figure was reached Jadwin bought a seat upon the Board of Trade.

He was now no longer an "outsider."

VII

ONE morning in November of the same year Laura joined her husband at breakfast, preoccupied and a little grave, her mind full of a subject about which, she told herself, she could no longer keep from speaking. So soon as an opportunity presented itself, which was when Jadwin laid down his paper and drew his coffee-cup toward him, Laura exclaimed:

"Curtis."

"Well, old girl?"

"Curtis, dear, . . . when is it all going to end—your speculating? You never used to be this way. It seems as though, nowadays, I never had you to myself. Even when you are not going over papers and reports and that, or talking by the hour to Mr. Gretry in the library—even when you are not doing all that, your mind seems to be away from me—down there in La Salle Street or the Board of Trade Building. Dearest, you don't know. I don't mean to complain, and I don't want to be exacting or selfish, but— sometimes I—I am lonesome. Don't interrupt," she said, hastily. "I want to say it all at once, and then never speak of it again. Last night when Mr. Gretry was here, you said, just after dinner, that you would be all through your talk in an hour. And I waited. . . . I waited till eleven, and then I went to bed. Dear, I—I—I was lonesome. The evening was long. I had put on my very prettiest gown, the one you said you liked so much, and you never seemed to notice. You told me Mr. Gretry was going by nine, and I had it all planned how we would spend the evening together."

But she got no further. Her husband had taken her in his arms, and had interrupted her words with blustering exclamations of self-reproach and self-condemnation. He was a brute, he cried, a senseless, selfish ass, who had no right to such a wife, who was not worth a single one of the tears that by now were trembling on Laura's lashes.

"Now we won't speak of it again," she began. "I suppose I am selfish—"

"Selfish, nothing!" he exclaimed. "Don't talk that way. I'm the one—"

"But," Laura persisted, "some time you will—get out of this speculating for good? Oh, I do look forward to it so! And, Curtis, what is the use? We're so rich now we can't spend our money. What do you want to make more for?"

"Oh, it's not the money," he answered. "It's the fun of the thing; the excitement—"

"That's just it, the 'excitement.' You don't know, Curtis. It is changing you. You are so nervous sometimes, and sometimes you don't listen to me when I talk to you. I can just see what's in your mind. It's wheat—wheat—wheat, wheat—wheat—wheat, all the time. Oh, if you knew how I hated and feared it!"

"Well, old girl, that settles it. I wouldn't make you unhappy a single minute for all the wheat in the world."

"And you will stop speculating?"

"Well, I can't pull out all in a moment, but just as soon as a chance comes I'll get out of the market. At any rate, I won't have any business of mine come between us. I don't like it any more than you do. Why, how long is it since we've read any book together, like we used to when you read aloud to me?"

"Not since we came back from the country."

"By George, that's so, that's so." He shook his head. "I've got to taper off. You're right, Laura. But you don't know, you haven't a guess how this trading in wheat gets a hold of you. And, then, what am I to do? What are we fellows, who have made our money, to do? I've got to be busy. I can't sit down and twiddle my thumbs. And I don't believe in lounging around clubs, or playing with race horses, or murdering game birds, or running some poor, helpless fox to death. Speculating seems to be about the only game, or the only business that's left open to me—that appears to be legitimate. I know I've gone too far into it, and I promise you I'll quit. But it's fine fun. When you know how to swing a deal, and can look ahead a little further than the other fellows, and can take chances they daren't, and plan and manœuvre, and then see it all come out just as you had known it would all along—I tell you it's absorbing."

"But you never do tell me," she objected. "I never know what you are doing. I hear through Mr. Court or Mr. Gretry, but never through you. Don't you think you could trust me? I want to enter into your life on its every side, Curtis. Tell me," she suddenly demanded, "what are you doing now?"

"Very well, then," he said, "I'll tell you. Of course you mustn't speak about it. It's nothing very secret, but it's always as well to keep quiet about these things."

She gave her word, and leaned her elbows on the table, prepared to listen intently. Jadwin crushed a lump of sugar against the inside of his coffee cup.

"Well," he began, "I've not been doing anything very exciting, except to buy wheat."

"What for?"

"To sell again. You see, I'm one of those who believe that wheat is going up. I was the very first to see it, I guess, 'way back last April. Now in August this year, while we were up at the lake, I bought three million bushels."

"Three—million—bushels!" she murmured. "Why, what do you do with it? Where do you put it?"

He tried to explain that he had merely bought the right to call for the grain on a certain date, but she could not understand this very clearly.

"Never mind," she told him, "go on."

"Well, then, at the end of August we found out that the wet weather in England would make a short crop there, and along in September came the news that Siberia would not raise enough to supply the southern provinces of Russia. That left only the United States and the Argentine Republic to feed pretty much the whole world. Of course that would make wheat valuable. Seems to be a short-crop year everywhere. I saw that wheat would go higher and higher, so I bought another million bushels in October, and another early in this month. That's all. You see, I figure that pretty soon those people over in England and Italy and Germany—the people that eat wheat—will be willing to pay us in America big prices for it, because it's so hard to get. They've got to have the wheat—it's bread 'n' butter to them."

"Oh, then why not give it to them?" she cried. "Give it to those poor people—your five million bushels. Why, that would be a god-send to them."

Jadwin stared a moment.

"Oh, that isn't exactly how it works out," he said.

Before he could say more, however, the maid came in and handed to Jadwin three despatches.

"Now those," said Laura, when the servant had gone out, "you get those every morning. Are these part of your business? What do they say?"

"I'll read them to you," he told her as he slit the first envelopes. "They are cablegrams from agents of mine in Europe. Gretry arranged to have them sent to me. Here now, this is from Odessa. It's in cipher, but"—he drew a narrow memorandum-book from his breast pocket—"I'll translate it for you."

He turned the pages of the key book a few moments, jotting down the translation on the back of an envelope with the gold pencil at the end of his watch chain.

"Here's how it reads," he said at last. " 'Cash wheat advanced one cent bushel on Liverpool buying, stock light. Shipping to interior. European price not attractive to sellers.' "

"What does that mean?" she asked.

"Well, that Russia will not export wheat, that she has no more than enough for herself, so that Western Europe will have to look to us for her wheat."

"And the others? Read those to me."

Again Jadwin translated.

"This is from Paris:

" 'Answer on one million bushels wheat in your market—stocks lighter than expected, and being cleared up.' "

"Which is to say?" she queried.

"They want to know how much I would ask for a million bushels. They find it hard to get the stuff over there—just as I said they would."

"Will you sell it to them?"

"Maybe. I'll talk to Sam about it."

"And now the last one."

"It's from Liverpool, and Liverpool, you must understand, is the great buyer of wheat. It's a tremendously influential place."

He began once more to consult the key book, one finger following the successive code words of the despatch.

Laura, watching him, saw his eyes suddenly contract.

"By George," he muttered, all at once, "by George, what's this?"
"What is it?" she demanded. "Is it important?"
But, all-absorbed, Jadwin neither heard nor responded. Three
times he verified the same word.
"Oh, please tell me," she begged.
Jadwin shook his head impatiently and held up a warning
hand.
"Wait, wait," he said. "Wait a minute."
Word for word he wrote out the translation of the cablegram,
and then studied it intently.
"That's it," he said, at last. Then he got to his feet. "I guess
I've had enough breakfast," he declared. He looked at his watch,
touched the call bell, and when the maid appeared said:
"Tell Jarvis to bring the buggy around right away."
"But, dear, what is it?" repeated Laura. "You said you would
tell me. You see," she cried, "it's just as I said. You've forgotten
my very existence. When it's a question of wheat I count for
nothing. And just now, when you read the despatch to yourself,
you were all different; such a look came into your face, so cruelly
eager, and triumphant and keen—"
"You'd be eager, too," he exclaimed, "if you understood. Look;
read it for yourself."
He thrust the cable into her hands. Over each code word he
had written its translation, and his wife read:
"Large firms here short and in embarrassing position, owing
to curtailment in Argentine shipments. Can negotiate for five million wheat if price satisfactory."
"Well?" she asked.
"Well, don't you see what that means? It's the 'European demand' at last. They must have wheat, and I've got it to give 'em—
wheat that I bought, oh, at seventy cents, some of it, and they'll
pay the market—that is, eighty cents, for it. Oh, they'll pay more.
They'll pay eighty-two if I want 'em to. France is after the stuff,
too. Remember that cable from Paris I just read. They'd bid
against each other. Why, if I pull this off, if this goes through—
and, by George," he went on, speaking as much to himself as to her,
new phases of the affair presenting themselves to him at every moment, "by George, I don't have to throw this wheat into the Pit and
break down the price—and Gretry has understandings with the
railroads, through the elevator gang, so we get big rebates. Why,
this wheat is worth eighty-two cents to them—and then there's this

'curtailment in Argentine shipments.' That's the first word we've
had about small crops there. Holy Moses, if the Argentine crop is
off, wheat will knock the roof clean off the Board of Trade!" The
maid reappeared in the doorway. "The buggy?" queried Jadwin.
"All right. I'm off, Laura, and—until it's over keep quiet about all
this, you know. Ask me to read you some more cables some day.
It brings good luck."

He gathered up his despatches and the mail and was gone.
Laura, left alone, sat looking out of the window a long moment.
She heard the front door close, and then the sound of the horses'
hoofs on the asphalt by the carriage porch. They died down, ceased,
and all at once a great silence seemed to settle over the house.

Laura sat thinking. At last she rose.

"It is the first time," she said to herself, "that Curtis ever forgot
to kiss me good-by."

The day, for all that the month was December, was fine. The
sun shone; underfoot the ground was dry and hard. The snow
which had fallen ten days before was practically gone. In fine, it
was a perfect day for riding. Laura called her maid and got
into her habit. The groom with his own horse and "Crusader"
were waiting for her when she descended.

That forenoon Laura rode further and longer than usual. Preoccupied at first, her mind burdened with vague anxieties, she
nevertheless could not fail to be aroused and stimulated by the
sparkle and effervescence of the perfect morning, and the cold, pure
glitter of Lake Michigan, green with an intense mineral hue, dotted
with whitecaps, and flashing under the morning sky. Lincoln Park
was deserted and still; a blue haze shrouded the distant masses of
leafless trees, where the gardeners were burning the heaps of leaves.
Under her the thoroughbred moved with an ease and a freedom that
were superb, throwing back one sharp ear at her lightest word; his
rippling mane caressed her hand and forearm, and as she looked
down upon his shoulder she could see the long, slender muscles,
working smoothly, beneath the satin sheen of the skin. At the
waterworks she turned into the long, straight road that leads to
North Lake, and touched Crusader with the crop, checking him
slightly at the same time. With a little toss of his head he broke
from a trot into a canter, and then, as she leaned forward in the
saddle, into his long, even gallop. There was no one to see; she
would not be conspicuous, so Laura gave the horse his head, and in
another moment he was carrying her with a swiftness that brought

the water to her eyes, and that sent her hair flying from her face.
She had him completely under control. A touch upon the bit, she
knew, would suffice to bring him to a standstill. She knew him to
be without fear and without nerves, knew that his every instinct
made for her safety, and that this morning's gallop was as much a
pleasure to him as to his rider. Beneath her and around her the
roadway and landscape flew; the cold air sang in her ears and
whipped a faint color to her pale cheeks; in her deep brown eyes a
frosty sparkle came and went, and throughout all her slender figure
the blood raced spanking and careering in a full, strong tide of
health and gayety.

She made a circle around North Lake, and came back by way of
the Linné monument and the Palm House, Crusader ambling quietly
by now, the groom trotting stolidly in the rear. Throughout all
her ride she had seen no one but the park gardeners and the single
gray-coated, mounted policeman whom she met each time she rode,
and who always touched his helmet to her as she cantered past.
Possibly she had grown a little careless in looking out for pedestri-
ans at the crossings, for as she turned eastward at the La Salle
statue, she all but collided with a gentleman who was traversing
the road at the same time.

She brought her horse to a standstill with a little start of apprehension, and started again as she saw that the gentleman was
Sheldon Corthell.

"Well," she cried, taken all aback, unable to think of formali-
ties, and relapsing all at once into the young girl of Barrington,
Massachusetts, "well, I never—of all the people."

But, no doubt, she had been more in his mind than he in hers,
and a meeting with her was for him an eventuality not at all remote. There was more of pleasure than of embarrassment in that
first look in which he recognized the wife of Curtis Jadwin.

The artist had changed no whit in the four years since last she
had seen him. He seemed as young as ever; there was the same
"elegance" to his figure; his hands were just as long and slim as
ever; his black beard was no less finely pointed, and the mustaches
were brushed away from his lips in the same French style that she
remembered he used to affect. He was, as always, carefully dressed.
He wore a suit of tweeds of a foreign cut, but no overcoat, a cloth
cap of greenish plaid was upon his head, his hands were gloved
in dogskin, and under his arm he carried a slender cane of varnished brown bamboo. The only unconventionality in his dress

was the cravat, a great bow of black silk that overflowed the lapels of his coat.

But she had no more than time to register a swift impression of the details, when he came quickly forward, one hand extended, the other holding his cap.

"I can not tell you how glad I am," he exclaimed.

It was the old Corthell beyond doubting or denial. Not a single inflection of his low-pitched, gently modulated voice was wanting; not a single infinitesimal mannerism was changed, even to the little tilting of the chin when he spoke, or the quick winking of the eyelids, or the smile that narrowed the corners of the eyes themselves, or the trick of perfect repose of his whole body. Even his handkerchief, as always, since first she had known him, was tucked into his sleeve at the wrist.

"And so you are back again," she cried. "And when, and how?"

"And so—yes—so I am back again," he repeated, as they shook hands. "Only day before yesterday, and quite surreptitiously. No one knows yet that I am here. I crept in—or my train did—under the cover of night. I have come straight from Tuscany."

"From Tuscany?"

"—and gardens and marble pergolas."

"Now, why any one should leave Tuscan gardens and—and all that kind of thing for a winter in Chicago, I can not see," she said.

"It is a little puzzling," he answered. "But I fancy that my gardens and pergolas and all the rest had come to seem to me a little—as the French would put it—*malle*. I began to long for a touch of our hard, harsh city again. Harshness has its place, I think, if it is only to cut one's teeth on."

Laura looked down at him, smiling.

"I should have thought you had cut yours long ago," she said.

"Not my wisdom teeth," he urged. "I feel now that I have come to that time of life when it is expedient to have wisdom."

"I have never known that feeling," she confessed, "and I live in the 'hard, harsh' city."

"Oh, that is because you have never known what it meant not to have wisdom," he retorted. "Tell me about everybody," he went on. "Your husband, he is well, of course, and distressfully rich. I heard of him in New York. And Page, our little, solemn Minerva of Dresden china?"

"Oh, yes, Page is well, but you will hardly recognize her; such a young lady nowadays."

"And Mr. Court, 'Landry'? I remember he always impressed me as though he had just had his hair cut; and the Cresslers, and Mrs. Wessels, and—"

"All well. Mrs. Cressler will be delighted to hear you are back. Yes, everybody is well."

"And, last of all, Mrs. Jadwin? But I needn't ask; I can see how well and happy you are."

"And Mr. Corthell," she queried, "is also well and happy?"

"Mr. Corthell," he responded, "is very well, and—tolerably —happy, thank you. One has lost a few illusions, but has managed to keep enough to grow old on. One's latter days are provided for."

"I shouldn't imagine," she told him, "that one lost illusions in Tuscan gardens."

"Quite right," he hastened to reply, smiling cheerfully. "One lost no illusions in Tuscany. One went there to cherish the few that yet remained. But," he added, without change of manner, "one begins to believe that even a lost illusion can be very beautiful sometimes—even in Chicago."

"I want you to dine with us," said Laura. "You've hardly met my husband, and I think you will like some of our pictures. I will have all your old friends there, the Cresslers and Aunt Wess' and all. When can you come?"

"Oh, didn't you get my note?" he asked. "I wrote you yesterday, asking if I might call to-night. You see, I am only in Chicago for a couple of days. I must go on to St. Louis to-morrow, and shall not be back for a week."

"Note? No, I've had no note from you. Oh, I know what happened. Curtis left in a hurry this morning, and he swooped all the mail into his pocket the last moment. I knew some of my letters were with his. There's where your note went. But, never mind, it makes no difference now that we've met. Yes, by all means, come to-night—to dinner. We're not a bit formal. Curtis won't have it. We dine at six; and I'll try to get the others. Oh, but Page won't be there, I forgot. She and Landry Court are going to have dinner with Aunt Wess', and they are all going to a lecture afterward."

The artist expressed his appreciation and accepted her invitation.

"Do you know where we live?" she demanded. "You know we've moved since."

"Yes, I know," he told her. "I made up my mind to take a long walk here in the Park this morning, and I passed your house on my way out. You see, I had to look up your address in the directory before writing. Your house awed me, I confess, and the style is surprisingly good."

"But tell me," asked Laura, "you never speak of yourself, what have you been doing since you went away?"

"Nothing. Merely idling, and painting a little, and studying some thirteenth century glass in Avignon and Sienna."

"And shall you go back?"

"Yes, I think so, in about a month. So soon as I have straightened out some little businesses of mine—which puts me in mind," he said, glancing at his watch, "that I have an appointment at eleven, and should be about it."

He said good-by and left her, and Laura cantered homeward in high spirits. She was very glad that Corthell had come back. She had always liked him. He not only talked well himself, but seemed to have the faculty of making her do the same. She remembered that in the old days, before she had met Jadwin, her mind and conversation, for undiscoverable reasons, had never been nimbler, quicker, nor more effective than when in the company of the artist.

Arrived at home, Laura (as soon as she had looked up the definition of "pergola" in the dictionary) lost no time in telephoning to Mrs. Cressler.

"What," this latter cried when she told her the news, "that Sheldon Corthell back again! Well, dear me, if he wasn't the last person in my mind. I do remember the lovely windows he used to paint, and how refined and elegant he always was—and the loveliest hands and voice."

"He's to dine with us to-night, and I want you and Mr. Cressler to come."

"Oh, Laura, child, I just simply can't. Charlie's got a man from Milwaukee coming here to-night, and I've got to feed him. Isn't it too provoking? I've got to sit and listen to those two, clattering commissions and percentages and all, when I might be hearing Sheldon Corthell talk art and poetry and stained glass. I declare, I never have any luck."

At quarter to six that evening Laura sat in the library, before the fireplace, in her black velvet dinner gown, cutting the pages of a new novel, the ivory cutter as it turned and glanced in her hand appearing to be a mere prolongation of her slender fingers. But she was not interested in the book, and from time to time glanced nervously at the clock upon the mantel-shelf over her head. Jadwin was not home yet, and she was distressed at the thought of keeping dinner waiting. He usually came back from downtown at five o'clock, and even earlier. To-day she had expected that quite possibly the business implied in the Liverpool cable of the morning might detain him, but surely he should be home by now; and as the minutes passed she listened more and more anxiously for the sound of hoofs on the driveway at the side of the house.

At five minutes of the hour, when Corthell was announced, there was still no sign of her husband. But as she was crossing the hall on her way to the drawing-room, one of the servants informed her that Mr. Jadwin had just telephoned that he would be home in half an hour.

"Is he on the telephone now?" she asked, quickly. "Where did he telephone from?"

But it appeared that Jadwin had "hung up" without mentioning his whereabouts.

"The buggy came home," said the servant. "Mr. Jadwin told Jarvis not to wait. He said he would come in the street cars."

Laura reflected that she could delay dinner a half hour, and gave orders to that effect.

"We shall have to wait a little," she explained to Corthell as they exchanged greetings in the drawing-room. "Curtis has some special business on hand to-day, and is half an hour late."

They sat down on either side of the fireplace in the lofty apartment, with its sombre hangings of wine-colored brocade and thick, muffling rugs, and for upward of three-quarters of an hour Corthell interested her with his description of his life in the cathedral towns of northern Italy. But at the end of that time dinner was announced.

"Has Mr. Jadwin come in yet?" Laura asked of the servant.

"No, madam."

She bit her lip in vexation.

"I can't imagine what can keep Curtis so late," she murmured. "Well," she added, at the end of her resources, "we must make the best of it. I think we will go in, Mr. Corthell, without waiting. Curtis must be here soon now."

But, as a matter of fact, he was not. In the great dining-room, filled with a dull crimson light, the air touched with the scent of lilies of the valley, Corthell and Mrs. Jadwin dined alone.

"I suppose," observed the artist, "that Mr. Jadwin is a very busy man."

"Oh, no," Laura answered. "His **real estate**, he says, runs itself, and, as a rule, Mr. Gretry manages most of his Board of Trade business. It is only occasionally that anything keeps him downtown late. I scolded him this morning, however, about his speculating, and made him promise not to do so much of it. I hate speculation. It seems to absorb some men so; and I don't believe it's right for a man to allow himself to become absorbed altogether in business."

"Oh, why limit one's absorption to business?" replied Corthell, sipping his wine. "Is it right for one to be absorbed 'altogether' in anything—even in art, even in religion?"

"Oh, religion, I don't know," she protested.

"Isn't that certain contribution," he hazarded, "which we make to the general welfare, over and above our own individual work, isn't that the essential? I suppose, of course, that we must hoe, each of us, his own little row, but it's the stroke or two we give to our neighbor's row—don't you think?—that helps most to cultivate the field."

"But doesn't religion mean more than a stroke or two?" she ventured to reply.

"I'm not so sure," he answered, thoughtfully. "If the stroke or two is taken from one's own work instead of being given in excess of it. One must do one's own hoeing first. That's the foundation of things. A religion that would mean to be 'altogether absorbed' in my neighbor's hoeing would be genuinely pernicious, surely. My row, meanwhile, would lie open to weeds."

"But if your neighbor's row grew flowers?"

"Unfortunately weeds grow faster than the flowers, and the weeds of my row would spread until they choked and killed my neighbor's flowers, I am sure."

"That seems selfish though," she persisted. "Suppose my neighbor were maimed or halt or blind? His poor little row would never be finished. My stroke or two would not help very much."

"Yes, but every row lies between two others, you know. The hoer on the far side of the cripple's row would contribute a stroke or two as well as you. No," he went on, "I am sure one's first duty is to do one's own work. It seems to me that a work accomplished benefits the whole world—the people—pro rata. If we help another at the expense of our work instead of in excess of it, we benefit only the individual, and, pro rata again, rob the people. A little good contributed by everybody to the race is of more, infinitely more, importance than a great deal of good contributed by one individual to another."

"Yes," she admitted, beginning at last to be convinced, "I see what you mean. But one must think very large to see that. It never occurred to me before. The individual—I, Laura Jadwin—counts for nothing. It is the type to which I belong that's important, the mold, the form, the sort of composite photograph of hundreds of thousands of Laura Jadwins. Yes," she continued, her brows bent, her mind hard at work, "what I am, the little things that distinguish me from everybody else, those pass away very quickly, are very ephemeral. But the type Laura Jadwin, that always remains, doesn't it? One must help building up only the permanent things. Then, let's see, the individual may deteriorate, but the type always grows better. . . . Yes, I think one can say that."

"At least the type never recedes," he prompted.

"Oh, it began good," she cried, as though at a discovery, "and can never go back of that original good. Something keeps it from going below a certain point, and it is left to us to lift it higher and higher. No, the type can't be bad. Of course the type is more important than the individual. And that something that keeps it from going below a certain point is God."

"Or nature."

"So that God and nature," she cried again, "work together? No, no, they are one and the same thing."

"There, don't you see," he remarked, smiling back at her, "how simple it is?"

"Oh-h," exclaimed Laura, with a deep breath, "isn't it beautiful?" She put her hand to her forehead with a little laugh of deprecation. "My," she said, "but those things make you think."

Dinner was over before she was aware of it, and they were still talking animatedly as they rose from the table.

"We will have our coffee in the art gallery," Laura said, "and please smoke."

He lighted a cigarette, and the two passed into the great glass-roofed rotunda.

"Here is the one I like best," said Laura, standing before the Bougereau.

"Yes?" he queried, observing the picture thoughtfully. "I suppose," he remarked, "it is because it demands less of you than some others. I see what you mean. It pleases you because it satisfies you so easily. You can grasp it without any effort."

"Oh, I don't know," she ventured.

"Bougereau 'fills a place.' I know it," he answered. "But I can not persuade myself to admire his art."

"But," she faltered, "I thought that Bougereau was considered the greatest—one of the greatest—his wonderful flesh tints, the drawing, and coloring—"

"But I think you will see," he told her, "if you think about it, that for all there is *in* his picture—back of it—a fine hanging, a beautiful vase would have exactly the same value upon your wall. Now, on the other hand, take this picture." He indicated a small canvas to the right of the bathing nymphs, representing a twilight landscape.

"Oh, that one," said Laura. "We bought that here in America, in New York. It's by a Western artist. I never noticed it much, I'm afraid."

"But now look at it," said Corthell. "Don't you know that the artist saw something more than trees and a pool and afterglow? He had that feeling of night coming on, as he sat there before his sketching easel on the edge of that little pool. He heard the frogs beginning to pipe, I'm sure, and the touch of the night mist was on his hands. And he was very lonely and even a little sad. In those deep shadows under the trees he put something of himself, the gloom and the sadness that he felt at the moment. And that little pool, still and black and sombre—why, the whole thing is the tragedy of a life full of dark, hidden secrets. And the little pool is a heart. No one can say how deep it is, or what dreadful thing one would find at the bottom, or what drowned hopes or what sunken ambitions. That little pool says one word as plain as if it were whispered in the ear—despair. Oh, yes, I prefer it to the nymphs."

"I am very much ashamed," returned Laura, "that I could not see it all before for myself. But I see it now. It is better, of course. I shall come in here often now and study it. Of all the rooms in our house, this is the one I like best. But, I am afraid, it has been more because of the organ than of the pictures."

Corthell turned about.

"Oh, the grand, noble organ," he murmured. "I envy you this of all your treasures. May I play for you? Something to compensate for the dreadful, despairing little tarn of the picture."

"I should love to have you," she told him.

He asked permission to lower the lights, and stepping outside the door an instant, pressed the buttons that extinguished all but a very few of them. After he had done this he came back to the organ and detached the self-playing "arrangement" without comment, and seated himself at the console.

Laura lay back in a long chair close at hand. The moment was propitious. The artist's profile silhouetted itself against the shade of a light that burned at the side of the organ, and that gave light to the keyboard. And on this keyboard, full in the reflection, lay his long, slim hands. They were the only things that moved in the room, and the chords and bars of Mendelssohn's "Consolation" seemed, as he played, to flow, not from the instrument, but, like some invisible ether, from his finger-tips themselves.

"You hear," he said to Laura, "the effect of question and answer in this. The questions are passionate and tumultuous and varied, but the answer is always the same, always calm and soothing and dignified."

She answered with a long breath, speaking just above a whisper: "Oh, yes, yes, I understand."

He finished and turned toward her a moment. "Possibly not a very high order of art," he said; "a little too 'easy,' perhaps, like the Bougereau, but 'Consolation' should appeal very simply and directly, after all. Do you care for Beethoven?"

"I—I am afraid—" began Laura, but he had continued without waiting for her reply.

"You remember this? The 'Appassionata,' the F minor sonata —just the second movement."

But when he had finished Laura begged him to continue.

"Please go on," she said. "Play anything. You can't tell how I love it."

"Here is something I've always liked," he answered, turning back to the keyboard. "It is the 'Mephisto Walzer' of Liszt. He has adapted it himself from his own orchestral score, very ingeniously. It is difficult to render on the organ, but I think you can get the idea of it." As he spoke he began playing, his head very slightly moving to the rhythm of the piece. At the beginning of each new theme, and without interrupting his playing, he offered a word of explanation:

"Very vivid and arabesque this, don't you think? . . . And now this movement; isn't it reckless and capricious, like a woman who hesitates and then takes the leap? Yet there's a certain nobility there, a feeling for ideals. You see it, of course. . . .

And all the while this undercurrent of the sensual, and that feline, eager sentiment . . . and here, I think, is the best part of it, the very essence of passion, the voluptuousness that is a veritable anguish. . . . These long, slow rhythms, tortured, languishing, really dying. It reminds one of 'Phèdre'—'Venus toute entière,' and the rest of it; and Wagner has the same. You find it again in Isolde's motif continually."

Laura was transfixed, all but transported. Here was something better than Gounod and Verdi, something above and beyond the obvious one, two, three, one, two, three of the opera scores as she knew them and played them. Music she understood with an intuitive quickness; and those prolonged chords of Liszt's, heavy and clogged and cloyed with passion, reached some hitherto untouched string within her heart, and with resistless power twanged it so that the vibration of it shook her entire being, and left her quivering and breathless, the tears in her eyes, her hands clasped till the knuckles whitened.

She felt all at once as though a whole new world were opened to her. She stood on Pisgah. And she was ashamed and confused at her ignorance of those things which Corthell tactfully assumed that she knew as a matter of course. What wonderful pleasures she had ignored! How infinitely removed from her had been the real world of art and artists of which Corthell was a part! Ah, but she would make amends now. No more Verdi and Bougereau. She would get rid of the "Bathing Nymphs." Never, never again would she play the "Anvil Chorus." Corthell should select her pictures, and should play to her from Liszt and Beethoven that music which evoked all the turbulent emotion, all the impetuosity and fire and exaltation that she felt was hers.

She wondered at herself. Surely, surely there were two Laura Jadwins. One calm and even and steady, loving the quiet life, loving her home, finding a pleasure in the duties of the housewife. This was the Laura who liked plain, homely, matter-of-fact Mrs. Cressler, who adored her husband, who delighted in Mr. Howells's novels, who abjured society and the formal conventions, who went to church every Sunday, and who was afraid of her own elevator.

But at moments such as this she knew that there was another Laura Jadwin—the Laura Jadwin who might have been a great actress, who had a "temperament," who was impulsive. This was the Laura of the "grand manner," who played the rôle of the great lady from room to room of her vast house, who read Meredith, who

reveled in swift gallops through the park on jet-black, long-tailed
horses, who affected black velvet, black jet, and black lace in her
gowns, who was conscious and proud of her pale, stately beauty—
the Laura Jadwin, in fine, who delighted to recline in a long chair
in the dim, beautiful picture gallery and listen with half-shut eyes
to the great golden organ thrilling to the passion of Beethoven and
Liszt.

The last notes of the organ sank and faded into silence—a
silence that left a sense of darkness like that which follows upon
the flight of a falling star, and after a long moment Laura sat
upright, adjusting the heavy masses of her black hair with thrusts
of her long, white fingers. She drew a deep breath.

"Oh," she said, "that was wonderful, wonderful. It is like
a new language—no, it is like new thoughts, too fine for
language."

"I have always believed so," he answered. "Of all the arts,
music, to my notion, is the most intimate. At the other end of the
scale you have architecture, which is an expression of and an appeal
to the common multitude, a whole people, the mass. Fiction and
painting, and even poetry, are affairs of the classes, reaching the
groups of the educated. But music—ah, that is different, it is one
soul speaking to another soul. The composer meant it for you and
himself. No one else has anything to do with it. Because his soul
was heavy and broken with grief, or bursting with passion, or
tortured with doubt, or searching for some unnamed ideal, he has
come to you—you of all the people in the world—with his message,
and he tells you of his yearnings and his sadness, knowing that you
will sympathize, knowing that your soul has, like his, been acquainted with grief, or with gladness; and in the music his soul
speaks to yours, beats with it, blends with it, yes, is even, spiritually,
married to it."

And as he spoke the electrics all over the gallery flashed out in
a sudden blaze, and Curtis Jadwin entered the room, crying out:

"Are you here, Laura? By George, my girl, we pulled it off,
and I've cleaned up five—hundred—thousand—dollars."

Laura and the artist faced quickly about, blinking at the sudden
glare, and Laura put her hand over her eyes.

"Oh, I didn't mean to blind you," said her husband, as he came
forward. "But I thought it wouldn't be appropriate to tell you the
good news in the dark."

Corthell rose, and for the first time Jadwin caught sight of him.

"This is Mr. Corthell, Curtis," Laura said. "You remember him, of course."

"Why, certainly, certainly," declared Jadwin, shaking Corthell's hand. "Glad to see you again. I hadn't an idea you were here." He was excited, elated, very talkative. "I guess I came in on you abruptly," he observed. "They told me Mrs. Jadwin was in here, and I was full of my good news. By the way, I do remember now. When I came to look over my mail on the way down town this morning, I found a note from you to my wife, saying you would call to-night. Thought it was for me, and opened it before I found the mistake."

"I knew you had gone off with it," said Laura.

"Guess I must have mixed it up with my own mail this morning. I'd have telephoned you about it, Laura, but upon my word I've been so busy all day I clean forgot it. I've let the cat out of the bag already, Mr. Corthell, and I might as well tell the whole thing now. I've been putting through a little deal with some Liverpool fellows to-day, and I had to wait down town to get their cables to-night. You got my telephone, did you, Laura?"

"Yes, but you said then you'd be up in half an hour."

"I know—I know. But those Liverpool cables didn't come till all hours. Well, as I was saying, Mr. Corthell, I had this deal on hand—it was that wheat, Laura, I was telling you about this morning—five million bushels of it, and I found out from my English agent that I could slam it right into a couple of fellows over there, if we could come to terms. We came to terms right enough. Some of that wheat I sold at a profit of fifteen cents on every bushel. My broker and I figured it out just now, before I started home, and, as I say, I'm a clean half million to the good. So much for looking ahead a little further than the next man." He dropped into a chair and stretched his arms wide. "Whoo! I'm tired, Laura. Seems as though I'd been on my feet all day. Do you suppose Mary, or Martha, or Maggie, or whatever her name is, could rustle me a good strong cup of tea?"

"Haven't you dined, Curtis?" cried Laura.

"Oh, I had a stand-up lunch somewhere with Sam. But we were both so excited we might as well have eaten sawdust. Heigho, I sure am tired. It takes it out of you, Mr. Corthell, to make five hundred thousand in about ten hours."

"Indeed I imagine so," assented the artist. Jadwin turned to his wife, and held her glance in his a moment. He was full

of triumph, full of the grim humor of the suddenly successful
American.

"Hey?" he said. "What do you think of that, Laura," he
clapped down his big hand upon his chair arm, "a whole half million—at one grab? Maybe they'll say down there in La Salle
Street now that I don't know wheat. Why, Sam—that's Gretry,
my broker, Mr. Corthell, of Gretry, Converse & Co.—Sam said to
me, Laura, to-night, he said, 'J.'—they call me 'J.' down there, Mr.
Corthell—'J., I take off my hat to you. I thought you were wrong
from the very first, but I guess you know this game better than I do.'
Yes, sir, that's what he said, and Sam Gretry has been trading in
wheat for pretty nearly thirty years. Oh, I knew it," he cried,
with a quick gesture; "I knew wheat was going to go up. I knew it
from the first, when all the rest of 'em laughed at me. I knew
this European demand would hit us hard about this time. I knew
it was a good thing to buy wheat; I knew it was a good thing to have
special agents over in Europe. Oh, they'll all buy now—when I've
showed 'em the way. Upon my word, I haven't talked so much in
a month of Sundays. You must pardon me, Mr. Corthell. I don't
make five hundred thousand every day."

"But this is the last—isn't it?" said Laura.

"Yes," admitted Jadwin, with a quick, deep breath. "I'm done
now. No more speculating. Let some one else have a try now.
See if they can hold five million bushels till it's wanted. My, my,
I am tired—as I've said before. D'that tea come, Laura?"

"What's that in your hand?" she answered, smiling.

Jadwin stared at the cup and saucer he held, whimsically.
"Well, well," he exclaimed, "I *must* be flustered. Corthell," he
declared between swallows, "take my advice. Buy May wheat.
It'll beat art all hollow."

"Oh, dear, no," returned the artist. "I should lose my senses if
I won, and my money if I didn't."

"That's so. Keep out of it. It's a rich man's game. And at
that, there's no fun in it unless you risk more than you can afford
to lose. Well, let's not talk shop. You're an artist, Mr. Corthell.
What do you think of our house?"

Later on, when they had said good-by to Corthell, and when
Jadwin was making the rounds of the library, art gallery, and drawing-rooms—a nightly task which he never would intrust to the
servants—turning down the lights and testing the window fasten-
ings, his wife said: "And now you are out of it—for good."

"I don't own a grain of wheat," he assured her. "I've got to be out of it."

The next day he went down town for only two or three hours in the afternoon. But he did not go near the Board of Trade building. He talked over a few business matters with the manager of his real estate office, wrote an unimportant letter or two, signed a few orders, was back at home by five o'clock, and in the evening took Laura, Page, and Landry Court to the theatre.

After breakfast the next morning, when he had read his paper, he got up, and, thrusting his hands in his pockets, looked across the table at his wife.

"Well," he said. "Now what'll we do?"

She put down at once the letter she was reading.

"Would you like to drive in the park?" she suggested. "It is a beautiful morning."

"M—m—yes," he answered slowly. "All right. Let's drive in the park."

But she could see that the prospect was not alluring to him.

"No," she said, "no. I don't think you want to do that."

"I don't think I do, either," he admitted. "The fact is, Laura, I just about know that park by heart. Is there anything good in the magazines this month?"

She got them for him, and he installed himself comfortably in the library, with a box of cigars near at hand.

"Ah," he said, fetching a long breath as he settled back in the deep-seated leather chair. "Now this is what I call solid comfort. Better than stewing and fussing about La Salle Street with your mind loaded down with responsibilities and all. This is my idea of life."

But an hour later, when Laura—who had omitted her ride that morning—looked into the room, he was not there. The magazines were helter-skeltered upon the floor and table, where he had tossed each one after turning the leaves. A servant told her that Mr. Jadwin was out in the stables.

She saw him through the window, in a cap and great-coat, talking with the coachman and looking over one of the horses. But he came back to the house in a little while, and she found him in his smoking-room with a novel in his hand.

"Oh, I read that last week," she said, as she caught a glimpse of the title. "Isn't it interesting? Don't you think it is good?"

"Oh—yes—pretty good," he admitted. "Isn't it about time for lunch? Let's go to the matinée this afternoon, Laura. Oh, that's so, it's Thursday; I forgot."

"Let me read that aloud to you," she said, reaching for the book. "I know you'll be interested when you get further along."

"Honestly, I don't think I would be," he declared. "I've looked ahead in it. It seems terribly dry. Do you know," he said, abruptly, "if the law was off I'd go up to Geneva Lake and fish through the ice. Laura, how would you like to go to Florida?"

"Oh, I tell you," she exclaimed. "Let's go up to Geneva Lake over Christmas. We'll open up the house and take some of the servants along and have a house party."

Eventually this was done. The Cresslers and the Gretrys were invited, together with Sheldon Corthell and Landry Court. Page and Aunt Wess' came as a matter of course. Jadwin brought up some of the horses and a couple of sleighs. On Christmas night they had a great tree, and Corthell composed the words and music for a carol which had a great success.

About a week later, two days after New Year's Day, when Landry came down from Chicago on the afternoon train, he was full of the tales of a great day on the Board of Trade. Laura, descending to the sitting-room just before dinner, found a group in front of the fireplace, where the huge logs were hissing and crackling. Her husband and Cressler were there, and Gretry, who had come down on an earlier train. Page sat near at hand, her chin on her palm, listening intently to Landry, who held the centre of the stage for the moment. In a far corner of the room Sheldon Corthell, in a dinner coat and patent leather pumps, a cigarette between his fingers, read a volume of Italian verse.

"It was the confirmation of the failure of the Argentine crop that did it," Landry was saying; "that and the tremendous foreign demand. She opened steady enough at eighty-three, but just as soon as the gong tapped we began to get it. Buy, buy, buy. Everybody is in it now. The public are speculating. For one fellow who wants to sell there are a dozen buyers. We had one of the hottest times I ever remember in the Pit this morning."

Laura saw Jadwin's eyes snap.

"I told you we'd get this, Sam," he said, nodding to the broker.

"Oh, there's plenty of wheat," answered Gretry, easily. "Wait till we get dollar wheat—if we do—and see it come out. The farmers haven't sold it all yet. There's always an army of ancient hayseeds who have the stuff tucked away—in old stockings, I guess

—and who'll dump it on you all right if you pay enough. There's plenty of wheat. I've seen it happen before. Work the price high enough, and, Lord, how they'll scrape the bins to throw it at you! You'd never guess from what out-of-the-way places it would come."

"I tell you, Sam," retorted Jadwin, "the surplus of wheat is going out of the country—and it's going fast. And some of these shorts will have to hustle lively for it pretty soon."

"The Crookes gang, though," observed Landry, "seem pretty confident the market will break. I'm sure they were selling short this morning."

"The idea," exclaimed Jadwin, incredulously, "the idea of selling short in face of this Argentine collapse, and all this Bull news from Europe!"

"Oh, there are plenty of shorts," urged Gretry. "Plenty of them."

Try as he would, the echoes of the rumbling of the Pit reached Jadwin at every hour of the day and night. The maelstrom there at the foot of La Salle Street was swirling now with a mightier rush than for years past. Thundering, its vortex smoking, it sent its whirling far out over the country, from ocean to ocean, sweeping the wheat into its currents, sucking it in, and spewing it out again in the gigantic pulses of its ebb flow.

And he, Jadwin, who knew its every eddy, who could foretell its every ripple, was out of it, out of it. Inactive, he sat there idle while the clamor of the Pit swelled daily louder, and while other men, men of little minds, of narrow imaginations, perversely, blindly shut their eyes to the swelling of its waters, neglecting the chances which he would have known how to use with such large, such vast results. That mysterious event which long ago he felt was preparing, was not yet consummated. The great Fact, the great Result which was at last to issue forth from all this turmoil was not yet achieved. Would it refuse to come until a master hand, all powerful, all daring, gripped the levers of the sluice gates that controlled the crashing waters of the Pit? He did not know. Was it the moment for a chief?

Was this upheaval a revolution that called aloud for its Napoleon? Would another, not himself, at last, seeing where so many shut their eyes, step into the place of high command?

Jadwin chafed and fretted in his inaction. As the time when the house party should break up drew to its close, his impatience harried him like a gadfly. He took long drives over the lonely country roads, or tramped the hills or the frozen lake, thoughtful, preoccupied. He still held his seat upon the Board of Trade. He still retained his agents in Europe. Each morning brought him fresh despatches, each evening's paper confirmed his forecasts.

"Oh, I'm out of it for good and all," he assured his wife. "But I know the man who could take up the whole jing-bang of that Crookes crowd in one hand and"—his large fist swiftly knotted as he spoke the words—"scrunch it like an eggshell, by George."

Landry Court often entertained Page with accounts of the doings on the Board of Trade, and about a fortnight after the Jadwins had returned to their city home he called on her one evening and brought two or three of the morning's papers.

"Have you seen this?" he asked. She shook her head.

"Well," he said, compressing his lips, and narrowing his eyes, "let me tell you, we are having pretty—lively—times—down there on the Board these days. The whole country is talking about it."

He read her certain extracts from the newspapers he had brought. The first article stated that recently a new factor had appeared in the Chicago wheat market. A "Bull" clique had evidently been formed, presumably of New York capitalists, who were ousting the Crookes crowd and were rapidly coming into control of the market. In consequence of this the price of wheat was again mounting.

Another paper spoke of a combine of St. Louis firms who were advancing prices, bulling the market. Still a third said, at the beginning of a half-column article:

"It is now universally conceded that an Unknown Bull has invaded the Chicago wheat market since the beginning of the month, and is now dominating the entire situation. The Bears profess to have no fear of this mysterious enemy, but it is a matter of fact that a multitude of shorts were driven ignominiously to cover on Tuesday last, when the Great Bull gathered in a long line of two million bushels in a single half-hour. Scalping and eighth-chasing are almost entirely at an end, the smaller traders dreading to be caught on the horns of the Unknown. The new operator's identity has been carefully concealed, but whoever he is, he is a wonderful trader and is possessed of consummate nerve. It has been rumored that he hails from New York, and is but one of a large clique who are inaugurating a Bull campaign. But our New York advices are emphatic in denying this report, and we can

safely state that the Unknown Bull is a native, and a present in-
habitant of the Windy City."

Page looked up at Landry quickly, and he returned her glance
without speaking. There was a moment's silence.

"I guess," Landry hazarded, lowering his voice, "I guess we're
both thinking of the same thing."

"But I know he told my sister that he was going to stop all that
kind of thing. What do you think?"

"I hadn't ought to think anything."

"Say 'shouldn't think,' Landry."

"Shouldn't think, then, anything about it. My business is to
execute Mr. Gretry's orders."

"Well, I know this," said Page, "that Mr. Jadwin is down town
all day again. You know he stayed away for a while."

"Oh, that may be his real estate business that keeps him down
town so much," replied Landry.

"Laura is terribly distressed," Page went on. "I can see that.
They used to spend all their evenings together in the library, and
Laura would read aloud to him. But now he comes home so tired
that sometimes he goes to bed at nine o'clock, and Laura sits there
alone reading till eleven and twelve. But she's afraid, too, of the
effect upon him. He's getting so absorbed. He don't care for
literature now as he did once, or was beginning to when Laura
used to read to him; and he never thinks of his Sunday-school.
And then, too, if you're to believe Mr. Cressler, there's a chance
that he may lose if he is speculating again."

But Landry stoutly protested:

"Well, don't think for one moment that Mr. Curtis Jadwin is
going to let any one get the better of him. There's no man—no,
nor gang of men—could down him. He's head and shoulders above
the biggest of them down there. I tell you he's Napoleonic. Yes,
sir, that's what he is, Napoleonic, to say the least. Page," he declared solemnly, "he's the greatest man I've ever known."

Very soon after this it was no longer a secret to Laura Jadwin
that her husband had gone back to the wheat market, and that, too,
with such impetuosity, such eagerness, that his rush had carried him
to the very heart's heart of the turmoil.

He was now deeply involved; his influence began to be felt.
Not an important move on the part of the "Unknown Bull," the
nameless mysterious stranger, that was not duly noted and discussed
by the entire world of La Salle Street.

Almost his very first move, carefully guarded, executed with profoundest secrecy, had been to replace the five million bushels sold to Liverpool by five million more of the May option. This was in January, and all through February and all through the first days of March, while the cry for American wheat rose, insistent and vehement, from fifty cities and centres of eastern Europe; while the jam of men in the Wheat Pit grew ever more frantic, ever more furious, and while the impassive hand on the great dial over the floor of the Board rose, resistless, till it stood at eighty-seven, he bought steadily, gathering in the wheat, calling for it, welcoming it, receiving full in the face and with opened arms the cataract that poured in upon the Pit from Iowa and Nebraska, Minnesota and Dakota, from the dwindling bins of Illinois and the fast-emptying elevators of Kansas and Missouri.

Then, squarely in the midst of the commotion, at a time when Curtis Jadwin owned some ten million bushels of May wheat, fell the Government report on the visible supply.

"Well," said Jadwin, "what do you think of it?"

He and Gretry were in the broker's private room in the offices of Gretry, Converse & Co. They were studying the report of the Government as to the supply of wheat, which had just been published in the editions of the evening papers. It was very late in the afternoon of a lugubrious March day. Long since the gas and electricity had been lighted in the office, while in the streets the lamps at the corners were reflected downward in long shafts of light upon the drenched pavements. From the windows of the room one could see directly up La Salle Street. The cable cars, as they made the turn into or out of the street at the corner of Monroe, threw momentary glares of red and green lights across the mists of rain, and filled the air continually with the jangle of their bells. Further on one caught a glimpse of the Court House rising from the pavement like a rain-washed cliff of black basalt, picked out with winking lights, and beyond that, at the extreme end of the vista, the girders and cables of the La Salle Street bridge.

The sidewalks on either hand were incumbered with the "six o'clock crowd" that poured out incessantly from the street entrances of the office buildings. It was a crowd almost entirely of men, and they moved only in one direction, buttoned to the chin in rain coats, their umbrellas bobbing, their feet scuffling through the little pools of wet in the depressions of the sidewalk. They streamed from out the brokers' offices and commission houses

on either side of La Salle Street, continually, unendingly, moving
with the dragging sluggishness of the fatigue of a hard day's work.
Under that gray sky and blurring veil of rain they lost their in-
dividualities, they became conglomerate—a mass, slow-moving,
black. All day long the torrent had seethed and thundered through
the street—the torrent that swirled out and back from that vast Pit
of roaring within the Board of Trade. Now the Pit was stilled,
the sluice gates of the torrent locked, and from out the thousands
of offices, from out the Board of Trade itself, flowed the black and
sluggish lees, the lifeless dregs that filtered back to their level for
a few hours' stagnation, till in the morning the whirlpool, revolving
once more, should again suck them back into its vortex.

The rain fell uninterruptedly. There was no wind. The cable
cars jolted and jostled over the tracks with a strident whir of vibrating window glass. In the street, immediately in front of the
entrance to the Board of Trade, a group of pigeons, garnet-eyed,
trim, with coral-colored feet and iridescent breasts, strutted and
fluttered, pecking at the handfuls of wheat that a porter threw
them from the windows of the floor of the Board.

"Well," repeated Jadwin, shifting with a movement of his lips
his unlighted cigar to the other corner of his mouth, "well, what
do you think of it?"

The broker, intent upon the figures and statistics, replied only
by an indefinite movement of the head.

"Why, Sam," observed Jadwin, looking up from the paper,
"there's less than a hundred million bushels in the farmers' hands.
. . . That's awfully small. Sam, that's awfully small."

"It *ain't*, as you might say, colossal," admitted Gretry.

There was a long silence while the two men studied the report
still further. Gretry took a pamphlet of statistics from a pigeon-
hole of his desk, and compared certain figures with those mentioned
in the report.

Outside the rain swept against the windows with the subdued
rustle of silk. A newsboy raised a Gregorian chant as he went
down the street.

"By George, Sam," Jadwin said again, "do you know that a
whole pile of that wheat has got to go to Europe before July. How
have the shipments been?"

"About five millions a week."

"Why, think of that, twenty millions a month, and it's—let's
see, April, May, June, July—four months before a new crop.

Eighty million bushels will go out of the country in the next four months—eighty million out of less than a hundred millions."

"Looks that way," answered Gretry.

"Here," said Jadwin, "let's get some figures. Let's get a squint on the whole situation. Got a 'Price Current' here? Let's find out what the stocks are in Chicago. I don't believe the elevators are exactly bursting, and, say," he called after the broker, who had started for the front office, "say, find out about the primary receipts, and the Paris and Liverpool stocks. Bet you what you like that Paris and Liverpool together couldn't show ten million to save their necks."

In a few moments Gretry was back again, his hands full of pamphlets and "trade" journals.

By now the offices were quite deserted. The last clerk had gone home. Without, the neighborhood was emptying rapidly. Only a few stragglers hurried over the glistening sidewalks; only a few lights yet remained in the façades of the tall, gray office buildings. And in the widening silence the cooing of the pigeons on the ledges and window-sills of the Board of Trade Building made itself heard with increasing distinctness.

Before Gretry's desk the two men leaned over the litter of papers. The broker's pencil was in his hand, and from time to time he figured rapidly on a sheet of note paper.

"And," observed Jadwin after a while, "and you see how the millers up here in the Northwest have been grinding up all the grain in sight. Do you see that?"

"Yes," said Gretry; then he added, "navigation will be open in another month up there in the straits."

"That's so, too," exclaimed Jadwin, "and what wheat there is here will be moving out. I'd forgotten that point. Ain't you glad you aren't short of wheat these days?"

"There's plenty of fellows that are, though," returned Gretry. "I've got a lot of short wheat on my books—a lot of it."

All at once as Gretry spoke Jadwin started, and looked at him with a curious glance.

"You have, hey?" he said. "There are a lot of fellows who have sold short?"

"Oh, yes, some of Crookes' followers—yes, quite a lot of them."

Jadwin was silent a moment, tugging at his mustache. Then suddenly he leaned forward, his finger almost in Gretry's face.

"Why, look here," he cried. "Don't you see? Don't you see—"

"See what?" demanded the broker, puzzled at the other's vehemence.

Jadwin loosened his collar with a forefinger.

"Great Scott! I'll choke in a minute. See what? Why, I own ten million bushels of this wheat already, and Europe will take eighty million out of the country. Why, there ain't going to be any wheat left in Chicago by May! If I get in now and buy a long line of cash wheat, where are all these fellows who've sold short going to get it to deliver to me? Say, where are they going to get it? Come on now, tell me, where are they going to get it?"

Gretry laid down his pencil and stared at Jadwin, looked long at the papers on his desk, consulted his penciled memoranda, then thrust his hands deep into his pockets, with a long breath. Bewildered, and as if stupefied, he gazed again into Jadwin's face.

"My God" he murmured at last.

"Well, where are they going to get it?" Jadwin cried once more, his face suddenly scarlet.

"J.," faltered the broker, "J., I—I'm damned if I know."

And then, all in the same moment, the two men were on their feet. The event which all those past eleven months had been preparing was suddenly consummated, suddenly stood revealed, as though a veil had been ripped asunder, as though an explosion had crashed through the air upon them, deafening, blinding.

Jadwin sprang forward, gripping the broker by the shoulder.

"Sam," he shouted, "do you know—great God!—do you know what this means? Sam, we can corner the market!"

VIII

On that particular morning in April, the trading around the Wheat Pit on the floor of the Chicago Board of Trade began practically a full five minutes ahead of the stroke of the gong; and the throng of brokers and clerks that surged in and about the Pit itself was so great that it overflowed and spread out over the floor between the wheat and corn pits, ousting the traders in oats from their traditional ground. The market had closed the day before with May wheat at ninety-eight and five-eighths, and the Bulls had prophesied and promised that the magic legend "Dollar wheat" would be on the Western Union wires before another twenty-four hours.

The indications pointed to a lively morning's work. Never for an instant during the past six weeks had the trading sagged or languished. The air of the Pit was surcharged with a veritable electricity; it had the effervescence of champagne, or of a mountain-top at sunrise. It was buoyant, thrilling.

The "Unknown Bull" was to all appearance still in control; the whole market hung upon his horns; and from time to time one felt the sudden upward thrust, powerful, tremendous, as he flung the wheat up another notch. The "tailers"—the little Bulls—were radiant. In the dark, they hung hard by their unseen and mysterious friend who daily, weekly, was making them richer. The Bears were scarcely visible. The Great Bull in a single superb rush had driven them nearly out of the Pit. Growling, grumbling, they had retreated, and only at a distance dared so much as to bare a claw. Just the formidable lowering of the Great Bull's frontlet sufficed, so it seemed, to check their every move of aggression or resistance. And all the while Liverpool, Paris, Odessa, and Buda-Pesth clamored ever louder and louder for the grain that meant food to the crowded streets and barren farms of Europe.

A few moments before the opening Charles Cressler was in the public room, in the southeast corner of the building, where smoking was allowed, finishing his morning's cigar. But as he heard the distant striking of the gong, and the roar of the Pit as it began to get under way, with a prolonged rumbling trepidation like the advancing of a great flood, he threw his cigar away and stepped out from the public room to the main floor, going on toward the front windows. At the sample tables he filled his pockets with wheat, and once at the windows raised the sash and spread the pigeons' breakfast on the granite ledge.

While he was watching the confused fluttering of flashing wings, that on the instant filled the air in front of the window, he was all at once surprised to hear a voice at his elbow, wishing him good-morning.

"Seem to know you, don't they?"

Cressler turned about.

"Oh," he said. "Hullo, hullo—yes, they know me all right. Especially that red and white hen. She's got a lame wing since yesterday, and if I don't watch, the others would drive her off. The pouter brute yonder, for instance. He's a regular pirate. Wants all the wheat himself. Don't ever seem to get enough."

"Well," observed the newcomer, laconically, "there are others."

The man who spoke was about forty years of age. His name was Calvin Hardy Crookes. He was very small and very slim. His hair was yet dark, and his face—smooth-shaven and triangulated in shape, like a cat's—was dark as well. The eyebrows were thin and black, and the lips too were thin and were puckered a little, like the mouth of a tight-shut sack. The face was secretive, impassive, and cold.

The man himself was dressed like a dandy. His coat and trousers were of the very newest fashion. He wore a white waistcoat, drab gaiters, a gold watch and chain, a jeweled scarf pin, and a seal ring. From the top pocket of his coat protruded the fingertips of a pair of unworn red gloves.

"Yes," continued Crookes, unfolding a brand-new pocket handkerchief as he spoke. "There are others—who never know when they've got enough wheat."

"Oh, you mean the 'Unknown Bull.'"

"I mean the unknown damned fool," returned Calvin Crookes placidly.

There was not a trace of the snob about Charles Cressler. No one could be more democratic. But at the same time, as this interview proceeded, he could not fight down nor altogether ignore a certain qualm of gratified vanity. Had the matter risen to the realm of his consciousness, he would have hated himself for this. But it went no further than a vaguely felt increase of self-esteem. He seemed to feel more important in his own eyes; he would have liked to have his friends see him just now talking with this man. "Crookes was saying to-day—" he would observe when next he met an acquaintance. For C. H. Crookes was conceded to be the "biggest man" in La Salle Street. Not even the growing importance of the new and mysterious Bull could quite make the market forget the Great Bear. Inactive during all this trampling and goring in the Pit, there were yet those who, even as they strove against the Bull, cast uneasy glances over their shoulders, wondering why the Bear did not come to the help of his own.

"Well, yes," admitted Cressler, combing his short beard, "yes, he is a fool."

The contrast between the two men was extreme. Each was precisely what the other was not. The one, long, angular, loose-jointed; the other, tight, trig, small, and compact. The one osseous, the other sleek; the one stoop-shouldered, the other erect as a corporal of infantry.

But as Cressler was about to continue Crookes put his chin in the air.

"Hark!" he said. "What's that?"

For from the direction of the Wheat Pit had come a sudden and vehement renewal of tumult. The traders as one man were roaring in chorus. There were cheers; hats went up into the air. On the floor by the lowest step two brokers, their hands trumpetwise to their mouths, shouted at top voice to certain friends at a distance, while above them, on the topmost step of the Pit, a half-dozen others, their arms at fullest stretch, threw the hand signals that interpreted the fluctuations in the price to their associates in the various parts of the building. Again and again the cheers rose, violent hip-hip-hurrahs and tigers, while from all corners and parts of the floor men and boys came scurrying up. Visitors in the gallery leaned eagerly upon the railing. Over in the provision pit trading ceased for the moment, and all heads were turned toward the commotion of the wheat traders.

"Ah," commented Crookes, "they did get it there at last."

For the hand on the dial had suddenly jumped another degree, and not a messenger boy, not a porter, not a janitor, none whose work or life brought him in touch with the Board of Trade that did not feel the thrill. The news flashed out to the world on a hundred telegraph wires; it was called to a hundred offices across the telephone lines. From every doorway, even, as it seemed, from every window of the building, spreading thence all over the city, the State, the Northwest, the entire nation, sped the magic words, "Dollar wheat."

Crookes turned to Cressler.

"Can you lunch with me to-day—at Kinsley's? I'd like to have a talk with you."

And as soon as Cressler had accepted the invitation, Crookes, with a succinct nod, turned upon his heel and walked away.

At Kinsley's that day, in a private room on the second floor, Cressler met not only Crookes, but his associate Sweeny, and another gentleman by the name of Freye, the latter one of his oldest and best-liked friends.

Sweeny was an Irishman, florid, flamboyant, talkative, who spoke with a faint brogue, and who tagged every observation, argument, or remark with the phrase, "Do you understand me, gen'lemen?" Freye, a German-American, was a quiet fellow, very handsome, with black side whiskers and a humorous, twinkling eye. The three were

members of the Board of Trade, and were always associated with
the Bear forces. Indeed, they could be said to be its leaders. Between them, as Cressler afterward was accustomed to say, "they
could have bought pretty much all of the West Side."

And during the course of the luncheon these three, with a sim-
plicity and a directness that for the moment left Cressler breathless,
announced that they were preparing to drive the Unknown Bull
out of the Pit, and asked him to become one of the clique.

Crookes, whom Cressler intuitively singled out as the leader, did
not so much as open his mouth till Sweeny had talked himself
breathless, and all the preliminaries were out of the way. Then he
remarked, his eye as lifeless as the eye of a fish, his voice as ex-
pressionless as the voice of Fate itself:

"I don't know who the big Bull is, and I don't care a curse.
But he don't suit my book. I want him out of the market. We've
let him have his way now for three or four months. We figured we'd let him run to the dollar mark. The May option
closed this morning at a dollar and an eighth. . . . Now *we*
take hold."

"But," Cressler hastened to object, "you forget—I'm not a speculator."

Freye smiled, and tapped his friend on the arm.

"I guess, Charlie," he said, "that there won't be much speculating about this."

"Why, gen'lemen," cried Sweeny, brandishing a fork, "we're
going to sell him right out o' the market, so we are. Simply
flood out the son-of-a-gun—you understand me, gen'lemen?"

Cressler shook his head.

"No," he answered. "No, you must count me out. I quit speculating years ago. And, besides, to sell short on this kind of market
—I don't need to tell you what you risk."

"Risk hell!" muttered Crookes.

"Well, now, I'll explain to you, Charlie," began Freye.

The other two withdrew a little from the conversation. Crookes,
as ever monosyllabic, took himself off in a little while, and Sweeny,
his chair tipped back against the wall, his hands clasped behind his
head, listened to Freye explaining to Cressler the plans of the proposed clique and the lines of their attack.

He talked for nearly an hour and a half, at the end of which
time the lunch table was one litter of papers—letters, contracts,
warehouse receipts, tabulated statistics, and the like.

"Well," said Freye at length, "well, Charlie, do you see the game? What do you think of it?"

"It's about as ingenious a scheme as I ever heard of, Billy," answered Cressler. "You can't lose, with Crookes back of it."

"Well, then, we can count you in, hey?"

"Count nothing," declared Cressler, stoutly. "I don't speculate."

"But have you thought of this?" urged Freye, and he went over the entire proposition, from a fresh point of view, winding up with the exclamation: "Why, Charlie, we're going to make our everlasting fortunes."

"I don't want any everlasting fortune, Billy Freye," protested Cressler. "Look here, Billy. You must remember I'm a pretty old cock. You boys are all youngsters. I've got a little money left and a little business, and I want to grow old quiet-like. I had my fling, you know, when you boys were in knickerbockers. Now you let me keep out of all this. You get some one else."

"No, we'll be jiggered if we do," exclaimed Sweeny. "Say, are ye scared we can't buy that trade journal? Why, we have it in our pocket, so we have. D'ye think Crookes, now, couldn't make Bear sentiment with the public, with just the lift o' one forefinger? Why, he owns most of the commercial columns of the dailies already. D'ye think he couldn't swamp that market with sellin' orders in the shorter end o' two days? D'ye think we won't all hold together, now? Is that the bug in the butter? Sure, now, listen. Let me tell you—"

"You can't tell me anything about this scheme that you've not told me before," declared Cressler. "You'll win, of course. Crookes & Co. are like Rothschild—earthquakes couldn't budge 'em. But I promised myself years ago to keep out of the speculative market, and I mean to stick by it."

"Oh, get on with you, Charlie," said Freye, good-humoredly, "you're scared."

"Of what," asked Cressler, "speculating? You bet I am, and when you're as old as I am, and have been through three panics, and have known what it meant to have a corner bust under you, you'll be scared of speculating too."

"But suppose we can prove to you," said Sweeny, all at once, "that we're not speculating—that the other fellow, this fool Bull, is doing the speculating?"

"I'll go into anything in the way of legitimate trading," an-

swered Cressler, getting up from the table. "You convince me that
your clique is not a speculative clique, and I'll come in. But I
don't see how your deal can be anything else."

"Will you meet us here to-morrow?" asked Sweeny, as they got
into their overcoats.

"It won't do you any good," persisted Cressler.

"Well, will you meet us just the same?" the other insisted. And
in the end Cressler accepted.

On the steps of the restaurant they parted, and the two leaders
watched Cressler's broad, stooped shoulders disappear down the
street.

"He's as good as in already," Sweeny declared. "I'll fix him
to-morrow. Once a speculator, always a speculator. He was the
cock of the cow-yard in his day, and the thing is in the blood. He
gave himself clean, clean away when he let out he was afraid o'
speculating. You can't be afraid of anything that ain't got a hold
on you. Y' understand me, now?"

"Well," observed Freye, "we've got to get him in."

"Talk to me about that now," Sweeny answered. "I'm new to
some parts o' this scheme o' yours yet. Why is Crookes so keen
on having him in? I'm not so keen. We could get along without
him. He ain't so god-awful rich, y' know."

"No, but he's a solid, conservative cash grain man," answered
Freye, "who hasn't been associated with speculating for years.
Crookes has got to have that element in the clique before we can
approach Stires & Co. We may have to get a pile of money from
them, and they're apt to be scary and cautious. Cressler being in,
do you see, gives the clique a substantial, conservative character.
You let Crookes manage it. He knows his business."

"Say," exclaimed Sweeny, an idea occurring to him, "I thought
Crookes was going to put us wise to-day. He must know by now
who the Big Bull is."

"No doubt he does know," answered the other. "He'll tell us
when he's ready. But I think I could copper the individual. There
was a great big jag of wheat sold to Liverpool a little while ago
through Gretry, Converse & Co., who've been acting for Curtis
Jadwin for a good many years."

"Oh, Jadwin, hey? Hi! we're after big game now, I'm thinking."

"But look here," warned Freye. "Here's a point. Cressler is
not to know by the longest kind of chalk; anyhow not until he's so

far in he can't pull out. He and Jadwin are good friends, I'm told. Hello, it's raining a little. Well, I've got to be moving. See you at lunch to-morrow."

As Cressler turned into La Salle Street the light sprinkle of rain suddenly swelled to a deluge, and he had barely time to dodge into the portico of the Illinois Trust to escape a drenching. All the passers-by close at hand were making for the same shelter, and among these Cressler was surprised to see Curtis Jadwin, who came running up the narrow lane from the café entrance of the Grand Pacific Hotel.

"Hello! Hello, J.," he cried, when his friend came panting up the steps, "as the whale said to Jonah, 'Come in out of the wet.'"

The two friends stood a moment under the portico, their coat collars turned up, watching the scurrying in the street.

"Well," said Cressler, at last, "I see we got 'dollar wheat' this morning."

"Yes," answered Jadwin, nodding, "'dollar wheat.'"

"I suppose," went on Cressler, "I suppose you are sorry, now, that you're not in any more?"

"Oh, no," replied Jadwin, nibbling off the end of a cigar. "No, I'm—I'm just as well out of it."

"And it's for good and all this time, eh?"

"For good and all."

"Well," commented Cressler, "some one else has begun where you left off, I guess. This Unknown Bull, I mean. All the boys are trying to find out who he is. Crookes, though, was saying to me—Cal Crookes, you know—he was saying he didn't care who he was. Crookes is out of the market, too, I understand—and means to keep out, he says, till the Big Bull gets tired. Wonder who the Big Bull is."

"Oh, there isn't any Big Bull," blustered Jadwin. "There's simply a lot of heavy buying, or maybe there might be a ring of New York men operating through Gretry. I don't know; and I guess I'm like Crookes, I don't care—now that I'm out of the game. Real estate is too lively now to think of anything else; keeps me on the keen jump early and late. I tell you what, Charlie, this city isn't half grown yet. And do you know, I've noticed another thing —cities grow to the westward. I've got a building and loan association going, out in the suburbs on the West Side, that's a dandy. Well, looks as though the rain had stopped. Remember me to madam. So long, Charlie."

On leaving Cressler Jadwin went on to his offices in The Rook-ery, close at hand. But he had no more than settled himself at his desk, when he was called up on his telephone.

"Hello!" said a small, dry transformation of Gretry's voice. "Hello, is that you, J.? Well, in the matter of that cash wheat in Duluth, I've bought that for you."

"All right," answered Jadwin, then he added, "I guess we had better have a long talk now."

"I was going to propose that," answered the broker. "Meet me this evening at seven at the Grand Pacific. It's just as well that we're not seen together nowadays. Don't ask for me. Go right into the smoking-room. I'll be there. And, by the way, I shall ex-pect a reply from Minneapolis about half-past five this afternoon. I would like to be able to get at you at once when that comes in. Can you wait down for that?"

"Well, I *was* going home," objected Jadwin. "I wasn't home to dinner last night, and Mrs. Jadwin—"

"This is pretty important, you know," warned the broker. "And if I call you up on your residence telephone, there's always the chance of somebody cutting in and overhearing us."

"Oh, very well, then," assented Jadwin. "I'll call it a day. I'll get home for luncheon to-morrow. It can't be helped. By the way, I met Cressler this afternoon, Sam, and he seemed sort of suspicious of things, to me—as though he had an inkling—"

"Better hang up," came back the broker's voice. "Better hang up, J. There's big risk telephoning like this. I'll see you to-night. Good-by."

And so it was that about half an hour later Laura was called to the telephone in the library.

"Oh, not coming home at all to-night?" she cried blankly in re-sponse to Jadwin's message.

"It's just impossible, old girl," he answered.

"But why?" she insisted.

"Oh, business; this building and loan association of mine."

"Oh, I know it can't be that. Why don't you let Mr. Gretry manage your—"

But at this point Jadwin, the warning of Gretry still fresh in his mind, interrupted quickly:

"I must hang up now, Laura. Good-by. I'll see you to-morrow noon and explain it all to you. Good-by. . . . Laura. . . . Hello! . . . Are you there yet? . . . Hello, Hello!"

But Jadwin had heard in the receiver the rattle and click as of a tiny door closing. The receiver was silent and dead; and he knew that his wife, disappointed and angry, had "hung up" without saying good-by.

The days passed. Soon another week had gone by. The wheat market steadied down after the dollar mark was reached, and for a few days a calmer period intervened. Down beneath the surface, below the ebb and flow of the currents, the great forces were silently at work reshaping the "situation." Millions of dollars were beginning to be set in motion to govern the millions of bushels of wheat. At the end of the third week of the month Freye reported to Crookes that Cressler was "in," and promptly negotiations were opened between the clique and the great banking house of the Stires. But meanwhile Jadwin and Gretry, foreseeing no opposition, realizing the incalculable advantage that their knowledge of the possibility of a "corner" gave them, were, quietly enough, gathering in the grain. As early as the end of March Jadwin, as incidental to his contemplated corner of May wheat, had bought up a full half of the small supply of cash wheat in Duluth, Chicago, Liverpool and Paris—some twenty million bushels; and against this had sold short an equal amount of the July option. Having the actual wheat in hand, he could not lose. If wheat went up, his twenty million bushels were all the more valuable; if it went down, he covered his short sales at a profit. And all the while, steadily, persistently, he bought May wheat, till Gretry's book showed him to be possessed of over twenty million bushels of the grain deliverable for that month.

But all this took not only his every minute of time, but his every thought, his every consideration. He who had only so short a while before considered the amount of five million bushels burdensome, demanding careful attention, was now called upon to watch, govern, and control the tremendous forces latent in a line of forty million. At times he remembered the Curtis Jadwin of the spring before his marriage, the Curtis Jadwin who had sold a pitiful million on the strength of the news of the French import duty, and had considered the deal "big." Well, he was a different man since that time. Then he had been suspicious of speculation, had feared it even. Now he had discovered that there were in him powers, capabilities, and a breadth of grasp hitherto unsuspected. He could control the Chicago wheat market; and the man who could do that might well call himself "great," without presumption.

He knew that he overtopped them all—Gretry, the Crookes gang, the arrogant, sneering Bears, all the men of the world of the Board of Trade. He was stronger, bigger, shrewder than them all. A few days now would show," when they would all wake up to the fact that wheat, which they had promised to deliver before they had it in hand, was not to be got except from him—and at whatever price he chose to impose. He could exact from them a hundred dollars a bushel if he chose, and they must pay him the price or become bankrupts.

By now his mind was upon this one great fact—May Wheat—continually. It was with him the instant he woke in the morning. It kept him company during his hasty breakfast; in the rhythm of his horses' hoofs, as the team carried him down town, he heard "Wheat—wheat—wheat, wheat—wheat—wheat." No sooner did he enter La Salle Street than the roar of traffic came to his ears as the roar of the torrent of wheat which drove through Chicago from the Western farms to the mills and bakeshops of Europe. There at the foot of the street the torrent swirled once upon itself, forty million strong, in the eddy which he told himself he mastered. The afternoon waned, night came on. The day's business was to be gone over; the morrow's campaign was to be planned; little, unexpected side issues, a score of them, a hundred of them, cropped out from hour to hour; new decisions had to be taken each minute. At dinner time he left the office, and his horses carried him home again, while again their hoofs upon the asphalt beat out unceasingly the monotone of the one refrain, "Wheat—wheat—wheat, wheat—wheat—wheat." At dinner table he could not eat. Between each course he found himself going over the day's work, testing it, questioning himself, "Was this rightly done?" "Was that particular decision sound?" "Is there a loophole here?" "Just what was the meaning of that despatch?" After the meal the papers, contracts, statistics and reports which he had brought with him in his Gladstone bag were to be studied. As often as not Gretry called, and the two, shut in the library, talked, discussed, and planned till long after midnight.

Then at last, when he had shut the front door upon his lieutenant and turned to face the empty, silent house, came the moment's reaction. The tired brain flagged and drooped; exhaustion, like a weight of lead, hung upon his heels. But somewhere a hall clock struck, a single, booming note, like a gong—like the signal that would unchain the tempest in the Pit to-morrow morning. Wheat

— wheat — wheat, wheat — wheat — wheat. Instantly the jaded
senses braced again, instantly the wearied mind sprang to its post.
He turned out the lights, he locked the front door. Long since
the great house was asleep. In the cold, dim silence of the earliest
dawn Curtis Jadwin went to bed, only to lie awake, staring up into
the darkness, planning, devising new measures, reviewing the day's
doings, while the faint tides of blood behind the eardrums murmured ceaselessly to the overdriven brain, "Wheat—wheat—wheat,
wheat—wheat—wheat. Forty million bushels, forty million, forty
million."

Whole days now went by when he saw his wife only at breakfast
and at dinner. At times she was angry, hurt, and grieved that
he should leave her so much alone. But there were moments when
she was sorry for him. She seemed to divine that he was not all
to blame.

What Laura thought he could only guess. She no longer spoke
of his absorption in business. At times he thought he saw re-
proach and appeal in her dark eyes, at times anger and a pride
cruelly wounded. A few months ago this would have touched him.
But now he all at once broke out vehemently:

"You think I am wilfully doing this! You don't know, you
haven't a guess. I corner the wheat! Great heavens, it is the wheat
that has cornered me! The corner made itself. I happened to
stand between two sets of circumstances, and they made me do
what I've done. I couldn't get out of it now, with all the good will
in the world. Go to the theatre to-night with you and the Cresslers? Why, old girl, you might as well ask me to go to Jericho.
Let that Mr. Corthell take my place."

And very naturally this is what was done. The artist sent a
great bunch of roses to Mrs. Jadwin upon the receipt of her invitation, and after the play had the party to supper in his apartments, that overlooked the Lake Front. Supper over, he escorted
her, Mrs. Cressler, and Page back to their respective homes.

By a coincidence that struck them all as very amusing, he was
the only man of the party. At the last moment Page had received
a telegram from Landry. He was, it appeared, sick, and in bed.
The day's work on the Board of Trade had quite used him up for
the moment, and his doctor forbade him to stir out of doors. Mrs.
Cressler explained that Charlie had something on his mind these
days, that was making an old man of him.

"He don't ever talk shop with me," she said. "I'm sure he

hasn't been speculating, but he's worried and fidgety to beat all I
ever saw, this last week; and now this evening he had to take himself off to meet some customer or other at the Palmer House."

They dropped Mrs. Cressler at the door of her home, and then
went on to the Jadwins'.

"I remember," said Laura to Corthell, "that once before the
three of us came home this way. Remember? It was the night
of the opera. That was the night I first met Mr. Jadwin."

"It was the night of the Helmick failure," said Page, seriously,
"and the office buildings were all lit up. See," she added, as
they drove up to the house, "there's a light in the library, and it
must be nearly one o'clock. Mr. Jadwin is up yet."

Laura fell suddenly silent. When was it all going to end, and
how? Night after night her husband shut himself thus in the
library, and toiled on till early dawn. She enjoyed no companionship with him. Her evenings were long, her time hung with in-
supportable heaviness upon her hands.

"Shall you be at home?" inquired Corthell, as he held her hand
a moment at the door. "Shall you be at home to-morrow evening?
May I come and play to you again?"

"Yes, yes," she answered. "Yes, I shall be home. Yes, do
come."

Laura's carriage drove the artist back to his apartments. All
the way he sat motionless in his place, looking out of the window
with unseeing eyes. His cigarette went out. He drew another
from his case, but forgot to light it.

Thoughtful and abstracted he slowly mounted the stairway—the
elevator having stopped for the night—to his studio, let himself in,
and, throwing aside his hat and coat, sat down without lighting the
gas in front of the fireplace, where (the weather being even yet
sharp) an armful of logs smouldered on the flagstones.

His man, Evans, came from out an inner room to ask if he
wanted anything. Corthell got out of his evening coat, and Evans
brought him his smoking-jacket and set the little table with its long
tin box of cigarettes and ash trays at his elbow. Then he lighted
the tall lamp of corroded bronze, with its heavy silk shade, that
stood on a table in the angle of the room, drew the curtains, put a
fresh log upon the fire, held the tiny silver alcohol burner to Corthell while the latter lighted a fresh cigarette, and then with a murmured "Good-night, sir," went out, closing the door with the precaution of a depredator.

This suite of rooms, facing the Lake Front, was what Corthell called "home." Whenever he went away, he left it exactly as it was, in charge of the faithful Evans; and no matter how long he was absent, he never returned thither without a sense of welcome and relief. Even now, perplexed as he was, he was conscious of a feeling of comfort and pleasure as he settled himself in his chair.

The lamp threw a dull illumination about the room. It was a picturesque apartment, carefully planned. Not an object that had not been chosen with care and the utmost discrimination. The walls had been treated with copper leaf till they produced a sombre, iridescent effect of green and faint gold, that suggested the depth of a forest glade shot through with the sunset. Shelves bearing eighteenth-century books in seal brown tree calf—Addison, the "Spectator," Junius and Racine, Rochefoucauld and Pascal hung against it here and there. On every hand the eye rested upon some small masterpiece of art or workmanship. Now it was an antique portrait bust of the days of decadent Rome, black marble with a bronze tiara; now a framed page of a fourteenth-century version of "Li Quatres Filz d'Aymon," with an illuminated letter of miraculous workmanship; or a Renaissance gonfalon of silk, once white, but now brown with age, yet in the centre blazing with the escutcheon and quarterings of a dead queen. Between the windows stood an ivory statuette of the "Venus of the Heel," done in the days of the magnificent Lorenzo. An original Cazin, and a chalk drawing by Baudry hung against the wall close by, together with a bronze tablet by Saint Gaudens; while across the entire end of the room opposite the fireplace, worked in the tapestry of the best period of the northern French school, Halcyone, her arms already blossoming into wings, hovered over the dead body of Ceyx, his long hair streaming like seaweed in the blue waters of the Ægean.

For a long time Corthell sat motionless, looking into the fire. In an adjoining room a clock chimed the half-hour of one, and the artist stirred, passing his long fingers across his eyes.

After a long while he rose, and going to the fireplace, leaned an arm against the overhanging shelf, and resting his forehead against it, remained in that position, looking down at the smouldering logs.

"She is unhappy," he murmured at length. "It is not difficult to see that. . . . Unhappy and lonely. Oh, fool, fool, to have left her when you might have stayed! Oh, fool, fool, not to find the strength to leave her now when you should not remain!"

The following evening Corthell called upon Mrs. Jadwin. She was alone, as he usually found her. He had brought a book of poems with him, and instead of passing the evening in the art gallery, as they had planned, he read aloud to her from Rossetti. Nothing could have been more conventional than their conversation, nothing more impersonal. But on his way home one feature of their talk suddenly occurred to him. It struck him as significant; but of what he did not care to put into words. Neither he nor Laura had once spoken of Jadwin throughout the entire evening.

Little by little the companionship grew. Corthell shut his eyes, his ears. The thought of Laura, the recollection of their last evening together, the anticipation of the next meeting filled all his waking hours. He refused to think; he resigned himself to the drift of the current. Jadwin he rarely saw. But on those few occasions when he and Laura's husband met, he could detect no lack of cordiality in the other's greeting. Once even Jadwin had remarked:

"I'm very glad you have come to see Mrs. Jadwin, Corthell. I have to be away so much these days, I'm afraid she would be lonesome if it wasn't for some one like you to drop in now and then and talk art to her."

By slow degrees the companionship trended toward intimacy. At the various theatres and concerts he was her escort. He called upon her two or three times each week. At his studio entertainments Laura was always present. How—Corthell asked himself—did she regard the affair? She gave him no sign; she never intimated that his presence was otherwise than agreeable. Was this tacit acquiescence of hers an encouragement? Was she willing to *afficher* herself, as a married woman, with a cavalier? Her married life was intolerable, he was sure of that; her husband uncongenial. He told himself that she detested him.

Once, however, this belief was rather shocked by an unexpected and (to him) an inconsistent reaction on Laura's part. She had made an engagement with him to spend an afternoon in the Art Institute, looking over certain newly acquired canvases. But upon calling for her an hour after luncheon he was informed that Mrs. Jadwin was not at home. When next she saw him she told him that she had spent the entire day with her husband. They had taken an early train and had gone up to Geneva Lake to look over their country house, and to prepare for its opening, later on in the spring. They had taken the decision so unexpectedly that she had no time

to tell him of the change in her plans. Corthell wondered if she
had—as a matter of fact—forgotten all about her appointment with
him. He never quite understood the incident, and afterward asked
himself whether or no he could be so sure, after all, of the estrange-
ment between the husband and wife. He guessed it to be possible
that on this occasion Jadwin had suddenly decided to give himself
a holiday, and that Laura had been quick to take advantage of it.
Was it true, then, that Jadwin had but to speak the word to have
Laura forget all else? Was it true that the mere nod of his head
was enough to call her back to him? Corthell was puzzled. He
would not admit this to be true. She was, he was persuaded, a
woman of more spirit, of more pride than this would seem to
indicate. Corthell ended by believing that Jadwin had, in some way,
coerced her; though he fancied that for the few days immediately
following the excursion Laura had never been gayer, more alert,
more radiant.

But the days went on, and it was easy to see that his business
kept Jadwin more and more from his wife. Often now, Corthell
knew, he passed the night down town, and upon those occasions
when he managed to get home after the day's work, he was exhausted, worn out, and went to bed almost immediately after dinner.
More than ever now the artist and Mrs. Jadwin were thrown
together.

On a certain Sunday evening, the first really hot day of the year,
Laura and Page went over to spend an hour with the Cresslers,
and—as they were all wont to do in the old days before Laura's
marriage—the party "sat out on the front stoop." For a wonder,
Jadwin was able to be present. Laura had prevailed upon him to
give her this evening and the evening of the following Wednesday
—on which latter occasion she had planned that they were to take
a long drive in the park in the buggy, just the two of them, as it
had been in the days of their courtship.

Corthell came to the Cresslers' quite as a matter of course. He
had dined with the Jadwins at the great North Avenue house and
afterward the three, preferring to walk, had come down to the
Cresslers' on foot.

But evidently the artist was to see but little of Laura Jadwin
that evening. She contrived to keep by her husband continually.
She even managed to get him away from the others, and the two,
leaving the rest upon the steps, sat in the parlor of the Cresslers'
house, talking.

By and by, Laura, full of her projects, exclaimed:

"Where shall we go? I thought, perhaps, we would not have dinner at home, but you could come back to the house just a little— a little bit—early, and you could drive me out to the restaurant there in the park, and we could have dinner there, just as though we weren't married—just as though we were sweethearts again. Oh, I do hope the weather will be fine."

"Oh," answered Jadwin, "you mean Wednesday evening. Dear old girl, honestly, I—I don't believe I can make it after all. You see, Wednesday—"

Laura sat suddenly erect.

"But you said," she began, her voice faltering a little, "you said—"

"Honey, I know I did, but you must let me off this time again."

She did not answer. It was too dark for him to see her face; but, uneasy at her silence, he began an elaborate explanation. Laura, however, interrupted. Calmly enough, she said:

"Oh, that's all right. No, no, I don't mind. Of course, if you are busy."

"Well, you see, don't you, old girl?"

"Oh, yes, yes, I see," she answered. She rose.

"I think," she said, "we had better be going home. Don't you?"

"Yes, I do," he assented. "I'm pretty tired myself. I've had a hard day's work. I'm thirsty, too," he added, as he got up. "Would you like to have a drink of water, too?"

She shook her head, and while he disappeared in the direction of the Cresslers' dining-room, she stood alone a moment in the darkened room looking out into the street. She felt that her cheeks were hot. Her hands, hanging at her sides, shut themselves into tight fists.

"What, you are all alone?" said Corthell's voice, behind her.

She turned about quickly.

"I must be going," he said. "I came to say good-night." He held out his hand.

"Good-night," she answered, as she gave him hers. Then all at once she added:

"Come to see me again—soon, will you? Come Wednesday night."

And then, his heart leaping to his throat, Corthell felt her hand, as it lay in his, close for an instant firmly about his fingers.

"I shall expect you Wednesday then?" she repeated.

He crushed her hand in his grip, and suddenly bent and kissed it. "Good-night," she said, quietly. Jadwin's step sounded at the doorway.

"Good-night," he whispered, and in another moment was gone. During these days Laura no longer knew herself. At every hour she changed; her moods came and went with a rapidity that bewildered all those who were around her. At times her gayety filled the whole of her beautiful house; at times she shut herself in her apartments, denying herself to every one, and, her head bowed upon her folded arms, wept as though her heart was breaking, without knowing why.

For a few days a veritable seizure of religious enthusiasm held sway over her. She spoke of endowing a hospital, of doing church work among the "slums" of the city. But no sooner had her friends readjusted their points of view to suit this new development than she was off upon another tangent, and was one afternoon seen at the races, with Mrs. Gretry, in her showiest victoria, wearing a great flaring hat and a bouquet of crimson flowers.

She never repeated this performance, however, for a new fad took possession of her the very next day. She memorized the rôle of Lady Macbeth, built a stage in the ballroom at the top of the house, and, locking herself in, rehearsed the part, for three days uninterruptedly, dressed in elaborate costume, declaiming in chest tones to the empty room:

" 'The raven himself is hoarse that croaks the entrance of Duncan under my battlements.' "

Then, tiring of Lady Macbeth, she took up Juliet, Portia, and Ophelia; each with appropriate costumes, studying with tireless avidity, and frightening Aunt Wess' with her declaration that "she might go on the stage after all." She even entertained the notion of having Sheldon Corthell paint her portrait as Lady Macbeth.

As often as the thought of the artist presented itself to her she fought to put it from her. Yes, yes, he came to see her often, very often. Perhaps he loved her yet. Well, suppose he did? He had always loved her. It was not wrong to have him love her, to have him with her. Without his company, great heavens, her life would be lonely beyond words and beyond endurance. Besides, was it to be thought, for an instant, that she, she, Laura Jadwin, in her pitch of pride, with all her beauty, with her quick, keen mind, was to pine, to droop, to fade in oblivion and neglect? Was she to blame? Let those who neglected her look to it. Her youth was all with her yet, and all her power to attract, to compel admiration.

When Corthell came to see her on the Wednesday evening in question, Laura said to him, after a few moments' conversation in the drawing-room:

"Oh, you remember the picture you taught me to appreciate—the picture of the little pool in the art gallery, the one you called 'Despair'? I have hung it in my own particular room upstairs—my sitting-room—so as to have it where I can see it always. I love it now. But," she added, "I am not sure about the light. I think it could be hung to better advantage." She hesitated a moment, then, with a sudden, impulsive movement, she turned to him.

"Won't you come up with me, and tell me where to hang it?"

They took the little elevator to the floor above, and Laura led the artist to the room in question—her "sitting-room," a wide, airy place, the polished floor covered with deep skins, the walls wainscoted half-way to the ceiling in dull woods. Shelves of books were everywhere, together with potted plants and tall brass lamps. A long "Madeira" chair stood at the window which overlooked the park and lake, and near to it a great round table of San Domingo mahogany, with tea things and almost diaphanous china.

"What a beautiful room," murmured Corthell, as she touched the button in the wall that opened the current, "and how much you have impressed your individuality upon it. I should have known that you lived here. If you were thousands of miles away and I had entered here, I should have known it was yours—and loved it for such."

"Here is the picture," she said, indicating where it hung. "Doesn't it seem to you that the light is bad?"

But he explained to her that it was not so, and that she had but to incline the canvas a little more from the wall to get a good effect.

"Of course, of course," she assented, as he held the picture in place. "Of course. I shall have it hung over again to-morrow."

For some moments they remained standing in the centre of the room, looking at the picture and talking of it. And then, without remembering just how it had happened, Laura found herself leaning back in the Madeira chair, Corthell seated near at hand by the round table.

"I am glad you like my room," she said. "It is here that I spend most of my time. Often lately I have had my dinner here. Page goes out a great deal now, and so I am left alone occasionally. Last night I sat here in the dark for a long time. The house was so still, everybody was out—even some of the servants. It was so warm, I raised the windows and I sat here for hours looking out over the lake. I could hear it lapping and washing against the shore—almost like a sea. And it was so still, so still; and I was thinking of the time when I was a little girl back at Barrington, years and years ago, picking whortleberries down in the 'water lot,' and how I got lost once in the corn—the stalks were away above my head—and how happy I was when my father would take me up on the hay wagon. Ah, I was happy in those days—just a freckled, black-haired slip of a little girl, with my frock torn and my hands all scratched with the berry bushes."

She had begun by dramatizing, but by now she was acting—acting with all her histrionic power at fullest stretch, acting the part of a woman unhappy amid luxuries, who looked back with regret and with longing toward a joyous, simple childhood. She was sincere and she was not sincere. Part of her—one of those two Laura Jadwins who at different times, but with equal right, called themselves "I," knew just what effect her words, her pose, would have upon a man who sympathized with her, who loved her. But the other Laura Jadwin would have resented as petty, as even wrong, the insinuation that she was not wholly, thoroughly sincere. All that she was saying was true. No one, so she believed, ever was placed before as she was placed now. No one had ever spoken as now she spoke. Her chin upon one slender finger, she went on, her eyes growing wide:

"If I had only known then that those days were to be the happiest of my life. . . . This great house, all the beauty of it, and all this wealth, what does it amount to?" Her voice was the voice of Phèdre, and the gesture of lassitude with which she let her arms fall into her lap was precisely that which only the day before she had used to accompany Portia's plaint of

"—my little body is a-weary of this great world."

Yet, at the same time, Laura knew that her heart was genuinely aching with real sadness, and that the tears which stood in her eyes were as sincere as any she had ever shed.

"All this wealth," she continued, her head dropping back upon the cushion of the chair as she spoke, "what does it matter; for what does it compensate? Oh, I would give it all gladly, gladly, to be that little black-haired girl again, back in Squire Dearborn's water lot; with my hands stained with the whortleberries and the nettles in my fingers—and my little lover, who called me his beau-heart and bought me a blue hair ribbon, and kissed me behind the pump house."

"Ah," said Corthell, quickly and earnestly, "that is the secret. It was love—even the foolish boy and girl love—love that after all made your life sweet then."

She let her hands fall into her lap, and, musing, turned the rings back and forth upon her fingers.

"Don't you think so?" he asked, in a low voice.

She bent her head slowly, without replying. Then for a long moment neither spoke. Laura played with her rings. The artist, leaning forward in his chair, looked with vague eyes across the room. And no interval of time since his return, no words that had ever passed between them, had been so fraught with significance, so potent in drawing them together as this brief, wordless moment.

At last Corthell turned toward her.

"You must not think," he murmured, "that your life is with-out love now. I will not have you believe that."

But she made no answer.

"If you would only see," he went on. "If you would only con-descend to look, you would know that there is a love which has infolded your life for years. You have shut it out from you always. But it has been yours, just the same; it has lain at your door, it has looked—oh, God knows with what longing!—through your win-dows. You have never stirred abroad that it has not followed you. Not a footprint of yours that it does not know and cherish. Do you think that your life is without love? Why, it is all around you—all around you, but voiceless. It has no right to speak, it only has the right to suffer."

Still Laura said no word. Her head turned from him, she looked out of the window, and once more the seconds passed while neither spoke. The clock on the table ticked steadily. In the distance, through the open window, came the incessant, mournful wash of the lake. All around them the house was still. At length Laura sat upright in her chair.

"I think I will have this room done over while we are away this summer," she said. "Don't you think it would be effective if the wainscoting went almost to the ceiling?"

He glanced critically about the room.

"Very," he answered, briskly "There is no background so beautiful as wood."

"And I might finish it off at the top with a narrow shelf."

"Provided you promised not to put brass 'plaques' or pewter kitchen ware upon it."

"Do smoke," she urged him. "I know you want to. You will find matches on the table."

But Corthell, as he lighted his cigarette, produced his own match box. It was a curious bit of antique silver, which he had bought in a Viennese pawnshop, heart-shaped and topped with a small ducal coronet of worn gold. On one side he had caused his name to be engraved in small script. Now, as Laura admired it, he held it toward her.

"An old pouncet-box, I believe," he informed her, "or possibly it held an ointment for her finger nails." He spilled the matches into his hand. "You see the red stain still on the inside; and—smell," he added, as she took it from him. "Even the odor of the sulphur matches can not smother the quaint old perfume, distilled perhaps three centuries ago."

An hour later Corthell left her. She did not follow him further than the threshold of the room, but let him find his way to the front door alone.

When he had gone she returned to the room, and for a little while sat in her accustomed place by the window overlooking the park and the lake. Very soon after Corthell's departure she heard Page, Landry Court, and Mrs. Wessels come in; then at length rousing from her reverie she prepared for bed. But, as she passed the round mahogany table, on her way to her bedroom, she was aware of a little object lying upon it, near to where she had sat.

"Oh, he forgot it," she murmured, as she picked up Corthell's heart-shaped match box. She glanced at it a moment, indifferently; but her mind was full of other things. She laid it down again upon the table, and going on to her own room, went to bed.

Jadwin did not come home that night, and in the morning Laura presided at breakfast table in his place. Landry Court, Page, and Aunt Wess' were there; for occasionally nowadays, when the trio went to one of their interminable concerts or lectures, Landry stayed overnight at the house.

"Any message for your husband, Mrs. Jadwin?" inquired Landry, as he prepared to go downtown after breakfast. "I always see him in Mr. Gretry's office the first thing. Any message for him?"

"No," answered Laura, simply.

"Oh, by the way," spoke up Aunt Wess', "we met that Mr. Corthell on the corner last night, just as he was leaving. I was real sorry not to get home here before he left. I've never heard him play on that big organ, and I've been wanting to for ever so long. I hurried home last night, hoping I might have caught him before he left. I was regularly disappointed."

"That's too bad," murmured Laura, and then, for obscure reasons, she had the stupidity to add: "And we were in the art gallery the whole evening. He played beautifully."

Toward eleven o'clock that morning Laura took her usual ride, but she had not been away from the house quite an hour before she turned back.

All at once she had remembered something. She returned homeward, now urging Crusader to a flying gallop, now curbing him to his slowest ambling walk. That which had so abruptly presented itself to her mind was the fact that Corthell's match box—his name engraved across its front—still lay in plain sight upon the table in her sitting-room—the peculiar and particular place of her privacy.

It was so much her own, this room, that she had given orders that the servants were to ignore it in their day's routine. She looked after its order herself. Yet, for all that, the maids or the housekeeper often passed through it, on their way to the suite beyond, and occasionally Page or Aunt Wess' came there to read, in her absence. The family spoke of the place sometimes as the "upstairs sitting-room," sometimes simply as "Laura's room."

Now, as she cantered homeward, Laura had it vividly in her mind that she had not so much as glanced at the room before leaving the house that morning. The servants would not touch the place. But it was quite possible that Aunt Wess' or Page—

Laura, the blood mounting to her forehead, struck the horse sharply with her crop. The pettiness of the predicament, the small meanness of her situation struck across her face like the flagellations of tiny whips. That she should stoop to this! She who had held her head so high.

Abruptly she reined in the horse again. No, she would not hurry. Exercising all her self-control, she went on her way with deliberate slowness, so that it was past twelve o'clock when she dismounted under the carriage porch.

Her fingers clutched tightly about her crop, she mounted to her sitting-room and entered, closing the door behind her.

She went directly to the table, and then, catching her breath, with a quick, apprehensive sinking of the heart, stopped short. The little heart-shaped match box was gone, and on the couch in the corner of the room Page, her book fallen to the floor beside her, lay curled up and asleep.

A loop of her riding-habit over her arm, the toe of her boot tapping the floor nervously, Laura stood motionless in the centre of the room, her lips tight pressed, the fingers of one gloved hand drumming rapidly upon her riding-crop. She was bewildered, and an anxiety cruelly poignant, a dread of something she could not name, gripped suddenly at her throat.

Could she have been mistaken? Was it upon the table that she had seen the match box after all? If it lay elsewhere about the room, she must find it at once. Never had she felt so degraded as now, when, moving with such softness and swiftness as she could in her agitation command, she went here and there about the room, peering into the corners of her desk, searching upon the floor, upon the chairs, everywhere, anywhere; her face crimson, her breath failing her, her hands opening and shutting.

But the silver heart with its crown of worn gold was not to be found. Laura, at the end of half an hour, was obliged to give over searching. She was certain the match box lay upon the mahogany table when last she left the room. It had not been mislaid; of that she was now persuaded.

But while she sat at the desk, still in habit and hat, rummaging for the fourth time among the drawers and shelves, she was all at once aware, even without turning around, that Page was awake and watching her. Laura cleared her throat.

"Have you seen my blue note paper, Page?" she asked. "I want to drop a note to Mrs. Cressler, right away."

"No," said Page, as she rose from the couch. "No, I haven't seen it." She came toward her sister across the room. "I thought, maybe," she added, gravely, as she drew the heart-shaped match box from her pocket, "that you might be looking for this. I took it. I knew you wouldn't care to have Mr. Jadwin find it here."

Laura struck the little silver heart from Page's hand, with a violence that sent it spinning across the room, and sprang to her feet.

"You took it!" she cried. "You took it! How dare you! What do you mean? What do I care if Curtis should find it here? What's it to me that he should know that Mr. Corthell came up here. Of course he was here."

But Page, though very pale, was perfectly calm under her sister's outburst.

"If you didn't care whether any one knew that Mr. Corthell came up here," she said quietly, "why did you tell us this morning at breakfast that you and he were in the art gallery the whole evening? I thought," she added, with elaborate blandness, "I thought I would be doing you a service in hiding the match box."

"A service! You! What have I to hide?" cried Laura, almost inarticulate. "Of course I said we were in the art gallery the whole evening. So we were. We did—I do remember now—we did come up here for an instant, to see how my picture hung. We went down stairs again at once. We did not so much as sit down. He was not in the room two minutes."

"He was here," returned Page, "long enough to smoke half a dozen times." She pointed to a silver pen tray on the mahogany table, hidden behind a book rack and littered with the ashes and charred stumps of some five or six cigarettes.

"Really, Laura," Page remarked. "Really, you manage very awkwardly, it seems to me."

Laura caught her riding-crop in her right hand.

"Don't you—don't you make me forget myself," she cried, breathlessly."

"It seems to me," observed Page, quietly, "that you've done that long since, yourself."

Laura flung the crop down and folded her arms.

"Now," she cried, her eyes blazing and riveted upon Page's. "Now, just what do you mean? Sit down," she commanded, flinging a hand toward a chair, "sit down and tell me just what you mean by all this."

But Page remained standing. She met her sister's gaze without wavering.

"Do you want me to believe," she answered, "that it made no difference to you that Mr. Corthell's match safe was here?"

"Not the least," exclaimed Laura. "Not the least."

"Then why did you search for it so when you came in. I was not asleep all of the time. I saw you."

"Because," answered Laura, "because—I—because—" Then all at once she burst out afresh: "Have I got to answer to you for what I do? Have I got to explain? All your life long you've pretended to judge your sister. Now you've gone too far. Now I forbid it—from this day on. What I do is my affair; I'll ask no-

body's advice. I'll do as I please, do you understand?" The tears
sprang to her eyes, the sobs strangled in her throat. "I'll do as I
please, as I please," and with the words she sank down in the chair
by her desk and struck her bare knuckles again and again upon the
open lid, crying out through her tears and her sobs, and from
between her tight-shut teeth: "I'll do as I please, do you understand? As I please, as I please! I will be happy. I will, I will, I
will!"

"Oh, darling, dearest—" cried Page, running forward. But
Laura, on her feet once more, thrust her back.

"Don't touch me," she cried. "I hate you!" She put her fists
to her temples and, her eyes closed, rocked herself to and fro.
"Don't you touch me. Go away from me; go away from me. I
hate you; I hate you all. I hate this house, I hate this life. You
are all killing me. Oh, my God, if I could only die!"

She flung herself full length upon the couch, face downward.
Her sobs shook her from head to foot.

Page knelt at her side, an arm about her shoulder, but to all her
sister's consolations Laura, her voice muffled in her folded arms,
only cried:

"Let me alone, let me alone. Don't touch me."

For a time Page tried to make herself heard; then, after a moment's reflection, she got up and drew out the pin in Laura's hat.
She took off the hat, loosened the scarf around Laura's neck, and
then deftly, silently, while her sister lay inert and sobbing beneath
her hands, removed the stiff, tight riding-habit. She brought a
towel dipped in cold water from the adjoining room and bathed
Laura's face and hands.

But her sister would not be comforted, would not respond to her
entreaties or caresses. The better part of an hour went by; Page,
knowing her sister's nature, in the end held her peace, waiting for
the paroxysm to wear itself out.

After a while Laura's weeping resolved itself into long, shuddering breaths, and at length she managed to say, in a faint, choked
voice:

"Will you bring me the cologne from my dressing-table, honey?
My head aches so."

And, as Page ran toward the door, she added: "And my hand
mirror, too. Are my eyes all swollen?"

And that was the last word upon the subject between the two
sisters.

But the evening of the same day, between eight and nine o'clock, while Laura was searching the shelves of the library for a book with which to while away the long evening that she knew impended, Corthell's card was brought to her.

"I am not at home," she told the servant. "Or—wait," she added. Then, after a moment's thought, she said: "Very well. Show him in here."

Laura received the artist, standing very erect and pale upon the great white rug before the empty fireplace. Her hands were behind her back when he came in, and as he crossed the room she did not move.

"I was not going to see you at first," she said. "I told the servant I was not at home. But I changed my mind—I wanted to say something to you."

He stood at the other end of the fireplace, an elbow upon an angle of the massive mantel, and as she spoke the last words he looked at her quickly. As usual, they were quite alone. The heavy, muffling curtain of the doorway shut them in effectually.

"I have something to say to you," continued Laura. Then quietly enough, she said:

"You must not come to see me any more."

He turned abruptly away from her, and for a moment did not speak. Then at last, his voice low, he faced her again and asked:

"Have I offended?"

She shook her head.

"No," he said quietly. "No, I knew it was not that." There was a long silence. The artist looked at the floor, his hand slowly stroking the back of one of the big leather chairs.

"I knew it must come," he answered at length, "sooner or later. You are right—of course. I should not have come back to America. I should not have believed that I was strong enough to trust myself. Then"—he looked at her steadily. His words came from his lips, one by one, very slowly. His voice was hardly more than a whisper. "Then, I am—never to see you—again. . . . Is that it?"

"Yes."

"Do you know what that means for me?" he cried. "Do you realize—" he drew in his breath sharply. "Never to see you again! To lose even the little that is left to me now. I—I—" He turned away quickly and walked to a window and stood a moment, his back turned, looking out, his hands clasped behind him. Then, after a long moment, he faced about. His manner was quiet again, his voice very low.

"But before I go," he said, "will you answer me, at least, this—it can do no harm now that I am to leave you—answer me, and I know you will speak the truth: Are you happy, Laura?"

She closed her eyes.

"You have not the right to know."

"You are not happy," he declared. "I can see it, I know it. If you were, you would have told me so. . . . If I promise you," he went on; "if I promise you to go away now, and never try to see you again, may I come once more—to say good-by?"

She shook her head.

"It is so little for you to grant," he pleaded, "and it is so incalculably much for me to look forward to in the little time that yet remains. I do not ask to see you alone. I will not harass you with any heroics."

"Oh, what good will it do," she cried, wearily, "for you to see me again? Why will you make me more unhappy than I am? Why did you come back?"

"Because," he answered, steadily, "because I love you more than—he partly raised a clinched fist and let it fall slowly upon the back of the chair, "more than any other consideration in the world."

"Don't!" she cried. "You must not. Never, never say that to me again. Will you go—please?"

"Oh, if I had not gone from you four years ago!" he cried. "If I had only stayed then! Not a day of my life since that I have not regretted it. You could have loved me then. I know it, I know it, and, God forgive me, but I know you could love me now—"

"Will you go?" she cried.

"I dare you to say you could not," he flashed out.

Laura shut her eyes and put her hands over her ears. "I could not, I could not," she murmured, monotonously, over and over again. "I could not; I could not."

She heard him start suddenly, and opened her eyes in time to see him come quickly toward her. She threw out a defensive hand, but he caught the arm itself to him and, before she could resist, had kissed it again and again through the interstices of the lace sleeve. Upon her bare shoulder she felt the sudden passion of his lips.

A quick, sharp gasp, a sudden qualm of breathlessness wrenched

through her, to her very finger tips, with a fierce leap of the blood,
a wild bound of the heart.

She tore back from him with a violence that rent away the lace
upon her arm, and stood off from him, erect and rigid, a fine, delicate, trembling vibrating through all her being. On her pale cheeks
the color suddenly flamed.

"Go, go," was all she had voice to utter.

"And may I see you once more—only once?"

"Yes, yes, anything, only go, go—if you love me!"

He left the room. In another moment she heard the front door
close.

"Curtis," said Laura, when next she saw her husband, "Curtis,
you could not—stay with me, that last time. Remember? When
we were to go for a drive. Can you spend this evening with me?
Just us two, here at home—or I'll go out with you. I'll do anything you say." She looked at him steadily an instant. "It is not—
not easy for a woman to ask—for me to ask favors like this. Each
time I tell myself it will be the last. I am—you must remember
this, Curtis, I am—perhaps I am a little proud. Don't you see?"

They were at the breakfast table again. It was the morning after
Laura had given Corthell his dismissal. As she spoke Jadwin
brought his hand down upon the table with a bang.

"You bet I will," he exclaimed; "you bet I'll stay with you to-
night. Business can go to the devil! And we won't go out, either;
we'll stay right here. You get something to read to me, and we'll
have one of our old evenings again. We—"

All at once Jadwin paused, laid down his knife and fork, and
looked strangely to and fro about the room.

"We'll have one of our old evenings again," he repeated slowly.

"What is it, Curtis?" demanded his wife. "What is the matter?"

"Oh—nothing," he answered.

"Why, yes there was. Tell me."

"No, no. I'm all right now," he returned, briskly enough.

"No," she insisted. "You must tell me. Are you sick?"

He hesitated a moment. Then:

"Sick?" he queried. "No, indeed. But—I'll tell you. Since a
few days I've had," he put his fingers to his forehead between his
eyes, "I've had a queer sensation right there. It comes and goes."

"A headache?"

"N-no. It's hard to describe. A sort of numbness. Sometimes
it's as though there was a heavy iron cap—a helmet on my head.

And sometimes it—I don't know, it seems as if there were fog, or something or other, inside. I'll take a good long rest this summer, as soon as we can get away. Another month or six weeks, and I'll have things ship-shape and so as I can leave them. Then we'll go up to Geneva, and, by Jingo, I'll loaf." He was silent for a moment, frowning, passing his hand across his forehead and winking his eyes. Then, with a return of his usual alertness, he looked at his watch.

"Hi!" he exclaimed. "I must be off. I won't be home to dinner to-night. But you can expect me by eight o'clock, sure. I promise I'll be here on the minute."

But as he kissed his wife good-by, Laura put her arms about his neck.

"Oh, I don't want you to leave me at all, ever, ever! Curtis, love me, love me always, dear. And be thoughtful of me and kind to me. And remember that you are all I have in the world; you are father and mother to me, and my dear husband as well. I know you do love me; but there are times— Oh," she cried, suddenly, "if I thought you did not love me—love me better than anything, anything—I could not love you; Curtis, I could not, I could not. No, no," she cried, "don't interrupt. Hear me out. Maybe it is wrong of me to feel that way, but I'm only a woman, dear. I love you, but I love Love, too. Women are like that, right or wrong, weak or strong, they must be—must be loved above everything else in the world. Now go, go to your business; you mustn't be *late*. Hark, there is Jarvis with the team. Go now. Good-by, good-by, and I'll expect you at eight."

True to his word, Jadwin reached his home that evening promptly at the promised hour. As he came into the house, however, the door-man met him in the hall, and, as he took his master's hat and stick, explained that Mrs. Jadwin was in the art gallery, and that she had said he was to come there at once.

Laura had planned a little surprise. The art gallery was darkened. Here and there behind the dull-blue shades a light burned low. But one of the movable reflectors that were used to throw a light upon the pictures in the topmost rows was burning brilliantly. It was turned from Jadwin as he entered, and its broad cone of intense white light was thrown full upon Laura, who stood over against the organ in the full costume of "Théodora."

For an instant Jadwin was taken all aback.

"What the devil!" he ejaculated, stopping short in the doorway.

Laura ran forward to him, the chains, ornaments, and swinging
pendants chiming furiously as she moved.

"I did surprise you, I did surprise you," she laughed. "Isn't it
gorgeous?" She turned about before him, her arms raised. "Isn't
it superb? Do you remember Bernhardt—and that scene in the
Emperor Justinian's box at the amphitheatre? Say now that your
wife isn't beautiful. I am, am I not?" she exclaimed defiantly, her
head raised. "Say it, say it."

"Well, what for a girl!" gasped Jadwin, "to get herself up—"

"Say that I am beautiful," commanded Laura.

"Well, I just about guess you are," he cried.

"The most beautiful woman you have ever known?" she insisted. Then on the instant added: "Oh, I may be really as plain
as a kitchen maid, but you must believe that I am not. I would
rather be ugly and have you think me beautiful, than to be the most
beautiful woman in the world and have you think me plain. Tell
me—am I not the most beautiful woman you ever saw?"

"The most beautiful I ever saw," he repeated fervently. "But—
Lord, what will you do next? What ever put it into your head to
get into this rig?"

"Oh, I don't know. I just took the notion. You've seen me in
every one of my gowns. I sent down for this, this morning, just
after you left. Curtis, if you hadn't made me love you enough to
be your wife, Laura Dearborn would have been a great actress. I
feel it in my finger tips. Ah!" she cried, suddenly flinging up her
head till the pendants of the crown flashed again. "I could have
been magnificent. You don't believe it. Listen. This is Athalia—
the queen in the Old Testament, you remember."

"Hold on," he protested. "I thought you were this Théodora
person."

"I know—but never mind. I am anything I choose. Sit down;
listen. It's from Racine's 'Athalie,' and the wicked queen has had
this terrible dream of her mother, Jezebel. It's French, but I'll
make you see."

And "taking stage," as it were, in the centre of the room, Laura
began:

> "*Son ombre vers mon lit a paru se baisser*
> *Et moi, je lui tendais les mains pour l'embrasser;*
> *Mais je n'ai plus trouvé qu'un horrible mélange*
> *D'os et de chair meurtris et trainés dans la fange,*
> *Des lambeaux pleins de sang, et des membres affreux*
> *Que les chiens dévorants se disputaient entre eux.*"

"Great God!" exclaimed Jadwin, ignorant of the words, yet, in spite of himself, carried away by the fury and passion of her rendering.

Laura struck her palms together.

"Just what 'Abner' says," she cried. "The very words."

"Abner?"

"In the play. I knew I could make you feel it."

"Well, well," murmured her husband, shaking his head, bewildered even yet. "Well, it's a strange wife I've got here."

"When you've realized that," returned Laura, "you've just begun to understand me."

Never had he seen her gayer. Her vivacity was bewildering.

"I wish," she cried, all at once, "I wish I had dressed as 'Carmen,' and I would have danced for you. Oh, and you could have played the air for me on the organ. I have the costume upstairs now. Wait! I will, I will! Sit right where you are—no, fix the attachment to the organ while I'm gone. Oh, be gay with me to-night," she cried, throwing her arms around him. "This is my night, isn't it? And I am to be just as foolish as I please."

With the words she ran from the room, but was back in an incredibly short time, gowned as Bizet's cigarette girl, a red rose in her black hair, castanets upon her fingers.

Jadwin began the bolero.

"Can you see me dance, and play at the same time?"

"Yes, yes. Go on. How do you know anything about a Spanish dance?"

"I learned it long ago. I know everything about anything I choose, to-night. Play, play it *fast*."

She danced as though she would never tire, with the same force of passion that she had thrown into "Athalie." Her yellow skirt was a flash of flame spurting from the floor, and her whole body seemed to move with the same wild, untamed spirit as a tongue of fire. The castanets snapped like the crackling of sparks; her black mantilla was a hovering cloud of smoke. She was incarnate flame, capricious and riotous, elusive and dazzling.

Then suddenly she tossed the castanets far across the room and dropped upon the couch, panting and laughing.

"There," she cried, "now I feel better. That had to come out. Come over here and sit by me. Now, maybe you'll admit that I can dance, too."

"You sure can," answered Jadwin, as she made a place for him among the cushions. "That was wonderful. But, at the same time, old girl, I wouldn't—wouldn't—"

"Wouldn't what?"

"Well, do too much of that. It's sort of overwrought—a little—and unnatural. I like you best when you are your old self, quiet, and calm, and dignified. It's when you are quiet that you are at your best. I didn't know you had this streak in you. You are that excitable to-night!"

"Let me be so then. It's myself, for the moment, whatever it is. But now I'll be quiet. Now we'll talk. Have you had a hard day? Oh, and did your head bother you again?"

"No, things were a little easier down town to-day. But that queer feeling in my head did come back as I was coming home—and my head aches a little now, besides."

"Your head aches!" she exclaimed. "Let me do something for it. And I've been making it worse with all my foolishness."

"No, no; that's all right," he assured her. "I tell you what we'll do. I'll lie down here a bit, and you play something for me. Something quiet. I get so tired down there in La Salle Street, Laura, you don't know."

And while he stretched out at full length upon the couch, his wife, at the organ, played the music she knew he liked best—old songs, "Daisy Dean," "Lord Lovell," "When Stars Are in the Quiet Sky," and "Open Thy Lattice to Me."

When at length she paused, he nodded his head with pleasure. "That's pretty," he said. "Ah, that *is* blame pretty. Honey, it's just like medicine to me," he continued, "to lie here, quiet like this, with the lights low, and have my dear girl play those old, old tunes. My old governor, Laura, used to play that 'Open the Lattice to Me,' that and 'Father, oh, Father, Come Home with Me Now'—used to play 'em on his fiddle." His arm under his head, he went on, looking vaguely at the opposite wall. "Lord love me, I can see that kitchen in the old farmhouse as plain! The walls were just logs and plaster, and there were upright supports in each corner, where we used to measure our heights—we children. And the fire-place was there," he added, gesturing with his arm, "and there was the wood box, and over here was an old kind of dresser with drawers, and the torty-shell cat always had her kittens under there. Honey, I was happy then. Of course, I've got you now, and that's all the difference in the world. But you're the only thing that does make a difference. We've got a fine place and a mint of money, I suppose—and I'm proud of it. But I don't know. . . . If they'd let me be and put us two—just you and me—back in the old house with the bare floors and the rawhide chairs and the shuck beds, I guess we'd manage. If you're happy, you're happy; that's about the size of it. And sometimes I think that we'd be happier— you and I—chumming along shoulder to shoulder, poor an' working hard, than making big money an' spending big money, why—oh, I don't know . . . if you're happy, that's the thing that counts, and if all this stuff," he kicked out a careless foot at the pictures, the heavy hangings, the glass cabinets of bibelots, "if all this stuff stood in the way of it—well—it could go to the devil! That's not poetry maybe, but it's the truth."

Laura came over to where her husband lay, and sat by him, and took his head in her lap, smoothing his forehead with her long white hands.

"Oh, if I could only keep you like this always," she murmured. "Keep you untroubled, and kind, and true. This is my husband again. Oh, you are a man, Curtis; a great, strong, kind-hearted man, with no little graces, nor petty culture, nor trivial fine speeches, nor false sham, imitation polish. I love you. Ah, I love you, love you, dear!"

"Old girl!" said Jadwin, stroking her hand.

"Do you want me to read to you now?" she asked.

"Just this is pretty good, it seems to me."

As he spoke, there came a step in the hall and a knock.

Laura sat up, frowning.

"I told them I was not to be disturbed," she exclaimed under her breath. Then, "Come in," she called.

"Mr. Gretry, sir," announced the servant. "Said he wished to see you at once, sir."

"Tell him," cried Laura, turning quickly to Jadwin, "tell him you're not at home—that you can't see him."

"I've got to see him," answered Jadwin, sitting up. "He wouldn't come here himself unless it was for something important."

"Can I come in, J.?" spoke the broker, from the hall. And even through the thick curtains they could hear how his voice rang with excitement and anxiety.

"Can I come in? I followed the servant right up, you see. I know—"

"Yes, yes. Come in," answered Jadwin. Laura, her face flushing, threw a fold of the couch cover over her costume as Gretry, his hat still on his head, stepped quickly into the room.

Jadwin met him half way, and Laura from her place on the couch heard the rapidly spoken words between the general and his lieutenant.

"Now we're in for it!" Gretry exclaimed.

"Yes—well?" Jadwin's voice was as incisive and quick as the fall of an axe.

"I've just found out," said Gretry, "that Crookes and his crowd are going to take hold to-morrow. There'll be hell to pay in the morning. They are going to attack us the minute the gong goes."

"Who's with them?"

"I don't know; nobody does. Sweeny, of course. But he has a gang back of him—besides, he's got good credit with the banks. I told you you'd have to fight him sooner or later."

"Well, we'll fight him, then. Don't get scared. Crookes ain't the Great Mogul."

"Holy Moses, I'd like to know who is, then."

"*I* am. And he's got to know it. There's not room for Crookes and me in this game. One of us two has got to control this market. If he gets in my way, by God, I'll smash him!"

"Well, then, J., you and I have got to do some tall talking to-night. You'd better come down to the Grand Pacific Hotel right away. Court is there already. It was him, nervy little cuss, that found out about Crookes. Can you come now, at once? Good-evening, Mrs. Jadwin. I'm sorry to take him from you, but business is business."

No, it was not. To the wife of the great manipulator, listening with a sinking heart to this courier from the front, it was battle. The Battle of the Streets was again in array. Again the trumpet sounded, again the rush of thousands of feet filled all the air. Even here, here in her home, her husband's head upon her lap, in the quiet and stillness of her hour, the distant rumble came to her ears. Somewhere, far off there in the darkness of the night, the great forces were manœuvring for position once more. To-morrow would come the grapple, and one or the other must fall—her husband or the enemy. How keep him to herself when the great conflict impended? She knew how the thunder of the captains and the shoutings appealed to him. She had seen him almost leap to his arms out of her embrace. He was all the man she had called him, and less strong, less eager, less brave, she would have loved him less.

Yet she had lost him again, lost him at the very moment she believed she had won him back.

"Don't go, don't go," she whispered to him, as he kissed her good-by. "Oh, dearest, don't go! This was my evening."

"I must, I must, Laura. Good-by, old girl. Don't keep me—see, Sam is waiting."

He kissed her hastily twice.

"Now, Sam," he said, turning toward the broker.

"Good-night, Mrs. Jadwin."

"Good-by, old girl."

They turned toward the door.

"You see, young Court was down there at the bank, and he noticed that checks—"

The voices died away as the hangings of the entrance fell to place. The front door clashed and closed.

Laura sat upright in her place, listening, one fist pressed against her lips.

There was no more noise. The silence of the vast empty house widened around her at the shutting of the door as the ripples widen on a pool with the falling of the stone. She crushed her knuckles tighter and tighter over her lips, she pressed her fingers to her eyes, she slowly clasped and reclasped her hands, listening for what she did not know. She thought of her husband hurrying away from her, ignoring her and her love for him in the haste and heat of battle. She thought of Corthell, whom she had sent from her, forever, shutting his love from out her life.

Crushed, broken, Laura laid herself down among the cushions, her face buried in her arm. Above her and around her rose the dimly lighted gallery, lowering with luminous shadows. Only a point or two of light illuminated the place. The gold frames of the pictures reflected it dully; the massive organ pipes, just outlined in faint blurs of light, towered far into the gloom above. The whole place, with its half-seen gorgeous hangings, its darkened magnificence, was like a huge, dim interior of Byzantium.

Lost, beneath the great height of the dome, and in the wide reach of the floor space, in her foolish finery of bangles, silks, high comb, and little rosetted slippers, Laura Jadwin lay half hidden among the cushions of the couch. If she wept, she wept in silence, and the muffling stillness of the lofty gallery was broken but once, when a cry, half whisper, half sob, rose to the deaf, blind darkness.

"Oh, now I am alone, alone, alone!"

IX

"WELL, that's about all then, I guess," said Gretry at last, as he pushed back his chair and rose from the table.

He and Jadwin were in a room on the third floor of the Grand Pacific Hotel, facing Jackson Street. It was three o'clock in the morning. Both men were in their shirt-sleeves; the table at which they had been sitting was scattered over with papers, telegraph blanks, and at Jadwin's elbow stood a lacquer tray filled with the stumps of cigars and burned matches, together with one of the hotel pitchers of ice water.

"Yes," assented Jadwin, absently, running through a sheaf of telegrams, "that's all we can do—until we see what kind of a game Crookes means to play. I'll be at your office by eight."

"Well," said the broker, getting into his coat, "I guess I'll go to my room and try to get a little sleep. I wish I could see how we'll be to-morrow night at this time."

Jadwin made a sharp movement of impatience.

"Damnation, Sam, aren't you ever going to let up croaking? If you're afraid of this thing, get out of it. Haven't I got enough to bother me?"

"Oh, say! Say, hold on, hold on, old man," remonstrated the broker, in an injured voice. "You're terrible touchy sometimes, J., of late. I was only trying to look ahead a little. Don't think I want to back out. You ought to know me by this time, J."

"There, there, I'm sorry, Sam," Jadwin hastened to answer, getting up and shaking the other by the shoulder. "I *am* touchy these days. There's so many things to think of, and all at the same time. I do get nervous. I never slept one little wink last night—and you know the night before I didn't turn in till two in the morning."

"Lord, you go swearing and damning round here like a pirate sometimes, J.," Gretry went on. "I haven't heard you cuss before in twenty years. Look out, now, that I don't tell on you to your Sunday-school superintendents."

"I guess they'd cuss, too," observed Jadwin, "if they were long forty million wheat, and had to know just where every hatful of it was every second of the time. It was all very well for us to whoop about swinging a corner that afternoon in your office. But the real thing—well, you don't have any trouble keeping awake. Do you suppose we can keep the fact of our corner dark much longer?"

"I fancy not," answered the broker, putting on his hat and thrusting his papers into his breast pocket. "If we bust Crookes, it'll come out—and it won't matter then. I think we've got all the shorts there are."

"I'm laying particularly for Dave Scannel," remarked Jadwin. "I hope he's in up to his neck, and if he is, by the Great Horn Spoon, I'll bankrupt him, or my name is not Jadwin! I'll wring him bone-dry. If I once get a twist of that rat, I won't leave him hide nor hair to cover the wart he calls his heart."

"Why, what all has Scannel ever done to you?" demanded the other, amazed.

"Nothing, but I found out the other day that old Hargus—poor old, broken-backed, half-starved Hargus—I found out that it was Scannel that ruined him. Hargus and he had a big deal on, you know—oh, ages ago—and Scannel sold out on him. Great God, it was the dirtiest, damnedest treachery I ever heard of! Scannel made his pile, and what's Hargus now? Why, he's a scarecrow. And he has a little niece that he supports, heaven only knows how. I've seen her, and she's pretty as a picture. Well, that's all right; I'm going to carry fifty thousand wheat for Hargus, and I've got another scheme for him, too. By God, the poor old boy won't go hungry again if I know it! But if I lay my hands on Scannel—if we catch him in the corner—holy, suffering Moses, but I'll make him squeal!"

Gretry nodded, to say he understood and approved.

"I guess you've got him," he remarked. "Well, I must get to bed. Good-night, J."

"Good-night, Sam. See you in the morning."

And before the door of the room was closed, Jadwin was back at the table again. Once more, painfully, toilfully, he went over his plans, retesting, altering, recombining, his hands full of lists, of despatches, and of endless columns of memoranda. Occasionally he murmured fragments of sentences to himself. "H'm . . . I must look out for that. . . . They can't touch us there. . . . The annex of that Nickel Plate elevator will hold— let's see . . . half a million. . . . If I buy the grain within five days after arrival I've got to pay storage, which is, let's see—three-quarters of a cent times eighty thousand. . . ."

An hour passed. At length Jadwin pushed back from the table, drank a glass of ice water, and rose, stretching.

"Lord, I must get some sleep," he muttered.

He threw off his clothes and went to bed, but even as he composed himself to sleep, the noises of the street in the awakening city invaded the room through the chink of the window he had left open. The noises were vague. They blended easily into a far-off murmur; they came nearer; they developed into a cadence:

"Wheat-wheat-wheat, wheat-wheat-wheat."

Jadwin roused up. He had just been dropping off to sleep. He rose and shut the window, and again threw himself down. He was weary to death; not a nerve of his body that did not droop and flag. His eyes closed slowly. Then, all at once, his whole body twitched sharply in a sudden spasm, a simultaneous recoil of every muscle. His heart began to beat rapidly, his breath failed him. Broad awake, he sat up in bed.

"H'm!" he muttered. "That was a start—must have been dreaming, surely."

Then he paused, frowning, his eyes narrowing; he looked to and fro about the room, lighted by the subdued glow that came in through the transom from a globe in the hall outside. Slowly his hand went to his forehead.

With almost the abruptness of a blow, that strange, indescribable sensation had returned to his head. It was as though he were struggling with a fog in the interior of his brain; or again it was a numbness, a weight, or sometimes it had more of the feeling of a heavy, tight-drawn band across his temples.

"Smoking too much, I guess," murmured Jadwin. But he knew this was not the reason, and as he spoke, there smote across his face the first indefinite sensation of an unnamed fear.

He gave a quick, short breath, and straightened himself, passing his hands over his face.

"What the deuce," he muttered, "does this mean?"

For a long moment he remained sitting upright in bed, looking from wall to wall of the room. He felt a little calmer. He shrugged his shoulders impatiently.

"Look here," he said to the opposite wall, "I guess I'm not a schoolgirl, to have nerves at this late date. High time to get to sleep, if I'm to mix things with Crookes to-morrow."

But he could not sleep. While the city woke to its multitudinous life below his windows, while the gray light of morning drowned the yellow haze from the gas jet that came through the transom, while the "early call" alarms rang in neighboring rooms, Curtis Jadwin lay awake, staring at the ceiling, now concentrating his thoughts upon the vast operation in which he found himself engaged, following out again all its complexities, its inconceivable ramifications, or now puzzling over the inexplicable numbness, the queer, dull weight that descended upon his brain so soon as he allowed its activity to relax.

By five o'clock he found it intolerable to remain longer in bed; he rose, bathed, ordered his breakfast, and, descending to the office of the hotel, read the earliest editions of the morning papers for half an hour.

Then, at last, as he sat in the corner of the office deep in an armchair, the tired shoulders began to droop, the wearied head to nod. The paper slipped from his fingers, his chin sank upon his collar.

To his ears the early clamor of the street, the cries of newsboys, the rattle of drays came in a dull murmur. It seemed to him that very far off a great throng was forming. It was menacing, shouting. It stirred, it moved, it was advancing. It came galloping down the street, shouting with insensate fury; now it was at the corner, now it burst into the entrance of the hotel. Its clamor was deafening, but intelligible. For a thousand, a million, forty million voices were shouting in cadence:

"Wheat-wheat-wheat, wheat-wheat-wheat."

Jadwin woke abruptly, half starting from his chair. The morning sun was coming in through the windows, the clock above the hotel desk was striking seven, and a waiter stood at his elbow, saying:

"Your breakfast is served, Mr. Jadwin."

He had no appetite. He could eat nothing but a few mouthfuls of toast, and long before the appointed hour he sat in Gretry's office, waiting for the broker to appear, drumming on the arm of his chair, plucking at the buttons of his coat, and wondering why it was that every now and then all the objects in his range of vision seemed to move slowly back and stand upon the same plane.

By degrees he lapsed into a sort of lethargy, a wretched counterfeit of sleep, his eyes half closed, his breath irregular. But, such as it was, it was infinitely grateful. The little, over-driven cogs and wheels of the mind, at least, moved more slowly. Perhaps by and by this might actually develop into genuine, blessed oblivion.

But there was a quick step outside the door. Gretry came in.

"Oh, J.! Here already, are you? Well, Crookes will begin to sell at the very tap of the bell."

"He will, hey?" Jadwin was on his feet. Instantly the jaded nerves braced taut again; instantly the tiny machinery of the brain spun again at its fullest limit. "He's going to try to sell us out, is he? All right. We'll sell, too. We'll see who can sell the most—Crookes or Jadwin."

"Sell! You mean buy, of course."

"No, I don't. I've been thinking it over since you left last night. Wheat is worth exactly what it is selling for this blessed day. I've not inflated it up one single eighth yet; Crookes thinks I have. Good Lord, I can read him like a book! He thinks I've boosted the stuff above what it's worth, and that a little shove will send it down. He can send it down to ten cents if he likes, but it'll jump back like a rubber ball. I'll sell bushel for bushel with him as long as he wants to keep it up."

"Heavens and earth, J.," exclaimed Gretry, with a long breath, "the risk is about as big as holding up the Bank of England. You are depreciating the value of about forty million dollars' worth of your property with every cent she breaks."

"You do as I tell you—you'll see I'm right," answered Jadwin. "Get your boys in here, and we'll give 'em the day's orders."

The "Crookes affair"—as among themselves the group of men who centred about Jadwin spoke of it—was one of the sharpest fights known on the Board of Trade for many a long day. It developed with amazing unexpectedness and was watched with breathless interest from every produce exchange between the oceans.

It occupied every moment of each morning's session of the Board of Trade for four furious, never-to-be-forgotten days. Promptly at half-past nine o'clock on Tuesday morning Crookes began to sell May wheat short, and instantly, to the surprise of every Pit trader on the floor, the price broke with his very first attack. In twenty minutes it was down half a cent. Then came the really big surprise of the day. Landry Court, the known representative of the firm which all along had fostered and encouraged the rise in the price, appeared in the Pit, and instead of buying, upset all precedent and all calculation by selling as freely as the Crookes men themselves. For three days the battle went on. But to the outside world—even to the Pit itself—it seemed less a battle than a rout. The "Unknown Bull" was down, was beaten at last.

He had inflated the price of the wheat, he had backed a false, an artificial, and unwarrantable boom, and now he was being broken. Ah, Crookes knew when to strike. Here was the great general— the real leader who so long had held back.

By the end of the Friday session, Crookes and his clique had sold five million bushels, "going short," promising to deliver wheat that they did not own, but expected to buy at low prices. The market that day closed at ninety-five.

Friday night, in Jadwin's room in the Grand Pacific, a conference was held between Gretry, Landry Court, two of Gretry's most trusted lieutenants, and Jadwin himself. Two results issued from this conference. One took the form of a cipher cable to Jadwin's Liverpool agent, which, translated, read: "Buy all wheat that is offered till market advances one penny." The other was the general order issued to Landry Court and the four other Pit traders for the Gretry-Converse house, to the effect that in the morning they were to go into the Pit and, making no demonstration, begin to buy back the wheat they had been selling all the week. Each of them was to buy one million bushels. Jadwin had, as Gretry put it, "timed Crookes to a split second," foreseeing the exact moment when he would make his supreme effort. Sure enough, on that very Saturday Crookes was selling more freely than ever, confident of breaking the Bull ere the closing gong should ring.

But before the end of the morning wheat was up two cents. Buying orders had poured in upon the market. The price had stiffened almost of itself. Above the indicator upon the great dial there seemed to be an invisible, inexplicable magnet that lifted it higher and higher, for all the strenuous efforts of the Bears to drag it down.

A feeling of nervousness began to prevail. The small traders, who had been wild to sell short during the first day of the movement, began on Monday to cover a little here and there.

"Now," declared Jadwin that night, "now's the time to open up all along the line *hard*. If we start her with a rush to-morrow morning, she'll go to a dollar all by herself."

Tuesday morning, therefore, the Gretry-Converse traders bought another five million bushels. The price under this stimulus went up with the buoyancy of a feather. The little shorts, more and more uneasy, and beginning to cover by the scores, forced it up even higher.

The nervousness of the "crowd" increased. Perhaps, after all,

Crookes was not so omnipotent.   Perhaps, after all, the Unknown
Bull had another fight in him.   Then the "outsiders" came into the
market.   All in a moment all the traders were talking "higher
prices."   Everybody now was as eager to buy as, a week before,
they had been eager to sell.   The price went up by convulsive
bounds.   Crookes dared not buy, dared not purchase the wheat
to make good his promises of delivery, for fear of putting up the
price on himself higher still.   Dismayed, chagrined, and humiliated,
he and his clique sat back inert, watching the tremendous reaction,
hoping against hope that the market would break again.

But now it became difficult to get wheat at all.   All of a sudden nobody was selling.   The buyers in the Pit commenced to bid
against each other, offering a dollar and two cents.   The wheat did
not "come out."   They bid a dollar two and a half, a dollar two and
five-eighths; still no wheat.   Frantic, they shook their fingers in the
very faces of Landry Court and the Gretry traders, shouting: "A
dollar, two and seven-eighths!   A dollar, three!   Three and an
eighth!   A quarter!   Three-eighths!   A half!"   But the others
shook their heads.   Except on extraordinary advances of a whole
cent at a time, there was no wheat for sale.

At the last-named price Crookes acknowledged defeat.   Somewhere in his big machine a screw had been loose.   Somehow he had
miscalculated.   So long as he and his associates sold and sold and
sold, the price would go down.   The instant they tried to cover
there was no wheat for sale, and the price leaped up again with an
elasticity that no power could control.

He saw now that he and his followers had to face a loss of
several cents a bushel on each one of the five million they had
sold.   They had not been able to cover one single sale, and the situation was back again exactly as before his onslaught, the Unknown
Bull in securer control than ever before.

But Crookes had, at last, begun to suspect the true condition of
affairs, and now that the market was hourly growing tighter and
more congested, his suspicion was confirmed.   Alone, locked in
his private office, he thought it out, and at last remarked to
himself:

"Somebody has a great big line of wheat that is not on the
market at all.   Somebody has got all the wheat there is.   I guess I
know his name.   I guess the visible supply of May wheat in the
Chicago market is cornered."

This was at a time when the price stood at a dollar and one

cent. Crookes—who from the first had managed and handled the operations of his confederates—knew very well that if he now bought in all the wheat his clique had sold short, the price would go up long before he could complete the deal. He said nothing to the others, further than that they should "hold on a little longer, in the hopes of a turn," but very quietly he began to cover his own personal sales—his share of the five million sold by his clique. Foreseeing the collapse of his scheme, he got out of the market; at a loss, it was true, but still no more than he could stand. If he "held on a little longer, in the hopes of a turn," there was no telling how deep the Bull would gore him. This was no time to think much about "obligations." It had got to be "every man for himself" by now.

A few days after this Crookes sat in his office in the building in La Salle Street that bore his name. It was about eleven o'clock in the morning. His dry, small, beardless face creased a little at the corners of the mouth as he heard the ticker chattering behind him. He knew how the tape read. There had been another flurry on the Board that morning, not half an hour since, and wheat was up again. In the last thirty-six hours it had advanced three cents, and he knew very well that at that very minute the "boys" on the floor were offering nine cents over the dollar for the May option—and not getting it. The market was in a tumult. He fancied he could almost hear the thunder of the Pit as it swirled. All La Salle Street was listening and watching, all Chicago, all the nation, all the world. Not a "factor" on the London 'Change who did not turn an ear down the wind to catch the echo of this turmoil, not an *agent de change* in the peristyle of the Paris Bourse, who did not strain to note the every modulation of its mighty diapason.

"Well," said the little voice of the man-within-the-man, who in the person of Calvin Harry Crookes sat listening to the ticker in his office, "well, let it roar. It sure can't hurt C. H. C."

"Can you see Mr. Cressler?" said the clerk at the door.

He came in with a hurried, unsteady step. The long, stooping figure was unkempt; was, in a sense, unjointed, as though some support had been withdrawn. The eyes were deep-sunk, the bones of the face were gaunt and bare; and from moment to moment the man swallowed quickly and moistened his lips.

Crookes nodded as his ally came up, and one finger raised, pointed to a chair. He himself was impassive, calm. He did not move. Taciturn as ever, he waited for the other to speak.

"I want to talk with you, Mr. Crookes," began Cressler hurriedly. "I—I made up my mind to it day before yesterday, but I put it off. I had hoped that things would come our way. But I can't delay now. . . . Mr. Crookes, I can't stand this any longer. I must get out of the clique. I haven't the ready money to stand this pace."

There was a silence. Crookes neither moved nor changed expression. His small eyes fixed upon the other, he waited for Cressler to go on.

"I might remind you," Cressler continued, "that when I joined your party I expressly stipulated that our operations should not be speculative."

"You knew—" began Crookes.

"Oh, I have nothing to say," Cressler interrupted. "I did know. I knew from the first it was to be speculation. I tried to deceive myself. I—well, this don't interest you. The point is I must get out of the market. I don't like to go back on you others"—Cressler's fingers were fiddling with his watch chain—"I don't like to—I mean to say you must let me out. You must let me cover—at once. I am—very nearly bankrupt now. Another half-cent raise, and I'm done for. It will take as it is—my—my—all my ready money—all my savings for the last ten years to buy in my wheat."

"Let's see. How much did I sell for you?" demanded Crookes. "Five hundred thousand?"

"Yes, five hundred thousand at ninety-eight—and we're at a dollar nine now. It's an eleven-cent jump. I—I can't stand another eighth. I must cover at once."

Crookes, without answering, drew his desk telephone to him.

"Hello!" he said after a moment. "Hello . . . Buy five hundred May, at the market, right away."

He hung up the receiver and leaned back in his chair.

"They'll report the trade in a minute," he said. "Better wait and see."

Cressler stood at the window, his hands clasped behind his back, looking down into the street. He did not answer. The seconds passed, then the minutes. Crookes turned to his desk and signed a few letters, the scrape of his pen the only noise to break the silence of the room. Then at last he observed:

"Pretty bum weather for this time of year."

Cressler nodded. He took off his hat, and pushed the hair back from his forehead with a slow, persistent gesture; then as the ticker began to tick again, he faced around quickly, and, crossing the room, ran the tape through his fingers.

"God," he muttered, between his teeth, "I hope your men didn't lose any time. It's up again."

There was a step at the door, and as Crookes called to come in the office messenger entered and put a slip of paper into his hands. Crookes looked at it, and pushed it across the desk toward Cressler.

"There you are," he observed. "That's your trade. Five hundred May, at a dollar ten. You were lucky to get it at that—or at any price."

"Ten!" cried the other as he took the paper.

Crookes turned away again, and glanced indifferently over his letters. Cressler laid the slip carefully down upon the ledge of the desk, and though Crookes did not look up, he could almost feel how the man braced himself, got a grip of himself, put all his resources to the stretch to meet this blow squarely in the front.

"And I said another eighth would bust me," Cressler remarked, with a short laugh. "Well," he added, grimly, "it looks as though I were busted. I suppose, though, we must all expect to get the knife once in a while—mustn't we? Well, there goes fifty thousand dollars of my good money."

"I can tell you who's got it, if you care to know," answered Crookes. "It's a pewter quarter to Government bonds that Gretry, Converse & Co. sold that wheat to you. They've got about all the wheat there is."

"I know, of course, they've been heavy buyers—for this Unknown Bull they talk so much about."

"Well, he ain't Unknown to me," declared Crookes. "I know him. It's Curtis Jadwin. He's the man we've been fighting all along, and all hell's going to break loose down here in three or four days. He's cornered the market."

"Jadwin! You mean J.—Curtis—my friend?"

Crookes grunted an affirmative.

"But—why, he told me he was out of the market—for good."

Crookes did not seem to consider that the remark called for any useless words. He put his hands in his pockets and looked at Cressler.

"Does he know?" faltered Cressler. "Do you suppose he could have heard that I was in this clique of yours?"

"Not unless you told him yourself."

Cressler stood up, clearing his throat.

"I have not told him, Mr. Crookes," he said. "You would do
me an especial favor if you would keep it from the public, from
everybody, from Mr. Jadwin, that I was a member of this ring."

Crookes swung his chair around and faced his desk.

"Hell! You don't suppose I'm going to talk, do you?"

"Well. . . . Good-morning, Mr. Crookes."

"Good-morning."

Left alone, Crookes took a turn the length of the room. Then
he paused in the middle of the floor, looking down thoughtfully at
his trim, small feet.

"Jadwin!" he muttered. "Hm! . . . Think you're boss of
the boat now, don't you? Think I'm done with you, hey? Oh, yes,
you'll run a corner in wheat, will you? Well, here's a point for
your consideration, Mr. Curtis Jadwin, 'Don't get so big that all
the other fellows can see you—they throw bricks.'"

He sat down in his chair, and passed a thin and delicate hand
across his lean mouth.

"No," he muttered, "I won't try to kill you any more. You've
cornered wheat, have you? All right. . . . Your own wheat,
my smart Aleck, will do all the killing I want."

Then at last the news of the great corner, authoritative, definite,
went out over all the country, and promptly the figure and name
of Curtis Jadwin loomed suddenly huge and formidable in the eye
of the public. There was no wheat on the Chicago market. He,
the great man, the "Napoleon of La Salle Street," had it all. He
sold it or hoarded it, as suited his pleasure. He dictated the price
to those men who must buy it of him to fill their contracts. His
hand was upon the indicator of the wheat dial of the Board of
Trade, and he moved it through as many or as few of the degrees
of the circle as he chose.

The newspapers, not only of Chicago, but of every city in the
Union, exploited him for "stories." The history of his corner, how
he had effected it, its chronology, its results, were told and retold,
till his name was familiar in the homes and at the firesides of un-
counted thousands. "Anecdotes" were circulated concerning him,
interviews—concocted for the most part in the editorial rooms—
were printed. His picture appeared. He was described as a cool,
calm man of steel, with a cold and calculating gray eye, "piercing
as an eagle's"; as a desperate gambler, bold as a buccaneer, his eye
black and fiery—a veritable pirate; as a mild, small man with a
weak chin and a deprecatory demeanor; as a jolly and roistering

"high roller," addicted to actresses, suppers, and to bathing in champagne.

In the Democratic press he was assailed as little better than a thief, vituperated as an oppressor of the people, who ground the faces of the poor, and battened in the luxury wrung from the toiling millions. The Republican papers spoke solemnly of the new era of prosperity upon which the country was entering, referred to the stimulating effect of the higher prices upon capitalized industry, and distorted the situation to an augury of a sweeping Republican victory in the next Presidential campaign.

Day in and day out Gretry's office, where Jadwin now fixed his headquarters, was besieged. Reporters waited in the anteroom for whole half days to get but a nod and a word from the great man. Promoters, inventors, small financiers, agents, manufacturers, even "crayon artists" and horse dealers, even tailors and yacht builders rubbed shoulders with one another outside the door marked "Private."

Farmers from Iowa or Kansas, come to town to sell their little quotas of wheat at the prices they once had deemed impossible, shook his hand on the street, and urged him to come out and see "God's own country."

But once, however, an entire deputation of these wheat growers found their way into the sanctum. They came bearing a presentation cup of silver, and their spokesman, stammering and horribly embarrassed in unwonted broadcloth and varnished boots, delivered a short address. He explained that all through the Middle West, all through the wheat belts, a great wave of prosperity was rolling because of Jadwin's corner. Mortgages were being paid off, new and improved farming implements were being bought, new areas seeded, new live stock acquired. The men were buying buggies again, the women parlor melodeons, houses and homes were going up; in short, the entire farming population of the Middle West was being daily enriched. In a letter that Jadwin received about this time from an old fellow living in "Bates Corners," Kansas, occurred the words:

"—and, sir, you must know that not a night passes that my little girl, now going on seven, sir, and the brightest of her class in the county seat grammar school, does not pray to have God bless Mister Jadwin, who helped papa save the farm."

If there was another side, if the brilliancy of his triumph yet threw a shadow behind it, Jadwin could ignore it. It was far from him, he could not see it. Yet for all this a story came to him about this time that for long would not be quite forgotten. It came through Corthell, but very indirectly, passed on by a dozen mouths before it reached his ears.

It told of an American, an art student, who at the moment was on a tramping tour through the north of Italy. It was an ugly story. Jadwin pished and pshawed, refusing to believe it, condemning it as ridiculous exaggeration, but somehow it appealed to an uncompromising sense of the probable; it rang true.

"And I met this boy," the student had said, "on the highroad, about a kilometre outside of Arezzo. He was a fine fellow of twenty or twenty-one. He knew nothing of the world. England he supposed to be part of the mainland of Europe. For him Cavour and Mazzini were still alive. But when I announced myself American, he roused at once.

"'Ah, American,' he said. 'We know of your compatriot, then, here in Italy—this Jadwin of Chicago, who has bought all the wheat. We have no more bread. The loaf is small as the fist, and costly. We can not buy it, we have no money. For myself, I do not care. I am young. I can eat lentils and cress. But'—and here his voice was a whisper—'but my mother—my mother!'"

"It's a lie!" Jadwin cried. "Of course it's a lie. Good God, if I were to believe every damned story the papers print about me these days I'd go insane."

Yet when he put up the price of wheat to a dollar and twenty cents, the great flour mills of Minnesota and Wisconsin stopped grinding, and finding a greater profit in selling the grain than in milling it threw their stores upon the market. Though the bakers did not increase the price of their bread as a consequence of this, the loaf—even in Chicago, even in the centre of that great Middle West that weltered in the luxury of production—was smaller, and from all the poorer districts of the city came complaints, protests, and vague grumblings of discontent.

On a certain Monday, about the middle of May, Jadwin sat at Gretry's desk (long since given over to his use) in the office on the ground floor of the Board of Trade, swinging nervously back and forth in the swivel chair, drumming his fingers upon the arms, and glancing continually at the clock that hung against the opposite wall. It was about eleven in the morning. The Board of Trade vibrated with the vast trepidation of the Pit, that for two hours had spun and sucked, and guttered and disgorged just overhead.

The waiting-room of the office was more than usually crowded. Parasites of every description polished the walls with shoulder and elbow. Millionaires and beggars jostled one another about the doorway. The vice-president of a bank watched the door of the private office covertly; the traffic manager of a railroad exchanged yarns with a group of reporters while waiting his turn.

As Gretry, the great man's lieutenant, hurried through the ante-room, conversation suddenly ceased, and half a dozen of the more impatient sprang forward. But the broker pushed his way through the crowd, shaking his head, excusing himself as best he might, and entering the office closed the door behind him.

At the clash of the lock Jadwin started half-way from his chair, then recognizing the broker, sank back with a quick breath.

"Why don't you knock, or something, Sam?" he exclaimed. "Might as well kill a man as scare him to death. Well, how goes it?"

"All right. I've fixed the warehouse crowd—and we just about 'own' the editorial and news sheets of these papers." He threw a memorandum down upon the desk. "I'm off again now. Got an appointment with the Northwestern crowd in ten minutes. Has Hargus or Scannel shown up yet?"

"Hargus is always out in your customers' room," answered Jadwin. I can get him whenever I want him. But Scannel has not shown up yet. I thought when we put up the price again Friday we'd bring him in. I thought you'd figured out that he couldn't stand that rise."

"He can't stand it," answered Gretry. "He'll be in to see you to-morrow or next day."

"To-morrow or next day won't do," answered Jadwin. "I want to put the knife into him to-day. You go out there on the floor and put the price up another cent. That will bring him, or I'll miss my guess."

Gretry nodded. "All right," he said, "it's your game. Shall I see you at lunch?"

"Lunch! I can't eat. But I'll drop around and hear what the Northwestern people had to say to you."

A few moments after Gretry had gone Jadwin heard the ticker on the other side of the room begin to chatter furiously; and at the same time he could fancy that the distant thunder of the Pit grew suddenly more violent, taking on a sharper, shriller note. He looked at the tape. The one-cent rise had been effected.

"You will hold out, will you, you brute?" muttered Jadwin. "See how you like that now." He took out his watch. "You'll be running in to me in just about ten minutes' time."

He turned about, and, calling a clerk, gave orders to have Hargus found and brought to him.

When the old fellow appeared Jadwin jumped up and gave him his hand as he came slowly forward.

His rusty top hat was in his hand; from the breast pocket of his faded and dirty frock coat a bundle of ancient newspapers protruded. His shoestring tie straggled over his frayed shirt front, while at his wrist one of his crumpled cuffs, detached from the sleeve, showed the bare, thin wrist between cloth and linen, and incumbered the fingers in which he held the unlighted stump of a fetid cigar.

Evidently bewildered as to the cause of this summons, he looked up perplexed at Jadwin as he came up, out of his dim, red-lidded eyes.

"Sit down, Hargus. Glad to see you," called Jadwin.

"Hey?"

The voice was faint and a little querulous.

"I say, sit down. Have a chair. I want to have a talk with you. You ran a corner in wheat once yourself."

"Oh. . . . Wheat."

"Yes, your corner. You remember?"

"Yes. Oh, that was long ago. In seventy-eight it was—the September option. And the Board made wheat in the cars 'regular.' "

His voice trailed off into silence, and he looked vaguely about on the floor of the room, sucking in his cheeks, and passing the edge of one large, osseous hand across his lips.

"Well, you lost all your money that time, I believe. Scannel, your partner, sold out on you."

"Hey? It was in seventy-eight. . . . The secretary of the Board announced our suspension at ten in the morning. If the Board had not voted to make wheat in the cars 'regular'—"

He went on and on, in an impassive monotone, repeating, word for word, the same phrases he had used for so long that they had lost all significance.

"Well," broke in Jadwin, at last, "it was Scannel, your partner, did for you. Scannel, I say. You know Dave Scannel."

The old man looked at him confusedly. Then, as the name

forced itself upon the atrophied brain, there flashed, for one instant, into the pale, blurred eye, a light, a glint, a brief, quick spark of an old, long-forgotten fire. It gleamed there an instant, but the next sank again.

Plaintively, querulously he repeated:

"It was in seventy-eight. . . . I lost three hundred thousand dollars."

"How's your little niece getting on?" at last demanded Jadwin.

"My little niece—you mean Lizzie? . . . Well and happy, well and happy. I—I got"—he drew a thick bundle of dirty papers from his pocket, envelopes, newspapers, circulars, and the like—"I—I—I got, I got her picture here somewheres."

"Yes, yes, I know, I know," cried Jadwin. "I've seen it. You showed it to me yesterday, you remember."

"I—I got it here somewheres . . . somewheres," persisted the old man, fumbling and peering, and as he spoke the clerk from the doorway announced:

"Mr. Scannel."

This latter was a large, thick man, red-faced, with white, short whiskers of an almost wiry texture. He had a small, gimlet-like eye, enormous, hairy ears, wore a "sack" suit, a highly polished top hat, and entered the office with a great flourish of manner and a defiant trumpeting, "Well, how do, Captain?"

Jadwin nodded, glancing up under his scowl.

"Hello!" he said.

The other subsided into a chair, and returned scowl for scowl.

"Oh, well," he muttered, "if that's your style."

He had observed Hargus sitting by the other side of the desk, still fumbling and mumbling in his dirty memoranda, but he gave no sign of recognition. There was a moment's silence, then in a voice from which all the first bluffness was studiously excluded, Scannel said:

"Well, you've rung the bell on me. I'm a sucker. I know it. I'm one of the few hundred other God-damned fools that you've managed to catch out shooting snipe. Now what I want to know is, how much is it going to cost me to get out of your corner? What's the figure? What do you say?"

"I've got a good deal to say?" remarked Jadwin, scowling again.

But Hargus had at last thrust a photograph into his hands.

"There it is," he said. "That's it. That's Lizzie."

Jadwin took the picture without looking at it, and as he continued to speak, held it in his fingers, and occasionally tapped it upon the desk.

"I know. I know, Hargus," he answered. "I got a good deal to say, Mr. David Scannel. Do you see this old man here?"

"Oh-h, cut it out!" growled the other.

"It's Hargus. You know him very well. You used to know him better. You and he together tried to swing a great big deal in September wheat once upon a time. Hargus! I say, Hargus!"

The old man looked up.

"Here's the man we were talking about—Scannel, you remember. Remember Dave Scannel, who was your partner in seventy-eight? Look at him. This is him now. He's a rich man now. Remember Scannel?"

Hargus, his bleared old eyes blinking and watering, looked across the desk at the other.

"Oh, what's the game?" exclaimed Scannel. "I ain't here on exhibition, I guess. I—"

But he was interrupted by a sharp, quick gasp that all at once issued from Hargus's trembling lips. The old man said no word, but he leaned far forward in his chair, his eyes fixed upon Scannel, his breath coming short, his fingers dancing against his chin.

"Yes, that's him, Hargus," said Jadwin. "You and he had a big deal on your hands a long time ago," he continued, turning suddenly upon Scannel, a pulse in his temple beginning to beat. "A big deal, and you sold him out—"

"It's a lie!" cried the other.

Jadwin beat his fist upon the arm of his chair. His voice was almost a shout as he answered:

"*You—sold—him—out*. I know you. I know the kind of bug you are. You ruined him to save your own dirty hide, and all his life since poor old Hargus has been living off the charity of the boys down here, pinched and hungry and neglected, and getting on, God knows how; yes, and supporting his little niece, too, while you, you have been loafing about your clubs, and sprawling on your steam yachts, and dangling round after your kept women—on the money you stole from him."

Scannel squared himself in his chair, his little eyes twinkling.

"Look here," he cried, furiously, "I don't take that kind of talk from the best man that ever wore shoe-leather. Cut it out, understand? Cut it out."

Jadwin's lower jaw set with a menacing click; aggressive, masterful, he leaned forward.

"You interrupt me again," he declared, "and you'll go out of that door a bankrupt. You listen to me and take my orders. That's what you're here to-day for. If you think you can get your wheat somewheres else, suppose you try."

Scannel sullenly settled himself in his place. He did not answer. Hargus, his eye wandering again, looked distressfully from one to the other. Then Jadwin, after shuffling among the papers of his desk, fixed a certain memorandum with his glance. All at once, whirling about and facing the other, he said quickly:

"You are short to our firm two million bushels at a dollar a bushel."

"Nothing of the sort," cried the other. "It's a million and a half."

Jadwin could not forbear a twinkle of grim humor as he saw how easily Scannel had fallen into the trap.

"You're short a million and a half, then," he repeated. "I'll let you have six hundred thousand of it at a dollar and a half a bushel."

"A dollar and a half! Why, my God, man! Oh, well"—Scannel spread out his hands nonchalantly—"I shall simply go into bankruptcy—just as you said."

"Oh, no, you won't," replied Jadwin, pushing back and crossing his legs. "I've had your financial standing computed very carefully, Mr. Scannel. You've got the ready money. I know what you can stand without busting, to the fraction of a cent."

"Why, it's ridiculous. That handful of wheat will cost me three hundred thousand dollars."

"Pre-cisely."

And then all at once Scannel surrendered. Stony, imperturbable, he drew his check-book from his pocket.

"Make it payable to bearer," said Jadwin.

The other complied, and Jadwin took the check and looked it over carefully.

"Now," he said, "watch here, Dave Scannel. You see this check? And now," he added, thrusting it into Hargus's hands, "you see where it goes. There's the principal of your debt paid off."

"The principal?"

"You haven't forgotten the interest, have you? I won't compound it, because that *might* bust you. But six per cent interest on three hundred thousand since 1878 comes to—let's see—three hundred and sixty thousand dollars. And you still owe me nine hundred thousand bushels of wheat." He ciphered a moment on a sheet of note paper. "If I charge you a dollar and forty a bushel for that wheat, it will come to that sum exactly. . . . Yes, that's correct. I'll let you have the balance of that wheat at a dollar forty. Make the check payable to bearer as before."

For a second Scannel hesitated, his face purple, his teeth grinding together, then muttering his rage beneath his breath, opened his check-book again.

"Thank you," said Jadwin as he took the check.

He touched his call bell.

"Kinzie," he said to the clerk who answered it, "after the close of the market to-day send delivery slips for a million and a half wheat to Mr. Scannel. His account with us has been settled."

Jadwin turned to the old man, reaching out the second check to him.

"Here you are, Hargus. Put it away carefully. You see what it is, don't you? Buy your Lizzie a little gold watch with a hundred of it, and tell her it's from Curtis Jadwin, with his compliments. . . . What, going, Scannel? Well, good-by to you, sir, and hey!" he called after him, "please don't slam the door as you go out."

But he dodged with a defensive gesture as the pane of glass almost leaped from its casing, as Scannel stormed across the threshold.

Jadwin turned to Hargus with a solemn wink.

"He did slam it after all, didn't he?"

The old fellow, however, sat fingering the two checks in silence. Then he looked up at Jadwin, scared and trembling.

"I—I don't know," he murmured, feebly. "I am a very old man. This—this is a great deal of money, sir. I—I can't say; I —I don't know. I'm an old man . . . an old man."

"You won't lose 'em, now?"

"No, no. I'll deposit them at once in the Illinois Trust. I shall ask—I should like—"

"I'll send a clerk with you."

"Yes, yes, that is about what—what I—what I was about to suggest. But I must say, Mr. Jadwin—"

He began to stammer his thanks. But Jadwin cut him off. Rising, he guided Hargus to the door, one hand on his shoulder, and at the entrance to the outer office called a clerk.

"Take Mr. Hargus over to the Illinois Trust, Kinzie, and introduce him. He wants to open an account."

The old man started off with the clerk, but before Jadwin had reseated himself at his desk was back again. He was suddenly all excitement, as if a great idea had abruptly taken possession of him. Stealthy, furtive, he glanced continually over his shoulder as he spoke, talking in whispers, a trembling hand shielding his lips.

"You—you are in—you are in control now," he said. "You could give—hey? You could give me—just a little—just one word. A word would be enough, hey? hey? Just a little tip. My God, I could make fifty dollars by noon."

"Why, man, I've just given you about half a million."

"Half a million? I don't know. But"—he plucked Jadwin tremulously by the sleeve—"just a word," he begged. "Hey, just yes or no."

"Haven't you enough with those two checks?"

"Those checks? Oh, I know, I know, I know. I'll salt 'em down. Yes, in the Illinois Trust. I won't touch 'em—not those. But just a little tip now, hey?"

"Not a word. Not a word. Take him along, Kinzie."

One week after this Jadwin sold, through his agents in Paris, a tremendous line of "cash" wheat at a dollar and sixty cents the bushel. By now the foreign demand was a thing almost insensate. There was no question as to the price. It was, "Give us the wheat, at whatever cost, at whatever figure, at whatever expense; only that it be rushed to our markets with all the swiftness of steam and steel." At home, upon the Chicago Board of Trade, Jadwin was as completely master of the market as of his own right hand. Everything stopped when he raised a finger; everything leaped to life with the fury of obsession when he nodded his head. His wealth increased with such stupefying rapidity that at no time was he able to even approximate the gains that accrued to him because of his corner. It was more than twenty million, and less than fifty million. That was all he knew. Nor were the everlasting hills more secure than he from the attack of any human enemy. Out of the ranks of the conquered there issued not so much as a whisper of hostility. Within his own sphere no Czar, no satrap, no Cæsar ever wielded power more resistless.

"Sam," said Curtis Jadwin, at length to the broker, "Sam, nothing in the world can stop me now. They think I've been doing something big, don't they, with this corner? Why, I've only just begun. This is just a feeler. Now I'm going to let 'em know just how big a gun C. J. really is. I'm going to swing this deal right over into July. I'm going to buy in my July shorts."

The two men were in Gretry's office as usual, and as Jadwin spoke, the broker glanced up incredulously.

"Now you are for sure crazy."

Jadwin jumped to his feet.

"Crazy!" he vociferated. "Crazy! What do you mean? Crazy! For God's sake, Sam, what— Look here, don't use that word to me. I—it don't suit. What I've done isn't exactly the work of— of—takes brains, let me tell you. And look here, look here, I say, I'm going to swing this deal right over into July. Think I'm going to let go now, when I've just begun to get a real grip on things? A pretty fool I'd look like to get out now—even if I could. Get out? How are we going to unload our big line of wheat without breaking the price on us? No, sir, not much. This market is going up to two dollars." He smote a knee with his clinched fist, his face going abruptly crimson. "I say two dollars," he cried. "Two dollars, do you hear? It will go there, you'll see, you'll see."

"Reports on the new crop will begin to come in in June." Gretry's warning was almost a cry. "The price of wheat is so high now that God knows how many farmers will plant it this spring. You may have to take care of a record harvest."

"I know better," retorted Jadwin. "I'm watching this thing. You can't tell me anything about it. I've got it all figured out, your 'new crop.'"

"Well, then, you're the Lord Almighty himself."

"I don't like that kind of joke. I don't like that kind of joke. It's blasphemous," exclaimed Jadwin. "Go, get it off on Crookes. He'd appreciate it, but I don't. But this new crop now—look here."

And for upward of two hours Jadwin argued and figured, and showed to Gretry endless tables of statistics to prove that he was right.

But at the end Gretry shook his head. Calmly and deliberately he spoke his mind.

"J., listen to me. You've done a big thing. I know it, and I know, too, that there've been lots of times in the last year or so when I've been wrong and you've been right. But now, J., so help me God, we've reached our limit. Wheat is worth a dollar and a half to-day, and not one cent more. Every eighth over that figure is inflation. If you run it up to two dollars—"

"It will go there of itself, I tell you."

"—if you run it up to two dollars, it will be that top-heavy, that the littlest kick in the world will knock it over. Be satisfied now with what you got. J., it's common sense. Close out your long line of May, and then stop. Suppose the price does break a little, you'd still make your pile. But swing this deal over into July, and it's ruin, ruin. I may have been mistaken before, but I know I'm right now. And do you realize, J., that yesterday in the Pit there were some short sales? There's some of them dared to go short of wheat against you—even at the very top of your corner—and there was more selling this morning. You've always got to buy, you know. If they all began to sell to you at once they'd bust you. It's only because you've got 'em so scared—I believe—that keeps 'em from it. But it looks to me as though this selling proved that they were picking up heart. They think they can get the wheat from the farmers when harvesting begins. And I tell you, J., you've put the price of wheat so high, that the wheat areas are extending all over the country'"

"You're scared," cried Jadwin. "That's the trouble with you, Sam. You've been scared from the start. Can't you see, man, can't you see that this market is a regular tornado?"

"I see that the farmers all over the country are planting wheat as they've never planted it before. Great Scott, J., you're fighting against the earth itself."

"Well, we'll fight it, then. I'll stop those hayseeds. What do I own all these newspapers and trade journals for? We'll begin sending out reports to-morrow that'll discourage any big wheat planting."

"And then, too," went on Gretry, "here's another point. Do you know, you ought to be in bed this very minute. You haven't got any nerves left at all. You acknowledge yourself that you don't sleep any more. And, good Lord, the moment any one of us contradicts you, or opposes you, you go off the handle to beat the Dutch. I know it's a strain, old man, but you want to keep yourself in hand if you go on with this thing. If you should break down now—well, I don't like to think of what would happen. You ought to see a doctor."

"Oh-h, fiddlesticks," exclaimed Jadwin, "I'm all right. I don't need a doctor, haven't time to see one, anyhow. Don't you bother about me. I'm all right."

Was he? That same night, the first he had spent under his own roof for four days, Jadwin lay awake till the clocks struck four, asking himself the same question. No, he was not all right. Something was very wrong with him, and whatever it might be, it was growing worse. The sensation of the iron clamp about his head was almost permanent by now, and just the walk between his room at the Grand Pacific and Gretry's office left him panting and exhausted. Then had come vertigoes and strange, inexplicable qualms, as if he were in an elevator that sank under him with terrifying rapidity.

Going to and fro in La Salle Street, or sitting in Gretry's office, where the roar of the Pit dinned forever in his ears, he could forget these strange symptoms. It was the night he dreaded—the long hours he must spend alone. The instant the strain was relaxed, the gallop of hoofs, the beat of ungovernable torrents began in his brain. Always the beat dropped to the same cadence, always the pulse spelled out the same words:

"Wheat-wheat-wheat, wheat-wheat-wheat."

And of late, during the long and still watches of the night, while he stared at the ceiling, or counted the hours that must pass before his next dose of bromide of potassium, a new turn had been given to the screw.

This was a sensation, the like of which he found it difficult to describe. But it seemed to be a slow, tense crisping of every tiniest nerve in his body. It would begin as he lay in bed—counting interminably to get himself to sleep—between his knees and ankles, and thence slowly spread to every part of him, creeping upward, from loin to shoulder, in a gradual wave of torture that was not pain, yet infinitely worse. A dry, prinkling aura as of billions of minute electric shocks crept upward over his flesh, till it reached his head, where it seemed to culminate in a white flash, which he felt rather than saw.

His body felt strange and unfamiliar to him. It seemed to have no weight, and at times his hands would appear to swell swiftly to the size of mammoth boxing-gloves, so that he must rub them together to feel that they were his own.

He put off consulting a doctor from day to day, alleging that he had not the time. But the real reason, though he never admitted it, was the fear that the doctor might tell him what he guessed to be the truth.

Were his wits leaving him? The horror of the question smote through him like the drive of a javelin. What was to happen? What nameless calamity impended?

"Wheat-wheat-wheat, wheat-wheat-wheat."

His watch under his pillow took up the refrain. How to grasp the morrow's business, how control the sluice gates of that torrent he had unchained, with this unspeakable crumbling and disintegrating of his faculties going on?

Jaded, feeble, he rose to meet another day. He drove down town, trying not to hear the beat of his horses' hoofs. Dizzy and stupefied, he gained Gretry's office, and alone with his terrors sat in the chair before his desk, waiting, waiting.

Then far away the great gong struck. Just over his head, penetrating wood and iron, he heard the mighty throe of the Pit once more beginning, moving. And then, once again, the limp and raveled fibres of his being grew tight with a wrench. Under the stimulus of the roar of the maelstrom, the flagging, wavering brain righted itself once more, and—how, he himself could not say—the business of the day was despatched, the battle was once more urged. Often he acted upon what he knew to be blind, unreasoned instinct. Judgment, clear reasoning, at times, he felt, forsook him. Decisions that involved what seemed to be the very stronghold of his situation, had to be taken without a moment's warning. He decided for or against without knowing why. Under his feet fissures opened. He must take the leap without seeing the other edge. Somehow he always landed upon his feet, somehow his great, cumbersome engine, lurching, swaying, in spite of loosened joints, always kept the track.

Luck, his golden goddess, the genius of glittering wings, was with him yet. Sorely tried, flouted even, she yet remained faithful, lending a helping hand to lost and wandering judgment.

So the month of May drew to its close. Between the twenty-fifth and the thirtieth Jadwin covered his July shortage, despite Gretry's protests and warnings. To him they seemed idle enough. He was too rich, too strong now to fear any issue. Daily the profits of the corner increased. The unfortunate shorts were wrung dry and drier. In Gretry's office they heard their sentences, and as time went on, and Jadwin beheld more and more of these broken speculators, a vast contempt for human nature grew within him.

Some few of his beaten enemies were resolute enough, accepting defeat with grim carelessness, or with sphinx-like indifference, or even with airy jocularity. But for the most part their alert, eager deference, their tame subservience, the abject humility and debasement of their bent shoulders drove Jadwin to the verge of

self-control. He grew to detest the business; he regretted even
the defiant brutality of Scannel, a rascal, but none the less keeping
his head high. The more the fellows cringed to him, the tighter
he wrenched the screw. In a few cases he found a pleasure in re-
lenting entirely, selling his wheat to the unfortunates at a price that
left them without loss; but in the end the business hardened his
heart to any distress his mercilessness might entail. He took his
profits as a Bourbon took his taxes, as if by right of birth. Somewhere, in a long-forgotten history of his brief school days, he had
come across a phrase that he remembered now, by some devious and
distant process of association, and when he heard of the calamities
that his campaign had wrought, of the shipwrecked fortunes and
careers that were sucked down by the Pit, he found it possible to say,
with a short laugh, and a lift of one shoulder:

"*Væ victis.*"

His wife he saw but seldom. Occasionally they breakfasted together; more often they met at dinner. But that was all. Jadwin's
life by now had come to be so irregular, and his few hours of sleep
so precious and so easily disturbed, that he had long since occupied
a separate apartment.

What Laura's life was at this time he no longer knew. She
never spoke of it to him; never nowadays complained of loneliness.
When he saw her she appeared to be cheerful. But this very cheer-
fulness made him uneasy, and at times, through the murk of the
chaff of wheat, through the bellow of the Pit, and the crash of
collapsing fortunes there reached him a suspicion that all was not
well with Laura.

Once he had made an abortive attempt to break from the turmoil of La Salle Street and the Board of Trade, and, for a time at
least, to get back to the old life they both had loved—to get back,
in a word, to her. But the consequences had been all but disastrous. Now he could not keep away.

"Corner wheat!" he had exclaimed to her, the following
day. "Corner wheat! It's the wheat that has cornered me.
It's like holding a wolf by the ears, bad to hold on, but worse
to let go."

But absorbed, blinded, deafened by the whirl of things, Curtis
Jadwin could not see how perilously well-grounded had been his
faint suspicion as to Laura's distress.

On the day after her evening with her husband in the art gallery, the evening when Gretry had broken in upon them like a

courier from the front, Laura had risen from her bed to look out
upon a world suddenly empty.

Corthell she had sent from her forever. Jadwin was once more
snatched from her side. Where, now, was she to turn? Jadwin
had urged her to go to the country—to their place at Geneva Lake—
but she refused. She saw the change that had of late come over
her husband, saw his lean face, the hot, tired eyes, the trembling
fingers and nervous gestures. Vaguely she imagined approaching
disaster. If anything happened to Curtis, her place was at his side.

During the days that Jadwin and Crookes were at grapples,
Laura found means to occupy her mind with all manner of small
activities. She overhauled her wardrobe, planned her summer
gowns, paid daily visits to her dressmakers, rode and drove in the
park, till every turn of the roads, every tree, every bush was familiar,
to the point of wearisome contempt.

Then suddenly she began to indulge in a mania for old books
and first editions. She haunted the stationers and second-hand book-
stores, studied the authorities, followed the auctions, and bought
right and left, with reckless extravagance. But the taste soon
palled upon her. With so much money at her command there was
none of the spice of the hunt in the affair. She had but to express a
desire for a certain treasure, and forthwith it was put into her hand.

She found it so in all other things. Her desires were gratified
with an abruptness that killed the zest of them. She felt none of
the joy of possession; the little personal relation between her and
her belongings vanished away. Her gowns, beautiful beyond all
she had ever imagined, were of no more interest to her than a
drawerful of outworn gloves. She bought horses till she could no
longer tell them apart; her carriages crowded three supplementary
stables in the neighborhood. Her flowers, miracles of laborious
cultivation, filled the whole house with their fragrance. Wherever
she went deference moved before her like a guard; her beauty, her
enormous wealth, her wonderful horses, her exquisite gowns made
of her a cynosure, a veritable queen.

And hardly a day passed that Laura Jadwin, in the solitude of
her own boudoir, did not fling her arms wide in a gesture of lassitude and infinite weariness, crying out:

"Oh, the ennui and stupidity of all this wretched life!"

She could look forward to nothing. One day was like the next.
No one came to see her. For all her great house and for all her
money, she had made but few friends. Her "grand manner" had

never helped her popularity. She passed her evenings alone in her "upstairs sitting-room," reading, reading till far into the night; or, the lights extinguished, sat at her open window listening to the monotonous lap and wash of the lake.

At such moments she thought of the men who had come into her life—of the love she had known almost from her girlhood. She remembered her first serious affair. It had been with the impecunious theological student who was her tutor. He had worn glasses and little black side whiskers, and had implored her to marry him and come to China, where he was to be a missionary. Every time that he came he had brought her a new book to read, and he had taken her for long walks up toward the hills where the old powder mill stood. Then it was the young lawyer—the "brightest man in Worcester County"—who took her driving in a hired buggy, sent her a multitude of paper novels (which she never read), with every love passage carefully underscored, and wrote very bad verse to her eyes and hair, whose "velvet blackness was the shadow of a crown." Or, again, it was the youthful cavalry officer met in a flying visit to her Boston aunt, who loved her on first sight, gave her his photograph in uniform and a bead belt of Apache workmanship. He was forever singing to her—to a guitar accompaniment—an old love song:

> "At midnight hour
> Beneath the tower
> He murmured soft,
> 'Oh nothing fearing
> With thine own true soldier fly.' "

Then she had come to Chicago, and Landry Court, with his bright enthusiasms and fine exaltations, had loved her. She had never taken him very seriously, but none the less it had been very sweet to know his whole universe depended upon the nod of her head, and that her influence over him had been so potent, had kept him clean and loyal and honest.

And after this Corthell and Jadwin had come into her life, the artist and the man of affairs. She remembered Corthell's quiet, patient, earnest devotion of those days before her marriage. He rarely spoke to her of his love, but by some ingenious subtlety he had filled her whole life with it. His little attentions, his undemonstrative solicitudes came precisely when and where they were most appropriate. He had never failed her. Whenever she had needed him, or even when through caprice or impulse she had turned to him, it always had been to find that long since he had carefully prepared for that very contingency. His thoughtfulness of her had been a thing to wonder at. He remembered for months, years even, her most trivial fancies, her unexpressed dislikes. He knew her tastes, as if by instinct; he prepared little surprises for her, and placed them in her way without ostentation, and quite as matters of course. He never permitted her to be embarrassed; the little annoying situations of the day's life he had smoothed away long before they had ensnared her. He never was off his guard, never disturbed, never excited.

And he amused her, he entertained her without seeming to do so. He made her talk, he made her think. He stimulated and aroused her, so that she herself talked and thought with a brilliancy that surprised herself. In fine, he had so contrived that she associated him with everything that was agreeable.

She had sent him away the first time, and he had gone without a murmur; only to come back loyal as ever, silent, watchful, sympathetic, his love for her deeper, stronger than before, and—as always timely—bringing to her a companionship at the moment of all others when she was most alone.

Now she had driven him from her again, and this time, she very well knew, it was to be forever. She had shut the door upon this great love.

Laura stirred abruptly in her place, adjusting her hair with nervous fingers.

And, last of all, it had been Jadwin, her husband. She rose and went to the window, and stood there a long moment, looking off into the night over the park. It was warm and very still. A few carriage lamps glimpsed among the trees like fireflies. Along the walks and upon the benches she could see the glow of white dresses and could catch the sound of laughter. Far off, somewhere in the shrubbery, she thought she heard a band playing. To the northeast lay the lake, shimmering under the moon, dotted here and there with the colored lights of steamers.

She turned back into the room. The great house was still. From all its suites of rooms, its corridors, galleries, and hallways there came no sound. There was no one upon the same floor as herself. She had read all her books. It was too late to go out—and there was no one to go with. To go to bed was ridiculous. She was never more wakeful, never more alive, never more ready to be amused, diverted, entertained.

She thought of the organ, and descending to the art gallery, played Bach, Palestrina, and Stainer for an hour; then suddenly she started from the console, with a sharp, impatient movement of her head.

"Why do I play this stupid music?" she exclaimed. She called a servant and asked:

"Has Mr. Jadwin come in yet?"

"Mr. Gretry just this minute telephoned that Mr. Jadwin would not be home to-night."

When the servant had gone out, Laura, her lips compressed, flung up her head. Her hands shut to hard fists, her eye flashed. Rigid, erect in the middle of the floor, her arms folded, she uttered a smothered exclamation over and over again under her breath.

All at once anger mastered her—anger and a certain defiant reck- lessness, an abrupt spirit of revolt. She straightened herself sud- denly, as one who takes a decision. Then, swiftly, she went out of the art gallery, and, crossing the hallway, entered the library and opened a great writing-desk that stood in a recess under a small stained window.

She pulled the sheets of note paper toward her and wrote a short letter, directing the envelope to Sheldon Corthell, The Fine Arts Building, Michigan Avenue.

"Call a messenger," she said to the servant who answered her ring, "and have him take—or send him in here when he comes."

She rested the letter against the inkstand, and leaned back in her chair, looking at it, her fingers plucking swiftly at the lace of her dress. Her head was in a whirl. A confusion of thoughts, im- pulses, desires, half-formed resolves, half-named regrets, swarmed and spun about her. She felt as though she had all at once taken a leap—a leap which had landed her in a place whence she could see a new and terrible country, an unfamiliar place—terrible, yet beau- tiful—unexplored, and for that reason all the more inviting, a place of shadows.

Laura rose and paced the floor, her hands pressed together over her heart. She was excited, her cheeks flushed, a certain breathless exhilaration came and went within her breast, and in place of the intolerable ennui of the last days, there came over her a sudden, an almost wild animation, and from out her black eyes there shot a kind of furious gayety.

But she was aroused by a step at the door. The messenger stood there, a figure ridiculously inadequate for the intensity of all that was involved in the issue of the hour—a weazened, stunted boy, in a uniform many sizes too large.

Laura, seated at her desk, held the note toward him resolutely. Now was no time to hesitate, to temporize. If she did not hold to her resolve now, what was there to look forward to? Could one's life be emptier than hers—emptier, more intolerable, more humiliating?

"Take this note to that address," she said, putting the envelope and a coin in the boy's hand. "Wait for an answer."

The boy shut the letter in his book, which he thrust into his breast pocket, buttoning his coat over it. He nodded and turned away.

Still seated, Laura watched him moving toward the door. Well, it was over now. She had chosen. She had taken the leap. What new life was to begin for her to-morrow? What did it all mean? With an inconceivable rapidity her thoughts began racing through her brain.

She did not move. Her hands, gripped tight together, rested upon the desk before her. Without turning her head, she watched the retreating messenger, from under her lashes. He passed out of the door, the curtain fell behind him.

And only then, when the irrevocableness of the step was all but an accomplished fact, came the reaction.

"Stop!" she cried, springing up. "Stop! Come back here. Wait a moment."

What had happened? She could neither understand nor explain. Somehow an instant of clear vision had come, and, in that instant a power within her that was herself and not herself, had laid hold upon her will. No, no, she could not, she could not, after all. She took the note back.

"I have changed my mind," she said abruptly. "You may keep the money. There is no message to be sent."

As soon as the boy had gone she opened the envelope and read what she had written. But now the words seemed the work of another mind than her own. They were unfamiliar; they were not the words of the Laura Jadwin she knew. Why was it that from the very first hours of her acquaintance with this man, and in every circumstance of their intimacy, she had always acted upon impulse? What was there in him that called into being all that was reckless in her?

And for how long was she to be able to control these impulses?

This time she had prevailed once more against that other impetuous self of hers. Would she prevail the next time? And in these struggles, was she growing stronger as she overcame, or weaker? She did not know. She tore the note into fragments, and making a heap of them in the pen tray, burned them carefully.

During the week following upon this, Laura found her trouble more than ever keen. She was burdened with a new distress. The incident of the note to Corthell, recalled at the last moment, had opened her eyes to possibilities of the situation hitherto unguessed. She saw now what she might be capable of doing in a moment of headstrong caprice, she saw depths in her nature she had not plumbed. Whether these hidden pitfalls were peculiarly hers, or whether they were common to all women placed as she now found herself, she did not pause to inquire. She thought only of results, and she was afraid.

But for the matter of that, Laura had long since passed the point of deliberate consideration or reasoned calculation. The reaction had been as powerful as the original purpose, and she was even yet struggling blindly, intuitively.

For what she was now about to do she could give no reason, and the motives for this final and supreme effort to conquer the league of circumstances which hemmed her in were obscure. She did not even ask what they were. She knew only that she was in trouble, and yet it was to the cause of her distress that she addressed herself. Blindly she turned to her husband; and all the woman in her roused itself, girded itself, called up its every resource in one last test, in one ultimate trial of strength between her and the terrible growing power of that blind, soulless force that roared and guttered and sucked, down there in the midst of the city.

She alone, one unaided woman, her only auxiliaries her beauty, her wit, and the frayed, strained bands of a sorely tried love, stood forth like a challenger, against Charybdis, joined battle with the Cloaca, held back with her slim, white hands against the power of the maelstrom that swung the Nations in its grip.

In the solitude of her room she took the resolve. Her troubles were multiplying; she, too, was in the current, the end of which was a pit—a pit black and without bottom. Once already its grip had seized her, once already she had yielded to the insidious drift. Now suddenly aware of a danger, she fought back, and her hands beating the air for help, turned toward the greatest strength she knew.

"I want my husband," she cried, aloud, to the empty darkness of the night. "I want my husband. I will have him; he is mine, he is mine. There shall nothing take me from him; there shall nothing take him from me."

Her first opportunity came upon a Sunday soon afterward. Jadwin, wakeful all the Saturday night, slept a little in the forenoon, and after dinner Laura came to him in his smoking-room, as he lay on the leather lounge trying to read. His wife seated herself at a writing-table in a corner of the room, and by and by began turning the slips of a calendar that stood at her elbow. At last she tore off one of the slips and held it up.

"Curtis."

"Well, old girl?"

"Do you see that date?"

He looked over to her.

"Do you see that date? Do you know of anything that makes that day different—a little—from other days? It's June thirteenth. Do you remember what June thirteenth is?"

Puzzled, he shook his head.

"No—no."

Laura took up a pen and wrote a few words in the space above the printed figures reserved for memoranda. Then she handed the slip to her husband, who read aloud what she had written.

"'Laura Jadwin's birthday.' Why, upon my word," he declared, sitting upright. "So it is, so it is. June thirteenth, of course. And I was beast enough not to realize it. Honey, I can't remember anything these days, it seems."

"But you are going to remember this time?" she said. "You are not going to forget it now. That evening is going to mark the beginning of—oh, Curtis, it is going to be a new beginning of everything. You'll see. I'm going to manage it. I don't know how, but you are going to love me so that nothing, no business, no money, no wheat will ever keep you from me. I will make you. And that evening, that evening of June thirteenth is mine. The day your business can have you, but from six o'clock on you are mine." She crossed the room quickly and took both his hands in hers and knelt beside him. "It is mine," she said, "if you love me. Do you understand, dear? You will come home at six o'clock, and whatever happens—oh, if all La Salle Street should burn to the ground, and all your millions of bushels of wheat with it—whatever happens, you—will—not—leave—me—nor think of anything else but just me, me. That evening is mine, and you will give it to

me, just as I have said. I won't remind you of it again. I won't
speak of it again. I will leave it to you. But—you will give me
that evening if you love me. Dear, do you see just what I mean?
. . . *If you love me.* . . . No—no, don't say a word, we won't
talk about it at all. No, no, please. Not another word. I don't
want you to promise, or pledge yourself, or anything like that.
You've heard what I said—and that's all there is about it. We'll
talk of something else. By the way, have you seen Mr. Cressler
lately?"

"No," he said, falling into her mood. "No, I haven't seen
Charlie in over a month. Wonder what's become of him?"

"I understand he's been sick," she told him. "I met Mrs.
Cressler the other day, and she said she was bothered about him."

"Well, what's the matter with old Charlie?"

"She doesn't know herself. He's not sick enough to go to
bed, but he doesn't or won't go downtown to his business. She
says she can see him growing thinner every day. He keeps telling
her he's all right, but for all that, she says, she's afraid he's going
to come down with some kind of sickness pretty soon."

"Say," said Jadwin, "suppose we drop around to see them this
afternoon? Wouldn't you like to? I haven't seen him in over a
month, as I say. Or telephone them to come up and have dinner.
Charlie's about as old a friend as I have. We used to be together
about every hour of the day when we first came to Chicago. Let's
go over to see him this afternoon and cheer him up."

"No," said Laura, decisively. "Curtis, you must have one day
of rest out of the week. You are going to lie down all the rest of
the afternoon, and sleep if you can. I'll call on them to-morrow."

"Well, all right," he assented. "I suppose I ought to sleep if I
can. And then Sam is coming up here, by five. He's going to
bring some railroad men with him. We've got a lot to do. Yes, I
guess, old girl, I'll try to get forty winks before they get here. And,
Laura," he added, taking her hand as she rose to go, "Laura, this is
the last lap. In just another month now—oh, at the outside, six
weeks—I'll have closed the corner, and then, old girl, you and I
will go somewheres, anywhere you like, and then we'll have a good
time together all the rest of our lives—all the rest of our lives,
honey. Good-by. Now I think I can go to sleep."

She arranged the cushions under his head and drew the curtains close over the windows, and went out, softly closing the door
behind her. And a half hour later, when she stole in to look at him,

she found him asleep at last, the tired eyes closed, and the arm, with its broad, strong hand, resting under his head. She stood a long moment in the middle of the room, looking down at him; and then slipped out as noiselessly as she had come, the tears trembling on her eyelashes.

Laura Jadwin did not call on the Cresslers the next day, nor even the next after that. For three days she kept indoors, held prisoner by a series of petty incidents; now the delay in the finishing of her new gowns, now by the excessive heat, now by a spell of rain. By Thursday, however, at the beginning of the second week of the month, the storm was gone, and the sun once more shone. Early in the afternoon Laura telephoned to Mrs. Cressler.

"How are you and Mr. Cressler?" she asked. "I'm coming over to take luncheon with you and your husband, if you will let me."

"Oh, Charlie is about the same, Laura," answered Mrs. Cressler's voice. "I guess the dear man has been working too hard, that's all. Do come over and cheer him up. If I'm not here when you come, you just make yourself at home. I've got to go downtown to see about railroad tickets and all. I'm going to pack my old man right off to Oconomowoc before I'm another day older. Made up my mind to it last night, and I don't want him to be bothered with tickets or time cards, or baggage or anything. I'll run down and do it all myself. You come right up whenever you're ready and keep Charlie company. How's your husband, Laura, child?"

"Oh, Curtis is well," she answered. "He gets very tired at times."

"Well, I can understand it. Lands alive, child, whatever are you going to do with all your money? They tell me that J. has made millions in the last three or four months. A man I was talking to last week said his corner was the greatest thing ever known on the Chicago Board of Trade. Well, good-by, Laura, come up whenever you're ready. I'll see you at lunch. Charlie is right here. He says to give you his love."

An hour later Laura's victoria stopped in front of the Cresslers' house, and the little footman descended with the agility of a monkey, to stand, soldier-like, at the steps, the lap robe over his arm.

Laura gave orders to have the victoria call for her at three, and ran quickly up the front steps. The front entrance was open, the screen door on the latch, and she entered without ceremony.

"Mrs. Cressler!" she called, as she stood in the hallway drawing off her gloves. "Mrs. Cressler! Carrie, have you gone yet?"

But the maid, Annie, appeared at the head of the stairs, on the landing of the second floor, a towel bound about her head, her duster in her hand.

"Mrs. Cressler has gone out, Mrs. Jadwin," she said. "She said you was to make yourself at home, and she'd be back by noon."

Laura nodded, and, standing before the hatrack in the hall, took off her hat and gloves, and folded her veil into her purse. The house was old-fashioned, very homelike and spacious, cool, with broad halls and wide windows. In the "front library," where Laura entered first, were steel engravings of the style of the seventies, "whatnots" crowded with shells, Chinese coins, lacquer boxes, and the inevitable sawfish bill. The mantel was mottled white marble, and its shelf bore the usual bronze and gilt clock, decorated by a female figure in classic draperies, reclining against a globe. An oil painting of a mountain landscape hung against one wall; and on a table of black walnut, with a red marble slab, that stood between the front windows, were a stereoscope and a rosewood music box.

The piano, an old style Chickering, stood diagonally across the far corner of the room, by the closed sliding doors, and Laura sat down here and began to play the "Mephisto Walzer," which she had been at pains to learn since the night Corthell had rendered it on her great organ in the art gallery.

But when she had played as much as she could remember of the music, she rose and closed the piano, and pushed back the folding-doors between the room she was in and the "back library," a small room where Mrs. Cressler kept her books of poetry.

As Laura entered the room she was surprised to see Mr. Cressler there, seated in his armchair, his back turned toward her.

"Why, I didn't know you were here, Mr. Cressler," she said, as she came up to him.

She laid her hand upon his arm. But Cressler was dead; and as Laura touched him the head dropped upon the shoulder and showed the bullet hole in the temple, just in front of the ear.

X

THE suicide of Charles Cressler had occurred on the tenth of June, and the report of it, together with the wretched story of his friend's final surrender to a temptation he had never outlived, reached Curtis Jadwin early on the morning of the eleventh.

He and Gretry were at their accustomed places in the latter's office, and the news seemed to shut out all the sunshine that had been flooding in through the broad plate-glass windows. After their first incoherent horror, the two sat staring at each other, speechless.

"My God, my God," groaned Jadwin, as if in the throes of a deadly sickness. "He was in the Crookes' ring, and we never knew it— I've killed him, Sam. I might as well have held that pistol myself." He stamped his foot, striking his fist across his forehead, "Great God—my best friend—Charlie—Charlie Cressler! Sam, I shall go mad if this—if this—"

"Steady, steady does it, J.," warned the broker, his hand upon his shoulder, "we got to keep a grip on ourselves to-day. We've got a lot to think of. We'll think about Charlie later. Just now . . . well, it's business now. Matthewson & Knight have called on us for margins—twenty thousand dollars."

He laid the slip down in front of Jadwin, as he sat at his desk.

"Oh, this can wait," exclaimed Jadwin. "Let it go till this afternoon. I can't talk business now. Think of Carrie—Mrs. Cressler, I—"

"No," answered Gretry, reflectively and slowly, looking anywhere but in Jadwin's face. "N—no, I don't think we'd better wait. I think we'd better meet these margin calls promptly. It's always better to keep our trades margined up."

Jadwin faced around.

"Why," he cried, "one would think, to hear you talk, as though there was danger of me busting here at any hour."

Gretry did not answer. There was a moment's silence. Then the broker caught his principal's eye and held it a second.

"Well," he answered, "you saw how freely they sold to us in the Pit yesterday. We've got to buy, and buy and buy, to keep our price up; and look here, look at these reports from our correspondents—everything points to a banner crop. There's been an increase of acreage everywhere, because of our high prices. See this from Travers"—he picked up a despatch and read: "Preliminary returns of spring wheat in two Dakotas, subject to revision, indicate a total area seeded of sixteen million acres, which, added to area in winter wheat States, makes total of forty-three million, or nearly four million acres greater than last year.'"

"Lot of damned sentiment," cried Jadwin, refusing to be convinced. "Two-thirds of that wheat won't grade, and Europe will take nearly all of it. What we ought to do is to send our men into the Pit and buy another million, buy more than these fools can offer. Buy 'em to a *standstill*."

"That takes a big pile of money then," said the broker. "More than we can lay our hands on this morning. The best we can do is to take all the Bears are offering, and support the market. The moment they offer us wheat and we don't buy it, that moment—as you know, yourself—they'll throw wheat at you by the train load, and the price will break, and we with it."

"Think we'll get rid of much wheat to-day?" demanded Jadwin.

By now it had become vitally necessary for Jadwin to sell out his holdings. His "long line" was a fearful expense, insurance and storage charges were eating rapidly into the profits. He *must* get rid of the load he was carrying, little by little. To do this at a profit, he had adopted the expedient of flooding the Pit with buying orders just before the close of the session, and then, as the price rose under this stimulus, selling quickly, before it had time to break. At first this had succeeded. But of late he must buy more and more to keep the price up, while the moment that he began to sell, the price began to drop; so that now, in order to sell one bushel, he must buy two.

"Think we can unload much on 'em to-day?" repeated Jadwin.

"I don't know," answered Gretry, slowly and thoughtfully. "Perhaps—there's a chance— Frankly, J., I don't think we can. The Pit is taking heart, that's the truth of it. Those fellows are not so scared of us as they were a while ago. It's the new crop, as I've said over and over again. We've put wheat so high that all the farmers have planted it, and are getting ready to dump it on us. The Pit knows that, of course. Why, just think, they are harvesting in some places. These fellows we've caught in the corner will be able to buy all the wheat they want from the farmers if they can hold out a little longer. And that Government report yesterday showed that the growing wheat is in good condition."

"Nothing of the sort. It was a little over eighty-six."

"Good enough," declared Gretry, "good enough so that it broke the price down to a dollar and twenty. Just think, we were at a dollar and a half a little while ago."

"And we'll be at two dollars in another ten days, I tell you."

"Do you know how we stand, J.?" said the broker gravely. "Do you know how we stand—financially? It's taken pretty nearly every cent of our ready money to support this July market. Oh, we can figure out our paper profits into the millions. We've got thirty, forty, fifty million bushels of wheat that's worth over a dollar a bushel, but if we can't sell it, we're none the better off—and that wheat is costing us six thousand dollars a day. Hell, old man, where's the money going to come from? You don't seem to realize that we are in a precarious condition." He raised an arm, and pointed above him, in the direction of the floor of the Board of Trade.

"The moment we can't give our boys—Landry Court, and the rest of 'em—the moment we can't give 'em buying orders, that Pit will suck us down like a chip. The moment we admit that we can't buy all the wheat that's offered, there's the moment we bust."

"Well, we'll buy it," cried Jadwin, through his set teeth. "I'll show those brutes. Look here, is it money we want? You cable to Paris and offer two million, at—oh, at eight cents below the market; and to Liverpool, and let 'em have twopence off on the same amount. They'll snap it up as quick as look at it. That will bring in one lot of money, and as for the rest, I guess I've got some real estate in this town that's pretty good security."

"What—you going to mortgage part of that?"

"No," cried Jadwin, jumping up with a quick, impatient gesture, "no, I'm going to mortgage all of it, and I'm going to do it to-day—this morning. If you say we're in a precarious condition, it's no time for half measures. I'll have more money than you'll know what to do with in the Illinois Trust by three o'clock this afternoon, and when the Board opens to-morrow morning I'm going to light into those cattle in the Pit there, so as they'll think a locomotive has struck 'em. They'd stand me off, would they? They'd try to sell me down; they won't cover when I turn the screw! I'll show 'em, Sam Gretry. I'll run wheat up so high before the next two days that the Bank of England can't pull it down, and before the Pit can catch its breath I'll sell our long line, and with the profits of that, by God! I'll run it up again. Two dollars! Why, it will be two fifty here so quick you won't know how it's happened. I've just been fooling with this crowd until now. *Now,* I'm really going to get down to business."

Gretry did not answer. He twirled his pencil between his fingers, and stared down at the papers on his desk. Once he started to speak, but checked himself. Then at last he turned about.

"All right," he said, briskly. "We'll see what that will do."

"I'm going over to the Illinois Trust now," said Jadwin, putting on his hat. "When your boys come in for their orders, tell them for to-day just to support the market. If there's much wheat offered they'd better buy it. Tell them not to let the market go below a dollar twenty. When I come back we'll make out those cables."

That day Jadwin carried out his programme so vehemently announced to his broker. Upon every piece of real estate that he owned he placed as heavy a mortgage as the property would stand. Even his old house on Michigan Avenue, even the "homestead" on North State Street were incumbered. The time was come, he felt, for the grand *coup,* the last huge strategical move, the concentration of every piece of heavy artillery. Never in all his multitude of operations on the Chicago Board of Trade had he failed. He knew he would not fail now; Luck, the golden goddess, still stayed at his shoulder. He did more than mortgage his property; he floated a number of promissory notes. His credit, always unimpeachable, he taxed to its furthest stretch; from every source he gathered in the sinews of the war he was waging. No sum was too great to daunt him, none too small to be overlooked. Reserves, van and rear, battle line and skirmish outposts he summoned together to form one single vast column of attack.

It was on this same day, while Jadwin, pressed for money, was leaving no stone unturned to secure ready cash, that he came across old Hargus in his usual place in Gretry's customers' room, reading a two days' old newspaper. Of a sudden an idea occurred to Jadwin. He took the old man aside. "Hargus," he said, "do you want a good investment for your money, that money I turned over to you? I can give you a better rate than the bank, and pretty good security. Let me have about a hundred thousand at—oh, ten per cent."

"Hey—what?" asked the old fellow querulously. Jadwin repeated his request.

But Hargus cast a suspicious glance at him and drew away.

"I—I don't lend my money," he observed.

"Why—you old fool," exclaimed Jadwin. "Here, is it more interest you want? Why, we'll say fifteen per cent, if you like."

"I don't lend my money," exclaimed Hargus, shaking his head. "I ain't got any to lend," and with the words he took himself off.

One source of help alone Jadwin left untried. Sorely tempted, he nevertheless kept himself from involving his wife's money in the hazard. Laura, in her own name, was possessed of a little fortune; sure as he was of winning, Jadwin none the less hesitated from seeking an auxiliary here. He felt it was a matter of pride. He could not bring himself to make use of a woman's succor.

But his entire personal fortune now swung in the balance. It was the last fight, the supreme attempt—the final consummate assault, and the thrill of a victory more brilliant, more conclusive, more decisive than any he had ever known, vibrated in Jadwin's breast, as he went to and fro in Jackson, Adams, and La Salle Streets all through that day of the eleventh.

But he knew the danger—knew just how terrible was to be the grapple. Once that same day a certain detail of business took him near to the entrance of the Floor. Though he did not so much as look inside the doors, he could not but hear the thunder of the Pit; and even in that moment of confidence, his great triumph only a few hours distant, Jadwin, for the instant, stood daunted. The roar was appalling, the whirlpool was again unchained, the maelstrom was again unleashed. And during the briefest of seconds he could fancy that the familiar bellow of its swirling had taken on another pitch. Out of that hideous turmoil, he imagined, there issued a strange, unwonted note; as it were, the first rasp and grind of a new avalanche just beginning to stir, a diapason more profound than any he had yet known, a hollow distant bourdon as of the slipping and sliding of some almighty and chaotic power.

It was the Wheat, the Wheat. It was on the move again. From the farms of Illinois and Iowa, from the ranches of Kansas and Nebraska, from all the reaches of the Middle West, the Wheat, like a tidal wave, was rising, rising. Almighty, blood-brother to the earthquake, coeval with the volcano and the whirlwind, that gigantic world-force, that colossal billow, Nourisher of the Nations, was swelling and advancing.

There in the Pit its first premonitory eddies already swirled and spun. If even the first ripples of the tide smote terribly upon the heart, what was it to be when the ocean itself burst through, on its

eternal way from west to east? For an instant came clear vision.
What were these shouting, gesticulating men of the Board of
Trade, these brokers, traders, and speculators? It was not these
he fought, it was that fatal New Harvest; it was the Wheat; it was
—as Gretry had said—the very Earth itself. What were those
scattered hundreds of farmers of the Middle West, who because he
had put the price so high had planted the grain as never before?
What had they to do with it? Why, the Wheat had grown itself;
demand and supply, these were the two great laws the Wheat
obeyed. Almost blasphemous in his effrontery, he had tampered
with these laws, and had roused a Titan. He had laid his puny
human grasp upon Creation, and the very earth herself, the great
mother, feeling the touch of the cobweb that the human insect had
spun, had stirred at last in her sleep and sent her omnipotence moving through the grooves of the world, to find and crush the dis-
turber of her appointed courses.

The new harvest was coming in; the new harvest of wheat, huge
beyond possibility of control; so vast that no money could buy it,
so swift that no strategy could turn it. But Jadwin hurried away
from the sound of the near roaring of the Pit. No, no. Luck was
with him; he had mastered the current of the Pit many times before—he would master it again. The day passed and the night, and
at nine o'clock the following morning he and Gretry once more met
in the broker's office.

Gretry turned a pale face upon his principal.

"I've just received," he said, "the answers to our cables to Liverpool and Paris. I offered wheat at both places, as you know,
cheaper than we've ever offered it there before."

"Yes—well?"

"Well," answered Gretry, looking gravely into Jadwin's eyes,
"well—they won't take it."

.   .   .   .

On the morning of her birthday—the thirteenth of the month—
when Laura descended to the breakfast room, she found Page
already there. Though it was barely half-past seven, her sister was
dressed for the street. She wore a smart red hat, and as she stood
by the French windows, looking out, she drew her gloves back and
forth between her fingers, with a nervous, impatient gesture.

"Why," said Laura, as she sat down at her place, "why, Pagie,
what is in the wind to-day?"

"Landry is coming," Page explained, facing about and glancing at the watch pinned to her waist. "He is going to take me down to see the Board of Trade—from the visitors' gallery, you know. He said this would probably be a great day. Did Mr. Jadwin come home last night?"

Laura shook her head, without speech. She did not choose to put into words the fact that for three days—with the exception of an hour or two, on the evening after that horrible day of her visit to the Cresslers' house—she had seen nothing of her husband.

"Landry says," continued Page, "that it is awful—down there, these days. He says that it is the greatest fight in the history of La Salle Street. Has Mr. Jadwin said anything to you? Is he going to win?"

"I don't know," answered Laura, in a low voice; "I don't know anything about it, Page."

She was wondering if even Page had forgotten. When she had come into the room her first glance had been toward her place at table. But there was nothing there, not even so much as an envelope; and no one had so much as wished her joy of the little anniversary. She had thought Page might have remembered, but her sister's next words showed that she had more on her mind than birthdays.

"Laura," she began, sitting down opposite to her, and unfolding her napkin, with laborious precision. "Laura—Landry and I— Well . . . we're going to be married in the fall."

"Why, Pagie," cried Laura, "I'm just as glad as I can be for you. He's a fine, clean fellow, and I know he will make you a good husband."

Page drew a deep breath.

"Well," she said, "I'm glad you think so, too. Before you and Mr. Jadwin were married I wasn't sure about having him care for me, because at that time—well—" Page looked up with a queer little smile, "I guess you could have had him—if you had wanted to."

"Oh, that," cried Laura. "Why, Landry never really cared for me. It was all the silliest kind of flirtation. The moment he knew you better, I stood no chance at all."

"We're going to take an apartment on Michigan Avenue, near the Auditorium," said Page, "and keep house. We've talked it all over, and know just how much it will cost to live and keep one servant. I'm going to serve the loveliest little dinners; I've learned the kind of cooking he likes already. Oh, I guess there he is now," she cried, as they heard the front door close.

Landry came in, carrying a great bunch of cut flowers, and a box of candy. He was as spruce as though he were already the bridegroom, his cheeks pink, his blond hair radiant. But he was thin and a little worn, a dull feverish glitter came and went in his eyes, and his nervousness, the strain and excitement which beset him, were in his every gesture, in every word of his speech.

"We'll have to hurry," he told Page. "I must be down there hours ahead of time this morning."

"How is Curtis?" demanded Laura. "Have you seen him lately? How is he getting on with—with his speculating?"

Landry made a sharp gesture of resignation.

"I don't know," he answered. "I guess nobody knows. We had a fearful day yesterday, but I think we controlled the situation at the end. We ran the price up and up and up till I thought it would never stop. If the Pit thought Mr. Jadwin was beaten, I guess they found out how they were mistaken. For a time there, we were just *driving* them. But then Mr. Gretry sent word to us in the Pit to sell, and we couldn't hold them. They came back at us like wolves; they beat the price down five cents, in as many minutes. We had to quit selling and buy again. But then Mr. Jadwin went at them with a rush. *Oh, it was grand!* We steadied the price at a dollar and fifteen, stiffened it up to eighteen and a half, and then sent it up again, three cents at a time, till we'd hammered it back to a dollar and a quarter."

"But Curtis himself?" inquired Laura, "is he all right, is he well?"

"I only saw him once," answered Landry. "He was in Mr. Gretry's office. Yes, he looked all right. He's nervous, of course. But Mr. Gretry looks like the sick man. He looks all frazzled out."

"I guess we'd better be going," said Page, getting up from the table. "Have you had your breakfast, Landry? Won't you have some coffee?"

"Oh, I breakfasted hours ago," he answered. "But you are right. We had better be moving. If you are going to get a seat in the gallery, you must be there half an hour ahead of time, to say the least. Shall I take any word to your husband from you, Mrs. Jadwin?"

"Tell him that I wish him good luck," she answered, "and— yes, ask him if he remembers what day of the month this is—or no, don't ask him that. Say nothing about it. Just tell him I send him my very best love, and that I wish him all the success in the world."

It was about nine o'clock when Landry and Page reached the foot of La Salle Street. The morning was fine and cool. The sky over the Board of Trade sparkled with sunlight, and the air was full of fluttering wings of the multitude of pigeons that lived upon the leakage of grain around the Board of Trade building.

"Mr. Cressler used to feed them regularly," said Landry, as they paused on the street corner opposite the Board. "Poor—poor Mr. Cressler—the funeral is to-morrow, you know."

Page shut her eyes.

"Oh," she murmured, "think, *think* of Laura finding him there like that. Oh, it would have killed me, it would have killed me."

"Somehow," abserved Landry, a puzzled expression in his eyes, "somehow, by George! she don't seem to mind very much. You'd have thought a shock like that would have made her sick."

"Oh! Laura," cried Page. "I don't know her any more these days, she is just like stone—just as though she were crowding down every emotion or any feeling she ever had. She seems to be holding herself in with all her strength—for something—and afraid to let go a finger, for fear she would give way altogether. When she told me about that morning at the Cresslers' house, her voice was just like ice; she said, "Mr. Cressler has shot himself. I found him dead in his library.' She never shed a tear, and she spoke, oh, in such a terrible monotone. Oh! *dear,"* cried Page, "I wish all this was over, and we could all get away from Chicago, and take Mr. Jadwin with us, and get him back to be as he used to be, always so light-hearted, and thoughtful and kindly. He used to be making jokes from morning till night. Oh, I loved him just as if he were my father."

They crossed the street, and Landry, taking her by the arm, ushered her into the corridor on the ground floor of the Board.

"Now, keep close to me," he said, "and see if we can get through somewhere here."

The stairs leading up to the main floor were already crowded with visitors, some standing in line close to the wall, others aimlessly wandering up and down, looking and listening, their heads in the air. One of these, a gentleman with a tall white hat, shook his head at Landry and Page as they passed by him.

"You can't get up there," he said, "even if they let you in. They're packed in like sardines already."

But Landry reassured Page with a knowing nod of his head.

"I told the guide up in the gallery to reserve a seat for you. I guess we'll manage."

But when they reached the staircase that connected the main floor with the visitors' gallery it became a question as to whether or not they could get even to the seat. The crowd was packed solidly upon the stairs, between the wall and the balustrades. There were men in top hats and women in silks; rough fellows of the poorer streets, and gaudily dressed queens of obscure neighborhoods, while mixed with these one saw the faded and shabby wrecks that perennially drifted about the Board of Trade, the failures who sat on the chairs of the customers' rooms day in and day out, reading old newspapers, smoking vile cigars. And there were young men of the type of clerks and bookkeepers, young men with drawn, worn faces, and hot, tired eyes, who pressed upward, silent, their lips compressed, listening intently to the indefinite echoing murmur that was filling the building.

For on this morning of the thirteenth of June the Board of Trade, its halls, corridors, offices, and stairways, were already thrilling with a vague and terrible sound. It was only a little after nine o'clock. The trading would not begin for another half hour but, even now, the mutter of the whirlpool, the growl of the Pit was making itself felt. The eddies were gathering; the thousands of subsidiary torrents that fed the cloaca were moving. From all over the immediate neighborhood they came, from the offices of hundreds of commission houses, from brokers' offices, from banks, from the tall, gray buildings of La Salle Street, from the street itself. And even from greater distances they came; auxiliary currents set in from all the reach of the Great Northwest, from Minneapolis, Duluth, and Milwaukee. From the Southwest, St. Louis, Omaha, and Kansas City contributed to the volume. The Atlantic Seaboard, New York, and Boston and Philadelphia sent out their tributary streams; London, Liverpool, Paris, and Odessa merged their influences with the vast world-wide flowing that bore down upon Chicago, and that now began slowly, slowly to centre and circle about the Wheat Pit of the Board of Trade.

Small wonder that the building to Page's ears vibrated to a strange and ominous humming. She heard it in the distant clicking of telegraph keys, in the echo of hurried whispered conversations held in dark corners, in the noise of rapid footsteps, in the trilling of telephone bells. These sounds came from all around her; they issued from the offices of the building below her, above her and on either side. She was surrounded with them, and they mingled together to form one prolonged and muffled roar, that from moment to moment increased in volume.

The Pit was getting under way; the whirlpool was forming, and the sound of its courses was like the sound of the ocean in storm, heard at a distance.

Page and Landry were still half-way up the last stairway. Above and below, the throng was packed dense and immobilized. But, little by little, Landry wormed a way for them, winning one step at a time. But he was very anxious; again and again he looked at his watch. At last he said:

"I've *got* to go. It's just madness for me to stay another minute. I'll give you my card."

"Well, leave me here," Page urged. "It can't be helped. I'm all right. Give me your card. I'll tell the guide in the gallery that you kept the seat for me—if I ever can get there. You must go. Don't stay another minute. If you can, come for me here in the gallery, when it's over. I'll wait for you. But if you can't come, all right. I can take care of myself."

He could but assent to this. This was no time to think of small things. He left her and bore back with all his might through the crowd, gained the landing at the turn of the balustrade, waved his hat to her and disappeared.

A quarter of an hour went by. Page, caught in the crowd, could neither advance nor retreat. Ahead of her, some twenty steps away, she could see the back rows of seats in the gallery. But they were already occupied. It seemed hopeless to expect to see anything of the floor that day. But she could no longer extricate herself from the press; there was nothing to do but stay where she was.

On every side of her she caught odds and ends of dialogues and scraps of discussions, and while she waited she found an interest in listening to these, as they reached her from time to time.

"Well," observed the man in the tall white hat, who had discouraged Landry from attempting to reach the gallery, "well, he's shaken 'em up pretty well. Whether he downs 'em or they down him, he's made a good fight."

His companion, a young man with eyeglasses, who wore a wonderful white waistcoat with queer glass buttons, assented, and Page heard him add:

"Big operator, that Jadwin."

"They're doing for him now, though."

"I ain't so sure. He's got another fight in him. You'll see."

"Ever see him?"

"No, no, he don't come into the Pit—these big men never do."

Directly in front of Page two women kept up an interminable discourse.

"Well," said the one, "that's all very well, but Mr. Jadwin made my sister-in-law—she lives in Dubuque, you know—a rich woman. She bought some wheat just for fun, you know, a long time ago, and held on till Mr. Jadwin put the price up to four times what she paid for it. Then she sold out. My, you ought to see the lovely house she's building, and her son's gone to Europe, to study art, if you please, and a year ago, my dear, they didn't have a cent, not a cent, but her husband's salary."

"There's the other side, too, though," answered her companion, adding in a hoarse whisper: "If Mr. Jadwin fails to-day—well, honestly, Julia, I don't know what Philip will do."

But, from another group at Page's elbow, a man's bass voice cut across the subdued chatter of the two women.

" 'Guess we'll pull through, somehow. Burbank & Co., though— by George! I'm not sure about them. They are pretty well involved in this thing, and there's two or three smaller firms that are dependent on them. If Gretry, Converse & Co. should suspend, Burbank would go with a crash sure. And there's that bank in Keokuk; they can't stand much more. Their depositors would run 'em quick as how-do-you-do if there was a smash here in Chicago."

"Oh, Jadwin will pull through."

"Well, I hope so—by Jingo! I hope so. Say, by the way, how did you come out?"

"Me! Hoh! Say, my boy, the next time I get into a wheat trade you'll know it. I was one of the merry paretics who believed that Crookes was the Great Lumtum. I tailed on to his clique. Lord love you! Jadwin put the knife into me to the tune of twelve thousand dollars. But, say, look here; aren't we ever going to get up to that blame gallery? We ain't going to see any of this, and I —hark!—by God! there goes the gong. They've begun. Say, say, hear 'em, will you! Holy Moses! say—listen to that! Did you ever hear—Lord! I wish we could see—could get somewhere where we could see something."

His friend turned to him and spoke a sentence that was drowned

in the sudden vast volume of sound that all at once shook the
building.

"Hey—what?"

The other shouted into his ear. But even then his friend could
not hear. Nor did he listen. The crowd upon the staircases had
surged irresistibly forward and upward. There was a sudden outburst of cries. Women's voices were raised in expostulation, and
even fear.

"Oh, oh—don't push so!"

"My arm! oh!—oh, I shall faint . . . please."

But the men, their escorts, held back furiously; their faces
purple, they shouted imprecations over their shoulders.

"Here, here, you damn fools, what you doing?"

"Don't crowd so!"

"Get back, back!"

"There's a lady fainted here. Get back you! We'll all have a
chance to see. Good Lord! ain't there a policeman anywheres?"

"Say, say! It's going down—the price. It broke three cents,
just then, at the opening, they say."

"This is the worst I ever saw or heard of."

"My God! if Jadwin can only *hold* 'em."

"You bet he'll hold 'em."

"Hold nothing!—Oh! say, my friend, it don't do you any good
to crowd like that."

"It's the people behind: I'm not doing it. Say, do you know
where they're at on the floor? The wheat, I mean, is it going up
or down?"

"Up, they tell me. There was a rally; I don't know. How can
we tell here? We—Hi! there they go again. Lord! that must
have been a smash. I guess the Board of Trade won't forget this
day in a hurry. Heavens, you can't hear yourself think!"

"Glad I ain't down there in the Pit."

But, at last, a group of policemen appeared. By main strength
they shouldered their way to the top of the stairs, and then began
pushing the crowd back. At every instant they shouted:

"Move on now, clear the stairway. No seats left!"

But at this Page, who by the rush of the crowd had been carried
almost to the top of the stairs, managed to extricate an arm from
the press, and hold Landry's card in the air. She even hazarded
a little deception:

"I have a pass. Will you let me through, please?"

Luckily one of the officers heard her. He bore down heavily with all the mass of his two hundred pounds and the majesty of the law he represented to the rescue and succor of this very pretty girl.

"Let the lady through," he roared, forcing a passage with both elbows. "Come right along, Miss. Stand back you, now. Can't you see the lady has a pass? Now then, Miss, and be quick about it, I can't keep 'em back forever."

Jostled and hustled, her dress crumpled, her hat awry, Page made her way forward, till the officer caught her by the arm, and pulled her out of the press. With a long breath she gained the landing of the gallery.

The guide, an old fellow in a uniform of blue, with brass buttons and a vizored cap, stood near by, and to him she presented Landry's card.

"Oh, yes, oh, yes," he shouted in her ear, after he had glanced it over. "You were the party Mr. Court spoke about. You just came in time. I wouldn't 'a' dared hold your seat a minute longer."

He led her down the crowded aisle between rows of theatre chairs, all of which were occupied, to one vacant seat in the very front row.

"You can see everything, now," he cried, making a trumpet of his palm. "You're Mister Jadwin's niece. I know, I know. Ah, it's a wild day, Miss. They ain't done much yet, and Mr. Jadwin's holding his own, just now. But I thought for a moment they had him on the run. You see that—my, my, there was a sharp rally. But he's holding on strong yet."

Page took her seat, and leaning forward looked down into the Wheat Pit.

Once free of the crowd after leaving Page, Landry ran with all the swiftness of his long legs down the stair, and through the corridors till, all out of breath, he gained Gretry's private office. The other Pit traders for the house, some eight or ten men, were already assembled, and just as Landry entered by one door the broker himself came in from the customers' room. Jadwin was nowhere to be seen.

"What are the orders for to-day, sir?"

Gretry was very pale. Despite his long experience on the Board of Trade, Landry could see anxiety in every change of his expression, in every motion of his hands. The broker before answering the question crossed the room to the water cooler and drank a brief swallow. Then emptying the glass he refilled it, moistened his lips again, and again emptied and filled the goblet. He put it down, caught it up once more, filled it, emptied it, drinking now in long draughts, now in little sips. He was quite unconscious of his actions, and Landry, as he watched, felt his heart sink. Things must, indeed, be at a desperate pass when Gretry, the calm, the clear-headed, the placid, was thus upset.

"Your orders?" said the broker, at last. "The same as yesterday; keep the market up—that's all. It must not go below a dollar fifteen. But act on the defensive. Don't be aggressive, unless I send word. There will probably be very heavy selling the first few moments. You can buy, each of you, up to half a million bushels apiece. If that don't keep the price up, if they still are selling after that . . . well"—Gretry paused a moment, irresolutely—"well," he added suddenly, "if they are still selling freely after you've each bought half a million, I'll let you know what to do. And, look here," he continued, facing the group, "look here—keep your heads cool . . . I guess to-day will decide things. Watch the Crookes crowd pretty closely. I understand they're up to something again. That's all, I guess."

Landry and the other Gretry traders hurried from the office up to the floor. Landry's heart was beating thick and slow and hard, his teeth were shut tight. Every nerve, every fibre of him braced itself with the rigidity of drawn wire, to meet the issue of the impending hours. Now was to come the last grapple. He had never lived through a crisis such as this before. Would he prevail, would he keep his head? Would he avoid or balk the thousand and one little subterfuges, tricks, and traps that the hostile traders would prepare for him—prepare with a quickness, a suddenness that all but defied the sharpest, keenest watchfulness?

Was the gong never going to strike? He found himself, all at once, on the edge of the Wheat Pit. It was jammed tight with the crowd of traders, and the excitement that disengaged itself from that tense, vehement crowd of white faces and glittering eyes was veritably sickening, veritably weakening. Men on either side of him were shouting mere incoherencies, to which nobody, not even themselves, were listening. Others silent, gnawed their nails to the quick, breathing rapidly, audibly even, their nostrils expanding and contracting. All around roared the vague thunder that since early morning had shaken the building. In the Pit the bids leaped to and fro, though the time of opening had not yet come; the very planks underfoot seemed spinning about in the first huge warning swirl of the Pit's centripetal convulsion. There was dizziness in the air. Something, some infinite immeasurable power, onrushing in its eternal courses, shook the Pit in its grasp. Something deafened the ears, blinded the eyes, dulled and numbed the mind, with its roar, with the chaff and dust of its whirlwind passage, with the stupefying sense of its power, coeval with the earthquake and glacier, merciless, all-powerful, a primal basic throe of creation itself, unassailable, inviolate, and untamed.

Had the trading begun? Had the gong struck? Landry never knew, never so much as heard the clang of the great bell. All at once he was fighting; all at once he was caught, as it were, from off the stable earth, and flung headlong into the heart and centre of the Pit.

What he did, he could not say; what went on about him, he could not distinguish. He only knew that roar was succeeding roar, that there was crashing through his ears, through his very brain, the combined bellow of a hundred Niagaras. Hands clutched and tore at him, his own tore and clutched in turn. The Pit was mad, was drunk and frenzied; not a man of all those who fought and scrambled and shouted who knew what he or his neighbor did. They only knew that a support long thought to be secure was giving way, not gradually, not evenly, but by horrible collapses, and equally horrible upward leaps. Now it held, now it broke, now it re-formed again, rose again, then again in hideous cataclysms fell from beneath their feet to lower depths than before. The official reporter leaned back in his place, helpless. On the wall overhead, the indicator on the dial was rocking back and forth, like the mast of a ship caught in a monsoon. The price of July wheat no man could so much as approximate. The fluctuations were no longer by fractions of a cent, but by ten cents, fifteen cents, twenty-five cents at a time. On one side of the Pit wheat sold at ninety cents, on the other at a dollar and a quarter.

And all the while, above the din upon the floor, above the tramplings and the shoutings in the Pit, there seemed to thrill and swell that appalling roar of the Wheat itself coming in, coming on like a tidal wave, bursting through, dashing barriers aside, rolling like a measureless, almighty river, from the farms of Iowa and the ranches of California, on to the East—to the bakeshops and hungry mouths of Europe.

Landry caught one of the Gretry traders by the arm.

"What shall we do?" he shouted. "I've bought up to my limit.

No more orders have come in. The market has gone from under us. What's to be done?"

"I don't know," the other shouted back, "I don't know. We're all gone to hell; looks like the last smash. There are no more supporting orders—something's gone wrong. Gretry hasn't sent any word."

Then, Landry, beside himself with excitement and with actual terror, hardly knowing even yet what he did, turned sharply about. He fought his way out of the Pit; he ran hatless and panting across the floor, in and out between the groups of spectators, down the stairs to the corridor below, and into the Gretry-Converse offices.

In the outer office a group of reporters and the representatives of a great commercial agency were besieging one of the heads of the firm. They assaulted him with questions.

"Just tell us where you are at—that's all we want to know."

"Just what is the price of July wheat?"

"Is Jadwin winning or losing?"

But the other threw out an arm in a wild gesture of helplessness.

"We don't know, ourselves," he cried. "The market has run clean away from everybody. You know as much about it as I do. It's simply hell broken loose, that's all. We can't tell where we are at for days to come."

Landry rushed on. He swung open the door of the private office and entered, slamming it behind him and crying out:

"Mr. Gretry, what are we to do? We've had no orders."

But no one listened to him. Of the group that gathered around Gretry's desk, no one so much as turned a head.

Jadwin stood there in the centre of the others, hatless, his face pale, his eyes congested with blood. Gretry fronted him, one hand upon his arm. In the remainder of the group Landry recognized the senior clerk of the office, one of the heads of a great banking house, and a couple of other men—confidential agents, who had helped to manipulate the great corner.

"But you can't," Gretry was exclaiming. "You can't; don't you see we can't meet our margin calls? It's the end of the game. You've got no more money."

"It's a lie!" Never so long as he lived did Landry forget the voice in which Jadwin cried the words: "It's a lie! Keep on buying, I tell you. Take all they'll offer. I tell you we'll touch the two-dollar mark before noon."

"Not another order goes up to that floor," retorted Gretry. "Why, J., ask any of these gentlemen here. They'll tell you."

"It's useless, Mr. Jadwin," said the banker quietly. "You were practically beaten two days ago."

"Mr. Jadwin," pleaded the senior clerk, "for God's sake listen to reason. Our firm—"

But Jadwin was beyond all appeal. He threw off Gretry's hand.

"Your firm, your firm—you've been cowards from the start. I know you, I know you. You have sold me out. Crookes has bought you. Get out of my way!" he shouted. "Get out of my way! Do you hear? I'll play my hand alone from now on."

"J., old man—why—see here, man," Gretry implored, still holding him by the arm; "here, where are you going?"

Jadwin's voice rang like a trumpet call:

"Into the Pit."

"Look here—wait—here. Hold him back, gentlemen. He don't know what he's about."

"If you won't execute my orders, I'll act myself. I'm going into the Pit, I tell you."

"J., you're mad, old fellow. You're ruined—don't you understand?—you're ruined."

"Then, God curse you, Sam Gretry, for the man who failed me in a crisis." And as he spoke, Curtis Jadwin struck the broker full in the face.

Gretry staggered back from the blow, catching at the edge of his desk. His pale face flashed to crimson for an instant, his fists clinched; then his hands fell to his sides.

"No," he said, "let him go, let him go. The man is merely mad."

But Jadwin, struggling for a second in the midst of the group that tried to hold him, suddenly flung off the restraining clasps, thrust the men to one side, and rushed from the room.

Gretry dropped into his chair before his desk.

"It's the end," he said simply.

He drew a sheet of note paper to him, and in a shaking hand wrote a couple of lines.

"Take that," he said, handing the note to the senior clerk, "take that to the secretary of the Board at once."

And straight into the turmoil and confusion of the Pit, to the scene of so many of his victories, the battleground whereon again and again, his enemies routed, he had remained the victor undisputed, undismayed came the "Great Bull." No sooner had he set

foot within the entrance to the Floor than the news went flashing
and flying from lip to lip. The galleries knew it, the public room,
and the Western Union knew it, the telephone booths knew it, and
lastly even the Wheat Pit, torn and tossed and rent asunder by
the force this man himself had unchained, knew it, and knowing
stood dismayed.

For even then, so great had been his power, so complete his
dominion, and so well-rooted the fear which he had inspired, that
this last move in the great game he had been playing, this unexpected, direct, personal assumption of control struck a sense of consternation into the heart of the hardiest of his enemies.

Jadwin himself, the great man, the "Great Bull" in the Pit!
What was about to happen? Had they been too premature in their
hope of his defeat? Had he been preparing some secret, unexpected
manœuvre? For a second they hesitated, then moved by a common impulse, feeling the push of the wonderful new harvest behind
them, they gathered themselves together for the final assault, and
again offered the wheat for sale; offered it by thousands upon
thousands of bushels; poured, as it were, the reapings of entire
principalities out upon the floor of the Board of Trade.

Jadwin was in the thick of the confusion by now. And the
avalanche, the undiked Ocean of the Wheat, leaping to the lash
of the hurricane, struck him fairly in the face.

He heard it now, he heard nothing else. The Wheat had broken
from his control. For months he had, by the might of his single
arm, held it back; but now it rose like the upbuilding of a colossal
billow. It towered, towered, hung poised for an instant, and then,
with a thunder as of the grind and crash of chaotic worlds, broke
upon him, burst through the Pit and raced past him, on and on to
the eastward and to the hungry nations.

And then, under the stress and violence of the hour, something
snapped in his brain. The murk behind his eyes had been suddenly
pierced by a white flash. The strange qualms and tiny nervous
paroxysms of the last few months all at once culminated in some
indefinite, indefinable crisis, and the wheels and cogs of all activities
save one lapsed away and ceased. Only one function of the complicated machine persisted; but it moved with a rapidity of vibration
that seemed to be tearing the tissues of being to shreds, while its
rhythm beat out the old and terrible cadence:

"Wheat—wheat—wheat, wheat—wheat—wheat."

Blind and insensate, Jadwin strove against the torrent of the

Wheat. There in the middle of the Pit, surrounded and assaulted by herd after herd of wolves yelping for his destruction, he stood braced, rigid upon his feet, his head up, his hand, the great bony hand that once had held the whole Pit in its grip, flung high in the air, in a gesture of defiance, while his voice, like the clangor of bugles sounding to the charge of the forlorn hope, rang out again and again, over the din of his enemies:

"Give a dollar for July—give a dollar for July!"

With one accord they leaped upon him. The little group of his traders was swept aside. Landry alone, Landry, who had never left his side since his rush from out Gretry's office, Landry Court, loyal to the last, his one remaining soldier, white, shaking, the sobs strangling in his throat, clung to him desperately. Another billow of wheat was preparing. They two—the beaten general and his young armor-bearer—heard it coming; hissing, raging, bellowing, it swept down upon them. Landry uttered a cry. Flesh and blood could not stand this strain. He cowered at his chief's side, his shoulders bent, one arm above his head, as if to ward off an actual physical force.

But Jadwin, iron to the end, stood erect. All unknowing what he did, he had taken Landry's hand in his and the boy felt the grip on his fingers like the contracting of a vise of steel. The other hand, as though holding up a standard, was still in the air, and his great deep-toned voice went out across the tumult, proclaiming to the end his battle-cry:

"Give a dollar for July—give a dollar for July!"

But, little by little, Landry became aware that the tumult of the Pit was intermitting. There were sudden lapses in the shouting, and in these lapses he could hear from somewhere out upon the floor voices that were crying: "Order—order, order, gentlemen."

But, again and again the clamor broke out. It would die down for an instant, in response to these appeals, only to burst out afresh as certain groups of traders started the pandemonium again, by the wild outcrying of their offers. At last, however, the older men in the Pit, regaining some measure of self-control, took up the word, going to and fro in the press, repeating "Order, order."

And then, all at once, the Pit, the entire floor of the Board of Trade, was struck dumb. All at once the tension was relaxed, the furious struggling and stamping were stilled. Landry, bewildered, still holding his chief by the hand, looked about him. On the floor, near at hand, stood the president of the Board of Trade himself, and with him the vice-president and a group of the directors. Evidently it had been these who had called the traders to order. But it was not toward them now that the hundreds of men in the Pit and on the floor were looking.

In the little balcony on the south wall opposite the visitors' gallery a figure had appeared, a tall grave man, in a long black coat— the secretary of the Board of Trade. Landry with the others saw him, saw him advance to the edge of the railing, and fix his glance upon the Wheat Pit. In his hand he carried a slip of paper.

And then in the midst of that profound silence the secretary announced:

"All trades with Gretry, Converse & Co. must be closed at once."

The words had not ceased to echo in the high vaultings of the roof before they were greeted with a wild, shrill yell of exultation and triumph, that burst from the crowding masses in the Wheat Pit.

Beaten; beaten at last, the Great Bull! Smashed! The great corner smashed! Jadwin busted! They themselves saved, saved, saved! Cheer followed upon cheer, yell after yell. Hats went into the air. In a frenzy of delight men danced and leaped and capered upon the edge of the Pit, clasping their arms about each other, shaking each others' hands, cheering and hurrahing till their strained voices became hoarse and faint.

Some few of the older men protested. There were cries of:

"Shame, shame!"

"Order—let him alone."

"Let him be; he's down now. Shame, shame!"

But the jubilee was irrepressible, they had been too cruelly pressed, these others; they had felt the weight of the Bull's hoof, the rip of his horn. Now they had beaten him, had pulled him down.

"Yah-h-h, whoop, yi, yi, yi. Busted, busted, busted. Hip, hip, hip, and a tiger!"

"Come away, sir. For God's sake, Mr. Jadwin, come away."

Landry was pleading with Jadwin, clutching his arm in both his hands, his lips to his chief's ear to make himself heard above the yelping of the mob.

Jadwin was silent now. He seemed no longer to see or hear; heavily, painfully he leaned upon the young man's shoulder.

"Come away, sir—for God's sake!"

The group of traders parted before them, cheering even while they gave place, cheering with eyes averted, unwilling to see the ruin that meant for them salvation.

"Yah-h-h. Yah-h-h, busted, busted!"

Landry had put his arm about Jadwin, and gripped him close as he led him from the Pit. The sobs were in his throat again, and tears of excitement, of grief, of anger and impotence were running down his face.

"Yah-h-h. Yah-h-h, he's done for, busted, busted!"

"Damn you all," cried Landry, throwing out a furious fist, "damn you all; you brutes, you beasts! If he'd so much as raised a finger a week ago, you'd have run for your lives."

But the cheering drowned his voice; and as the two passed out of the Pit upon the floor, the gong that closed the trading struck, and, as it seemed, put a period definite and final to the conclusion of Curtis Jadwin's career as speculator.

Across the floor toward the doorway Landry led his defeated captain. Jadwin was in a daze, he saw nothing, heard nothing. Quietly he submitted to Landry's guiding arm. The visitors in the galleries bent far over to see him pass, and from all over the floor, spectators, hangers-on, corn-and-provision traders, messenger boys, clerks and reporters came hurrying to watch the final exit of the Great Bull, from the scene of his many victories and his one over-whelming defeat.

In silence they watched him go by. Only in the distance from the direction of the Pit itself came the sound of dying cheers. But at the doorway stood a figure that Landry recognized at once—a small man, lean-faced, trimly dressed, his clean-shaven lips pursed like the mouth of a shut money bag, imperturbable as ever, cold, unexcited—Calvin Crookes himself.

And as Jadwin passed, Landry heard the Bear leader say:

"They can cheer now, all they want. *They* didn't do it. It was the wheat itself that beat him; no combination of men could have done it—go on, cheer, you damn fools! He was a bigger man than the best of us."

With the striking of the gong, and the general movement of the crowd in the galleries toward the exits, Page rose, drawing a long breath, pressing her hands an instant to her burning cheeks. She had seen all that had happened, but she had not understood. The whole morning had been a whirl and a blur. She had looked down upon a jam of men, who for three hours had done nothing but shout and struggle. She had seen Jadwin come into the Pit, and almost at once the shouts had turned to cheers. That must have meant, she thought, that Jadwin had done something to please those excited men. They were all his friends, no doubt. They were cheering him—cheering his success. He had won then! And yet that announcement from the opposite balcony, to the effect that business with Mr. Gretry must be stopped, immediately! That had an ominous ring. Or, perhaps, that meant only a momentary check.

As she descended the stairways, with the departing spectators, she distinctly heard a man's voice behind her exclaim:

"Well, that does for *him!*"

Possibly, after all, Mr. Jadwin had lost some money that morning. She was desperately anxious to find Landry, and to learn the truth of what had happened, and for a long moment after the last visitors had disappeared she remained at the foot of the gallery stairway, hoping that he would come for her. But she saw nothing of him, and soon remembered she had told him to come for her only in case he was able to get away. No doubt he was too busy now. Even if Mr. Jadwin had won, the morning's work had evidently been of tremendous importance. This had been a great day for the wheat speculators. It was not surprising that Landry should be detained. She would wait till she saw him the next day to find out all that had taken place.

Page returned home. It was long past the hour for luncheon when she came into the dining-room of the North Avenue house.

"Where is my sister?" she asked of the maid, as she sat down to the table; "has she lunched yet?"

But it appeared that Mrs. Jadwin had sent down word to say that she wanted no lunch, that she had a headache and would remain in her room.

Page hurried through with her chocolate and salad, and ordering a cup of strong tea, carried it up to Laura's "sitting-room" herself.

Laura, in a long tea-gown, lay back in the Madeira chair, her hands clasped behind her head, doing nothing apparently but looking out of the window. She was paler even than usual, and to Page's mind seemed preoccupied, and in a certain indefinite way tense and hard. Page, as she had told Landry that morning, had remarked this tenseness, this rigidity on the part of her sister, of late. But to-day it was more pronounced than ever. Something surely was the matter with Laura. She seemed like one who had staked everything upon a hazard and, blind to all else, was keeping

back emotion with all her strength, while she watched and waited
for the issue. Page guessed that her sister's trouble had to do with
Jadwin's complete absorption in business, but she preferred to hold
her peace. By nature the young girl "minded her own business,"
and Laura was not a woman who confided her troubles to anybody.
Only once had Page presumed to meddle in her sister's affairs, and
the result had not encouraged a repetition of the intervention. Since
the affair of the silver match box she had kept her distance.

Laura on this occasion declined to drink the tea Page had
brought. She wanted nothing, she said; her head ached a little, she
only wished to lie down and be quiet.

"I've been down to the Board of Trade all the morning," Page
remarked.

Laura fixed her with a swift glance; she demanded quickly:

"Did you see Curtis?"

"No—or, yes, once; he came out on the floor. Oh, Laura, it
was so exciting there this morning. Something important happened, I know. I can't believe it's that way all the time. I'm afraid
Mr. Jadwin lost a great deal of money. I heard some one behind
me say so, but I couldn't understand what was going on. For
months I've been trying to get a clear idea of wheat trading, just
because it was Landry's business, but to-day I couldn't make anything of it at all."

"Did Curtis say he was coming home this evening?"

"No. Don't you understand, I didn't see him to talk to."

"Well, why didn't you, Page?"

"Why, Laura, honey, don't be cross. You don't know now
rushed everything was. I didn't even try to see Landry."

"Did he seem very busy?"

"Who, Landry? I—"

"No, no, no, Curtis."

"Oh, I should say so. Why, Laura, I think, honestly, I think
wheat went down to—oh, 'way down. They say that means so much
to Mr. Jadwin, and it went down, down, down. It looked that
way to me. Don't that mean that he'll lose a great deal of money?
And Landry seemed so brave and courageous through it all. Oh, I
felt for him so; I just wanted to go right into the Pit with him and
stand by his shoulder."

Laura started up with a sharp gesture of impatience and ex-
asperation, crying:

"Oh, what do I care about wheat—about this wretched scrambling for money. Curtis was busy, you say? He looked that way?"

Page nodded: "Everybody was," she said. Then she hazarded: "I wouldn't worry, Laura. Of course, a man must give a great deal of time to business. I didn't mind when Landry couldn't come home with me."

"Oh—Landry," murmured Laura.

On the instant Page bridled, her eyes snapping.

"I think that was very uncalled for," she exclaimed, sitting bolt upright, "and I can tell you this, Laura Jadwin, if you did care a little more about wheat—about your husband's business—if you had taken more of an interest in his work, if you had tried to enter more into his life, and be a help to him—and—and sympathize— and—" Page caught her breath, a little bewildered at her own vehemence and audacity. But she had committed herself now; recklessly she plunged on. "Just think; he may be fighting the battle of his life down there in La Salle Street, and you don't know anything about it—no, nor want to know. 'What do you care about wheat,' that's what you said. Well, I don't care either, just for the wheat itself, but it's Landry's business, his work; and right or wrong—" Page jumped to her feet, her fists tight shut, her face scarlet, her head upraised, "right or wrong, good or bad, I'd put my two hands into the fire to help him."

"What business—" began Laura; but Page was not to be interrupted. "And if he did leave me alone sometimes," she said; "do you think I would draw a long face, and think only of my own troubles. I guess he's got his own troubles, too. If my husband had a battle to fight, do you think I'd mope and pine because he left me at home; no, I wouldn't. I'd help him buckle his sword on, and when he came back to me I wouldn't tell him how lonesome I'd been, but I'd take care of him and cry over his wounds, and tell him to be brave—and—and—and I'd help him."

And with the words, Page, the tears in her eyes and the sobs in her throat, flung out of the room, shutting the door violently behind her.

Laura's first sensation was one of anger only. As always, her younger sister had presumed again to judge her, had chosen this day of all others to annoy her. She gazed an instant at the closed door, then rose and put her chin in the air. She was right, and Page, her husband, everybody, were wrong. She had been flouted, ignored. She paced the length of the room a couple of times, then threw herself down upon the couch, her chin supported on her palm.

As she crossed the room, however, her eye had been caught by an opened note from Mrs. Cressler, received the day before, and apprising her of the date of the funeral. At the sight, all the tragedy leaped up again in her mind and recollection, and in fancy she stood again in the back parlor of the Cressler home; her fingers pressed over her mouth to shut back the cries, horror and the terror of sudden death rending her heart, shaking the brain itself. Again and again since that dreadful moment had the fear come back, mingled with grief, with compassion, and the bitter sorrow of a kind friend gone forever from her side. And then, her resolution girding itself, her will power at fullest stretch, she had put the tragedy from her. Other and—for her—more momentous events impended. Everything in life, even death itself, must stand aside while her love was put to the test. Life and death were little things. Love only existed; let her husband's career fail; what did it import so only love stood the strain and issued from the struggle triumphant? And now, as she lay upon her couch, she crushed down all compunction for the pitiful calamity whose last scene she had discovered, her thoughts once more upon her husband and herself. Had the shock of that spectacle in the Cresslers' house, and the wearing suspense in which she had lived of late, so torn and disordered the delicate feminine nerves that a kind of hysteria animated and directed her impulses, her words, and actions? Laura did not know. She only knew that the day was going and that her husband neither came near her nor sent her word.

Even if he had been very busy, this was her birthday—though he had lost millions! Could he not have sent even the foolishest little present to her, even a line—three words on a scrap of paper? But she checked herself. The day was not over yet; perhaps, perhaps he would remember her, after all, before the afternoon was over. He was managing a little surprise for her, no doubt. He knew what day this was. After their talk that Sunday in his smoking-room he would not forget. And, besides, it was the evening that he had promised should be hers. "If he loved her," she had said, he would give that evening to her. Never, never would Curtis fail her when conjured by that spell.

Laura had planned a little dinner for that night. It was to be served at eight. Page would have dined earlier; only herself and her husband were to be present. It was to be her birthday

dinner. All the noisy, clamorous world should be excluded; no
faintest rumble of the Pit would intrude. She would have him all
to herself. He would, so she determined, forget everything else in
his love for her. She would be beautiful as never before—brilliant,
resistless, and dazzling. She would have him at her feet, her own,
her own again, as much her own as her very hands. And before
she would let him go he would forever and forever have abjured the
Battle of the Street that had so often caught him from her. The
Pit should not have him; the sweep of that great whirlpool should
never again prevail against the power of love.

Yes, she had suffered, she had known the humiliation of a
woman neglected. But it was to end now; her pride would never
again be lowered, her love never again be ignored.

But the afternoon passed and evening drew on without any
word from him. In spite of her anxiety, she yet murmured over
and over again as she paced the floor of her room, listening for the
ringing of the door bell:

"He will send word, he will send word. I know he will."

By four o'clock she had begun to dress. Never had she made
a toilet more superb, more careful. She disdained a "costume" on
this great evening. It was not to be "Théodora" now, nor "Juliet,"
nor "Carmen." It was to be only Laura Jadwin—just herself, unaided by theatricals, unadorned by tinsel. But it seemed consistent
none the less to choose her most beautiful gown for the occasion, to
panoply herself in every charm that was her own. Her dress, that
closely sheathed the low, flat curves of her body and that left her
slender arms and neck bare, was one shimmer of black scales, iridescent, undulating with light to her every movement. In the coils
and masses of her black hair she fixed her two great *cabochons* of
pearls, and clasped about her neck her palm-broad collaret of pearls
and diamonds. Against one shoulder nodded a bunch of Jacque-
minots, royal red, imperial.

It was hard upon six o'clock when at last she dismissed her
maid. Left alone, she stood for a moment in front of her long
mirror that reflected her image from head to foot, and at the sight
she could not forbear a smile and a sudden proud lifting of her
head. All the woman in her preened and plumed herself in the consciousness of the power of her beauty. Let the Battle of the Street
clamor never so loudly now, let the suction of the Pit be never so
strong, Eve triumphed. *Venus toute entière s'attachait à sa proie.*

These women of America, these others who allowed business to draw their husbands from them more and more, who submitted to those cruel conditions that forced them to be content with the wreckage left after the storm and stress of the day's work—the jaded mind, the exhausted body, the faculties dulled by overwork—she was sorry for them. They, less radiant than herself, less potent to charm, could not call their husbands back. But she, Laura, was beautiful; she knew it; she gloried in her beauty. It was her strength. She felt the same pride in it as the warrior in a finely tempered weapon.

And to-night her beauty was brighter than ever. It was a veritable aureole that crowned her. She knew herself to be invincible. So only that he saw her thus, she knew that she would conquer. And he would come. "If he loved her," she had said. By his love for her he had promised; by his love she knew she would prevail.

And then at last, somewhere out of the twilight, somewhere out of those lowest, unplumbed depths of her own heart, came the first tremor of doubt, came the tardy vibration of the silver cord which Page had struck so sharply. Was it—after all—Love that she cherished and strove for—love, or self-love? Ever since Page had spoken she seemed to have fought against the intrusion of this idea. But, little by little, it rose to the surface. At last, for an instant, it seemed to confront her.

Was this, after all, the right way to win her husband back to her—this display of her beauty, this parade of dress, this exploitation of self?

Self, self. Had she been selfish from the very first? What real interest had she taken in her husband's work? "Right or wrong, good or bad, I would put my two hands into the fire to help him." Was this the way? Was not this the only way? Win him back to her? What if there were more need for her to win back to him? Oh, once she had been able to say that love, the supreme triumph of a woman's life, was less a victory than a capitulation. Had she ordered her life upon that ideal? Did she even believe in the ideal at this day? Whither had this cruel cult of self led her?

Dimly Laura Jadwin began to see and to understand a whole new conception of her little world. The birth of a new being within her was not for that night. It was conception only—the sensation of a new element, a new force that was not herself, somewhere in the inner chambers of her being.

The woman in her was too complex, the fibres of character too intricate and mature to be wrenched into new shapes by any sudden revolution. But just so surely as the day was going, just so surely as the New Day would follow upon the night, conception had taken place within her. Whatever she did that evening, whatever came to her, through whatever crises she should hurry, she would not now be quite the same. She had been accustomed to tell herself that there were two Lauras. Now suddenly, behold, she seemed to recognize a third—a third that rose above and forgot the other two, that in some beautiful, mysterious way was identity ignoring self.

But the change was not to be abrupt. Very, very vaguely the thoughts came to her. The change would be slow, slow—would be evolution, not revolution. The consummation was to be achieved in the coming years. For to-night she was—what was she? Only a woman, weak, torn by emotion, driven by impulse, and entering upon what she imagined was a great crisis in her life.

But meanwhile the time was passing. Laura descended to the library and, picking up a book, composed herself to read. When six o'clock struck, she made haste to assure herself that of course she could not expect him exactly on the hour. No, she must make allowances; the day—as Page had suspected—had probably been an important one. He would be a little late, but he would come soon. "If you love me, you will come," she had said.

But an hour later Laura paced the room with tight-shut lips and burning cheeks. She was still alone; her day, her hour, was passing, and he had not so much as sent word. For a moment the thought occurred to her that he might perhaps be in great trouble, in great straits, that there was an excuse. But instantly she repudiated the notion.

"No, no," she cried, beneath her breath. "He should come, no matter what has happened. Or even, at the very least, he could send word."

The minutes dragged by. No roll of wheels echoed under the carriage porch; no step sounded at the outer door. The house was still, the street without was still, the silence of the midsummer evening widened, unbroken around her, like a vast calm pool. Only the musical Gregorians of the newsboys chanting the evening's extras from corner to corner of the streets rose into the air from time to time. She was once more alone. Was she to fail again? Was she to be set aside once more, as so often heretofore—set aside, flouted, ignored, forgotten? "If you love me," she had said.

And this was to be the supreme test. This evening was to decide which was the great influence of his life—was to prove whether or not love was paramount. This was the crucial hour. "And he knows it," cried Laura. "He knows it. He did not forget, could not have forgotten."

The half hour passed, then the hour, and as eight o'clock chimed from the clock over the mantel-shelf Laura stopped, suddenly rigid, in the midst of the floor.

Her anger leaped like fire within her. All the passion of the woman scorned shook her from head to foot. At the very moment of her triumph she had been flouted, in the pitch of her pride! And this was not the only time. All at once the past disappointments, slights, and humiliations came again to her memory. She had pleaded, and had been rebuffed again and again; she had given all and had received neglect—she, Laura, beautiful beyond other women, who had known love, devoted service, and the most thoughtful consideration from her earliest girlhood, had been cast aside.

Suddenly she bent her head quickly, listening intently. Then she drew a deep breath, murmuring, "At last, at last!"

For the sound of a footstep in the vestibule was unmistakable. He had come after all. But so late, so late! No, she could not be gracious at once; he must be made to feel how deeply he had offended; he must sue humbly, very humbly, for pardon. The servant's step sounded in the hall on the way toward the front door.

"I am in here, Matthew," she called. "In the library. Tell him I am in here."

She cast a quick glance at herself in the mirror close at hand, touched her hair with rapid fingers, smoothed the agitation from her forehead, and sat down in a deep chair near the fireplace, opening a book, turning her back toward the door.

She heard him come in, but did not move. Even as he crossed the floor she kept her head turned away. The footsteps paused near at hand. There was a moment's silence. Then slowly Laura, laying down her book, turned and faced him.

"With many very, very happy returns of the day," said Sheldon Corthell, as he held toward her a cluster of deep-blue violets.

Laura sprang to her feet, a hand upon her cheek, her eyes wide and flashing.

"You?" was all she had breath to utter. "You?"

The artist smiled as he laid the flowers upon the table.

"I am going away again to-morrow," he said, "for always, I

think. Have I startled you? I only came to say good-by—and to wish you a happy birthday."

"Oh, you remembered!" she cried. "*You* remembered! I might have known *you* would."

But the revulsion had been too great. She had been wrong after all. Jadwin had forgotten. Emotions to which she could put no name swelled in her heart and rose in a quick, gasping sob to her throat. The tears sprang to her eyes. Old impulses, forgotten impetuosities whipped her on.

"Oh, you remembered, you remembered!" she cried again, holding out both her hands.

He caught them in his own.

"Remembered!" he echoed. "I have never forgotten."

"No, no," she replied, shaking her head, winking back the tears. "You don't understand. I spoke before I thought. You don't understand."

"I do, believe me, I do," he exclaimed. "I understand you better than you understand yourself."

Laura's answer was a cry.

"Oh, then, why did you ever leave me—you who did understand me? Why did you leave me only because I told you to go? Why didn't you make me love you then? Why didn't you make me understand myself?" She clasped her hands tight together upon her breast; her words, torn by her sobs, came all but incoherent from behind her shut teeth. "No, no!" she exclaimed, as he made toward her. "Don't touch me, don't touch me! It is too late!"

"It is not too late. Listen—listen to me."

"Oh, why weren't you a man, strong enough to know a woman's weakness? You can only torture me now. Ah, I hate you! I hate you!"

"You love me! I tell you, you love me!" he cried, passionately, and before she was aware of it she was in his arms, his lips were against her lips, were on her shoulders, her neck.

"You love me!" he cried. "You love me! I defy you to say you do not."

"Oh, *make* me love you, then," she answered. "*Make* me believe that you do love me."

"Don't you know," he cried, "don't you know how I have loved you? Oh, from the very first! My love has been my life, has been my death, my one joy, and my one bitterness. It has always

been you, dearest, year after year, hour after hour. And now I've
found you again. And now I shall never, never let you go."

"No, no! Ah, don't, don't!" she begged. "I implore you. I
am weak, weak. Just a word, and I would forget everything."

"And I do speak that word, and your own heart answers me in
spite of you, and you will forget—forget everything of unhappiness
in your life—"

"Please, please," she entreated, breathlessly. Then, taking the
leap: "Ah, I love you, I love you!"

"—Forget all your unhappiness," he went on, holding her close
to him. "Forget the one great mistake we both made. Forget
everything, everything, everything but that we love each other."

"Don't let me think, then," she cried. "Don't let me think.
Make me forget everything, every little hour, every little moment
that has passed before this day. Oh, if I remembered once, I
would kill you, kill you with my hands. I don't know what I am
saying," she moaned, "I don't know what I am saying. I am mad,
I think. Yes—I—it must be that." She pulled back from him,
looking into his face with wide-opened eyes.

"What have I said, what have we done, what are you here for?"

"To take you away," he answered, gently, holding her in his
arms, looking down into her eyes. "To take you far away with
me. To give my whole life to making you forget that you were
ever unhappy."

"And you will never leave me alone—never once?"

"Never, never once."

She drew back from him, looking about the room with unseeing
eyes, her fingers plucking and tearing at the lace of her dress; her
voice was faint and small, like the voice of a little child.

"I—I am afraid to be alone. Oh, I must never be alone again
so long as I shall live. I think I should die."

"And you never shall be; never again. Ah, this is my birthday, too, sweetheart. I am born again to-night."

Laura clung to his arm; it was as though she were in the dark,
surrounded by the vague terrors of her girlhood. "And you will
always love me, love me, love me?" she whispered. "Sheldon, Sheldon, love me always, always, with all your heart and soul and
strength."

Tears stood in Corthell's eyes as he answered:

"God forgive whoever—whatever has brought you to this pass,"
he said.

And, as if it were a realization of his thought, there suddenly came to the ears of both the roll of wheels upon the asphalt under the carriage porch and the trampling of iron-shod hoofs.

"Is that your husband?" Corthell's quick eye took in Laura's disarranged coiffure, one black lock low upon her neck, the roses at her shoulder crushed and broken, and the bright spot on either cheek.

"Is that your husband?"

"My husband—I don't know." She looked up at him with unseeing eyes. "Where is my husband? I have no husband. *You are letting me remember,*" she cried, in terror. "You are letting me remember. Ah, no, no, you don't love me! I hate you!"

Quickly he bent and kissed her.

"I will come for you to-morrow evening," he said. "You will be ready then to go with me?"

"Ready then? Yes, yes, to go with you anywhere."

He stood still a moment, listening. Somewhere a door closed. He heard the hoofs upon the asphalt again.

"Good-by," he whispered. "God bless you! Good-by till to-morrow night." And with the words he was gone. The front door of the house closed quietly.

Had he come back again? Laura turned in her place on the long divan at the sound of a heavy tread by the door of the library.

Then an uncertain hand drew the heavy curtain aside. Jadwin, her husband, stood before her, his eyes sunken deep in his head, his face dead white, his hand shaking. He stood for a long instant in the middle of the room, looking at her. Then at last his lips moved:

"Old girl. . . . Honey."

Laura rose, and all but groped her way toward him, her heart beating, the tears streaming down her face.

"My husband, my husband!"

Together they made their way to the divan, and sank down upon it side by side, holding to each other, trembling and fearful, like children in the night.

"Honey," whispered Jadwin, after a while. "Honey, it's dark, it's dark. Something happened. . . . I don't remember," he put his hand uncertainly to his head, "I can't remember very well; but it's dark—a little."

"It's dark," she repeated, in a low whisper. "It's dark, dark. Something happened. Yes. I must not remember."

They spoke no further. A long time passed. Pressed close

together, Curtis Jadwin and his wife sat there in the vast, gorgeous room, silent and trembling, ridden with unnamed fears, groping in the darkness.

And while they remained thus, holding close by one another, a prolonged and wailing cry rose suddenly from the street and passed on through the city under the stars and the wide canopy of the darkness.

"Extra, oh-h-h, extra! All about the Smash of the Great Wheat Corner! All about the Failure of Curtis Jadwin!"

CONCLUSION

The evening had closed in wet and misty. All day long a chill wind had blown across the city from off the lake, and by eight o'clock, when Laura and Jadwin came down to the dismantled library, a heavy rain was falling.

Laura gave Jadwin her arm as they made their way across the room—their footsteps echoing strangely from the uncarpeted floor. "There, dear," she said. "Give me the valise. Now sit down on the packing box there. Are you tired? You had better put your hat on. It is full of draughts here, now that all the furniture and curtains are out."

"No, no. I'm all right, old girl. Is the hack there yet?"

"Not yet. You're sure you're not tired?" she insisted. "You had a pretty bad siege of it, you know, and this is only the first week you've been up. You remember how the doctor—"

"I've had too good a nurse," he answered, stroking her hand, "not to be as fine as a fiddle by now. You must be tired yourself, Laura. Why, for whole days there—and nights, too, they tell me—you never left the room."

She shook her head, as though dismissing the subject.

"I wonder," she said, sitting down upon a smaller packing-box and clasping a knee in her hands, "I wonder what the West will be like. Do you know, I think I am going to like it, Curtis?"

"It will be starting in all over again, old girl," he said, with a warning shake of his head. "Pretty hard at first, I'm afraid."

She laughed an almost contemptuous note.

"Hard! Now?" She took his hand and laid it to her cheek.

"By all the rules you ought to hate me," he began. "What have I done for you but hurt you and, at last, bring you to—"

But she shut her gloved hand over his mouth.

"Stop!" she cried. "Hush, dear. You have brought me the greatest happiness of my life."

Then under her breath, her eyes wide and thoughtful, she murmured:

"A capitulation and not a triumph, and I have won a victory by surrendering."

"Hey—what?" demanded Jadwin. "I didn't hear."

"Never mind," she answered. "It was nothing. 'The world is all before us where to choose,' now, isn't it? And this big house and all the life we have led in it was just an incident in our lives—an incident that is closed."

"Looks like it, to look around this room," he said, grimly. "Nothing left but the wall paper. What do you suppose are in these boxes?"

"They're labeled 'books and portières.' "

"Who bought 'em, I wonder? I'd have thought the party who bought the house would have taken them. Well, it was a wrench to see the place and all go so *dirt* cheap, and the 'Thetis,' too, by George! But I'm glad now. It's as though we had lightened ship." He looked at his watch. "That hack ought to be here pretty soon. I'm glad we checked the trunks from the house; gives us more time."

"Oh, by the way," exclaimed Laura, all at once opening her satchel, "I had a long letter from Page this morning, from New York. Do you want to hear what she has to say? I've only had time to read part of it myself. It's the first one I've had from her since their marriage."

He lighted a cigar.

"Go ahead," he said, settling himself on the box. "What does Mrs. Court have to say?"

" 'My dearest sister,' " began Laura. " 'Here we are, Landry and I, in New York at last. Very tired and mussed after the ride on the cars, but in a darling little hotel where the proprietor is head cook and everybody speaks French. I know my accent is improving, and Landry has learned any quantity of phrases already. We are reading George Sand out loud, and are making up the longest vocabulary. To-night we are going to a concert, and I've found out that there's a really fine course of lectures to be given soon on "Literary Tendencies," or something like that. *Quel chance.* Landry is intensely interested. You've no idea what a deep mind he has, Laura—a real thinker.

" 'But here's really a big piece of news. We may not have to give up our old home where we lived when we first came to Chicago. Aunt Wess' wrote the other day to say that, if you were willing, she would rent it, and then sublet all the lower floor to Landry and me, so we could have a real house over our heads and not the under side of the floor of the flat overhead. And she is such an old dear, I know we could all get along beautifully. Write me about this as soon as you can. I know you'll be willing, and Aunt Wess' said she'd agree to whatever rent you suggested.

" 'We went to call on Mrs. Cressler day before yesterday. She's been here nearly a fortnight by now, and is living with a maiden sister of hers in a very beautiful house fronting Central Park (not so beautiful as our palace on North Avenue. Never, never will I forget that house). She will probably stay here now always. She says the very sight of the old neighborhoods in Chicago would be more than she could bear. Poor Mrs. Cressler! How fortunate for her that her sister—' and so on, and so on," broke in Laura,

"Read it, read it," said Jadwin, turning sharply away. "Don't skip a line. I want to hear every word."

"That's all there is to it," Laura returned. " 'We'll be back,' " she went on, turning a page of the letter, " 'in about three weeks, and Landry will take up his work in that railroad office. No more speculating for him, he says. He talks of Mr. Jadwin continually. You never saw or heard of such devotion. He says that Mr. Jadwin is a genius, the greatest financier in the country, and that he knows he could have won if they all hadn't turned against him that day. He never gets tired telling me that Mr. Jadwin has been a father to him—the kindest, biggest-hearted man he ever knew—' "

Jadwin pulled his mustache rapidly.

"Pshaw, pish, nonsense—little fool!" he blustered.

"He simply worshiped you from the first, Curtis," commented Laura. "Even after he knew I was to marry you. He never once was jealous, never once would listen to a word against you from any one."

"Well—well, what else does Mrs. Court say?".

" 'I am glad to hear,' " read Laura, " 'that Mr. Gretry did not fail, though Landry tells me he must have lost a great deal of money. Landry tells me that eighteen brokers' houses failed in Chicago the day after Mr. Gretry suspended. Isabel sent us a wedding present—a lovely medicine chest full of homœopathic medicines, little pills and things, you know. But, as Landry and I are never sick and both laugh at homœopathy, I declare I don't know just what we will do with it. Landry is as careful of me as though I were a wax doll. But I do wish he would think more of his own health. He never will wear his mackintosh in rainy weather. I've been studying his tastes so carefully. He likes French light opera better than English, and bright colors in his cravats, and he simply adores stuffed tomatoes.

" 'We both send our love, and Landry especially wants to be
remembered to Mr. Jadwin. I hope this letter will come in time for
us to wish you both *bon voyage* and *bon succès*. How splendid of
Mr. Jadwin to have started his new business even while he was
convalescent! Landry says he knows he will make two or three
more fortunes in the next few years.

" 'Good-by, Laura, dear. Ever your loving sister,
" 'PAGE COURT.

" 'P. S.—I open this letter again to tell you that we met Mr.
Corthell on the street yesterday. He sails for Europe to-day.' "

"Oh," said Jadwin, as Laura put the letter quickly down, "Corthell—that artist chap. By the way, whatever became of him?"
Laura settled a comb in the back of her hair.
"He went away," she said. "You remember—I told you—told
you all about it."
She would have turned away her head, but he laid a hand upon
her shoulder.
"I remember," he answered, looking squarely into her eyes, "I
remember nothing—only that I have been to blame for everything.
I told you once—long ago—that I *understood*. And I understand
now, old girl, understand as I never did before. I fancy we both
have been living according to a wrong notion of things. We started
right when we were first married, but I worked away from it somehow and pulled you along with me. But we've both been through
a great big change, honey, a great big change, and we're starting all
over again. . . . Well, there's the carriage, I guess."
They rose, gathering up their valises.
"Hoh!" said Jadwin. "No servants now, Laura, to carry our
things down for us and open the door, and it's a hack, old girl,
instead of the victoria or coupé."
"What if it is?" she cried. "What do 'things,' servants, money,
and all amount to now?"
As Jadwin laid his hand upon the knob of the front door, he
all at once put down his valise and put his arm about his wife.
She caught him about the neck and looked deep into his eyes a
long moment. And then, without speaking, they kissed each other.
In the outer vestibule he raised the umbrella and held it over
her head.
"Hold it a minute, will you, Laura?" he said.
He gave it into her hand and swung the door of the house shut

behind him. The noise woke a hollow echo throughout all the series of empty, denuded rooms. Jadwin slipped the key in his pocket.

"Come," he said.

They stepped out from the vestibule. It was already dark. The rain was falling in gentle slants through the odorous, cool air. Across the street in the park the first leaves were beginning to fall; the lake lapped and washed quietly against the stone embankments, and a belated bicyclist stole past across the asphalt, with the silent flitting of a bat, his lamp throwing a fan of orange-colored haze into the mist of rain.

In the street in front of the house the driver, descending from the box, held open the door of the hack. Jadwin handed Laura in, gave an address to the driver, and got in himself, slamming the door after. They heard the driver mount to his seat and speak to his horses.

"Well," said Jadwin, rubbing the fog from the window pane of the door, "look your last at the old place, Laura. You will never see it again."

But she would not look.

"No, no," she said. "I'll look at you, dearest, at you, and our future, which is to be happier than any years we have ever known."

Jadwin did not answer other than by taking her hand in his, and in silence they drove through the city toward the train that was to carry them to the new life. A phase of the existences of each was closed definitely. The great corner was a thing of the past; the great corner with the long train of disasters its collapse had started. The great failure had precipitated smaller failures, and the aggregate of smaller failures had pulled down one business house after another. For weeks afterward, the successive crashes were like the shock and reverberation of undermined buildings toppling to their ruin. An important bank had suspended payment, and hundreds of depositors had found their little fortunes swept away. The ramifications of the catastrophe were unbelievable. The whole tone of financial affairs seemed changed. Money was "tight" again, credit was withdrawn. The business world began to speak of hard times, once more.

But Laura would not admit her husband was in any way to blame. He had suffered, too. She repeated to herself his words, again and again:

"The wheat cornered itself. I simply stood between two sets of circumstances. The wheat cornered me, not I the wheat."

And all those millions and millions of bushels of Wheat were gone now. The Wheat that had killed Cressler, that had engulfed Jadwin's fortune and all but unseated reason itself; the Wheat that had intervened like a great torrent to drag her husband from her side and drown him in the roaring vortices of the Pit, had passed on, resistless, along its ordered and predetermined courses from West to East, like a vast Titanic flood, had passed, leaving Death and Ruin in its wake, but bearing Life and Prosperity to the crowded cities and centres of Europe.

For a moment, vague, dark perplexities assailed her, questionings as to the elemental forces, the forces of demand and supply that ruled the world. This huge resistless Nourisher of the Nations— why was it that it could not reach the People, could not fulfil its destiny, unmarred by all this suffering, unattended by all this misery?

She did not know. But as she searched, troubled and disturbed, for an answer, she was aware of a certain familiarity in the neighborhood the carriage was traversing. The strange sense of having lived through this scene, these circumstances, once before, took hold upon her.

She looked out quickly, on either hand, through the blurred glasses of the carriage doors. Surely, surely this locality had once before impressed itself upon her imagination. She turned to her husband, an exclamation upon her lips; but Jadwin, by the dim light of the carriage lanterns, was studying a railroad folder.

All at once, intuitively, Laura turned in her place, and raising the flap that covered the little window at the back of the carriage, looked behind. On either side of the vista in converging lines stretched the tall office buildings, lights burning in a few of their windows even yet. Over the end of the street the lead-colored sky was broken by a pale faint haze of light, and silhouetted against this rose a sombre mass, unbroken by any glimmer, rearing a black and formidable façade against the blur of the sky behind it.

And this was the last impression of the part of her life that that day brought to a close; the tall gray office buildings, the murk of rain, the haze of light in the heavens, and raised against it, the pile of the Board of Trade building, black, monolithic, crouching on its foundations like a monstrous sphinx with blind eyes, silent, grave— crouching there without a sound, without sign of life, under the night and the drifting veil of rain.

THE END

A Deal in Wheat

AND OTHER STORIES
OF THE NEW AND
OLD WEST

BY

FRANK NORRIS

ILLUSTRATED BY

REMINGTON, LEYENDECKER,
HITCHCOCK AND HOOPER

A DEAL IN WHEAT

I

THE BEAR—WHEAT AT SIXTY–TWO

As Sam Lewiston backed the horse into the shafts of his buck-board and began hitching the tugs to the whiffletree, his wife came out from the kitchen door of the house and drew near, and stood for some time at the horse's head, her arms folded and her apron rolled around them. For a long moment neither spoke. They had talked over the situation so long and so comprehensively the night before that there seemed to be nothing more to say.

The time was late in the summer, the place a ranch in south-western Kansas, and Lewiston and his wife were two of a vast population of farmers, wheat growers, who at that moment were passing through a crisis—a crisis that at any moment might culminate in tragedy. Wheat was down to sixty-six.

At length Emma Lewiston spoke.

"Well," she hazarded, looking vaguely out across the ranch toward the horizon, leagues distant; "well, Sam, there's always that offer of brother Joe's. We can quit—and go to Chicago—if the worst comes."

"And give up!" exclaimed Lewiston, running the lines through the torets. "Leave the ranch! Give up! After all these years!"

His wife made no reply for the moment. Lewiston climbed into the buckboard and gathered up the lines. "Well, here goes for the last try, Emmie," he said. "Good-by, girl. Maybe things will look better in town to-day."

"Maybe," she said gravely. She kissed her husband good-by and stood for some time looking after the buckboard traveling toward the town in a moving pillar of dust.

"I don't know," she murmured at length; "I don't know just how we're going to make out."

When he reached town, Lewiston tied the horse to the iron

railing in front of the Odd Fellows' Hall, the ground floor of which was occupied by the post-office, and went across the street and up the stairway of a building of brick and granite—quite the most pretentious structure of the town—and knocked at a door upon the first landing. The door was furnished with a pane of frosted glass, on which, in gold letters, was inscribed "Bridges & Co., Grain Dealers."

Bridges himself, a middle-aged man who wore a velvet skull-cap and who was smoking a Pittsburg stogie, met the farmer at the counter and the two exchanged perfunctory greetings.

"Well," said Lewiston, tentatively, after a while.

"Well, Lewiston," said the other, "I can't take that wheat of yours at any better than sixty-two."

"Sixty-*two*."

"It's the Chicago price that does it, Lewiston. Truslow is bearing the stuff for all he's worth. It's Truslow and the bear clique that stick the knife into us. The price broke again this morning. We've just got a wire."

"Good heavens," murmured Lewiston, looking vaguely from side to side. "That—that ruins me. I *can't* carry my grain any longer—what with storage charges and—and— Bridges, I don't see just how I'm going to make out. Sixty-two cents a bushel! Why, man, what with this and with that it's cost me nearly a dollar a bushel to raise that wheat, and now Truslow—"

He turned away abruptly with a quick gesture of infinite discouragement.

He went down the stairs, and making his way to where his buckboard was hitched, got in, and, with eyes vacant, the reins slipping and sliding in his limp, half-open hands, drove slowly back to the ranch. His wife had seen him coming, and met him as he drew up before the barn.

"Well?" she demanded.

"Emmie," he said as he got out of the buckboard, laying his arm across her shoulder, "Emmie, I guess we'll take up with Joe's offer. We'll go to Chicago. We're cleaned out!"

II

THE BULL—WHEAT AT A DOLLAR-TEN

. . . —— and said Party of the Second Part further covenants and agrees to merchandise such wheat in foreign ports, it being understood and agreed between the Party of the First Part and the Party of the Second Part that the wheat hereinbefore mentioned is released and sold to the Party of the Second Part for export purposes only, and not for consumption or distribution within the boundaries of the United States of America or of Canada.

"Now, Mr. Gates, if you will sign for Mr. Truslow, I guess that'll be all," remarked Hornung when he had finished reading.

Hornung affixed his signature to the two documents and passed them over to Gates, who signed for his principal client, Truslow—or, as he had been called ever since he had gone into the fight against Hornung's corner—the Great Bear. Hornung's secretary was called in and witnessed the signatures, and Gates thrust the contract into his Gladstone bag and stood up, smoothing his hat.

"You will deliver the warehouse receipts for the grain," began Gates.

"I'll send a messenger to Truslow's office before noon," interrupted Hornung. "You can pay by certified check through the Illinois Trust people."

When the other had taken himself off, Hornung sat for some moments gazing abstractedly toward his office windows, thinking over the whole matter. He had just agreed to release to Truslow, at the rate of one dollar and ten cents per bushel, one hundred thousand out of the two million and odd bushels of wheat that he, Hornung, controlled, or actually owned. And for the moment he was wondering if, after all, he had done wisely in not goring the Great Bear to actual financial death. He had made him pay one hundred thousand dollars. Truslow was good for this amount. Would it not have been better to have put a prohibitive figure on the grain and forced the Bear into bankruptcy? True, Hornung would then be without his enemy's money, but Truslow would have been eliminated from the situation, and that—so Hornung told himself—was always a consummation most devoutly, strenuously and diligently to be striven for. Truslow once dead was dead, but the Bear was never more dangerous than when desperate.

"But so long as he can't get *wheat*," muttered Hornung at the end of his reflections, "he can't hurt me. And he can't get it. That I *know*."

For Hornung controlled the situation. So far back as the February of that year an "unknown bull" had been making his presence felt on the floor of the Board of Trade. By the middle of March the commercial reports of the daily press had begun to speak of "the powerful bull clique"; a few weeks later that legendary condition of affairs implied and epitomized in the magic words "Dollar Wheat" had been attained, and by the first of April, when the price had been boosted to one dollar and ten cents a bushel, Hornung had disclosed his hand, and in place of mere rumors, the definite and authoritative news that May wheat had been cornered in the Chicago Pit went flashing around the world from Liverpool to Odessa and from Duluth to Buenos Ayres.

It was—as the veteran operators were persuaded—Truslow himself who had made Hornung's corner possible. The Great Bear had for once overreached himself, and, believing himself all-powerful, had hammered the price just the fatal fraction too far down. Wheat had gone to sixty-two—for the time, and under the circumstances, an abnormal price. When the reaction came it was tremendous. Hornung saw his chance, seized it, and in a few months had turned the tables, had cornered the product, and virtually driven the bear clique out of the pit.

On the same day that the delivery of the hundred thousand bushels was made to Truslow, Hornung met his broker at his lunch club.

"Well," said the latter, "I see you let go that line of stuff to Truslow."

Hornung nodded; but the broker added:

"Remember, I was against it from the very beginning. I know we've cleared up over a hundred thou'. I would have fifty times preferred to have lost twice that and *smashed Truslow dead*. Bet you what you like he makes us pay for it somehow."

"Huh!" grunted his principal. "How about insurance and warehouse charges, and carrying expenses on that lot? Guess we'd have had to pay those, too, if we'd held on."

But the other put up his chin, unwilling to be persuaded. "I won't sleep easy," he declared, "till Truslow is busted."

III

THE PIT

JUST as Going mounted the steps on the edge of the pit the great gong struck, a roar of a hundred voices developed with the swiftness of successive explosions, the rush of a hundred men surging downward to the centre of the pit filled the air with the stamp and grind of feet, a hundred hands in eager strenuous gestures tossed upward from out the brown of the crowd, the official reporter in his cage on the margin of the pit leaned far forward with straining ear to catch the opening bid, and another day of battle was begun.

Since the sale of the hundred thousand bushels of wheat to Truslow the "Hornung crowd" had steadily shouldered the price higher until on this particular morning it stood at one dollar and a half. That was Hornung's price. No one else had any grain to sell.

But not ten minutes after the opening, Going was surprised out of all countenance to hear shouted from the other side of the pit these words:

"Sell May at one-fifty."

Going was for the moment touching elbows with Kimbark on one side and with Merriam on the other, all three belonging to the "Hornung crowd." Their answering challenge of *"Sold"* was as the voice of one man. They did not pause to reflect upon the strangeness of the circumstance. (That was for afterward.) Their response to the offer was as unconscious as reflex action and almost as rapid, and before the pit was well aware of what had happened the transaction of one thousand bushels was down upon Going's trading-card and fifteen hundred dollars had changed hands. But here was a marvel—the whole available supply of wheat cornered, Hornung master of the situation, invincible, unassailable; yet behold a man willing to sell, a Bear bold enough to raise his head.

"That was Kennedy, wasn't it, who made that offer?" asked Kimbark, as Going noted down the trade—"Kennedy, that new man?"

"Yes; who do you suppose he's selling for; who's willing to go short at this stage of the game?"

"Maybe he ain't short."

"Short! Great heavens, man; where'd he get the stuff?"

"Blamed if I know. We can account for every handful of May. Steady! Oh, there he goes again."

"Sell a thousand May at one-fifty," vociferated the bear-broker, throwing out his hand, one finger raised to indicate the number of "contracts" offered. This time it was evident that he was attacking the Hornung crowd deliberately, for, ignoring the jam of traders that swept toward him, he looked across the pit to where Going and Kimbark were shouting *"Sold! Sold!"* and nodded his head.

A second time Going made memoranda of the trade, and either the Hornung holdings were increased by two thousand bushels of May wheat or the Hornung bank account swelled by at least three thousand dollars of some unknown short's money.

Of late—so sure was the bull crowd of its position—no one had even thought of glancing at the inspection sheet on the bulletin board. But now one of Going's messengers hurried up to him with the announcement that this sheet showed receipts at Chicago for that morning of twenty-five thousand bushels, and not credited to Hornung. Some one had got hold of a line of wheat overlooked by the "clique" and was dumping it upon them.

"Wire the Chief," said Going over his shoulder to Merriam. This one struggled out of the crowd, and on a telegraph blank scribbled:

"Strong bear movement—New man—Kennedy—Selling in lots of five contracts—Chicago receipts twenty-five thousand."

The message was despatched, and in a few moments the answer came back, laconic, of military terseness.

"Support the market."

And Going obeyed, Merriam and Kimbark following, the new broker fairly throwing the wheat at them in thousand-bushel lots.

"Sell May at 'fifty; sell May; sell May." A moment's indecision, an instant's hesitation, the first faint suggestion of weakness, and the market would have broken under them. But for the better part of four hours they stood their ground, taking all that was offered, in constant communication with the Chief, and from time to time stimulated and steadied by his brief, unvarying command:

"Support the market."

At the close of the session they had bought in the twenty-five thousand bushels of May. Hornung's position was as stable as a rock, and the price closed even with the opening figure—one dollar and a half.

But the morning's work was the talk of all La Salle Street. Who was back of the raid? What was the meaning of this unexpected selling? For weeks the Pit trading had been merely nominal. Truslow, the Great Bear, from whom the most serious attack might have been expected, had gone to his country seat at Geneva Lake, in Wisconsin, declaring himself to be out of the market entirely. He went bass fishing every day.

IV

THE BELT LINE

On a certain day toward the middle of the month, at a time when the mysterious Bear had unloaded some eighty thousand bushels upon Hornung, a conference was held in the library of Hornung's home. His broker attended it, and also a clean-faced, bright-eyed individual whose name of Cyrus Ryder might have been found upon the pay-roll of a rather well-known detective agency. For upward of half an hour after the conference began the detective spoke, the other two listening attentively, gravely.

"Then, last of all," concluded Ryder, "I made out I was a hobo, and began stealing rides on the Belt Line Railroad. Know the road? It just circles Chicago. Truslow owns it. Yes? Well, then I began to catch on. I noticed that cars of certain numbers— thirty-one naught thirty-four, thirty-two one ninety—well, the numbers don't matter, but anyhow, these cars were always switched on to the sidings by Mr. Truslow's main elevator D soon as they came in. The wheat was shunted in, and they were pulled out again. Well, I spotted one car and stole a ride on her. Say, look here, *that car went right around the city on the Belt, and came back to D again, and the same wheat in her all the time.* The grain was reinspected —it was raw, I tell you—and the warehouse receipts made out just as though the stuff had come in from Kansas or Iowa."

"The same wheat all the time!" interrupted Hornung.

"The same wheat—your wheat, that you sold to Truslow."

"Great snakes!" ejaculated Hornung's broker. "Truslow never took it abroad at all."

"Took it abroad! Say, he's just been running it around Chicago, like the supers in 'Shenandoah,' round an' round, so you'd think it was a new lot, an' selling it back to you again."

"No wonder we couldn't account for so much wheat."

"Bought it from us at one-ten, and made us buy it back—our own wheat—at one-fifty."

Hornung and his broker looked at each other in silence for a moment. Then all at once Hornung struck the arm of his chair with his fist and exploded in a roar of laughter. The broker stared for one bewildered moment, then followed his example.

"Sold! Sold!" shouted Hornung almost gleefully. "Upon my soul it's as good as a Gilbert and Sullivan show. And we— Oh, Lord! Billy, shake on it, and hats off to my distinguished friend, Truslow. He'll be President some day. Hey! What? Prosecute him? Not I."

"He's done us out of a neat hatful of dollars for all that," observed the broker, suddenly grave.

"Billy, it's worth the price."

"We've got to make it up somehow."

"Well, tell you what. We were going to boost the price to one seventy-five next week, and make that our settlement figure."

"Can't do it now. Can't afford it."

"No. Here; we'll let out a big link; we'll put wheat at two dollars, and let it go at that."

"Two it is, then," said the broker.

V

THE BREAD LINE

THE street was very dark and absolutely deserted. It was a district on the "South Side," not far from the Chicago River, given up largely to wholesale stores, and after nightfall was empty of all life. The echoes slept but lightly hereabouts, and the slightest footfall, the faintest noise, woke them upon the instant and sent them clamoring up and down the length of the pavement between the iron-shuttered fronts. The only light visible came from the side door of a certain "Vienna" bakery, where at one o'clock in the morning loaves of bread were given away to any who should ask.

Every evening about nine o'clock the outcasts began to gather about the side door. The stragglers came in rapidly, and the line—the "bread line," as it was called—began to form. By midnight it was usually some hundred yards in length, stretching almost the entire length of the block.

Toward ten in the evening, his coat collar turned up against the fine drizzle that pervaded the air, his hands in his pockets, his elbows gripping his sides, Sam Lewiston came up and silently took his place at the end of the line.

Unable to conduct his farm upon a paying basis at the time when Truslow, the "Great Bear," had sent the price of grain down to sixty-two cents a bushel, Lewiston had turned over his entire property to his creditors, and, leaving Kansas for good, had abandoned farming, and had left his wife at her sister's boarding-house in Topeka with the understanding that she was to join him in Chicago so soon as he had found a steady job. Then he had come to Chicago and had turned workman. His brother Joe conducted a small hat factory on Archer Avenue, and for a time he found there a meagre employment. But difficulties had occurred, times were bad, the hat factory was involved in debts, the repealing of a certain import duty on manufactured felt overcrowded the home market with cheap Belgian and French products, and in the end his brother had assigned and gone to Milwaukee.

Thrown out of work, Lewiston drifted aimlessly about Chicago, from pillar to post, working a little, earning here a dollar, there a dime, but always sinking, sinking, till at last the ooze of the lowest bottom dragged at his feet and the rush of the great ebb went over him and engulfed him and shut him out from the light, and a park bench became his home and the "bread line" his chief makeshift of subsistence.

He stood now in the infolding drizzle, sodden, stupefied with fatigue. Before and behind stretched the line. There was no talking. There was no sound. The street was empty. It was so still that the passing of a cable-car in the adjoining thoroughfare grated like prolonged rolling explosions, beginning and ending at immeasurable distances. The drizzle descended incessantly. After a long time midnight struck.

There was something ominous and gravely impressive in this interminable line of dark figures, close-pressed, soundless; a crowd, yet absolutely still; a close-packed, silent file, waiting, waiting in the vast deserted night-ridden street; waiting without a word, without a movement, there under the night and under the slow-moving mists of rain.

Few in the crowd were professional beggars. Most of them were workmen, long since out of work, forced into idleness by long-continued "hard times," by ill luck, by sickness. To them the "bread line" was a godsend. At least they could not starve. Between jobs here in the end was something to hold them up—a small platform, as it were, above the sweep of black water, where for a moment they might pause and take breath before the plunge.

The period of waiting on this night of rain seemed endless to those silent, hungry men; but at length there was a stir. The line moved. The side door opened. Ah, at last! They were going to hand out the bread.

But instead of the usual white-aproned under-cook with his crowded hampers there now appeared in the doorway a new man—a young fellow who looked like a bookkeeper's assistant. He bore in his hand a placard, which he tacked to the outside of the door. Then he disappeared within the bakery, locking the door after him.

A shudder of poignant despair, an unformed, inarticulate sense of calamity, seemed to run from end to end of the line. What had happened? Those in the rear, unable to read the placard, surged forward, a sense of bitter disappointment clutching at their hearts.

The line broke up, disintegrated into a shapeless throng—a throng that crowded forward and collected in front of the shut door whereon the placard was affixed. Lewiston, with the others, pushed forward. On the placard he read these words:

"Owing to the fact that the price of grain has been increased to two dollars a bushel, there will be no distribution of bread from this bakery until further notice."

Lewiston turned away, dumb, bewildered. Till morning he walked the streets, going on without purpose, without direction. But now at last his luck had turned. Overnight the wheel of his fortunes had creaked and swung upon its axis, and before noon he had found a job in the street-cleaning brigade. In the course of time he rose to be first shift-boss, then deputy inspector, then inspector, promoted to the dignity of driving a red wagon with rubber tires and drawing a salary instead of mere wages. The wife was sent for and a new start made.

But Lewiston never forgot. Dimly he began to see the significance of things. Caught once in the cogs and wheels of a great and terrible engine, he had seen—none better—its workings. Of all the men who had vainly stood in the "bread line" on that rainy night in early summer, he, perhaps, had been the only one who had struggled up to the surface again. How many others had gone down in the great ebb? Grim question; he dared not think how many.

He had seen the two ends of a great wheat operation—a battle between Bear and Bull. The stories (subsequently published in the city's press) of Truslow's counter move in selling Hornung his own wheat, supplied the unseen section. The farmer—he who raised the wheat—was ruined upon one hand; the working-man—he who consumed it—was ruined upon the other. But between the two, the great operators, who never saw the wheat they traded in, bought and sold the world's food, gambled in the nourishment of entire nations, practiced their tricks, their chicanery and oblique shifty "deals," were reconciled in their differences, and went on through their appointed way, jovial, contented, enthroned, and unassailable.

THE WIFE OF CHINO

I

CHINO'S WIFE

On the back porch of the "office," young Lockwood—his boots, stained with the mud of the mines and with candle drippings, on the rail—sat smoking his pipe and looking off down the cañon.

It was early in the evening. Lockwood, because he had heard the laughter and horseplay of the men of the night shift as they went down the cañon from the bunk-house to the tunnel-mouth, knew that it was a little after seven. It would not be necessary to go indoors and begin work on the columns of figures of his payroll for another hour yet. He knocked the ashes out of his pipe, refilled and lighted it—stoppering with his match-box—and shot a wavering blue wreath out over the porch railing. Then he resettled himself in his tilted chair, hooked his thumbs into his belt, and fetched a long breath.

For the last few moments he had been considering, in that comfortable spirit of relaxed attention that comes with the after-dinner tobacco, two subjects: first, the beauty of the evening; second, the temperament, character, and appearance of Felice Zavalla.

As for the evening, there could be no two opinions about that. It was charming. The Hand-over-fist Gravel Mine, though not in the higher Sierras, was sufficiently above the level of the mere foothills to be in the sphere of influence of the greater mountains. Also, it was remote, difficult of access. Iowa Hill, the nearest post-office, was a good eight miles distant, by trail, across the Indian River. It was sixteen miles by stage from Iowa Hill to Colfax, on the line of the Overland Railroad, and all of a hundred miles from Colfax to San Francisco.

To Lockwood's mind this isolation was in itself an attraction. Tucked away in this fold of the Sierras, forgotten, remote, the little community of a hundred souls that comprised the *personnel* of the Hand-over-fist lived out its life with the completeness of an inde-

(320)

pendent State, having its own government, its own institutions and customs. Besides all this, it had its own dramas as well—little complications that developed with the swiftness of whirlpools, and that trended toward culmination with true Western directness. Lockwood, college-bred—he was a graduate of the Columbia School of Mines—found the life interesting.

On this particular evening he sat over his pipe rather longer than usual, seduced by the beauty of the scene and the moment. It was very quiet. The prolonged rumble of the mine's stamp-mill came to his ears in a ceaseless diapason, but the sound was so much a matter of course that Lockwood no longer heard it. The millions of pines and redwoods that covered the flanks of the mountains were absolutely still. No wind was stirring in their needles. But the chorus of tree-toads, dry, staccato, was as incessant as the pounding of the mill. Far-off—thousands of miles, it seemed—an owl was hooting, three velvet-soft notes at exact intervals. A cow in the stable near at hand lay down with a long breath, while from the back veranda of Chino Zavalla's cabin came the clear voice of Felice singing "The Spanish Cavalier" while she washed the dishes.

The twilight was fading; the glory that had blazed in cloudless vermilion and gold over the divide was dying down like receding music. The mountains were purple-black. From the cañon rose the night mist, pale blue, while above it stood the smoke from the mill, a motionless plume of sable, shot through by the last ruddiness of the afterglow.

The air was full of pleasant odors—the smell of wood fires from the cabins of the married men and from the ovens of the cookhouse, the ammoniacal whiffs from the stables, the smell of ripening apples from "Boston's" orchard—while over all and through all came the perfume of the witch-hazel and tar-weed from the forests and mountain sides, as pungent as myrrh, as aromatic as aloes.

> "And if I should fall,
> In vain I would call,"

sang Felice.

Lockwood took his pipe from his teeth and put back his head to listen. Felice had as good a voice as so pretty a young woman should have had. She was twenty-two or twenty-three years of age, and was incontestably the beauty of the camp. She was Mexican-Spanish, tall and very slender, black-haired, as lithe as a cat, with a cat's green eyes and with all of a cat's purring, ingratiating insinuation.

Lockwood could not have told exactly just how the first familiarity between him and Felice had arisen. It had grown by almost imperceptible degrees up to a certain point; now it was a chance meeting on the trail between the office and the mill, now a fragment of conversation apropos of a letter to be mailed, now a question as to some regulation of the camp, now a detail of repairs done to the cabin wherein Felice lived. As said above, up to a certain point the process of "getting acquainted" had been gradual, and on Lockwood's part unconscious; but beyond that point affairs had progressed rapidly.

At first Felice had been, for Lockwood, a pretty woman, neither more nor less; but by degrees she emerged from this vague classification: she became a very pretty woman. Then she became a personality; she occupied a place within the circle which Lockwood called his world, his life. For the past months this place had perforce to be enlarged. Lockwood allowed it to expand. To make room for Felice, he thrust aside, or allowed the idea of Felice to thrust aside, other objects which long had sat secure. The invasion of the woman into the sphere of his existence developed at the end into a thing veritably headlong. Deep-seated convictions, old-established beliefs and ideals, even the two landmarks, right and wrong, were hustled and shouldered about as the invasion widened and penetrated. This state of affairs was further complicated by the fact that Felice was the wife of Chino Zavalla, shift-boss of No. 4 gang in the new workings.

II

MADNESS

It was quite possible that, though Lockwood could not have told when and how the acquaintance between him and Felice began and progressed, the young woman herself could. But this is guesswork. Felice being a woman, and part Spanish at that, was vastly more self-conscious, more disingenuous, than the man, the Anglo-Saxon. Also she had that fearlessness that very pretty women have. In her more refined and city-bred sisters this fearlessness would be called poise, or, at the most, "cheek."

And she was quite capable of making young Lockwood, the superintendent, her employer, and nominally the ruler of her little world, fell in love with her. It is only fair to Felice to say that she would not do this deliberately. She would be more conscious of the business than the man, than Lockwood; but in affairs such as this, involving women like Felice, there is a distinction between deliberately doing a thing and consciously doing it. Admittedly this is complicated, but it must be understood that Felice herself was complex, and she could no more help attracting men to her than the magnet the steel filings. It made no difference whether the man was the "breed" boy who split logging down by the engine-house or the young superintendent with his college education, his white hands and dominating position; over each and all who came within range of her influence Felice, with her black hair and green eyes, her slim figure and her certain indefinite "cheek"—which must not by any manner of means be considered as "boldness"—cast the weird of her kind.

If one understood her kind, knew how to make allowances, knew just how seriously to take her eyes and her "cheek," no great harm was done. Otherwise, consequences were very apt to follow.

Hicks was one of those who from the very first had understood. Hicks was the manager of the mine, and Lockwood's chief—in a word, *the boss*. He was younger even than Lockwood, a boy virtually, but a wonderful boy—a boy such as only America, western America at that, could produce, masterful, self-controlled, incredibly capable, as taciturn as a sphinx, strong of mind and of muscle, and possessed of a cold gray eye that was as penetrating as chilled steel.

To this person, impersonal as force itself, Felice had once, by some mysterious feminine art, addressed, in all innocence, her little manœuvre of fascination. One lift of the steady eyelid, one quiet glint of that terrible cold gray eye, that poniarded her every tissue of complexity, inconsistency, and coquetry, had been enough. Felice had fled the field from this young fellow, so much her junior, and then afterward, in a tremor of discomfiture and distress, had kept her distance.

Hicks understood Felice. Also the great majority of the miners—shift-bosses, chuck tenders, bed-rock cleaners, and the like—understood. Lockwood did not.

It may appear difficult of belief that the men, the crude, simple workmen, knew how to take Felice Zavalla, while Lockwood, with all his education and superior intelligence, failed in his estimate of her. The explanation lies no doubt in the fact that in these man-and-woman affairs instinct is a surer guide than education and intelligence, unless, indeed, the intelligence is preternaturally keen. Lockwood's student life had benumbed the elemental instinct, which in the miners, the "men," yet remained vigorous and unblunted, and by means of which they assessed Felice and her harmless blandishments at their true worth. For all Lockwood's culture, his own chuck-tenders, unlettered fellows, cumbersome, slow-witted, "knew women"—at least, women of their own world, like Felice—better than he. On the other hand, his intelligence was no such perfected instrument as Hicks's, as exact as logarithms, as penetrating as a scalpel, as uncolored by emotions as a steel trap.

Lockwood's life had been a narrow one. He had studied too hard at Columbia to see much of the outside world, and he had come straight from his graduation to take his first position. Since then his life had been spent virtually in the wilderness, now in Utah, now in Arizona, now in British Columbia, and now, at last, in Placer County, California. His lot was the common lot of young mining engineers. It might lead one day to great wealth, but meanwhile it was terribly isolated.

Living thus apart from the world, Lockwood very easily allowed his judgment to get, as it were, out of perspective. Class distinctions lost their sharpness, and one woman—as, for instance, Felice—was very like another—as, for instance, the girls his sisters knew "back home" in New York.

As a last result, the passions were strong. Things were done "for all they were worth" in Placer County, California. When a man worked, he worked hard; when he slept, he slept soundly; when he hated, he hated with primeval intensity; and when he loved he grew reckless.

It was all one that Felice was Chino's wife. Lockwood swore between his teeth that she should be *his* wife. He had arrived at this conclusion on the night that he sat on the back porch of his office and watched the moon coming up over the Hog Back. He stood up at length and thrust his pipe into his pocket, and putting an arm across the porch pillar, leaned his forehead against it and looked out far in the purple shadows.

"It's madness," he muttered; "yes, I know it—sheer madness; but, by the Lord! I *am* mad—and I don't care."

III

CHINO GOES TO TOWN

As time went on the matter became more involved. Hicks was away. Chino Zavalla, stolid, easy-going, came and went about his work on the night shift, always touching his cap to Lockwood when the two crossed each other's paths, always good-natured, always respectful, seeing nothing but his work.

Every evening, when not otherwise engaged, Lockwood threw a saddle over one of the horses and rode in to Iowa Hill for the mail, returning to the mine between ten and eleven. On one of these occasions, as he drew near to Chino's cabin, a slim figure came toward him down the road and paused at his horse's head. Then he was surprised to hear Felice's voice asking " 'Ave you a letter for me, then, Meester Lockwude?"

Felice made an excuse of asking thus for her mail each night that Lockwood came from town, and for a month they kept up appearances; but after that they dropped even that pretence, and as often as he met her Lockwood dismounted and walked by her side till the light in the cabin came into view through the chaparral.

At length Lockwood made a mighty effort. He knew how very far he had gone beyond the point where between the two landmarks called right and wrong a line is drawn. He contrived to keep away from Felice. He sent one of the men into town for the mail, and he found reasons to be in the mine itself whole half-days at a time. Whenever a moment's leisure impended, he took his shotgun and tramped the mine ditch for leagues, looking for quail and gray squirrels. For three weeks he so managed that he never once caught sight of Felice's black hair and green eyes, never once heard the sound of her singing.

But the madness was upon him none the less, and it rode and roweled him like a hag from dawn to dark and from dark to dawn again, till in his complete loneliness, in the isolation of that simple, primitive life, where no congenial mind relieved the monotony by so much as a word, morbid, hounded, tortured, the man grew desperate—was ready for anything that would solve the situation.

Once every two weeks Lockwood "cleaned up and amalgamated"—that is to say, the mill was stopped and the "ripples" where the gold was caught were scraped clean. Then the ore was sifted out, melted down, and poured into the mold, whence it emerged as the "brick," a dun-colored rectangle, rough-edged, immensely heavy, which represented anywhere from two to six thousand dollars. This was sent down by express to the smelting-house.

But it was necessary to take the brick from the mine to the express office at Iowa Hill.

This duty devolved upon Lockwood and Chino Zavalla. Hicks had from the very first ordered that the Spaniard should accompany the superintendent upon this mission. Zavalla was absolutely trustworthy, as honest as the daylight, strong physically, cool-headed, discreet, and—to Hicks's mind a crowning recommendation—close-mouthed. For about the mine it was never known when the brick went to town or who took it. Hicks had impressed this fact upon Zavalla. He was to tell nobody that he was delegated to this duty. "Not even"—Hicks had leveled a forefinger at Chino, and the cold eyes drove home the injunction as the steam-hammer drives the rivet—"not even your wife." And Zavalla had promised. He would have trifled with dynamite sooner than with one of Hicks's orders.

So the fortnightly trips to town in company with Lockwood were explained in various fashions to Felice. She never knew that the mail-bag strapped to her husband's shoulders on those occasions carried some five thousand dollars' worth of bullion.

On a certain Friday in early June Lockwood had amalgamated, and the brick, duly stamped, lay in the safe in the office. The following night he and Chino, who was relieved from mine duty on these occasions, were to take it in to Iowa Hill.

Late Saturday afternoon, however, the engineer's boy brought word to Chino that the superintendent wanted him at once. Chino found Lockwood lying upon the old lounge in the middle room of the office, his foot in bandages.

"Here's luck, Chino," he exclaimed, as the Mexican paused on the threshold. "Come in and—shut the door," he added in a lower voice.

"*Dios!*" murmured Chino. "An accident?"

"Rather," growled Lockwood. "That fool boy, Davis's kid—the car-boy, you know—ran me down in the mine. I yelled at him. Somehow he couldn't stop. Two wheels went over my foot—and the car loaded, too."

Chino shuddered politely.

"Now here's the point," continued Lockwood. "Um—there's nobody round outside there? Take a look, Chino, by the window there. All clear, eh? Well, here's the point. That brick ought to go in to-night just the same, hey?"

"Oh—of a surety, of a surety." Chino spoke in Spanish.

"Now I don't want to let any one else take my place—you never can tell—the beggars will talk. Not all like you, Chino."

"*Gracias, signor.* It is an honor."

"Do you think you can manage alone? I guess you can, hey? No reason why you couldn't."

Chino shut his eyes tight and put up a palm. "Rest assured of that, Signor Lockwude. Rest assured of that."

"Well, get around here about nine."

"It is understood, signor."

Lockwood, who had a passable knowledge of telegraphy, had wired to the Hill for the doctor. About suppertime one appeared, and Lockwood bore the pain of the setting with such fortitude as he could command. He had his supper served in the office. The doctor shared it with him and kept him company.

During the early hours of the evening Lockwood lay on the sofa trying to forget the pain. There was no easier way of doing this than by thinking of Felice. Inevitably his thoughts reverted to her. Now that he was helpless, he could secure no diversion by plunging into the tunnel, giving up his mind to his work. He could not now take down his gun and tramp the ditch. Now he was supine, and the longing to break through the mesh, wrestle free from the complication, gripped him and racked him with all its old-time force.

Promptly at nine o'clock, the faithful Chino presented himself at the office. He had one of the two horses that were used by Lockwood as saddle animals, and as he entered he opened his coat and tapped the hilt of a pistol showing from his trousers pocket, with a wink and a grin. Lockwood took the brick from the safe, strapped it into the mail-bag, and Chino, swinging it across his shoulders, was gone, leaving Lockwood to hop back to the sofa, there to throw himself down and face once more his trouble.

IV

A DESPATCH FROM THE EXPRESS MESSENGER

WHAT made it harder for Lockwood just now was that even on that very day, in spite of all precaution, in spite of all good resolutions, he had at last seen Felice. Doubtless the young woman herself had contrived it; but, be that as it may, Lockwood, returning from a tour of inspection along the ditch, came upon her not far from camp, but in a remote corner, and she had, of course, demanded why he kept away from her. What Lockwood said in response he could not now remember; nor, for that matter, was any part of the conversation very clear to his memory. The reason for this was that, just as he was leaving her, something of more importance than conversation had happened. Felice had looked at him.

And she had so timed her look, had so insinuated it into the little, brief, significant silences between their words, that its meaning had been very clear. Lockwood had left her with his brain dizzy, his teeth set, his feet stumbling and fumbling down the trail, for now he knew that Felice wanted him to know that she regretted the circumstance of her marriage to Chino Zavalla; he knew that she wanted him to know that the situation was as intolerable for her as for him.

All the rest of the day, even at this moment, in fact, this new phase of the affair intruded its pregnant suggestions upon his mind, to the exclusion of everything else. He felt the drift strong around him; he knew that in the end he would resign himself to it. At the same time he sensed the abyss, felt the nearness of some dreadful, nameless cataclysm, a thing of black shadow, bottomless, terrifying.

"Lord!" he murmured, as he drew his hand across his forehead, "Lord! I wonder where this thing is going to fetch up."

As he spoke, the telegraph key on his desk, near at hand, began all at once to click off his call. Groaning and grumbling, Lockwood heaved himself up, and, with his right leg bent, hobbled from chair-back to chair-back over to the desk. He rested his right knee on his desk chair, reached for his key, opened the circuit, and answered. There was an instant's pause, then the instrument began to click again. The message was from the express messenger at Iowa Hill. Word by word Lockwood took it off as follows:

"Reno—Kid—will—attempt—hold-up—of—brick—on—trail—to-night—do—not—send—till—advised—at—this—end."

Lockwood let go the key and jumped back from the desk, lips compressed, eyes alight, his fists clinched till the knuckles grew white. The whole figure of him stiffened as tense as drawn wire, braced rigid like a finely bred hound "making game."

Chino was already half an hour gone by the trail, and the Reno Kid was a desperado of the deadliest breed known to the West. How he came to turn up here there was no time to inquire. He was on hand, that was the point; and Reno Kid always "shot to kill." This would be no mere hold-up; it would be murder.

Just then, as Lockwood snatched open a certain drawer of his desk where he kept his revolver, he heard from down the road, in the direction of Chino's cabin, Felice's voice singing:

"To the war I must go
To fight for my country and you, dear."

Lockwood stopped short, his arm at full stretch, still gripping tight the revolver that he had half pulled from the drawer—stopped short and listened.

The solution of everything had come.

He saw it in a flash. The knife hung poised over the knot—even at that moment was falling. Nothing was asked of him—nothing but inertia.

For an instant, alone there in that isolated mining-camp, high above the world, lost and forgotten in the gloom of the cañons and redwoods, Lockwood heard the crisis of his life come crashing through the air upon him like the onslaught of a whirlwind. For an instant, and no more, he considered. Then he cried aloud:

"No, no; I can't, I *can't*—not this way!" And with the words he threw the belt of the revolver about his hips and limped and scampered from the room, drawing the buckle close.

How he gained the stable he never knew, nor how he backed the horse from the building, nor how, hopping on one leg, he got the headstall on and drew the cinches tight.

But the wrench of pain in his foot as, swinging up at last, he tried to catch his off stirrup, was reality enough to clear any confusion of spirit. Hanging on as best he might with his knees and one foot, Lockwood, threshing the horse's flanks with the stinging quirt that tapered from the reins of the bridle, shot from the camp in a swirl of clattering hoofs, flying pebbles and blinding clouds of dust.

V

THE TRAIL

THE night was black dark under the redwoods, so impenetrable that he could not see his horse's head, and braced even as he was for greater perils it required all his courage to ride top-speed at this vast-slab of black that like a wall he seemed to charge head down with every leap of his bronco's hoofs.

For the first half-hour the trail mounted steadily, then, by the old gravel-pits, it topped the divide and swung down over more open slopes, covered only with chaparral and second growths. Here it was lighter, and Lockwood uttered a fervent "Thank God!" when, a few moment later, the moon shouldered over the mountain crests ahead of him and melted the black shadows to silver-gray. Beyond the gravel-pits the trail turned and followed the flank of the slope, level here for nearly a mile. Lockwood set his teeth against the agony of his foot and gave the bronco the quirt with all his strength.

In another half-hour he had passed Cold Cañon, and twenty minutes after that had begun the descent into Indian River. He forded the river at a gallop, and, with the water dripping from his very hat-brim, drove laboring under the further slope.

Then he drew rein with a cry of bewilderment and apprehension. The lights of Iowa Hill were not two hundred yards distant. He had covered the whole distance from the mine, and where was Chino?

There was but one answer: back there along the trail somewhere, at some point by which Lockwood had galloped headlong and unheeding, lying up there in the chaparral with Reno's bullets in his body.

There was no time now to go on to the Hill. Chino, if he was not past help, needed it without an instant's loss of time. Lockwood spun the horse about. Once more the ford, once more the cañon slopes, once more the sharp turn by Cold Cañon, once more the thick darkness under the redwoods. Steadily he galloped on, searching the roadside.

Then all at once he reined in sharply, bringing the horse to a standstill, one ear turned down the wind. The night's silence was broken by a multitude of sounds—the labored breathing of the spent bronco, the saddle creaking as the dripping flanks rose and fell, the touch of wind in the tree-tops and the chorusing of the myriad tree-toads. But through all these, distinct, as precise as a clock-tick, Lockwood had heard, and yet distinguished, the click of a horse's hoofs drawing near, and the horse was at a gallop; Reno at last.

Lockwood drew his pistol. He stood in thick shadow. Only some twenty yards in front of him was there any faintest break in the darkness; but at that point the blurred moonlight made a grayness across the trail, just a tone less deep than the redwoods' shadows.

With his revolver cocked and trained upon this patch of grayness, Lockwood waited, holding his breath.

The gallop came blundering on, sounding in the night's silence as loud as the passage of an express train; and the echo of it, flung back from the cañon side, confused it and distorted it till, to Lockwood's morbid alertness, it seemed fraught with all the madness of flight, all the hurry of desperation.

Then the hoof-beats rose to a roar, and a shadow just darker than the darkness heaved against the grayness that Lockwood held covered with his pistol. Instantly he shouted aloud:

"Halt! Throw up your hands!"

His answer was a pistol shot.

He dug his heels to his horse, firing as the animal leaped forward. The horses crashed together, rearing, plunging, and Lockwood, as he felt the body of a man crush by him on the trail, clutched into the clothes of him, and, with the pistol pressed against the very flesh, fired again, crying out as he did so:

"Drop your gun, Reno! I know you. I'll kill you if you move again!"

And then it was that a wail rose into the night, a wail of agony and mortal apprehension:

"Signor Lockwude, Signor Lockwude, for the love of God, don't shoot! 'Tis I—Chino Zavalla."

VI

THE DISCOVERY OF FELICE

An hour later, Felice, roused from her sleep by loud knocking upon her door, threw a blanket about her slim body, serape fashion, and opened the cabin to two gaunt scarecrows, who, the one, half supported by the other, himself far spent and all but swooning, lurched by her across the threshold and brought up wavering and bloody in the midst of the cabin floor.

"*Por Dios! Por Dios!*" cried Felice. "Ah, love of God! what misfortune has befallen Chino!" Then in English, and with a swift leap of surprise and dismay: "Ah, Meester Lockwude, air you hurt? Eh, tell me-a! Ah, it is too draidful!"

"No, no," gasped Lockwood, as he dragged Chino's unconscious body to the bed Felice had just left. "No; I—I've shot him. We met—there on the trail." Then the nerves that had stood strain already surprisingly long snapped and crisped back upon themselves like broken harp-strings.

"*I've shot him! I've shot him!*" he cried. "Shot him, do you understand? Killed him, it may be. Get the doctor, quick! He's at the office. I passed Chino on the trail over to the Hill. He'd hid in the bushes as he heard me coming from behind, then when I came back I took him. Oh, I'll explain later. Get the doctor, quick."

Felice threw on such clothes as came to her hand and ran over to the office, returning with the doctor, half-dressed and blinking in the lantern-light. He went in to the wounded man at once, and Lockwood, at the end of all strength, dropped into the hammock on the porch, stretching out his leg to ease the anguish of his broken foot. He leaned back and closed his eyes wearily, aware only of a hideous swirl of pain, of intolerable anxiety as to Chino's wound, and, most of all, of a mere blur of confusion wherein the sights and sounds of the last few hours tore through his brain with the plunge of a wild galloping such as seemed to have been in his ears for years and years.

But as he lay thus he heard a step at his side. Then came the touch of Felice's long brown hand upon his face. He sat up, opening his eyes.

"You aisk me-a," she said, "eef I do onderstaind, eh. Yais, I onderstaind. You—" her voice was a whisper—"you shoot Chino, eh? I know. You do those thing' for me-a. I am note angri, no-a. You ver' sharp man, eh? All for love oaf Felice, eh? Now we be happi, maybe; now we git married soam day byne-by, eh? Ah, you one brave man, Signor Lockwude!"

She would have taken his hand, but Lockwood, the pain all forgot, the confusion all vanishing, was on his feet. It was as though a curtain that for months had hung between him and the blessed light of clear understanding had suddenly been rent in twain by her words. The woman stood revealed. All the baseness of her tribe, all the degraded savagery of a degenerate race, all the capabilities for wrong, for sordid treachery, that lay dormant in her, leaped to life at this unguarded moment, and in that new light, that now at last she had herself let in, stood pitilessly revealed, a loathsome thing, hateful as malevolence itself.

"What," shouted Lockwood, "you think—think that I—that I could—oh-h, it's monstrous—you—" He could find no words to voice his loathing. Swiftly he turned away from her, the last spark of an evil love dying down forever in his breast.

It was a transformation, a thing as sudden as a miracle, as conclusive as a miracle, and with all a miracle's sense of uplift and power. In a second of time the scales seemed to fall from the man's eyes, fetters from his limbs; he saw, and he was free.

At the door Lockwood met the doctor:

"Well?"

"He's all right; only a superficial wound. He'll recover. But you—how about you? All right? Well, that is a good hearing. You've had a lucky escape, my boy."

"I *have* had a lucky escape," shouted Lockwood. "You don't know just how lucky it was."

A BARGAIN WITH PEG-LEG

"HEY, youse!" shouted the car-boy. He brought his trundling, jolting, loose-jointed car to a halt by the face of the drift. "Hey, youse!" he shouted again.

Bunt shut off the Burly air-drill and nodded.

"Chaw," he remarked to me.

We clambered into the car, and, as the boy released the brake, rolled out into the main tunnel of the Big Dipple, and banged and bumped down the long incline that led to the mouth.

"Chaw" was dinner. It was one o'clock in the morning, and the men on the night shift were taking their midnight spell off. Bunt was back at his old occupation of miner, and I—the one loafer of all that little world of workers—had brought him a bottle of beer to go with the "chaw"; for Bunt and I were ancient friends.

As we emerged from the cool, cave-like dampness of the mine and ran out into the wonderful night air of the Sierra foothills, warm, dry, redolent of witch-hazel, the car-boy began to cough, and, after we had climbed out of the car and had sat down on the embankment to eat and drink, Bunt observed:

"D'ye hear that bark? That kid's a one-lunger for fair. Which ain't no salubrious graft for him—this hiking cars about in the bowels of the earth. Some day he'll sure up an' quit. Ought to go down to Yuma a spell."

The engineer in the mill was starting the stamps. They got under way with broken, hiccoughing dislocations, bumping and stumbling like the hoofs of a group of horses on the cattle-deck in a gale. Then they jumped to a trot, then to a canter, and at last settled down to the prolonged roaring gallop that reverberated far off over the entire cañon.

"I knew a one-lunger once," Bunt continued, as he uncorked the bottle, "and the acquaintance was some distressful by reason of its bringing me into strained relations with a cow-rustlin', hair-liftin', only-one-born-in-captivity, man-eatin' brute of a one-legged Greaser which he was named Peg-leg Smith. He was shy a leg because of a shotgun that the other man thought wasn't loaded. And this here happens, lemme tell you, 'way down in the Panamint country, where they wasn't no doctor within twenty miles, and Peg-leg outs with his bowie and amputates that leg hisself, then later makes a wood stump outa a ole halter and a table-leg. I guess the whole jing-bang of it turned his head, for he goes bad and loco thereafter, and begins shootin' and r'arin' up an' down the hull Southwest, a-roarin' and a-bellerin' and a-takin' on amazin'. We dasn't say boo to a yaller pup while he's round. I never see such mean blood. Jus' let the boys know that Peg-leg was anyways adjacent an' you can gamble they walked chalk.

"Y'see, this Peg-leg lay it out as how he couldn't abide no cussin' an' swearin'. He said if there was any tall talkin' done he wanted to do it. And he sure could. I've seed him hold on for six minutes by the watch an' never repeat hisself once. An' shoot! Say, lemme tell you he did for two Greasers once in a barroom at La Paz, one in front o' him, t'other straight behind, *him* standing between with a gun in each hand, and shootin' both guns *at the same time.* Well, he was just a terror," declared Bunt solemnly, "and when he was in real good form there wa'n't a man south o' Leadville dared to call his hand.

"Now, the way I met up with this skunkin' little dewdrop was this-like. It was at Yuma, at a time when I was a kid of about nineteen. It was a Sunday mornin'; Peg-leg was in town. He was asleep on a lounge in the back room o' Bud Overick's Grand Transcontinental Hotel. (I used to guess Bud called it that by reason that it wa'n't grand, nor transcontinental, nor yet a hotel—it was a bar.) This was twenty year ago, and in those days I knowed a one-lunger in Yuma named Clarence. (He couldn't help that—he was a good kid—but his name *was* Clarence.) We got along first-rate. Yuma was a great consumptive place at that time. They used to come in on every train; yes, and go out, too—by freight.

"Well, findin' that they couldn't do much else than jes' sit around an' bark and keep their shawls tight, these 'ere chaps kinda drew together, and lay it out to meet every Sunday morning at Bud's to sorta talk it over and have a quiet game. One game they had that they played steady, an' when I drifted into Bud's that morning they was about a dozen of 'em at it—Clarence, too. When I came in, there they be, all sittin' in a circle round a table with a cigar-box on it. They'd each put four bits into the box. That was the pot.

"A stranger wouldn't 'a' made nothin' very excitin' out of that game, nor yet would 'a' caught on to what it were. For them pore yaps jes' sat there, each with his little glass thermometer in his mouth, awaitin' and awaitin' and never sayin' a word. Then bime-by Bud, who's a-holdin' of the watch on 'em, sings out 'Time!' an' they all takes their thermometers out an' looks at 'em careful-like to see where they stand.

" 'Mine's ninety-nine," says one.

"An' another says:

" 'Mine's a hundred.'

"An' Clarence pipes up—coughin' all the time:

" 'Mine's a hundred 'n' one 'n' 'alf.'

"An', no one havin' a higher tempriture than that, Clarence captures the pot. It was a queer kind o' game.

"Well, on that particular Sunday morning they's some unpleasantness along o' one o' the other one-lungers layin' it out as how Clarence had done some monkey-business to make his tempriture so high. It was said as how Clarence had took and drunk some hot tea afore comin' into the game at Bud's. They all began to discuss that same p'int.

"Naturally, they don't go at it polite, and to make their remarks p'inted they says a cussword occasional, and Clarence, bein' a high-steppin' gent as takes nobody's dust, slings it back some forceful.

"Then all at once they hears Peg-leg beller from where he's layin' on the lounge (they ain't figured on his bein' so contiguous), and he gives it to be understood, does Peg-leg, as how the next one-lunger that indulges in whatsoever profanity will lose his voice abrupt.

"They all drops out at that, bar the chap who had the next highest tempriture to Clarence. Him having missed the pot by only a degree or so is considerable sore.

" 'Why,' says he, 'I've had a reg'lar *fever* since yesterday afternoon, an' only just dodged a hem'rage by a squeak. I'm all legitimate, I am; an' if you-alls misdoubts as how my tempriture ain't normal you kin jes' ask the doctor. I don't take it easy that a strappin', healthy gesabe whose case ain't nowheres near the hopeless p'int yet steps in here with a scalded mouth and plays it low.'

"Clarence he r'ars right up at that an' forgits about Peg-leg an' expresses doubts, not to say convictions, about the one-lunger's chances of salvation. He puts it all into about three words, an' just as quick as look at it we hears ol' Peg-leg's wooden stump a-comin'. We stampedes considerable prompt, but Clarence falls over a chair, an' before he kin get up Peg-leg has him by the windpipe.

"Now I ain't billin' myself as a all-round star hero an' general grand-stand man. But I was sure took with Clarence, an' I'd 'a' been real disappointed if Peg-leg 'ud a-killed him that morning—which he sure was tryin' to do when I came in for a few chips.

"I don' draw on Peg-leg, him being down on his knees over Clarence, an' his back turned, but without sensin' very much *what* I'm a-doin' of I grabs holt o' the first part o' Peg-leg that comes handy, which, so help me, Bob, is his old wooden leg. I starts to pull him off o' Clarence, but instead o' that I pulls off the wooden leg an' goes a-staggerin' back agin the wall with the thing in my fist.

"Y'know how it is now with a fightin' pup if you pull his tail while he's a-chewin' up the other pup. Ye can bat him over the head till you're tired, or kick him till you w'ars your boot out, an' he'll go right on chawin' the harder. But monkey with his tail an' he's that sensitive an' techy about it that he'll take a interest right off.

"Well, it were just so with Peg-leg—though I never knew it. Just by accident I'd laid holt of him where he was tender; an' when he felt that leg go—say, lemme tell you, he was some excited. He forgits all about Clarence, and he lines out for me, a-clawin' the air. Lucky he'd left his gun in the other room.

"Well, sir, y'ought to have seen him, a-hoppin' on one foot, and banging agin the furniture, jes' naturally black in the face with rage, an' doin' his darnedest to lay his hands on me, roarin' all the whiles like a steer with a kinked tail.

"Well, I'm skeered, and I remarks that same without shame. I'm skeered. I don't want to come to no grapples with Peg-leg in his wrath, an' I knows that so long as he can't git his leg he can't take after me very fast. Bud's saloon backs right up agin the bluff over the river. So what do I do but heave that same wooden leg through one o' the back windows, an' down she goes (as I *thought*) mebbe seventy feet into the cañon o' the Colorado? And then, mister man, *I skins out—fast*.

"I takes me headlong flight by way o' the back room and *on-root* pitches Peg-leg's gun over into the cañon, too, an' then whips around the corner of the saloon an' fetches out ag'in by the street in front. With his gun gone an' his leg gone, Peg-leg—so lon's y'ain't within arm's reach—is as harmless as a horned toad. So I kinda hangs 'round the neighborhood jes' to see what-all mout turn up.

"Peg-leg, after hoppin' back to find that his gun was gone, to look for his leg, comes out by the front door, hoppin' from one chair to another, an' seein' me standin' there across the street makes remarks; an' he informs me that because of this same little turn-up this mornin' I ain't never goin' to live to grow hair on my face. His observations are that vigorous an' p'inted that I sure begin to see it that way, too, and I says to myself:

"'Now you, Bunt McBride, you've cut it out for yourself good and hard, an' the rest o' your life ain't goin' to be free from nervousness. Either y'ought to 'a' let this here hell-roarin' maverick alone or else you should 'a' put him clean out o' business when you had holt o' his shootin'-iron. An' I ain't a bit happy.' An' then jes' at this stage o' the proceedings occurs what youse 'ud call a diversion.

"It seemed that that wood stump didn't go clean to the river as I first figured, but stuck three-fourths the way down. An' a-course there's a fool half-breed kid who's got to chase after it, thinkin' to do Peg-leg a good turn.

"I don't know nothin' about this, but jes' stand there talkin' back to Peg-leg, an' pretendin' I ain't got no misgivings, when I sees this kid comin' a-cavoortin' an' a-cayoodlin' down the street with the leg in his hands, hollerin' out:

"'Here's your leg, Mister Peg-leg! I went an' got it for you, Mister Peg-leg!'

"It ain't so likely that Peg-leg could 'a' caught me even if he'd had his leg, but I wa'n't takin' no chances. An' as Peg-leg starts for the kid I start, too—with my heart knockin' agin my front teeth, you can bet.

"I never knew how fast a man could hop till that mornin', an', lookin' at Peg-leg with the tail o' my eye as I ran, it seemed to me as how he was a-goin' over the ground like a ole he-kangaroo. But somehow he gets off his balance and comes down all of a smash like a rickety table, an' I reaches the kid first an' takes the leg away from him.

"I guess Peg-leg must 'a' begun to lay it out by then that I held a straight flush to his ace high, for he sits down on the edge of the sidewalk an', being some winded, too, he just glares. Then bymeby he says:

"'You think you are some smart now, sonny, but I'm a-studyin'

of your face so's I'll know who to look for when I git a new leg;
an' believe me, I'll know it, m'son—yours an' your friend's too'
(he meant Clarence)—'an' I guess you'll both be kind o' sick afore
I'm done with you. *You!*' he goes on, tremendous disgustful.
'You! an' them one-lungers a-swearin' an' a-cussin' an' bedamnin'
an' bedevilin' one a-other. Ain't ye just ashamed o' yourselves?' (he
thought I was a one-lunger, too) ; 'ain't ye ashamed—befoulin' your
mouths, an' disturbin' the peace along of a quiet Sunday mornin',
an' you-alls waist over in your graves? I'm fair sick o' my job,'
he remarks, goin' kind o' thoughtful. 'Ten years now I've been
range-ridin' all this yere ranch, a-doin' o' my little feeble, or'nary
best to clean out the mouths o' you men an' purify the atmosphere
o' God's own country, but I ain't made *one* convert. I've pounded
'em an' booted 'em, an' busted 'em an' shot 'em up, an' they go on
cussin' each other out harder'n ever. I don't know w'at all to do
an' I sometimes gets plumb discouraged-like.'

"Now, hearin' of him talk that-a-way, an' a-knowin' of his weakness, I gits a idea. It's a chanst and mebbee it don't pan out, but I
puts it up as a bluff. I don't want, you see, to spend the rest o'
my appointed time in this yere vale o' tears a-dodgin' o' Peg-leg
Smith, an' in the end, after all, to git between the wind and a forty-
eight calibre do-good, sure not. So I puts up a deal. Says I: 'Peg-
leg, I'll make a bargint along o' you. You lays it out as how you
ain't never converted nobody out o' his swearin' habits. Now if
you wants, 'ere's a chanst. You gimmee your word as a gent and a
good-man-an'-true, as how you won't never make no play to shoot
me up, in nowise whatsoever, so long as we both do live, an' promise
never to bust me, or otherwise, an' promise never to rustle me or
interfere with my life, liberty, and pursuit o' happiness, an' thereunto
you set your seal an' may Lord 'a' mercy on your soul—you promise that, an' I will agree an' covenant with the party o' the first part
to abstain an' abjure, early or late, dry or drinkin', in liquor or out,
out o' luck or in, rangin' or roundin', from all part an' parcel o'
profanity, cuss-words, little or big, several an' separate, bar none:
this yere agreement to be considered as bindin' an' obligatory till
the day o' your demise, decease or death. *There!*' says I, 'there's a
fair bargint put up between man an' man, an' I puts it to you fair.
You comes in with a strong ante an' you gets a genuine, guaran-
teed an' high-grade convert—the real article. You stays out, an'
not only you loses a good chanst to cut off an' dam up as vigorous a
stream o' profanity as is found between here an' Laredo, but you

loses a hand-made, copper-bound, steel-riveted, artificial limb—
which in five minutes o' time,' says I, windin' up, 'will sure feed
the fire. There's the bargint.'

"Well, the ol' man takes out time for about as long as a thirsty
horse-rustler could put away half a dozen drinks an' he studies the
proposition sideways and endways an' down side up. Then at last
he ups an' speaks out decided-like:

" 'Son,' he says, 'son, it's a bargint. Gimmee my leg.'

"Somehow neither o' us misdoubts as how the other man won't
keep his word; an' I gives him his stump, an' he straps her on
joyful-like, just as if he'd got back a ole friend. Then later on he
hikes out for Mojave and I don' see him no more for mebbee three
years."

"And then?" I prompted.

"Well, I'll tell you," continued Bunt, between mouthfuls of
pie, "I'll tell you. This yere prejudice agin profanity is the only
thing about this yere Peg-leg that ain't pizen bad, an' *that* prejudice, you got to know, was just along o' his being loco on that one
subjeck. 'Twa'n't as if he had any real principles or convictions
about the thing. It was just a loco prejudice. Just as some
gesabes has feelin's agin cats an' snakes, or agin seein' a speckled
nigger. It was just on-reasonable. So what I'm aimin' to have
you understand is the fact that it was extremely appropriate that
Peg-leg should die, that it was a blamed good thing, and somethin' to be celebrated by free drinks all round.

"You can say he treated me white, an' took my unsupported
word. Well, so he did; but that was in spite o' what he really was
hisself, 'way on the inside o' him. Inside o' him he was black-bad,
and it wa'n't a week after we had made our bargint that he did for
a little Mojave kid in a way I don't like to think of.

"So when he took an' died like as how I'm a-going to tell you
of, I was plumb joyful, not only because I could feel at liberty to
relieve my mind when necessary in a manner as is approved of and
rightful among gents—not only because o' that, but because they
was one less bad egg in the cow-country.

"Now the manner o' Peg-leg's dying was sure hilarious-like.
I didn't git over laughin' about it for a month o' Sundays—an' I
ain't done yet. It was sure a joke on Peg-leg. The cutest joke
that was ever played off on him.

"It was in Sonora—Sonora, Arizona, I mean. They'd a-been
a kind o' gold excitement there, and all the boys had rounded up.

The town was full—chock-a-block. Peg-leg he was there, too, drunk all the time an' bullyin' everybody, an' slambangin' around in his same old way. That very day he'd used a friend o' his—his best friend—cruel hard; just mean and nasty, you know.

"Well, I'm sitting into a little game o' faro about twelve o'clock at night, me an' about a dozen o' the boys. We're good an' interested, and pretty much to the good o' the game, an' somebody's passin' drinks when all at once there's a sure big rumpus out in the street, an' a gent sticks his head thro' the door an' yells out:

" 'Hi, there, they's a fire! The Golden West Hotel is on fire!'

"We draws the game as soon as convenient and hikes out, an', my word, you'd 'a' thought from the looks o' things as how the whole town was going. But it was only the hotel—the Golden West, where Peg-leg was stayin'; an' when we got up we could hear the ol' murderer bellerin' an' ragin', and him drunk—of course.

"Well, I'm some excited. Lord love you, I'd as soon 'a' seen Peg-leg shot as I would eat, an' when I remembers the little Mojave kid I'm glad as how his time is at hand. Saved us the trouble o' lynchin' that sooner or later had to come.

"Peg-leg's room was in the front of the house on the fourth floor, but the fire was all below, and what with the smoke comin' out the third-story winders he couldn't see down into the street, no more'n the boys could see him—only they just heard him bellerin'.

"Then some one of 'em sings out:

" 'Hey, Peg-leg, jump! We got a blanket here.'

"An' sure enough he does jump!' "

Here Bunt chuckled grimly, muttering,

"Yes, sir, sure enough he did jump."

"I don't quite see," I observed, "where the laugh comes in. What was the joke of it?"

"The joke of it was," finished Bunt, "that they hadn't any blanket."

THE PASSING OF COCK-EYE
BLACKLOCK

"WELL, m'son," observed Bunt about half an hour after supper, "if your provender has shook down comfortable by now, we might as well jar loose and be moving along out yonder."

We left the fire and moved toward the hobbled ponies, Bunt complaining of the quality of the outfit's meals. "Down in the Panamint country," he growled, "we had a Chink that was a sure frying-pan expert; but *this* Dago—my word! That ain't victuals, that supper. That's just a' ingenious device for removing superfluous appetite. Next time I assimilate nutriment in this camp I'm sure going to take chloroform beforehand. Careful to draw your cinch tight on that pinto bronc' of yours. She always swells up same as a horned toad soon as you begin to saddle up."

We rode from the circle of the camp-fire's light and out upon the desert. It was Bunt's turn to ride the herd that night, and I had volunteered to bear him company.

Bunt was one of a fast-disappearing type. He knew his West as the cockney knows his Piccadilly. He had minded with and for Ralston, had soldiered with Crook, had turned cards in a faro game at Laredo, and had known the Apache Kid. He had fifteen separate and different times driven the herds from Texas to Dodge City, in the good old, rare old, wild old days when Dodge was the headquarters for the cattle trade, and as near to heaven as the cowboy cared to get. He had seen the end of gold and the end of the buffalo, the beginning of cattle, the beginning of wheat, and the spreading of the barbed-wire fence, that, in the end, will take from him his occupation and his revolver, his chaparejos and his usefulness, his lariat and his reason for being. He had seen the rise of a new period, the successive stages of which, singularly enough, tally exactly with the progress of our own world-civilization: first the nomad and hunter, then the herder, next and last the husbandman. He had passed the mid-mark of his life. His mustache was gray. He had four friends—his horse, his pistol, a teamster in the Indian Territory Panhandle named Skinny, and me.

The herd—I suppose all told there were some two thousand head—we found not far from the water-hole. We relieved the other watch and took up our night's vigil. It was about nine o'clock. The night was fine, calm. There was no cloud. Toward the middle watches one could expect a moon. But the stars, the stars! In Idaho, on those lonely ranches of desert and range, where the shadow of the sun by day and the courses of the constellations by night are the only things that move, these stars are a different matter from those bleared pin-points of the city after dark, seen through dust and smoke and the glare of electrics and the hot haze of fire-signs. On such a night as that when I rode the herd with Bunt *anything* might have happened; one could have believed in fairies then, and in the buffalo-ghost, and in all the weirds of the craziest Apache "Messiah" that ever made medicine.

One remembered astronomy and the "measureless distances" and the showy problems, including the rapid moving of a ray of light and the long years of its travel between star and star, and smiled incredulously. Why, the stars were just above our heads, were not much higher than the flat-topped hills that barred the horizons. Venus was a yellow lamp hung in a tree; Mars a red lantern in a clock-tower.

One listened instinctively for the tramp of the constellations, Orion, Cassiopeia and Ursa Major marched to and fro on the vault like cohorts of legionaries, seemingly within call of our voices, and all without a sound.

But beneath these quiet heavens the earth disengaged multitudinous sounds—small sounds, minimized as it were by the muffling of the night. Now it was the yap of a coyote leagues away; now the snapping of a twig in the sage-brush; now the mysterious, indefinable stir of the heat-ridden land cooling under the night. But more often it was the confused murmur of the herd itself—the click of a horn, the friction of heavy bodies, the stamp of a hoof, with now and then the low complaining note of a cow with a calf, or the subdued noise of a steer as it lay down, first lurching to the knees, then rolling clumsily upon the haunch, with a long, stertorous breath of satisfaction.

Slowly at Indian trot we encircle the herd. Earlier in the evening a prairie-wolf had pulled down a calf, and the beasts were still restless.

Little eddies of nervousness at long intervals developed here and there in the mass—eddies that not impossibly might widen at any time with perilous quickness to the maelstrom of a stampede. So as he rode Bunt sang to these great brutes, literally to put them to sleep—sang an old grandmother's song, with all the quaint modulations of sixty, seventy, a hundred years ago:

> "With her ogling winks
> And bobbling blinks,
> Her quizzing glass,
> Her one eye idle,
> Oh, she loved a bold dragoon,
> With his broadsword, saddle, bridle.
> *Whack*, fol-de-rol!"

I remember that song. My grandmother—so they tell me—used to sing it in Carolina, in the thirties, accompanying herself on a harp, if you please:

> "Oh, she loved a bold dragoon,
> With his broadsword, saddle, bridle."

It was in Charleston, I remembered, and the slave-ships used to discharge there in those days. My grandmother had sung it then to her beaux; officers they were; no wonder she chose it—"Oh, she loved a bold dragoon"—and now I heard it sung on an Idaho cattle-range to quiet two thousand restless steers.

Our talk at first, after the cattle had quieted down, ran upon all manner of subjects. It is astonishing to note what strange things men will talk about at night and in a solitude. That night we covered religion, of course, astronomy, love affairs, horses, travel, history, poker, photography, basket-making, and the Darwinian theory. But at last inevitably we came back to cattle and the pleasures and dangers of riding the herd.

"I rode herd once in Nevada," remarked Bunt, "and I was caught into a blizzard, and I was sure freezing to death. Got to where I couldn't keep my eyes open, I was that sleepy. Tell you what I did. Had some eating-tobacco along, and I'd chew it a spell, then rub the juice into my eyes. Kept it up all night. Blame near blinded me, but I come through. Me and another man named Blacklock—Cock-eye Blacklock we called him, by reason of his having one eye that was some out of line. Cock-eye sure ought to have got it that night, for he went bad afterward, and did a heap of killing before he *did* get it. He was a bad man for sure, and the way he died is a story in itself."

There was a long pause. The ponies jogged on. Rounding on the herd, we turned southward.

"He did 'get it' finally, you say," I prompted.

"He certainly did," said Bunt, "and the story of it is what a man with a' imaginary mind like you ought to make into one of your friction tales."

"Is it about a treasure?" I asked with apprehension. For ever since I once made a tale (of friction) out of one of Bunt's stories of real life, he has been ambitious for me to write another, and is forever suggesting motifs which invariably—I say invariably—imply the discovery of great treasures. With him fictitious literature must always turn upon the discovery of hidden wealth.

"No," said he, "it ain't about no treasure, but just about the origin, hist'ry and development—and subsequent decease—of as mean a Greaser as ever stole stock, which his name was Cock-eye Blacklock.

"You see, this same Blacklock went bad about two summers after our meet-up with the blizzard. He worked down Yuma way and over into New Mexico, where he picks up with a sure-thing gambler, and the two begin to devastate the population. They do say that when he and his running mate got good and through with that part of the Land of the Brave, men used to go round trading guns for commissary, and clothes for ponies, and cigars for whisky and such. There just wasn't any money left *anywhere*. Those sharps had drawed the landscape clean. Some one found a dollar in a floor-crack in a saloon, and the barkeep' gave him a gallon of forty-rod for it, and used to keep it in a box for exhibition, and the crowd would get around it and paw it over and say: 'My, my! Whatever in the world is this extremely cu-roos coin?'

"Then Blacklock cuts loose from his running mate, and plays a lone hand through Arizona and Nevada, up as far as Reno again, and there he stacks up against a kid—a little tenderfoot kid so new he ain't cracked the green paint off him—and *skins* him. And the kid, being foolish and impulsive-like, pulls out a pea-shooter. It was a *twenty-two*," said Bunt solemnly. "Yes, the kid was just that pore, pathetic kind to carry a dinky twenty-two, and with the tears runnin' down his cheeks begins to talk tall. Now, what does that Cock-eye do? Why, that pore kid that he had skinned couldn't 'a' hurt him with his pore little bric-à-brac. Does Cock-eye take his little parlor ornament away from him, and spank him, and tell him to go home? No, he never. The kid's little tin pop-shooter explodes right in his hand before he can crook his forefinger twice, and while he's a-wondering what-all has happened Cock-eye gets his two guns on him, slow and deliberate like, mind you, and throws forty-eights into him till he ain't worth shooting at no more. Murders him like the mud-eating, horse-thieving snake of a Greaser that he is; but being within the law, the kid drawing on him first, he don't stretch hemp the way he should.

"Well, fin'ly this Blacklock blows into a mining-camp in Placer County, California, where I'm chuck-tending on the night shift. This here camp is maybe four miles across the divide from Iowa Hill, and it sure is named a cu-roos name, which it is Why-not. They is a barn contiguous, where the mine horses are kep', and, blame me! if there ain't a weather-cock on top of that same—a golden trotting-horse—*upside down*. When the stranger an' pilgrim comes in, says he first off: 'Why'n snakes they got that weather-cock horse upside down—why?' says he. 'Why-not,' says you, and the drinks is on the pilgrim.

"That all went very lovely till some gesabe opens up a placer drift on the far side the divide, starts a rival camp, an' names her Because. The Boss gets mad at that, and rights up the weather-cock and renames the camp Ophir, and you don't work no more pilgrims.

"Well, as I was saying, Cock-eye drifts into Why-not and begins diffusing trouble. He skins some of the boys in the hotel over in town, and a big row comes of it, and one of the bed-rock cleaners cuts loose with both guns. Nobody hurt but a quarter-breed, who loses a' eye. But the marshal don't stand for no short-card men, an' closes Cock-eye up some prompt. Him being forced to give the boys back their money is busted an' can't get away from camp. To raise some wind he begins depredating.

"He robs a pore half-breed of a cayuse, and shoots up a Chink who's panning tailings, and generally and variously becomes too pronounced, till he's run outen camp. He's sure stony-broke, not being able to turn a card because of the marshal. So he goes to live in a ole cabin up by the mine ditch, and sits there doing a heap o' thinking, and hatching trouble like a' ole he-hen.

"Well, now, with that deporting of Cock-eye comes his turn of bad luck, and it sure winds his clock up with a loud report. I've narrated special of the scope and range of this 'ere Blacklock, so as you'll understand why it was expedient and desirable that he should up an' die. You see, he always managed, with all his killings and robbings and general and sundry flimflamming, to be just within the law. And if anybody took a notion to shoot him up, why, his luck saw him through, and the other man's shooting-iron missed fire, or exploded, or threw wild, or such like, till it seemed as if he sure did bear a charmed life; and so he did till a pore yeller tamale of a fool dog did for him what the law of the land couldn't do. Yes, sir, a fool dog, a pup, a blame yeller pup named Sloppy Weather, did for Cock-eye Blacklock, sporting character, three-card-monte man, sure-thing sharp, killer, and general bedeviler.

"You see, it was this way. Over in American Cañon, some five miles maybe back of the mine, they was a creek called the American River, and it was sure chock-a-block full of trouts. The Boss used for to go over there with a dinky fish-pole like a buggy-whip about once a week, and scout that stream for fish and bring back a basket-ful. He was sure keen on it, and had bought some kind of privilege or other, so as he could keep other people off.

"Well, I used to go along with him to pack the truck, and one Saturday, about a month after Cock-eye had been run outen camp, we hiked up over the divide, and went for to round up a bunch o' trouts. When we got to the river there was a mess for your life. Say, that river was full of dead trouts, floating atop the water; and they was some even on the bank. Not a scratch on 'em; just dead. The Boss had the papsy-lals. I never *did* see a man so rip-r'aring, snorting mad. *I* hadn't a guess about what we were up against, but he knew, and he showed down. He said somebody had been shooting the river for fish to sell down Sacramento way to the market. A mean trick; kill more fish in one shoot than you can possibly pack.

"Well, we didn't do much fishing that day—couldn't get a bite, for that matter—and took off home about noon to talk it over. You see, the Boss, in buying the privileges or such for that creek, had made himself responsible to the Fish Commissioners of the State, and 'twasn't a week before they were after him, camping on his trail incessant, and wanting to know how about it. The Boss was some worried, because the fish were being killed right along, and the Commission was making him weary of living. Twicet after-ward we prospected along that river and found the same lot of dead fish. We even put a guard there, but it didn't do no manner of good.

"It's the Boss who first suspicions Cock-eye. But it don't take no seventh daughter of no seventh daughter to trace trouble where Blacklock's about. He sudden shows up in town with a bunch of simoleons, buying bacon and tin cows* and such provender, and generally giving it away that he's come into money. The Boss, who's watching his movements sharp, says to me one day:

" 'Bunt, the storm-centre of this here low area is a man with a cock-eye, an' I'll back that play with a paint horse against a paper dime.'

" 'No takers,' says I. 'Dirty work and a cock-eyed man are two heels of the same mule.'

" 'Which it's a-kicking of me in the stummick frequent and painful,' he remarks, plenty wrathful.

" 'On general principles,' I said, 'it's a royal flush to a pair of deuces as how this Blacklock bird ought to stop a heap of lead, and I know the man to throw it. He's the only brother of my sister, and tends chuck in a placer mine. How about if I take a day off and drop round to his cabin and interview him on the fleetin' and unstable nature of human life?'

"But the Boss wouldn't hear of that.

" 'No,' says he; 'that's not the bluff to back in this game. You an' me an' Mary-go-round'—that was what we called the marshal, him being so much all over the country—'you an' me an' Mary-go-round will have to stock a sure-thing deck against that maverick.'

"So the three of us gets together an' has a talky-talk, an' we lays it out as how Cock-eye must be watched and caught red-handed.

"Well, let me tell you, keeping case on that Greaser sure did lack a certain indefinable charm. We tried him at sun-up, an' again at sundown, an' nights, too, laying in the chaparral an' tarweed, an' scouting up an' down that blame river, till we were sore. We built surreptitious a lot of shooting-boxes up in trees on the far side of the cañon, overlooking certain an' sundry pools in the river where Cock-eye would be likely to pursue operations, an' we took turns watching. I'll be a Chink if that bad egg didn't put it on us same as previous, an' we'd find new-killed fish all the time. I tell you we were *fitchered;* and it got on the Boss's nerves. The Commission began to talk of withdrawing the privilege, an' it was up to him to make good or pass the deal. We *knew* Blacklock was shooting the river, y' see, but we didn't have no evidence. Y' see, being

---

* Condensed milk.

shut off from card-sharping, he was up against it, and so took to pot-hunting to get along. It was as plain as red paint.

"Well, things went along sort of catch-as-catch-can like this for maybe three weeks, the Greaser shooting fish regular, an' the Boss b'iling with rage, and laying plans to call his hand, and getting bluffed out every deal.

"And right here I got to interrupt, to talk some about the pup dog, Sloppy Weather. If he hadn't got caught up into this Blacklock game, no one'd ever thought enough about him to so much as kick him. But after it was all over, we began to remember this same Sloppy an' to recall what he was; no big job. He was just a worthless fool pup, yeller at that, everybody's dog, that just hung round camp, grinning and giggling and playing the goat, as half-grown dogs will. He used to go along with the car-boys when they went swimmin' in the resevoy, an' dash along in an' yell an' splash round just to show off. He thought it was a keen stunt to get some gesabe to throw a stick in the resevoy so's he could paddle out after it. They'd trained him always to bring it back an' fetch it to whichever party throwed it. He'd give it up when he'd retrieved it, an' yell to have it throwed again. That was his idea of fun—just like a fool pup.

"Well, one day this Sloppy Weather is off chasing jack-rabbits an' don't come home. Nobody thinks anything about that, nor even notices it. But we afterward finds out that he'd met up with Blacklock that day, an' stopped to visit with him—sorry day for Cockeye. Now, it was the very next day after this that Mary-go-round an' the Boss plans another scout. I'm to go, too. It was a Wednesday, an' we lay it out that the Cock-eye would prob-ly shoot that day so's as to get his fish down to the railroad Thursday, so they'd reach Sacramento Friday—fish day, see. It wasn't much to go by, but it was the high card in our hand, an' we allowed to draw to it.

"We left Why-not afore daybreak, an' worked over into the cañon about sun-up. They was one big pool we hadn't covered for some time, an' we made out we'd watch that. So we worked down to it, an' clumb up into our trees, an' set out to keep guard.

"In about an hour we heard a shoot some mile or so up the creek. They's no mistaking dynamite, leastways not to miners, an' we knew that shoot was dynamite an' nothing else. The Cock-eye was at work, an' we shook hands all round. Then pretty soon a fish or so began to go by—big fellows, some of 'em, dead an' floatin', with their eyes popped 'way out same as knobs—sure sign they'd been shot.

"The Boss took and grit his teeth when he see a three-pounder go by, an' made remarks about Blacklock.

" 'Sh!' says Mary-go-round, sudden like. 'Listen!'

"We turned ear down the wind, an' sure there was the sound of some one scrambling along the bowlders by the riverside. Then we heard a pup yap.

" 'That's our man,' whispers the Boss.

"For a long time we thought Cock-eye had quit for the day an' had coppered us again, but byne-by we heard the manzanita crack on the far side the cañon, an' there at last we see Blacklock working down toward the pool, Sloppy Weather following an' yapping and cayoodling just as a fool dog will.

"Blacklock comes down to the edge of the water quiet-like. He lays his big scoop-net an' his sack—we can see it half-full already—down behind a bowlder, and takes a good squinting look all around, and listens maybe twenty minutes, he's that cute, same's a coyote stealing sheep. We lies low an' says nothing, fear he might see the leaves move.

"Then byne-by he takes his stick of dynamite out his hip pockèt —he was just that reckless kind to carry it that way—an' ties it careful to a couple of stones he finds handy. Then he lights the fuse an' heaves her into the drink, an' just there's where Cock-eye makes the mistake of his life. He ain't tied the rocks tight enough, an' the loop slips off just as he swings back his arm, the stones drop straight down by his feet, and the stick of dynamite whirls out right enough into the pool.

"Then the funny business begins.

"Blacklock ain't made no note of Sloppy Weather, who's been sizing up the whole game an' watchin' for the stick. Soon as Cock-eye heaves the dynamite into the water, off goes the pup after it, just as he'd been taught to do by the car-boys.

" 'Hey, you fool dog!' yells Blacklock.

"A lot that pup cares. He heads out for that stick of dynamite same as if for a veal cutlet, reaches it, grabs hold of it, an' starts back for shore, with the fuse sputterin' like hot grease. Blacklock heaves rocks at him like one possessed, capering an' dancing; but the pup comes right on. The Cock-eye can't stand it no longer, but lines out. But the pup's got to shore an' takes after him. Sure; why not? He thinks it's all part of the game. Takes after Cock-eye, running to beat a' express, while we-all whoops and yells an' nearly falls out the trees for laffing. Hi! Cock-eye did scratch gravel for sure. But 'tain't no manner of use. He can't run through that rough ground like Sloppy Weather, an' that fool pup comes a-cavartin' along, jumpin' up against him, an' him a-kickin' him away, an' r'arin', an' dancin', an' shakin' his fists, an' the more he r'ars the more fun the pup thinks it is. But all at once something big happens, an' the whole bank of the cañon opens out like a big wave, and slops over into the pool, an' the air is full of trees an' rocks and cart-loads of dirt an' dogs and Blacklocks and rivers an' smoke an' fire generally. The Boss got a clod o' river-mud spang in the eye, an' went off his limb like's he was trying to bust a bucking bronc' an' couldn't; and ol' Mary-go-round was shooting off his gun on general principles, glarin' round wild-eyed an' like as if he saw a' Injun devil.

"When the smoke had cleared away an' the trees and rocks quit falling, we clumb down from our places an' started in to look for Blacklock. We found a good deal of him, but they wasn't hide nor hair left of Sloppy Weather. We didn't have to dig no grave, either. They was a big enough hole in the ground to bury a horse an' wagon, let alone Cock-eye. So we planted him there, an' put up a board, an' wrote on it:

Here lies most

of

C. BLACKLOCK

who died of a'

entangling alliance with

a

stick of dynamite.

Moral: A hook and line is good enough
fish-tackle for any honest man.

"That there board lasted for two years, till the freshet of '82, when the American River— Hello, there's the sun!"

All in a minute the night seemed to have closed up like a great book. The east flamed roseate. The air was cold, nimble. Some of the sage-brush bore a thin rim of frost. The herd, aroused, the dew glistening on flank and horn, were chewing the first cud of the

day, and in twos and threes moving toward the water-hole for the
morning's drink. Far off toward the camp the breakfast fire sent
a shaft of blue smoke straight into the moveless air. A jack-rabbit,
with erect ears, limped from the sage-brush just out of pistol-shot
and regarded us a moment, his nose wrinkling and trembling. By
the time that Bunt and I, putting our ponies to a canter, had pulled
up by the camp of the Bar-circle-Z outfit, another day had begun
in Idaho.

A MEMORANDUM OF SUDDEN DEATH

THE manuscript of the account that follows belongs to a harness-maker in Albuquerque, Juan Tejada by name, and he is welcome to whatever of advertisement this notice may bring him. He is a good fellow, and his patented martingale for stage horses may be recommended. I understand he got the manuscript from a man named Bass, or possibly Bass left it with him for safe-keeping. I know that Tejada has some things of Bass's now—things that Bass left with him last November: a mess-kit, a lantern, and a broken theodolite—a whole saddle-box full of contraptions. I forgot to ask Tejada how Bass got the manuscript, and I wish I had done so now, for the finding of it might be a story itself. The probabilities are that Bass simply picked it up page by page off the desert, blown about the spot where the fight occurred and at some little distance from the bodies. Bass, I am told, is a bone-gatherer by profession, and one can easily understand how he would come across the scene of the encounter in one of his tours into western Arizona. My interest in the affair is impersonal, but none the less keen. Though I did not know young Karslake, I knew his stuff—as everybody still does, when you come to that. For the matter of that, the mere mention of his pen-name, "Anson Qualtraugh," recalls at once to thousands of the readers of a certain world-famous monthly magazine of New York articles and stories he wrote for it while he was alive; as, for instance, his admirable descriptive work called "Traces of the Aztecs on the Mogolon Mesa," in the October number of 1890. Also, in the January issue of 1892 there are two specimens of his work, one signed Anson Qualtraugh and the other Justin Blisset. Why he should have used the Blisset signature I do not know. It occurs only this once in all his writings. In this case it is signed to a very indifferent New Year's story. The Qualtraugh "stuff" of the same number is, so the editor writes to me, a much shortened transcript of a monograph on "Primitive Methods of Moki Irrigation," which are now in the archives of the

Smithsonian. The admirable novel, "The Peculiar Treasure of Kings," is of course well known. Karslake wrote it in 1888-89, and the controversy that arose about the incident of the third chapter is still—sporadically and intermittently—continued.

The manuscript that follows now appears, of course, for the first time in print, and I acknowledge herewith my obligations to Karslake's father, Mr. Patterson Karslake, for permission to publish.

I have set the account down word for word, with all the hiatuses and breaks that by nature of the extraordinary circumstances under which it was written were bound to appear in it. I have allowed it to end precisely as Karslake was forced to end it, in the middle of a sentence. God knows the real end is plain enough and was not far off when the poor fellow began the last phrase that never was to be finished.

The value of the thing is self-apparent. Besides the narrative of incidents it is a simple setting forth of a young man's emotions in the very face of violent death. You will remember the distinguished victim of the guillotine, a lady who on the scaffold begged that she might be permitted to write out the great thoughts that began to throng her mind. She was not allowed to do so, and the record is lost. Here is a case where the record is preserved. But Karslake, being a young man not very much given to introspection, his work is more a picture of things seen than a transcription of things thought. However, one may read between the lines; the very breaks are eloquent, while the break at the end speaks with a significance that no words could attain.

The manuscript in itself is interesting. It is written partly in pencil, partly in ink (no doubt from a fountain pen), on sheets of manila paper torn from some sort of long and narrow account-book. In two or three places there are smudges where the powder-blackened finger and thumb held the sheets momentarily. I would give much to own it, but Tejada will not give it up without Bass's permission, and Bass has gone to the Klondike.

As to Karslake himself. He was born in Raleigh, in North Carolina, in 1868, studied law at the State University, and went to the Bahamas in 1885 with the members of a Government coast survey commission. Gave up the practice of law and "went in" for fiction and the study of the ethnology of North America about 1887. He was unmarried.

The reasons for his enlisting have long been misunderstood. It was known that at the time of his death he was a member of B

Troop of the Sixth Regiment of United States Cavalry, and it was
assumed that because of this fact Karslake was in financial difficulties and not upon good terms with his family. All this, of course,
is untrue, and I have every reason to believe that Karslake at this
time was planning a novel of military life in the Southwest, and,
wishing to get in closer touch with the *milieu* of the story, actually
enlisted in order to be able to write authoritatively. He saw no
active service until the time when his narrative begins. The year
of his death is uncertain. It was in the spring probably of 1896,
in the twenty-eighth year of his age.

There is no doubt he would have become in time a great writer.
A young man of twenty-eight who had so lively a sense of the value
of accurate observation, and so eager a desire to produce that in the
very face of death he could faithfully set down a description of his
surroundings, actually laying down the rifle to pick up the pen, certainly was possessed of extraordinary faculties.

"They came in sight early this morning just after we had had
breakfast and had broken camp. The four of us—'Bunt,' 'Idaho,'
Estorijo, and myself—were jogging on to the southward and had
just come up out of the dry bed of some water-hole—the alkali was
white as snow in the crevices—when Idaho pointed them out to us,
three to the rear, two on one side, one on the other and—very far
away—two ahead. Five minutes before, the desert was as empty
as the flat of my hand. They seemed literally to have *grown* out
of the sage-brush. We took them in through my field-glasses and
Bunt made sure they were an outlying band of Hunt-in-the-Morning's Bucks. I had thought, and so had all of us, that the rest of
the boys had rounded up the whole of the old man's hostiles long
since. We are at a loss to account for these fellows here. They
seem to be well mounted.

"We held a council of war from the saddle without halting, but
there seemed very little to be done but to go right along and
wait for developments. At about eleven we found water—just a
pocket in the bed of a dried stream—and stopped to water the
ponies. I am writing this during the halt.

"We have one hundred and sixteen rifle cartridges. Yesterday
was Friday, and all day, as the newspapers say, 'the situation remained unchanged.' We expected surely that the night would see
some rather radical change, but nothing happened, though we stood
watch and watch till morning. Of yesterday's eight only six are

in sight and we bring up reserves. We now have two to the front, one on each side, and two to the rear, all far out of rifle-range.

[*The following paragraph is in an unsteady script and would appear to have been written in the saddle. The same peculiarity occurs from time to time in the narrative, and occasionally the writing is so broken as to be illegible.*]

"On again after breakfast. It is about eight-fifteen. The other two have come back—without 'reserves,' thank God. Very possibly they did not go away at all, but were hidden by a dip in the ground. I can not see that any of them are nearer. I have watched one to the left of us steadily for more than half an hour and I am sure that he has not shortened the distance between himself and us. What their plans are Hell only knows, but this silent, persistent escorting tells on the nerves. I do not think I am afraid— as yet. It does not seem possible but that we will ride into La Paz at the end of the fortnight exactly as we had planned, meet Greenock according to arrangements and take the stage on to the railroad. Then next month I shall be in San Antonio and report at headquarters. Of course, all this is to be, of course; and this business of to-day will make a good story to tell. It's an experience —good 'material.' Very naturally I can not now see how I am going to get out of this" [*the word "alive" has here been erased*], "but of course I *will*. Why 'of course'? I don't know. Maybe I am trying to deceive myself. Frankly, it looks like a situation insoluble; but the solution will surely come right enough in good time.

"Eleven o'clock.—No change.

"Two-thirty P. M.—We are halted to tighten girths and to take a single swallow of the canteens. One of them rode in a wide circle from the rear to the flank, about ten minutes ago, conferred a moment with his fellow, then fell back to his old position. He wears some sort of red cloth or blanket. We reach no more water till day after to-morrow. But we have sufficient. Estorijo has been telling funny stories en route.

"Four o'clock P. M.—They have closed up perceptibly, and we have been debating about trying one of them with Idaho's Winchester. No use; better save the ammunition. It looks . . ." [*the next words are undecipherable, but from the context they would appear to be "as if they would attack to-night"*] " . . . we have come to know certain of them now by nicknames. We speak of the Red One, or the Little One, or the One with the Feather, and Idaho has named a short thickset fellow on our right 'Little

Willie.' By God, I wish something would turn up—relief or fight.
I don't care which. How Estorijo can cackle on, reeling off his
senseless, pointless funny stories, is beyond me. Bunt is almost as
bad. They understand the fix we are in, I *know*, but how they can
take it so easily is the staggering surprise. I feel that I am as courageous as either of them, but levity seems horribly inappropriate.
I could kill Estorijo joyfully.

"Sunday morning.—Still no developments. We were so sure of
something turning up last night that none of us pretended to sleep.
But nothing stirred. There is no sneaking out of the circle at night.
The moon is full. A jack-rabbit could not have slipped by them
unseen last night.

"Nine o'clock (in the saddle).—We had coffee and bacon as
usual at sunrise; then on again to the southeast just as before. For
half an hour after starting the Red One and two others were well
within rifle-shot, nearer than ever before. They had worked in
from the flank. But before Idaho could get a chance at them they
dipped into a shallow arroyo, and when they came out on the other
side were too far away to think of shooting.

"Ten o'clock.—All at once we find there are nine instead of
eight; where and when this last one joined the band we can not
tell. He wears a sombrero and army trousers, but the upper part
of his body is bare. Idaho calls him 'Half-and-half.' He is riding
a— They're coming.

"Later.—For a moment we thought it was the long-expected
rush. The Red One—he had been in the front—wheeled quick as
a flash and came straight for us, and the others followed suit.
Great Heavens, how they rode! We could hear them yelling on
every side of us. We jumped off our ponies and stood behind
them, the rifles across the saddles. But at four hundred yards they
all pivoted about and cantered off again leisurely. Now they followed us as before—three in the front, two in the rear, and two on
either side. I do not think I am going to be frightened when the
rush does come. I watched myself just now. I was excited, and
I remember Bunt saying to me, 'Keep your shirt on, m'son'; but I
was not afraid of being killed. Thank God for that! It is something I've long wished to find out, and now that I know it I am
proud of it. Neither side fired a shot. I was not afraid. It's
glorious. Estorijo is all right.

"Sunday afternoon, one-thirty.—No change. It is unspeakably
hot.

"Three-fifteen.—The One with the Feather is walking, leading his pony. It seems to be lame." [*With this entry Karslake ended page five, and the next page of the manuscript is numbered seven. It is very probable, however, that he made a mistake in the numerical sequence of his pages, for the narrative is continuous, and, at this point at least, unbroken. There does not seem to be any sixth page.*]

"Four o'clock.—Is it possible that we are to pass another night of suspense? They certainly show no signs of bringing on the crisis, and they surely would not attempt anything so late in the afternoon as this. It is a relief to feel that we have nothing to fear till morning, but the tension of watching all night long is fearful.

"Later.—Idaho has just killed the Little One.

"Later.—Still Firing.

"Later.—Still at it.

"Later, about five.—A bullet struck within three feet of me.

"Five-ten.—Still firing.

"Seven-thirty P. M., in camp.—It happened so quickly that it was all over before I realized. We had our first interchange of shots with them late this afternoon. The Little One was riding from the front to the flank. Evidently he did not think he was in range—nor did any of us. All at once Idaho tossed up his rifle and let go without aiming—or so it seemed to me. The stock was not at his shoulder before the report came. About six seconds after the smoke had cleared away we could see the Little One begin to lean backward in the saddle, and Idaho said grimly, 'I guess I got *you*.' The Little One leaned further and further till suddenly his head dropped back between his shoulder-blades. He held to his pony's mane with both hands for a long time and then all at once went off feet first. His legs bent under him like putty as his feet touched the ground. The pony bolted.

"Just as soon as Idaho fired the others closed right up and began riding around us at top speed, firing as they went. Their aim was bad as a rule, but one bullet came very close to me. At about half-past five they drew off out of range again and we made camp right where we stood. Estorijo and I are both sure that Idaho hit the Red One, but Idaho himself is doubtful, and Bunt did not see the shot. I could swear that the Red One all but went off his pony. However, he seems active enough now.

"Monday morning.—Still another night without attack. I have

not slept since Friday evening. The strain is terrific. At day-break this morning, when one of our ponies snorted suddenly, I cried out at the top of my voice. I could no more have repressed it than I could have stopped my blood flowing; and for half an hour afterward I could feel my flesh crisping and prinkling, and there was a sickening weakness at the pit of my stomach. At breakfast I had to force down my coffee. They are still in place, but now there are two on each side, two in the front, two in the rear. The killing of the Little One seems to have heartened us all wonderfully. I am sure we will get out—somehow. But oh! the suspense of it.

"Monday morning, nine-thirty.—Under way for over two hours. There is no new development. But Idaho has just said that they seem to be edging in. We hope to reach water to-day. Our supply is low, and the ponies are beginning to hang their heads. It promises to be a blazing hot day. There is alkali all to the west of us, and we just commence to see the rise of ground miles to the south-ward that Idaho says are the San Jacinto Mountains. Plenty of water there. The desert hereabout is vast and lonesome beyond words; leagues of sparse sage-brush, leagues of leper-white alkali, leagues of baking gray sand, empty, heat-ridden, the abomination of desolation; and always—in whichever direction I turn my eyes—always, in the midst of this pale-yellow blur, a single figure in the distance, blanketed, watchful, solitary, standing out sharp and distinct against the background of sage and sand.

"Monday, about eleven o'clock.—No change. The heat is appalling. There is just a—

"Later.—I was on the point of saying that there was just a mouthful of water left for each of us in our canteens when Estorijo and Idaho both at the same time cried out that they were moving in. It is true. They are within rifle-range, but do not fire. We, as well, have decided to reserve our fire until something more positive happens.

"Noon.—The first shot—for to-day—from the Red One. We are halted. The shot struck low and to the left. We could see the sand spout up in a cloud just as though a bubble had burst on the surface of the ground.

"They have separated from each other, and the whole eight of them are now in a circle around us. Idaho believes the Red One fired as a signal. Estorijo is getting ready to take a shot at the One with the Feather. We have the ponies in a circle around us. It looks as if now at last this was the beginning of the real business.

"Later, twelve-thirty-five.—Estorijo missed. Idaho will try with the Winchester as soon as the One with the Feather halts. He is galloping toward the Red One.

"All at once, about two o'clock, the fighting began. This is the first let-up. It is now—God knows what time. They closed up suddenly and began galloping about us in a circle, firing all the time. They rode like madmen. I would not have believed that Indian ponies could run so quickly. What with their yelling and the incessant crack of their rifles and the mud of their ponies' feet our horses at first became very restless, and at last Idaho's mustang bolted clean away. We all stood to it as hard as we could. For about the first fifteen minutes it was hot work. The Spotted One is hit. We are certain of that much, though we do not know whose gun did the work. My poor old horse is bleeding dreadfully from the mouth. He has two bullets in the stomach, and I do not believe he can stand much longer. They have let up for the last few minutes, but are still riding around us, their guns at 'ready.' Every now and then one of us fires, but the heat-shimmer has come up over the ground since noon and the range is extraordinarily deceiving.

"Three-ten.—Estorijo's horse is down, shot clean through the head. Mine has gone long since. We have made a rampart of the bodies.

"Three-twenty.—They are at it again, tearing around us incredibly fast, every now and then narrowing the circle. The bullets are striking everywhere now. I have no rifle, do what I can with my revolver, and try to watch what is going on in front of me and warn the others when they press in too close on my side." [*Karslake nowhere accounts for the absence of his carbine. That a U. S. trooper should be without his gun while traversing a hostile country is a fact difficult to account for.*]

"Three-thirty.—They have winged me—through the shoulder. Not bad, but it is bothersome. I sit up to fire, and Bunt gives me his knee on which to rest my right arm. When it hangs it is painful.

"Quarter to four.—It is horrible. Bunt is dying. He can not speak, the ball having gone through the lower part of his face, but back, near the neck. It happened through his trying to catch his horse. The animal was struck in the breast and tried to bolt. He reared up, backing away, and as we had to keep him close to us to serve as a bulwark Bunt followed him out from the little circle that we formed, his gun in one hand, his other gripping the bridle. I suppose every one of the eight fired at him simultaneously, and down he went. The pony dragged him a little ways, still clutching the bridle, then fell itself, its whole weight rolling on Bunt's chest. We have managed to get him in and secure his rifle, but he will not live. None of us knows him very well. He only joined us about a week ago, but we all liked him from the start. He never spoke of himself, so we can not tell much about him. Idaho says he has a wife in Torreon, but that he has not lived with her for two years; they did not get along well together, it seems. This is the first violent death I have ever seen, and it astonishes me to note how *unimportant* it seems. How little anybody cares—after all. If I had been told of his death—the details of it, in a story or in the form of fiction—it is easily conceivable that it would have impressed me more with its importance than the actual scene has done. Possibly my mental vision is scaled to a larger field since Friday, and as the greater issues loom up one man more or less seems to be but a unit—more or less—in an eternal series. When he was hit he swung back against the horse, still holding by the rein. His feet slid from under him, and he cried out, 'My *God!*' just once. We divided his cartridges between us, and Idaho passed me his carbine. The barrel was scorching hot.

"They have drawn off a little, and for fifteen minutes, though they still circle us slowly, there has been no firing. Forty cartridges left. Bunt's body (I think he is dead now) lies just back of me, and already the gnats—I can't speak of it."

[*Karslake evidently made the next few entries at successive intervals of time, but neglected in his excitement to note the exact hour as above. We may gather that "They" made another attack and then repeated the assault so quickly that he had no chance to record it properly. I transcribe the entries in exactly the disjointed manner in which they occur in the original. The reference to the "fire" is unexplainable.*]

"I shall do my best to set down exactly what happened and what I do and think, and what I see.

"The heat-shimmer spoiled my aim, but I am quite sure that either

"This last rush was the nearest. I had started to say that though the heat-shimmer was bad, either Estorijo or myself wounded one of their ponies. We saw him stumble.

"Another rush—

"Our ammunition.

"Only a few cartridges left.

"The Red One like a whirlwind only fifty yards away.

"We fire separately now as they sneak up under cover of our smoke.

"We put the fire out. Estorijo—" [*It is possible that Karslake had begun here to chronicle the death of the Mexican.*]

"I have killed the Spotted One. Just as he wheeled his horse I saw him in a line with the rifle-sights and let him have it squarely. It took him straight in the breast. I could *feel* that shot strike. He went down like a sack of lead weights. By God, it was superb!

"Later.—They have drawn off out of range again, and we are allowed a breathing spell. Our ponies are either dead or dying, and we have dragged them around us to form a barricade. We lie on the ground behind the bodies and fire over them. There are twenty-seven cartridges left.

"It is now mid-afternoon. Our plan is to stand them off if we can till night and then to try an escape between them. But to what purpose? They would trail us so soon as it was light.

"We think now that they followed us without attacking for so long because they were waiting till the lay of the land suited them. They wanted—no doubt—an absolutely flat piece of country, with no depressions, no hills or stream-beds in which we could hide, but which should be high upon the edges, like an amphitheatre. They would get us in the centre and occupy the rim themselves. Roughly, this is the bit of desert which witnesses our 'last stand.' On three sides the ground swells a very little—the rise is not four feet. On the third side it is open, and so flat that even lying on the ground as we do we can see (leagues away) the San Jacinto hills—'from whence cometh no help.' It is all sand and sage, forever and forever. Even the sage is sparse—a bad place even for a coyote. The whole is flagellated with an intolerable heat and—now that the shooting is relaxed—oppressed with a benumbing, sodden silence—the silence of a primordial world. Such a silence as must have brooded over the Face of the Waters on the Eve of Creation—desolate, desolate, as though a colossal, invisible pillar—a pillar of the Infinitely Still, the pillar of Nirvana—rose forever into the empty blue, human life an atom of microscopic dust crushed under its basis, and at the summit God Himself. And I find time to ask myself why, at this of all moments of my tiny life-span, I am able to write as I do, registering impressions, keeping a

"ONLY A FEW CARTRIDGES LEFT"

The last stand of three troopers and a scout overtaken by a band of hostile Indians

finger upon the pulse of the spirit. But oh! if I had time now—
time to write down the great thoughts that do throng the brain.
They are there, I feel them, know them. No doubt the supreme
exaltation of approaching death is the stimulus that one never
experiences in the humdrum business of the day-to-day existence.
Such mighty thoughts! Unintelligible, but if I had time I could
spell them out, *and how I could write then!* I feel that the whole
secret of Life is within my reach; I can almost grasp it; I seem to
feel that in just another instant I can see it all plainly, as the arch-
angels see it all the time, as the great minds of the world, the great
philosophers, have seen it once or twice, vaguely—a glimpse here
and there, after years of patient study. Seeing thus I should be the
equal of the gods. But it is not meant to be. There is a sacrilege
in it. I almost seem to understand why it is kept from us. But
the very reason of this withholding is in itself a part of the secret.
If I could only, only set it down!—for whose eyes? Those of a
wandering hawk? God knows. But never mind. I should have
spoken—once; should have said the great Word for which the
World since the evening and the morning of the First Day has
listened. God knows. God knows. What a whirl is this? Monstrous incongruity. Philosophy and fighting troopers. The Infinite and dead horses. There's humor for you. The Sublime
takes off its hat to the Ridiculous. Send a cartridge clashing into
the breech and speculate about the Absolute. Keep one eye on your
sights and the other on Cosmos. Blow the reek of burned powder
from before you so you may look over the edge of the abyss of the
Great Primal Cause. Duck to the whistle of a bullet and commune
with Schopenhauer. Perhaps I am a little mad. Perhaps I am
supremely intelligent. But in either case I am not understandable
to myself. How, then, be understandable to others? If these
sheets of paper, this incoherence, is ever read, the others will understand it about as much as the investigating hawk. But none the
less be it of record that I, Karslake, saw. It reads like Revela-
tions: 'I, John, saw.' It is just that. There is something apoca-
lyptic in it all. I have seen a vision, but can not—there is the pitch
of anguish in the impotence—bear record. If time were allowed to
order and arrange the words of description, this exaltation of spirit,
in that very space of time, would relax, and the describer lapse
back to the level of the average again before he could set down the
things he saw, the things he thought. The machinery of the mind
that could coin the great Word is automatic, and the very force

that brings the die near the blank metal supplies the motor power
of the reaction before the impression is made . . . I stopped
for an instant, looking up from the page, and at once the great
vague panorama faded. I lost it all. Cosmos has dwindled again
to an amphitheatre of sage and sand, a vista of distant purple hills,
the shimmer of scorching alkali, and in the middle distance there,
those figures, blanketed, beaded, feathered, rifle in hand.

"But for a moment I stool on Patmos.

"The Ridiculous jostles the elbow of the Sublime and shoulders
it from place as Idaho announces that he has found two more cartridges in Estorijo's pockets.

"They rushed again. Eight more cartridges gone. Twenty-one
left. They rush in this manner—at first they circle, rapid beyond
expression, one figure succeeding the other so swiftly that the dizzied vision loses count and instead of seven of them there appear
to be seventy. Then suddenly, on some indistinguishable signal,
they contract this circle, and through the jets of powder-smoke
Idaho and I see them whirling past our rifle-sights not one hundred
yards away. Then their fire suddenly slackens, the smoke drifts
by, and we see them in the distance again, moving about us at a
slow canter. Then the blessed breathing-spell, while we peer out
to know if we have killed or not, and count our cartridges. We
have laid the twenty-one loaded shells that remain in a row between
us, and after our first glance outward to see if any of them are
down, our next is inward at that ever-shrinking line of brass and
lead. We do not talk much. This is the end. We know it now.
All of a sudden the conviction that I am to die here has hardened
within me. It is, all at once, absurd that I should ever have supposed that I was to reach La Paz, take the east-bound train and
report at San Antonio. It seems to me that I *knew,* weeks ago,
that our trip was to end thus. I knew it—somehow—in Sonora,
while we were waiting orders, and I tell myself that if I had only
stopped to really think of it I could have foreseen to-day's bloody
business.

"Later.—The Red One got off his horse and bound up the
creature's leg. One of us hit him, evidently. A little higher, it
would have reached the heart. Our aim is ridiculously bad—the
heat-shimmer—

"Later.—Idaho is wounded. This last time, for a moment, I
was sure the end had come. They were within revolver range and
we could feel the vibration of the ground under their ponies' hoofs.

But suddenly they drew off. I have looked at my watch; it is four o'clock.

"Four o'clock.—Idaho's wound is bad—a long, raking furrow in the right forearm. I bind it up for him, but he is losing a great deal of blood and is very weak.

"They seem to know that we are only two by now, for with each rush they grow bolder. The slackening of our fire must tell them how scant is our ammunition.

"Later.—This last was magnificent. The Red One and one other with lines of blue paint across his cheek galloped right at us. Idaho had been lying with his head and shoulders propped against the neck of his dead pony. His eyes were shut, and I thought he had fainted. But as he heard them coming he struggled up, first to his knees and then to his feet—to his full height—dragging his revolver from his hip with his left hand. The whole right arm swung useless. He was so weak that he could only lift the revolver half way—could not get the muzzle up. But though it sagged and dropped in his grip, he *would* die fighting. When he fired the bullet threw up the sand not a yard from his feet, and then he fell on his face across the body of the horse. During the charge I fired as fast as I could, but evidently to no purpose. They must have thought that Idaho was dead, for as soon as they saw him getting to his feet they sheered their horses off and went by on either side of us. I have made Idaho comfortable. He is unconscious; have used the last of the water to give him a drink. He does not seem—

"They continue to circle us. Their fire is incessant, but very wild. So long as I keep my head down I am comparatively safe.

"Later.—I think Idaho is dying. It seems he was hit a second time when he stood up to fire. Estorijo is still breathing; I thought him dead long since.

"Four-ten.—Idaho gone. Twelve cartridges left. Am all alone now.

"Four-twenty-five.—I am very weak." [*Karslake was evidently wounded some time between ten and twenty-five minutes after four. His notes make no mention of the fact.*] "Eight cartridges remain. I leave my library to my brother, Walter Patterson Karslake; all my personal effects to my parents, except the picture of myself taken in Baltimore in 1897, which I direct to be" [*the next lines are undecipherable*] " . . . at Washington, D. C., as soon as possible. I appoint as my literary

"Four forty-five.—Seven cartridges. Very weak and unable to

move lower part of my body. Am in no pain. They rode in very close. The Red One is— An intolerable thirst—

"I appoint as my literary executor my brother, Patterson Karslake. The notes on 'Coronado in New Mexico' should be revised.

"My death occurred in western Arizona, April 15th, at the hands of a roving band of Hunt-in-the-Morning's bucks. They have—

"Five o'clock.—The last cartridge gone.

"Estorijo still breathing. I cover his face with my hat. Their fire is incessant. Am much weaker. Convey news of death to Patterson Karslake, care of Corn Exchange Bank, New York City.

"Five-fifteen—about.—They have ceased firing, and draw together in a bunch. I have four cartridges left" [see conflicting note dated five o'clock], "but am extremely weak. Idaho was the best friend I had in all the Southwest. I wish it to be known that he was a generous, open-hearted fellow, a kindly man, clean of speech, and absolutely unselfish. He may be known as follows: Sandy beard, long sandy hair, scar on forehead, about six feet one inch in height. His real name is James Monroe Herndon; his profession that of government scout. Notify Mrs. Herndon, Trinidad, New Mexico.

"The writer is Arthur Staples Karslake, dark hair, height five feet eleven, body will be found near that of Herndon.

"Luis Estorijo, Mexican—

"Later.—Two more cartridges.

Five-thirty.—Estorijo dead.

"It is half-past five in the afternoon of April fifteenth. They followed us from the eleventh—Friday—till to-day. It will

[The MS. ends here.]

TWO HEARTS THAT BEAT AS ONE

"Which I puts it up as how you ain't never heard about that time that Hardenberg and Strokher—the Englisher—had a friendly go with bare knuckles—ten rounds it was—all along o' a feemale woman?"

It is a small world and I had just found out that my friend, Bunt McBride—horse-wrangler, miner, faro-dealer, and bone-gatherer—whose world was the plains and ranges of the Great Southwest, was known of the Three Black Crows, Hardenberg, Strokher, and Ally Bazan, and had even foregathered with them on more than one of their ventures for Cyrus Ryder's Exploitation Agency—ventures that had nothing of the desert in them, but that involved the sea, and the schooner, and the taste of the great-lunged canorous trades.

"Ye ain't never crossed the trail o' that mournful history?"

I professed my ignorance and said:

"They fought?"

"Mister Man," returned Bunt soberly, as one broaching a subject not to be trifled with, "they sure did. Friendly-like, y'know—like as how two high-steppin', sassy gents figures out to settle any little strained relations—friendly-like, but considerable keen."

He took a pinch of tobacco from his pouch and a bit of paper and rolled a cigarette in the twinkling of an eye, using only one hand, in true Mexican style.

"Now," he said, as he drew the first long puff to the very bottom of the leathern valves he calls his lungs. "Now, I'm a-goin' for to relate that same painful proceedin' to you, just so as you kin get a line on the consumin' and devourin' foolishness o' male humans when they's a woman in the wind. Woman," said Bunt, wagging his head thoughtfully at the water, "woman is a weather-breeder. Mister Dixon, they is three things I'm skeered of. The last two I don't just rightly call to mind at this moment, but the first is woman. When I meets up with a feemale woman on my trail, I sheers off some prompt, Mr. Dixon; I sheers off. An' Hardenberg," he added irrelevantly, "would a-took an' married this woman, so he would. Yes, an' Strokher would, too."

"Was there another man?" I asked.

"No," said Bunt. Then he began to chuckle behind his mustaches. "Yes, they was." He smote a thigh. "They sure was another man for fair. Well, now, Mr. Man, lemmee tell you the whole 'how.'

"It began with me bein' took into a wild-eyed scheme that that maverick, Cy Ryder, had cooked up for the Three Crows. They was a row down Gortamalar way. Same gesabe named Palachi— Barreto Palachi—findin' times dull an' the boys some off their feed, ups an' says to hisself, "Exercise is wot I needs. I will now take an' overthrow the blame Gover'ment.' Well, this same Palachi rounds up a bunch o' *insurrectos* an' begins pesterin' an' badgerin' an' hectorin' the Gover'ment, an' r'aring 'round and bellerin' an' makin' a procession of hisself, till he sure pervades the landscape; an before you knows what, lo'n beholt, here's a reel live Revolution-Thing cayoodlin' in the scenery, an' the Gover'ment is plum bothered.

"They rounds up the gesabe at last at a place on the coast, but he escapes as easy as how-do-you-do. He can't, howsomever, git back to his *insurrectos;* the blame Gover'ment being in possession of all the trails leadin' into the hinterland; so says he, 'What for a game would it be for me to hyke up to 'Frisco an' git in touch with my financial backers an' conspirate to smuggle down a load o' arms?' Which the same he does, and there's where the Three Black Crows an' me begin to take a hand.

"Cy Ryder gives us the job o' taking the schooner down to a certain point on the Gortamalar coast and there delivering to the agent o' the gazabo three thousand stand o' forty-eight Winchesters.

"When we gits this far into the game Ryder ups and says:

" 'Boys, here's where I cashes right in. You sets right to me for the schooner and the cargo. But you goes to Palachi's agent over 'crost the bay for instructions and directions.'

" 'But,' says the Englisher, Strokher, 'this bettin' a blind play don't suit our hand. Why not,' says he, 'make right up to Mister Palachi hisself?'

" 'No,' says Ryder; 'no, boys. Ye can't. The Signor is lying as low as a toad in a wheeltrack these days, because o' the pryin' and meddlin' disposition o' the local authorities. No,' he says, 'ye

must have your palaver with the agent which she is a woman,'
an' thereon I groans low and despairin'.

"So soon as he mentions 'feemale' I *knowed* trouble was in the
atmosphere. An' right there is where I sure looses my presence o'
mind. What I should a-done was to say, 'Mister Ryder, Hardenberg, and gents all: You're good boys an' you drinks and deals
fair, an' I loves you all with a love that can never, never die for the
terms o' your natural lives, an' may God have mercy on your souls;
but I ain't keepin' case on this 'ere game no longer. Woman and
me is mules an' music. We ain't never made to ride in the same
go-cart. Good-by.' That-all is wot I should ha' said. But I didn't.
I walked right plum into the sloo, like the mudhead that I was, an'
got mired for fair—jes as I might a-knowed I would.

"Well, Ryder gives us a address over across the bay an' we
fair hykes over there all along o' as crool a rain as ever killed
crops. We finds the place after a while, a lodgin'-house all lorn
and loony, set down all by itself in the middle o' some real estate
extension like a tepee in a 'barren'—crazy 'modern' house all gim-
crack and woodwork and frostin', with never another place in so far
as you could hear a coyote yelp.

"Well, we bucks right up an' asks o' the party at the door if
the Signorita Esperanza Ulivarri—that was who Ryder had told
us to ask for—might be concealed about the premises, an' we shows
Cy Ryder's note. The party that opened the door was a Greaser,
the worst looking I ever clapped eyes on—looked like the kind wot
'ud steal the coppers off his dead grandmother's eyes. Anyhow, he
says to come in, gruff-like, an' to wait, *poco tiempo*.

"Well, we waited *moucho tiempo—muy moucho*, all a-settin' on
the edge of the sofy, with our hats on our knees, like philly-loo birds
on a rail, and a-countin' of the patterns in the wall-paper to pass
the time along. An' Hardenberg, who's got to do the talkin', gets
the fidgets byne-by; and because he's only restin' the toes o' his feet
on the floor, his knees begin jiggerin'; an' along o' watchin' him, *my*
knees begin to go, an' then Strokher's and then Ally Bazan's. An'
there we sat all in a row and jiggered an' jiggered. Great snakes,
it makes me sick to the stummick to think o' the idjeets we were.

"Then after a long time we hears a rustle o' silk petticoats, an'
we all grabs holt o' one another an' looks scared-like, out from under
our eyebrows. An' then—then, Mister Man, they walks into that
bunk-house parlor the loveliest-lookin' young feemale woman that
ever wore hair.

"She was lovelier than Mary Anderson; she was lovelier than Lotta. She was tall, an' black-haired, and had a eye . . . well, I dunno; when she gave you the littlest flicker o' that same eye, you felt it was about time to take an' lie right down an' say, 'I would esteem it, ma'am, a sure smart favor if you was to take an' wipe your boots on my waistcoat, jus' so's you could hear my heart a-beatin'. That's the kind o' feemale woman *she* was.

"Well, when Hardenberg had caught his second wind, we begins to talk business.

"'An' you're to take a passenger back with you,' says Esperanza after a while.

"'What for a passenger might it be?' says Hardenberg.

"She fished out her calling-card at that and tore it in two an' gave Hardenberg one-half.

"'It's the party,' she says, 'that'll come aboard off San Diego on your way down an' who will show up the other half o' the card— the half I have here an' which the same I'm goin' to mail to him. An' you be sure the halves fit before you let him come aboard. An' when that party comes aboard,' she says, 'he's to take over charge.'

"'Very good,' says Hardenberg, mincing an' silly like a chessy cat lappin' cream. 'Very good, ma'am; your orders shall be obeyed.' He sure said it just like that, as if he spoke out o' a story-book. An' I kicked him under the table for it.

"Then we palavers a whole lot an' settles the way the thing is to be run, an' fin'ly, when we'd got as far as could be that day, the Sigñorita stood up an' says:

"'Now, me good fellers.' 'Twas Spanish she spoke. 'Now, me good fellows, you must drink a drink with me.' She herds us all up into the dining-room and fetches out—not whiskey, mind you— but a great, fat, green-and-gold bottle o' champagne, an' when Ally Bazan has fired it off, she fills our glasses—dinky little flat glasses that looked like flower vases. Then she stands up there before us, fine an' tall, all in black silk, an' puts her glass up high an' sings out—

"'To the Revolution!'

"An' we all solemn-like says, 'To the Revolution,' an' crooks our elbows. When we-all comes to, about half an hour later, we're in the street outside, havin' jus' said good-by to the Sigñorita. We-all are some quiet the first block or so, and then Hardenberg says— stoppin' dead in his tracks:

"'I pauses to remark that when a certain young feemale party

havin' black hair an' a killin' eye gets good an' ready to travel up
the centre aisle of a church, I know the gent to show her the way,
which he is six feet one in his stocking-feet, some freckled across the
nose, an' shoots with both hands.'

"'Which the same observation,' speaks up Strokher, twirlin'
his yeller lady-killer, 'which the same observation,' he says, 'has
my hearty indorsement an' co-operation savin' in the particular of
the description o' the gent. The gent is five foot eleven high, three
feet thick, is the only son of my mother, an' has yeller mustaches and
a buck tooth.'

"'He don't qualify,' puts in Hardenberg. 'First, because he's a
Englisher, and second, because he's up again a American—and
besides, he has a tooth that's bucked.'

"'Buck or no buck,' flares out Strokher, 'wot might be the mean-
in' o' that remark concernin' being a Englisher?'

"'The fact o' his bein' English,' says Hardenberg, 'is only half
the hoe-handle. 'Tother half being the fact that the first-named gent
is all American. No Yank ain't never took no dust from aft a Englisher, whether it were war, walking'-matches, or women.'

"'But they's a Englisher,' sings out Strokher, 'not forty miles
from here as can nick the nose o' a freckled Yank if so be occasion
require.'

"Now, ain't that plum foolish-like?" observed Bunt, philosophi-
cally. "Ain't it plum foolish-like o' them two gesabes to go flyin'
up in the air like two he-hens on a hot plate—for nothin' in the
world but because a neat lookin' feemale woman has looked at 'em
some soft?"

"Well, naturally, we others—Ally Bazan an' me—we others
throws it into 'em pretty strong about bein' more kinds of blame
fools than a pup with a bug; an' they simmers down some, but
along o' the way home I kin see as how they're a-glarin' at each
other, an' a-drawin' theirselves up proud-like an' presumptchoous,
an' I groans again, not loud but deep, as the Good Book says.

"We has two or three more palavers with the Signorita Esperanza and stacks the deck to beat the harbor police and the Customs
people an' all, an' to nip down the coast with our contraband. An'
each time we chins with the Signorita there's them two locoes steppin' and sidle'n' around her, actin' that silly-like that me and Ally
Bazan takes an' beats our heads agin' the walls so soon as we're
alone just because we're that pizen mortified.

"Fin'ly comes the last talky-talk an' we're to sail away next day an' mebbee snatch the little Joker through or be took an' hung by the *Costa Guardas.*

"An' 'Good-by,' says Hardenberg to Esperanza, in a faintin', die-away voice like a kitten with a cold. 'An' ain't we goin' to meet no more?'

" 'I sure hopes as much,' puts in Strokher, smirkin' so's you'd think he was a he-milliner sellin' a bonnet. 'I hope,' says he, 'our delightful acquaintanceship ain't a-goin' for to end abrupt this-a-way.'

" 'Oh, you nice, big Mister Men,' pipes up the Signorita in English, 'we will meet down there in Gortamalar soon again, yes, because I go down by the vapor carriages to-morrow.'

" 'Unprotected, too,' says Hardenberg, waggin' his fool head. 'An' so young!'

"Holy Geronimo! I don't know what more fool drivelin' they had, but they fin'ly comes away. Ally Bazan and me rounds 'em up and conducts 'em to the boat an' puts 'em to bed like as if they was little—or drunk, an' the next day—or next night, rather—about one o'clock, we slips the heel ropes and hobbles o' the schooner quiet as a mountain-lion stalking a buck, and catches the out-tide through the gate o' the bay. Lord, we was some keyed up, lemmee tell you, an' Ally Bazan and Hardenberg was at the fore end o' the boat with their guns ready in case o' bein' asked impert'-nent questions by the patrol-boats.

"Well, how-some-ever, we nips out with the little Jokers (they was writ in the manifest as minin' pumps) an' starts south. This 'ere *pasear* down to Gortamalar is the first time I goes a-gallying about on what the Three Crows calls 'blue water'; and when that schooner hit the bar I begins to remember that my stummick and inside arrangements ain't made o' no chilled steel, nor yet o' rawhide. First I gits plum sad, and shivery, and I feels as mean an' pore as a prairie-dog w'ich 'as eat a horned toad back'ards. I goes to Ally Bazan and gives it out as how I'm going for to die, an' I puts it up that I'm sure sad and depressed-like; an' don't care much about life nohow; an' that present surroundin's lack that certain undescribable charm. I tells him that I *knows* the ship is goin' to sink afore we git over the bar. Waves!—they was higher'n the masts; and I've rode some fair lively sun-fishers in my time, but I ain't never struck anythin' like the r'arin' and buckin' and high-an'-lofty tumblin' that that same boat went through with those first few hours after we had come out.

"But Ally Bazan tells me to go downstairs in the boat an' lie up quiet, an' byne-by I do feel better. By next day I kin sit up and take solid food again. An' then's when I takes special notice o' the everlastin' foolishness o' Strokher and Hardenberg.

"You'd 'a' thought each one o' them two mush-heads was tryin' to act the part of a ole cow which has had her calf took. They goes a-moonin' about the boat that mournful it 'ud make you yell jus' out o' sheer nervousness. First one 'ud up an' hold his head on his hand an' lean on the fence-rail that ran around the boat, and sigh till he'd raise his pants clean outa the top o' his boots. An' then the other 'ud go off in another part o' the boat an' *he'd* sigh an' moon an' take on fit to sicken a coyote.

"But byne-by—we're mebbee six days to the good o' 'Frisco— byne-by they two gits kind o' sassy along o' each t'other, an' they has a heart-to-heart talk and puts it up as how either one o' 'em 'ud stand to win so only the t'other was out o' the game.

"'It's double or nothing,' says Hardenberg, who is somethin' o' a card-sharp, 'for either you or me, Stroke; an' if you're agreeable I'll play you a round o' jack for the chance at the Signorita—the loser to pull out o' the running for good an' all.'

"No, Strokher don't come in on no such game, he says. He wins her, as a man, and not as no poker player. No, nor he won't throw no dice for the chance o' winnin' Esperanza, nor he won't flip no coin, nor yet 'rastle. 'But,' says he all of a sudden, 'I'll tell you which I'll do. You're a big, thick, strappin' hulk o' a two-fisted dray-horse, Hardie, an' I ain't no effete an' digenerate one-lunger myself. Here's wot I propose—that we-all takes an' lays out a sixteen-foot ring on the quarter-deck, an' that the raw-boned Yank and the stodgy Englisher strips to the waist, an' all-friendly-like, settles the question by Queensbury rules an' may the best man win.'

"Hardenberg looks him over.

"'An' wot might be your weight?' says he. 'I don't figure on hurtin' of you, if so be you're below my class.'

"'I fights at a hunder and seventy,' says Strokher.

"'An' me,' says Hardenberg, 'at a hunder an' seventy-five. We're matched.'

"'Is it a go?' inquires Strokher.

"'You bet your great-gran'mammy's tortis-shell chessy cat it's a go,' says Hardenberg, prompt as a hop-frog catching flies.

"We don't lose no time trying to reason with 'em, for they is

sure keen on havin' the go. So we lays out a ring by the rear
end o' the deck, an' runs the schooner in till we're in the lee o' the
land, an' she ridin' steady on her pins.

"Then along o' about four o'clock on a fine still day we lays
the boat to, as they say, an' folds up the sail, an' havin' scattered
resin in the ring (which it ain't no ring, but a square o' ropes on
posts), we says all is ready.

"Ally Bazan, he's referee, an' me, I'm the time-keeper, which
I has to ring the ship's bell every three minutes to let 'em know to
quit an' that the round is over.

"We gets 'em into the ring, each in his own corner, squattin' on
a bucket, the time-keeper bein' second to Hardenberg an' the referee
being second to Strokher. An' then, after they has shuk hands, I
climbs up on the chicken-coop an' hollers 'Time,' an' they begins.

"Mister Man, I've saw Tim Henan at his best, an' I've saw
Sayres when he was a top-notcher, an' likewise several other ir-
regler boxin' sharps that were sure tough terriers. Also I've saw
two short-horn bulls arguin' about a question o' leadership, but—so
help me Bob—the fight I saw that day made the others look like a
young ladies' quadrille. Oh, I ain't goin' to tell o' that mill in detail, nor by rounds. Rounds! After the first five minutes they
wa'n't no rounds. I rung the blame bell till I rung her loose an'
Ally Bazan yells 'Break-a-way' an' 'Time's up' till he's black in the
face, but you could no more separate them two than you could put
the brakes on a blame earthquake.

"At about supper time we pulled 'em apart. We could do it by
then, they was both so gone; an' jammed each one o' 'em down in
their corners. I rings my bell good an' plenty, an' Ally Bazan
stands up on a bucket in the middle o' the ring an' says:

" 'I declare this 'ere glove contest a draw.'

"An' draw it sure was. They fit for two hours stiddy an' never
a one got no better o' the other. They give each other lick for
lick as fast an' as steady as they could stand to it. 'Rastling, borin'
in, boxin'—all was alike. The one was just as good as 'tother.
An' both willin' to the very last.

"When Ally Bazan calls it a draw, they gits up and wobbles toward each other an' shakes hands, and Hardenberg he says:

" 'Stroke, I thanks you a whole lot for as neat a go as ever I
mixed in.'

"An' Strokher answers up:

" 'Hardie, I loves you better'n ever. You'se the first man I've

met up with which I couldn't do for—an' I've met up with some
scraggy propositions in my time, too.'

"Well, they two is a sorry-lookin' pair o' birds by the time we
runs into San Diego harbor next night. They was fine lookin' objects for fair, all bruises and bumps. You remember now we was
to take on a party at San Diego who was to show t'other half o'
Esperanza's card, an' thereafterward to boss the job.

"Well, we waits till nightfall an' then slides in an' lays to off
a certain pile o' stone, an' shows two green lights and one white
every three and a half minutes for half a hour—this being a signal.

"They is a moon, an' we kin see pretty well.   After we'd
signaled about a hour, mebbee, we gits the answer—a one-minute
green flare, and thereafterward we makes out a rowboat putting
out and comin' toward us.   They is two people in the boat.   One
is the gesabe at the oars an' the other a party sitting in the hinder
end.

"Ally Bazan an' me, an' Strokher an' Hardenberg, we's all lean-
in' over the fence a-watchin'; when all to once I ups an' groans
some sad.   The party in the hinder end o' the boat bein' feemale.

" 'Ain't we never goin' to git shut of 'em?' says I; but the
words ain't no more'n off my teeth when Strokher pipes up:

" 'It's she,' says he, gaspin' as though shot hard.

" 'Wot!' cries Hardenberg, sort of mystified, 'Oh, I'm sure
a-dreamin'!' he says, just that silly-like.

" 'An' the mugs we've got!' says Strokher.   An' they both sets
to swearin' and cussin' to beat all I ever heard.

" 'I can't let her see me so bunged up,' says Hardenberg, dole-
ful-like.   'Oh, whatever is to be done?'

" 'An' I look like a real genuine blown-in-the-bottle pug,' whim-
pers Strokher.   'Never mind,' says he, 'we must face the music.
We'll tell her these are sure honorable scars, got because we fit for
her.'

"Well, the boat comes up an' the feemale party jumps out and
comes up the let-down stairway, on to the deck.   Without sayin' a
word she hands Hardenberg the half o' the card and he fishes out
his half an' matches the two by the light o' a lantern.

"By this time the rowboat has gone a little ways off, an' then at
last Hardenberg says:

" 'Welkum aboard, Signorita.'

"And Strokher cuts in with—

" 'We thought it was to be a man that 'ud join us here to take

command, but *you,*' he says—an' oh, butter wouldn't a-melted in his
mouth—'but *you,*' he says, 'is always our mistress.'

" 'Very right, *bueno.* Me good fellows,' says the Signorita,
'but don't you be afraid that they's no man at the head o' this
business.' An' with that the party chucks off hat an' skirts, *and
I'll be Mexican if it wa'n't a man after all!*

" 'I'm the Signor Barreto Palachi, gentlemen,' says he. 'The
gringo police who wanted for to arrest me made the disguise necessary. Gentlemen, I regret to have been obliged to deceive such
gallant *compadres,* but war knows no law.'

"Hardenberg and Strokher gives one look at the Signor and
another at their own spiled faces, then:

" 'Come back here with the boat!' roars Hardenberg over the
side, and with that—(upon me word you'd a-thought they two both
were moved with the same spring)—over they goes into the water
and strikes out hands over hands for the boat as hard as ever they
kin lay to it. The boat meets 'em—Lord knows what the party at
the oars thought—they climbs in an' the last I sees of 'em they was
puttin' for shore—each havin' taken a oar from the boatman, an' they
sure was makin' that boat *hum.*

"Well, we sails away eventually without 'em; an' a year or
more afterward I crosses their trail again in Cy Ryder's office in
'Frisco."

"Did you ask them about it all?" said I.

"Mister Man," observed Bunt. "I'm several kinds of a fool; I
know it. But sometimes I'm wise. I wishes for to live as long as
I can, an' die when I can't help it. I does *not,* neither there, nor
thereafterward, ever make no joke, nor yet no alloosion about, or
concerning the Signorita Esperanza Palachi in the hearin' o' Hardenberg an' Strokher. I've seen—(ye remember)—both those boys
use their fists—an' likewise Hardenberg, as he says hisself, shoots
with both hands."

THE DUAL PERSONALITY OF
SLICK DICK NICKERSON

I

On a certain morning in the spring of the year, the three men who were known as the Three Black Crows called at the office of "The President of the Pacific and Oriental Flotation Company," situated in an obscure street near San Francisco's water-front. They were Strokher, the tall, blond, solemn, silent Englishman; Hardenberg, the American, dry of humor, shrewd, resourceful, who bargained like a Vermonter and sailed a schooner like a Gloucester codfisher; and in their company, as ever inseparable from the other two, came the little colonial, nicknamed, for occult reasons, "Ally Bazan," a small, wiry man, excitable, vociferous, who was without fear, without guile and without money.

When Hardenberg, who was always spokesman for the Three Crows, had sent in their names, they were admitted at once to the inner office of the "President." The President was an old man, bearded like a prophet, with a watery blue eye and a forehead wrinkled like an orang's. He spoke to the Three Crows in the manner of one speaking to friends he has not seen in some time.

"Well, Mr. Ryder," began Hardenberg. "We called around to see if you had anything fer us this morning. I don't mind telling you that we're at liberty jus' now. Anything doing?"

Ryder fingered his beard distressfully. "Very little, Joe; very little."

"Got any wrecks?"

"Not a wreck."

Hardenberg turned to a great map that hung on the wall by Ryder's desk. It was marked in places by red crosses, against which were written certain numbers and letters. Hardenberg put his finger on a small island south of the Marquesas group and demanded: "What might be H. 33, Mr. President?"

"Pearl Island," answered the President. "Davidson is on that job."

"Or H. 125?" Hardenberg indicated a point in the Gilbert group.

"Guano deposits. That's promised."

"Hallo! You're up in the Aleutians, I make out. 20 A.—what's that?"

"Old government telegraph wire—line abandoned—finest drawn-copper wire. I've had three boys at that for months."

"What's 301? This here, off the Mexican coast?"

The President, unable to remember, turned to his one clerk: "Hyers, what's 301? Isn't that Peterson?"

The clerk ran his finger down a column. "No, sir; 301 is the Whiskey Ship."

"Ah! So it is. I remember. *You* remember, too, Joe. Little schooner, the 'Tropic Bird'—sixty days out from Callao—five hundred cases of whiskey aboard—sunk in squall. It was thirty years ago. Think of five hundred cases of thirty-year-old whiskey! There's money in that if I can lay my hands on the schooner. Suppose you try that, you boys—on a twenty per cent basis. Come now, what do you say?"

"Not for *five* per cent," declared Hardenberg. "How'd we raise her? How'd we know how deep she lies? Not for Joe. What's the matter with landing arms down here in Central America for Bocas and his gang?"

"I'm out o' that, Joe. Too much competition."

"What's doing here in Tahiti—No. 88? It ain't lettered."

Once more the President consulted his books. "Ah!—88. Here we are. Cache o' illicit pearls. I had it looked up. Nothing in it."

"Say, Cap'n!"—Hardenberg's eye had traveled to the upper edge of the map—"whatever did you strike up here in Alaska? At Point Barrow, s'elp me Bob! It's 48 B."

The President stirred uneasily in his place. "Well, I ain't quite worked that scheme out, Joe. But I smell the deal. There's a Russian post along there some'eres. Where they catch sea-otters. And the skins o' sea-otters are selling this very day for seventy dollars at any port in China."

"I s'y," piped up Ally Bazan, "I knows a bit about that gyme. They's a bally kind o' Lum-tums among them Chinese as sports those syme skins on their bally clothes—as a mark o' rank, d'ye see."

"Have you figured at all on the proposition, Cap'n?" inquired Hardenberg.

"There's risk in it, Joe; big risk," declared the President nervously. "But I'd only ask fifteen per cent."

"You *have* worked out the scheme, then?"

"Well—ah—y'see, there's the risk, and—ah—" Suddenly Ryder leaned forward, his watery blue eyes glinting: "Boys, it's a *jewel*. It's just your kind. I'd a-sent for you, to try on this very scheme, if you hadn't shown up. You kin have the "Bertha Miller"—I've a year's charter o' her from Wilbur—and I'll only ask you fifteen per cent of the *net* profits—*net*, mind you."

"I ain't buyin' no dead horse, Cap'n," returned Hardenberg, "but I'll say this: we pay no fifteen per cent."

"Banks and the Ruggles were daft to try it and give me twenty-five."

"An' where would Banks land the scheme? I know him. You put him on that German cipher-code job down Honolulu way, an' it cost you about a thousand before you could pull out. We'll give you seven an' a half."

"Ten," declared Ryder, "ten, Joe, at the very least. Why, how much do you suppose just the stores would cost me? And Point Barrow—why, Joe, that's right up in the Arctic. I got to run the risk o' you getting the "Bertha" smashed in the ice."

"What do *we* risk?" retorted Hardenberg; and it was the monosyllabic Strokher who gave the answer:

"Chokee, by Jove!"

"Ten is fair. It's ten or nothing," answered Hardenberg.

"Gross, then, Joe. Ten on the gross—or I give the job to the Ruggles and Banks."

"Who's your bloomin' agent?" put in Ally Bazan.

"Nickerson. I sent him with Peterson on that "Mary Archer" wreck scheme. An' you know what Peterson says of him—didn't give him no trouble at all. One o' my best men, boys."

"There have been," observed Strokher stolidly, "certain stories told about Nickerson. Not that *I* wish to seem suspicious, but I put it to you as man to man.

"Ay," exclaimed Ally Bazan. "He was fair nutty once, they tell me. Threw some kind o' bally fit an' come aout all skewjee'd in his mind. Forgot his nyme an' all. I s'y, how abaout him, anyw'y?"

"Boys," said Ryder, "I'll tell you. Nickerson—yes, I know the yarns about him. It was this way—y'see, I ain't keeping anything from you, boys. Two years ago he was a Methody preacher in Santa Clara. Well, he was what they call a revivalist, and he was holding forth one blazin' hot day out in the sun when all to once he goes down, *flat,* an' don't come round for the better part o' two days. When he wakes up he's *another person;* he'd forgot his name, forgot his job, forgot the whole blamed shooting-match. *And he ain't never remembered them since.* The doctors have names for that kind o' thing. It seems it does happen now and again. Well, he turned to and began sailoring first off—soon as the hospitals and medicos were done with him—an' him not having any friends as you might say, he was let go his own gait. He got to be third mate of some kind o' dough-dish down Mexico way, and then I got hold o' him an' took him into the comp'ny. He's been with me ever since. He ain't got the faintest kind o' recollection o' his Methody days, an' believes he's always been a sailorman. Well, that's *his* business, ain't it? If he takes my orders an' walks chalk, what do I care about his Methody game? There, boys, is the origin, history and development of Slick Dick Nickerson. If you take up this sea-otter deal and go to Point Barrow, naturally Nick has got to go as owner's agent and representative of the Comp'ny. But I couldn't send a easier fellow to get along with. Honest, now, I couldn't. Boys, you think over the proposition between now and to-morrow an' then come around and let me know."

And the upshot of the whole matter was that one month later the "Bertha Millner," with Nickerson, Hardenberg, Strokher and Ally Bazan on board, cleared from San Francisco, bound—the papers were beautifully precise—for Seattle and Tacoma with a cargo of general merchandise.

As a matter of fact, the bulk of her cargo consisted of some odd hundreds of very fine lumps of rock—which as ballast is cheap by the ton—and some odd dozen cases of conspicuously labeled champagne.

The Pacific and Oriental Flotation Company made this champagne out of Rhine wine, effervescent salts, raisins, rock candy and alcohol. It was from the same stock of wine of which Ryder had sold some thousand cases to the Coreans the year before.

II

"NOT that I care a curse," said Strokher, the Englishman. "But I put it to you squarely that this voyage lacks that certain indescribable charm."

The "Bertha Millner" was a fortnight out, and the four adventurers—or, rather, the three adventurers and Nickerson—were lame in every joint, red-eyed from lack of sleep, half-starved, wholly wet and unequivocally disgusted. They had had heavy weather from the day they bade farewell to the whistling buoy off San Francisco Bay until the moment when even patient, docile, taciturn Strokher had at last—in his own fashion—rebelled.

"Ain't I a dam' fool? Ain't I a proper lot? Gard strike me if I don't chuck fer fair after this. Wot'd I come to sea fer—an' this 'ere go is the worst I *ever* knew—a baoat no bigger'n a bally bath-tub, head seas, livin' gyles the clock 'round, wet food, wet clothes, wet bunks. Caold till, by cricky! I've lost the feel o' mee feet. An' wat for? For the bloomin' good chanst o' a slug in mee guts. That's wat for."

At little intervals the little vociferous colonial, Ally Bazan—he was read-haired and speckled—capered with rage, shaking his fist.

But Hardenberg only shifted his cigar to the other corner of his mouth. He knew Ally Bazan, and knew that the little fellow would have jeered at the offer of a first-cabin passage back to San Francisco in the swiftest, surest, steadiest passenger steamer that ever wore paint. So he remarked: "I ain't ever billed this promenade as a Coney Island picnic, I guess."

Nickerson—Slick Dick, the supercargo—was all that Hardenberg, who captained the schooner, could expect. He never interfered, never questioned; never protested in the name or interests of the Company when Hardenberg "hung on" in the bleak, bitter squalls till the "Bertha" was rail under and the sails hard as iron.

If it was true that he had once been a Methody revivalist, no one, to quote Ally Bazan, "could 'a' smelled it off'n him." He was a black-bearded, scrawling six-footer, with a voice like a steam siren and a fist like a sledge. He carried two revolvers, spoke of the Russians at Point Barrow as the "Boomskys," and boasted if it came to *that* he'd engage to account for two of them, would shove their heads into their boot-legs and give them the running scrag, by God so he would!

Slowly, laboriously, beset in blinding fogs, swept with icy rains, buffeted and mauled and man-handled by the unending assaults of the sea, the "Bertha Millner" worked her way northward up that iron coast—till suddenly she entered an elysium.

Overnight she seemed to have run into it; it was a world of green, wooded islands, of smooth channels, of warm and steady winds, of cloudless skies. Coming on deck upon the morning of the "Bertha's" first day in this new region, Ally Bazan gazed open-mouthed. Then: "I s'y!" he yelled. "Hey! By crickey! Look!" He slapped his thighs. "S'trewth! This is 'eavenly."

Strokher was smoking his pipe on the hatch combings. "Rather," he observed. "An' I put it to you—we've deserved it."

In the main, however, the northward flitting was uneventful. Every fifth day Nickerson got drunk—on the Company's Corean champagne. Now that the weather had sweetened, the Three Black Crows had less to do in the way of handling and nursing the schooner. Their plans when the "Boomskys" should be reached were rehearsed over and over again. Then came spells of card and checker playing, story-telling, or hours of silent inertia when, man fashion, they brooded over pipes in a patch of sun, somnolent, the mind empty of all thought.

But at length the air took on a keener tang; there was a bite to the breeze, the sun lost his savor and the light of him lengthened till Hardenberg could read off logarithms at ten in the evening. Great-coats and sweaters were had from the chests, and it was no man's work to reef when the wind came down from out the north.

Each day now the schooner was drawing nearer the Arctic Circle. At length snow fell, and two days later they saw their first iceberg.

Hardenberg worked out their position on the chart and bore to the eastward till he made out the Alaskan coast—a smudge on the horizon. For another week he kept this in sight, the schooner dodging the bergs that by now drove by in squadrons, and even bumping and butting through drift and slush ice.

Seals were plentiful, and Hardenberg and Strokher promptly revived the quarrel of their respective nations. Once even they slew a mammoth bull walrus—astray from some northern herd—and played poker for the tusks. Then suddenly they pulled themselves sharply together, and, as it were, stood "attention." For more than a week the schooner, following the trend of the far-distant coast, had headed eastward, and now at length, looming out of the snow and out of the mist, a sombre bulwark, black, vast, ominous, rose the scarps and crags of that which they came so far to see—Point Barrow.

Hardenberg rounded the point, ran in under the lee of the land and brought out the chart which Ryder had given him. Then he shortened sail and moved west again till Barrow was "hull down" behind him. To the north was the Arctic, treacherous, nursing hurricanes, ice-sheathed; but close aboard, not a quarter of a mile off his counter, stretched a gray and gloomy land, barren, bleak as a dead planet, inhospitable as the moon.

For three days they crawled along the edge, keeping their glasses trained upon every bay, every inlet. Then at length, early one morning, Ally Bazan, who had been posted at the bows, came scrambling aft to Hardenberg at the wheel. He was gasping for breath in his excitement.

"Hi! There we are," he shouted. "O Lord! Oh, I s'y! Now we're in fer it. That's them! That's them! By the great jumpin' jimminy Christmas, that's them fer fair! Strike me blind for a bleedin' gutter-cat if it eyent. O Lord! S'y, I gotta to get drunk. S'y, what-all's the first jump in the bally game now?"

"Well, the first thing, little man," observed Hardenberg, "is for your mother's son to hang the monkey on to the safety-valve. Keep y'r steam and watch y'r uncle."

"Scrag the Boomskys," said Slick Dick encouragingly.

Strokher pulled the left end of his viking mustache with the fingers of his right hand.

"We must now talk," he said.

A last conference was held in the cabin, and the various parts of the comedy rehearsed. Also the three looked to their revolvers.

"Not that I expect a rupture of diplomatic relations," commented Strokher; "but if there's any shooting done, as between man and man, I choose to do it."

"All understood, then?" asked Hardenberg, looking from face to face. "There won't be no chance to ask questions once we set foot ashore."

The others nodded.

It was not difficult to get in with the seven Russian sea-otter fishermen at the post. Certain of them spoke a macerated English, and through these Hardenberg, Ally Bazan, and Nickerson—Strok-

her remained on board to look after the schooner—told to the
"Boomskys" a lamentable tale of the reported wreck of a vessel,
described by Hardenberg, with laborious precision, as a steam
whaler from San Francisco—the "Tiber" by name, bark-rigged,
seven hundred tons burden, Captain Henry Ward Beecher, mate Mr.
James Boss Tweed.   They, the visitors, were the officers of the
relief-ship on the lookout for castaways and survivors.

But in the course of these preliminaries it became necessary to
restrain Nickerson—not yet wholly recovered from a recent incur-
sion into the store of Corean champagne. It presented itself to his
consideration as facetious to indulge (when speaking to the Russians) in strange and elaborate distortions of speech.

"And she sunk-avitch in a hundred fathom o' water-owski."

"—All on board-erewski."

"—hell of dam' bad storm-onavna."

And he persisted in the idiocy till Hardenberg found an excuse
for taking him aside and cursing him into a realization of his
position.

In the end—inevitably—the schooner's company were invited to
dine at the post.

It was a strange affair—a strange scene. The coast, flat, gray,
dreary beyond all power of expression, lonesome as the interstellar
space, and quite as cold, and in all that limitless vastness of the
World's Edge, two specks—the hut, its three windows streaming
with light, and the tiny schooner rocking in the offing.   Over all
flared the pallid incandescence of the auroras.

The Company drank steadily, and Strokher, listening from the
schooner's quarterdeck, heard the shouting and the songs faintly
above the wash and lapping under the counter. Two hours had
passed since the moment he guessed that the feast had been laid.
A third went by. He grew uneasy. There was no cessation of the
noise of carousing. He even fancied he heard pistol shots. Then
after a long time the noise by degrees wore down; a long silence
followed. The hut seemed deserted; nothing stirred; another hour
went by.

Then at length Strokher saw a figure emerge from the door of
the hut and come down to the shore.. It was Hardenberg. Strokher
saw him wave his arm slowly, now to the left, now to the right, and
he took down the wig-wag as follows: "Stand—in—closer—we—
have—the—skins."

III

DURING the course of the next few days Strokher heard the different versions of the affair in the hut over and over again till he knew its smallest details. He learned how the "Boomskys" fell upon Ryder's champagne like wolves upon a wounded buck, how they drank it from "enameled-ware" coffee-cups, from tin dippers, from the bottles themselves; how at last they even dispensed with the tedium of removing the corks and knocked off the heads against the table-ledge and drank from the splintered bottoms; how they quarreled over the lees and dregs, how ever and always fresh supplies were forthcoming, and how at last Hardenberg, Ally Bazan, and Slick Dick stood up from the table in the midst of the seven inert bodies; how they ransacked the place for the priceless furs; how they failed to locate them; how the conviction grew that this was the wrong place after all, and how at length Hardenberg discovered the trap-door that admitted to the cellar, where in the dim light of the uplifted lanterns they saw, corded in tiny bales and packages, the costliest furs known to commerce.

Ally Bazan had sobbed in his excitement over that vision and did not regain the power of articulate speech till the "loot" was safely stowed in the 'tween-decks and Hardenberg had given order to come about.

"Now," he had observed dryly, "now, lads, it's Hong-kong—or bust."

The tackle had fouled aloft and the jib hung slatting over the sprit like a collapsed balloon.

"Cast off up there, Nick!" called Hardenberg from the wheel.

Nickerson swung himself into the rigging, crying out in a mincing voice as, holding to a rope's end, he swung around to face the receding hut: "By-bye-skevitch. We've had *such* a charming evening. *Do* hope-sky we'll be able to come again-off." And as he spoke the lurch of the "Bertha" twitched his grip from the rope. He fell some thirty feet to the deck, and his head carromed against an iron cleat with a resounding crack.

"Here's luck," observed Hardenberg, twelve hours later, when Slick Dick, sitting on the edge of his bunk, looked stolidly and with fishy eyes from face to face. "We wa'n't quite short-handed enough, it seems."

"Dotty for fair. Dotty for fair," exclaimed Ally Bazan; "clean off 'is nut. I s'y, Dick-ol'-chap, wyke-up, naow. Buck up. Buck up. *'Ave* a drink."

But Nickerson could only nod his head and murmur: "A few more—consequently—and a good light—" Then his voice died down to unintelligible murmurs.

"We'll have to call at Juneau," decided Hardenberg two days later. "I don't figure on navigating this 'ere bath-tub to no Hong-kong whatsoever, with three hands. We gotta pick up a couple o' A. B.'s in Juneau, if so be we can."

"How about the loot?" objected Strokher. "If one of those hands gets between decks he might smell—a sea-otter, now. I put it to you he might."

"My son," said Hardenberg, "I've handled A. B.'s before"; and that settled the question.

During the first part of the run down, Nickerson gloomed silently over the schooner, looking curiously about him, now at his comrades' faces, now at the tumbling gray-green seas, now—and this by the hour—at his own hands. He seemed perplexed, dazed, trying very hard to get his bearings. But by and by he appeared, little by little, to come to himself. One day he pointed to the rigging with an unsteady forefinger, then, laying the same finger doubtfully upon his lips, said to Strokher: "A ship?"

"Quite so, quite so, me boy."

"Yes," muttered Nickerson absently, "a ship—of course."

Hardenberg expected to make Juneau on a Thursday. Wednesday afternoon Slick Dick came to him. He seemed never more master of himself. "How did I come aboard?" he asked.

Hardenberg explained.

"What have we been doing?"

"Why, don't you remember?" continued Hardenberg. He outlined the voyage in detail. "Then you remember," he went on, "we got up there to Point Barrow and found where the Russian fellows had their post, where they caught sea-otters, and we went ashore and got 'em all full and lifted all the skins they had—"

" 'Lifted'? You mean *stole* them."

"Come here," said the other. Encouraged by Nickerson's apparent convalescence, Hardenberg decided that the concrete evidence of things done would prove effective. He led him down into

"'ERE'S 'ELL TO PAY!'"

the 'tween-decks. "See now," he said. "See this packing-case"—
he pried up a board—"see these 'ere skins. Take one in y'r hand.
Remember how we found 'em all in the cellar and hyked 'em out
while the beggars slept?"

"*Stole* them? You say we got—that is *you* did—got somebody
intoxicated and stole their property, and now you are on your way
to dispose of it."

"Oh, well, if you want to put it thataway. Sure we did."

"I understand— Well— Let's go back on deck. I want to
think this out."

The "Bertha Millner" crept into the harbor of Juneau in a fog,
with ships' bells tolling on every side, let go her anchor at last in
desperation and lay up to wait for the lifting. When this came the
Three Crows looked at one another wide-eyed. They made out the
drenched town and the dripping hills behind it. The quays, the custom house, the one hotel, and the few ships in the harbor. There
were a couple of whalers from 'Frisco, a white, showily painted
passenger boat from the same port, a Norwegian bark, and a
freighter from Seattle grimy with coal-dust. These, however, the
"Bertha's" company ignored. Another boat claimed all their attention. In the fog they had let go not a pistol-shot from her anchor-
age. She lay practically beside them. She was the United States
revenue cutter "Bear."

"But so long as they can't *smell* sea-otter skin," remarked
Hardenberg, "I don't know that we're any the worse."

"All the syme," observed Ally Bazan, "I don't want to lose no
bloomin' tyme a-pecking up aour bloomin' A. B.'s."

"I'll stay aboard and tend the baby," said Hardenberg with a
wink. "You two move along shore and get what you can—Scoovies
for choice. Take Slick Dick with you. I reckon a change o' air
might buck him up."

When the three had gone, Hardenberg, after writing up the
painfully doctored log, set to work to finish a task on which the
adventurers had been engaged in their leisure moments since leaving Point Barrow. This was the counting and sorting of the skins.
The packing-case had been broken open, and the scanty but precious
contents littered an improvised table in the hold. Pen in hand,
Hardenberg counted and ciphered and counted again. He could
not forbear to chuckle when the net result was reached. The lot of
the skins—the pelt of the sea-otter is ridiculously small in propor-
tion to its value—was no heavy load for the average man. But

Hardenberg knew that once the "loot" was safely landed at the Hong-kong pierhead the Three Crows would share between them close upon ten thousand dollars. Even—if they had luck, and could dispose of the skins singly or in small lots—that figure might be doubled.

"And I call it a neat turn," observed Hardenberg. He was aroused by the noise of hurried feet upon the deck, and there was that in their sound that brought him upright in a second, hand on hip. Then, after a second, he jumped out on deck to meet Ally Bazan and Strokher, who had just scrambled over the rail.

"Bust. B-u-s-t!" remarked the Englishman.

"'Ere's 'ell to pay," cried Ally Bazan in a hoarse whisper, glancing over at the revenue cutter.

"Where's Nickerson?" demanded Hardenberg.

"That's it," answered the colonial. "That's where it's 'ell. Listen naow. He goes ashore along o' us, quiet and peaceable like, never battin' a eye, we givin' him a bit o' jolly, y' know, to keep him chirked up as ye might s'y. But so soon as ever he sets foot on shore, abaout faice he gaoes, plumb into the Customs orfice. I s'ys, 'Wot all naow, messmite? Come along aout o' that.' But he turns on me like a bloomin' babby an' s'ys he: 'Hands orf, wretch!' Ay, them's just his words. Just like that, 'Hands orf, wretch!' And then he nips into the orfice an' marches fair up to the desk an' sy's like this—we heerd him, havin' followed on to the door—he s'ys, just like this:

"'Orfficer, I am a min'ster o' the gospel, o' the Methodis' denomineye-tion, an' I'm deteyined agin my will along o' a pirate ship which has robbed certain parties o' val'able goods. Which syme I'm pre-pared to attest afore a no'try publick, an' lodge informeye-tion of crime. An',' s'ys he, 'I demand the protection o' the authorities an' arsk to be directed to the American consul."

"S'y, we never wyted to hear no more, but hyked awye hot foot. S'y, wot all now. Oh, mee Gord! eyen't it a rum gao for fair? S'y, let's get aout o' here, Hardy, dear."

"Look there," said Hardenberg, jerking his head toward the cutter, "how far'd we get before the customs would 'a' passed the tip to her and she'd started to overhaul us? That's what they feed her for—to round up the likes o' us."

"We got to do something rather soon," put in Strokher. "Here comes the custom house dinghy now."

As a matter of fact, a boat was putting off from the dock. At her stern fluttered the custom house flag.

"Bitched—bitched for fair!" cried Ally Bazan.

"Quick, now!" exclaimed Hardenberg. "On the jump! Overboard with that loot!—or no. Steady! That won't do. There's that dam' cutter. They'd see it go. Here!—into the galley. There's a fire in the stove. Get a move on!"

"Wot!" wailed Ally Bazan. "Burn the little joker. Gord! I can't, Hardy, I can't. It's agin human nature."

"You can do time in San Quentin, then, for felony," retorted Strokher as he and Hardenberg dashed by him, their arms full of the skins. "You can do time in San Quentin else. Make your choice. I put it to you as between man and man."

With set teeth, and ever and again glancing over the rail at the oncoming boat, the two fed their fortune to the fire. The pelts, partially cured and still fatty, blazed like crude oil, the hair crisping, the hides melting into rivulets of grease. For a minute the schooner reeked of the smell and a stifling smoke poured from the galley stack. Then the embers of the fire guttered and a long whiff of sea wind blew away the reek. A single skin, fallen in the scramble, still remained on the floor of the galley. Hardenberg snatched it up, tossed it into the flames and clapped the door to. "Now, let him squeal," he declared. "You fellows, when that boat gets here, let me talk; keep your mouths shut or, by God, we'll all wear stripes."

The Three Crows watched the boat's approach in a silence broken only once by a long whimper from Ally Bazan. "An' it was a-workin' out as lovely as Billy-oh," he said, "till that syme underbred costermonger's swipe remembered he was Methody—an' him who, only a few d'ys back, went raound s'yin' 'scrag the "Boomskys"!' A couple o' thousand pounds gone as quick as look at it. Oh, I eyen't never goin' to git over this."

The boat came up and the Three Crows were puzzled to note that no brass-buttoned personage sat in the sternsheets, no harbor police glowered at them from the bow, no officer of the law fixed them with the eye of suspicion. The boat was manned only by a couple of freight-handlers in woolen Jerseys, upon the breasts of which were affixed the two letters, "C. H."

"Say," called one of the freight-handlers, "is this the 'Bertha Millner'?"

"Yes," answered Hardenberg, his voice at a growl. "An' what might you want with her, my friend?"

"Well, look here," said the other, "one of your hands came ashore mad as a coot and broke into the house of the American Consul, and resisted arrest and raised hell generally. The inspector says you got to send a provost guard or something ashore to take him off. There's been several mix-ups among ships' crews lately and the town—"

The tide drifted the boat out of hearing, and Hardenberg sat down on the capstan head, turning his back to his comrades. There was a long silence. Then he said:

"Boys, let's go home. I—I want to have a talk with President Ryder."

THE SHIP THAT SAW A GHOST

VERY much of this story must remain untold, for the reason
that if it were definitely known what business I had aboard the
tramp steam-freighter "Glarus," three hundred miles off the South
American coast on a certain summer's day, some few years ago, I
would very likely be obliged to answer a great many personal and
direct questions put by fussy and impertinent experts in maritime
law—who are paid to be inquisitive. Also, I would get "Ally
Bazan," Strokher, and Hardenberg into trouble.

Suppose on that certain summer's day you had asked of Lloyds'
agency where the "Glarus" was, and what was her destination and
cargo. You would have been told that she was twenty days out
from Callao, bound north to San Francisco in ballast; that she had
been spoken by the bark "Medea" and the steamer "Benevento";
that she was reported to have blown out a cylinder head, but
being manageable was proceeding on her way under sail.

That is what Lloyds would have answered.

If you know something of the ways of ships and what is expected of them, you will understand that the "Glarus," to be some
half a dozen hundred miles south of where Lloyds' would have her,
and to be still going south, under full steam, was a scandal that
would have made her brothers and sisters ostracize her finally and
forever.

And that is curious, too. Humans may indulge in vagaries
innumerable, and may go far afield in the way of lying; but a ship
may not so much as quibble without suspicion. The least lapse
of "regularity," the least difficulty in squaring performance with
intuition, and behold she is on the black list, and her captain,
owners, officers, agents, and consignors, and even supercargoes,
are asked to explain.

And the "Glarus" was already on the black list. From the beginning her stars had been malign. As the "Breda," she had first
lost her reputation, seduced into a filibustering escapade down the
South American coast, where in the end a plain-clothes United

States detective—that is to say, a revenue cutter—arrested her off Buenos Ayres and brought her home, a prodigal daughter, besmirched and disgraced.

After that she was in some dreadful black-birding business in a far quarter of the South Pacific; and after that—her name changed finally to the "Glarus"—poached seals for a syndicate of Dutchmen who lived in Tacoma, and who afterward built a club-house out of what she earned.

And after that we got her.

We got her, I say, through Ryder's South Pacific Exploitation Company. The "President" had picked out a lovely little deal for Hardenberg, Strokher and Ally Bazan (the Three Black Crows), which he swore would make them "independent rich" the rest of their respective lives. It is a promising deal (B. 300 it is on Ryder's map), and if you want to know more about it you may write to ask Ryder what B. 300 is. If he chooses to tell you, that is his affair.

For B. 300—let us confess it—is, as Hardenberg puts it, as crooked as a dog's hind leg. It is as risky as barratry. If you pull it off you may—after paying Ryder his share—divide sixty-five, or possibly sixty-seven, thousand dollars between you and your associates. If you fail, and you are perilously like to fail, you will be sure to have a man or two of your companions shot, maybe yourself obliged to pistol certain people, and in the end fetch up at Tahiti, prisoner in a French patrol-boat.

Observe that B. 300 is spoken of as still open. It is so, for the reason that the Three Black Crows did not pull it off. It still stands marked up in red ink on the map that hangs over Ryder's desk in the San Francisco office; and any one can have a chance at it who will meet Cyrus Ryder's terms. Only he can't get the "Glarus" for the attempt.

For the trip to the island after B. 300 was the last occasion on which the "Glarus" will smell blue water or taste the trades. She will never clear again. She is lumber.

And yet the "Glarus" on this very blessed day of 1902 is riding to her buoys off Sausalito in San Francisco Bay, complete in every detail (bar a broken propeller shaft), not a rope missing, not a screw loose, not a plank started—a perfectly equipped steamfreighter.

But you may go along the "Front" in San Francisco from Fisherman's Wharf to the China steamships' docks and shake your dollars under the seamen's noses, and if you so much as whisper "Glarus" they will edge suddenly off and look at you with scared suspicion, and then, as like as not, walk away without another word. No pilot will take the "Glarus" out; no captain will navigate her; no stoker will feed her fires; no sailor will walk her decks. The "Glarus" is suspect. She has seen a ghost.

. . . .

It happened on our voyage to the island after this same B. 300. We had stood well off from shore for day after day, and Hardenberg had shaped our course so far from the track of navigation that since the "Benevento" had hulled down and vanished over the horizon no stitch of canvas nor smudge of smoke had we seen. We had passed the equator long since, and would fetch a long circuit to the southward, and bear up against the island by a circuitous route. This to avoid being spoken. It was tremendously essential that the "Glarus" should not be spoken.

I suppose, no doubt, that it was the knowledge of our isolation that impressed me with the dreadful remoteness of our position. Certainly the sea in itself looks no different at a thousand than at a hundred miles from shore. But as day after day I came out on deck at noon, after ascertainng our position on the chart (a mere pin-point in a reach of empty paper), the sight of the ocean weighed down upon me with an infinitely great awesomeness—and I was no new hand to the high seas even then.

But at such times the "Glarus" seemed to me to be threading a loneliness beyond all worlds and beyond all conception desolate. Even in more populous waters, when no sail notches the line of the horizon, the propinquity of one's kind is nevertheless a thing understood, and to an unappreciated degree comforting. Here, however, I knew we were out, far out in the desert. Never a keel for years upon years before us had parted these waters; never a sail had bellied to these winds. Perfunctorily, day in and day out we turned our eyes through long habit toward the horizon. But we knew, before the look, that the searching would be bootless. Forever and forever, under the pitiless sun and cold blue sky stretched the indigo of the ocean floor. The ether between the planets can be no less empty, no less void.

I never, till that moment, could have so much as conceived the imagination of such loneliness, such utter stagnant abomination of desolation. In an open boat, bereft of comrades, I should have gone mad in thirty minutes.

I remember to have approximated the impression of such empty immensity only once before, in my younger days, when I lay on my back on a treeless, bushless mountain-side and stared up into the sky for the better part of an hour.

You probably know the trick. If you do not, you must understand that if you look up at the blue long enough, the flatness of the thing begins little by little to expand, to give here and there; and the eye travels on and on and up and up, till at length (well for you that it lasts but the fraction of a second) you all at once see space. You generally stop there and cry out, and—your hands over your eyes—are only too glad to grovel close to the good old solid earth again. Just as I, so often on short voyage, was glad to wrench my eyes away from that horrid vacancy, to fasten them upon our sailless masts and stack, or to lay my grip upon the sooty smudged taffrail of the only thing that stood between me and the Outer Dark.

For we had come at last to that region of the Great Seas where no ship goes, the silent sea of Coleridge and the Ancient One, the unplumbed, untracked, uncharted Dreadfulness, primordial, hushed, and we were as much alone as a grain of star-dust whirling in the empty space beyond Uranus and the ken of the greater telescopes.

So the "Glarus" plodded and churned her way onward. Every day and all day the same pale-blue sky and the unwinking sun bent over that moving speck. Every day and all day the same black-blue water-world, untouched by any known wind, smooth as a slab of syenite, colorful as an opal, stretched out and around and beyond and before and behind us, forever, illimitable, empty. Every day the smoke of our fires veiled the streaked whiteness of our wake. Every day Hardenberg (our skipper) at noon pricked a pin-hole in the chart that hung in the wheel-house, and that showed we were so much further into the wilderness. Every day the world of men, of civilization, of newspapers, policemen, and street-railways receded, and we steamed on alone, lost and forgotten in that silent sea.

"Jolly lot o' room to turn raound in," observed Ally Bazan, the colonial, "withaout steppin' on y'r neighbor's toes."

"We're clean, clean out o' the track o' navigation," Hardenberg told him. "An' a blessed good thing for us, too. Nobody ever comes down into these waters. Ye couldn't pick no course here. Everything leads to nowhere."

"Might as well be in a bally balloon," said Strokher.

I shall not tell of the nature of the venture on which the "Glarus" was bound, further than to say it was not legitimate. It had to do with an ill thing done more than two centuries ago. There was money in the venture, but it was not to be gained by a violation of metes and bounds which are better left intact.

The island toward which we were heading is associated in the minds of men with a Horror. A ship had called there once, two hundred years in advance of the "Glarus"—a ship not much unlike the crank high-prowed caravel of Hudson, and her company had landed, and having accomplished the evil they had set out to do, made shift to sail away. And then, just after the palms of the island had sunk from sight below the water's edge, the unspeakable had happened. The Death that was not Death had arisen from out the sea and stood before the ship, and over it, and the blight of the thing lay along the decks like mould, and the ship sweated in the terror of that which is yet without a name.

Twenty men died in the first week, all but six in the second. These six, with the shadow of insanity upon them, made out to launch a boat, returned to the island and died there, after leaving a record of what had happened.

The six left the ship exactly as she was, sails all set, lanterns all lighted—left her in the shadow of the Death that was not Death.

She stood there, becalmed, and watched them go. She was never heard of again.

Or was she—well, that's as may be.

But the main point of the whole affair, to my notion, has always been this. The ship was the last friend of those six poor wretches who made back for the island with their poor chests of plunder. She was their guardian, as it were, would have defended and befriended them to the last; and also we, the Three Black Crows and myself, had no right under heaven, nor before the law of men, to come prying and peeping into this business—into this affair of the dead and buried past. There was sacrilege in it. We were no better than body-snatchers.

.   .   .   .

When I heard the others complaining of the loneliness of our surroundings, I said nothing at first. I was no sailorman, and I was on board only by tolerance. But I looked again at the maddening sameness of the horizon—the same vacant, void horizon that we had seen now for sixteen days on end, and felt in my wits and in my nerves that same formless rebellion and protest such as comes when the same note is reiterated over and over again.

It may seem a little thing that the mere fact of meeting with no other ship should have ground down the edge of the spirit. But let the incredulous—bound upon such a hazard as ours—sail straight into nothingness for sixteen days on end, seeing nothing but the sun, hearing nothing but the thresh of his own screw, and then put the question.

And yet, of all things, we desired no company. Stealth was our one great aim. But I think there were moments—toward the last —when the Three Crows would have welcomed even a cruiser.

Besides, there was more cause for depression, after all, than mere isolation.

On the seventh day Hardenberg and I were forward by the cat-head, adjusting the grain with some half-formed intent of spearing the porpoises that of late had begun to appear under our bows, and Hardenberg had been computing the number of days we were yet to run.

"We are some five hundred odd miles off that island by now," he said, "and she's doing her thirteen knots handsome. All's well so far—but do you know, I'd just as soon raise that point o' land as soon as convenient."

"How so?" said I, bending on the line. "Expect some weather?"

"Mr. Dixon," said he, giving me a curious glance, "the sea is a queer proposition, put it any ways. I've been a seafarin' man since I was big as a minute, and I know the sea, and what's more, the Feel o' the sea. Now, look out yonder. Nothin', hey? Nothin' but the same ol' skyline we've watched all the way out. The glass is as steady as a steeple, and this ol' hooker, I reckon, is as sound as the day she went off the ways. But just the same if I were to home now, a-foolin' about Gloucester way in my little dough-dish—d'ye know what? I'd put into port. I sure would. Because why? Because I got the Feel o' the Sea, Mr. Dixon. I got the Feel o' the Sea."

I had heard old skippers say something of this before, and I cited to Hardenberg the experience of a skipper captain I once knew who had turned turtle in a calm sea off Trincomalee. I ask him what this Feel of the Sea was warning him against just now (for on the high sea any premonition is a premonition of evil, not of good). But he was not explicit.

"I don't know," he answered moodily, and as if in great perplexity, coiling the rope as he spoke. "I don't know. There's some blame thing or other close to us, I'll bet a hat. I don't know the name of it, but there's a big Bird in the air, just out of sight som'-eres, and," he suddenly exclaimed, smacking his knee and leaning forward, "I—don't—like—it—one—dam'—bit."

The same thing came up in our talk in the cabin that night, after the dinner was taken off and we settled down to tobacco. Only, at this time, Hardenberg was on duty on the bridge. It was Ally Bazan who spoke instead.

"Seems to me," he hazarded, "as haow they's somethin' or other a-goin' to bump up pretty blyme soon. I shouldn't be surprised, naow, y'know, if we piled her up on some bally uncharted reef along o' to-night and went strite daown afore we'd had a bloomin' charnce to s'y 'So long, gen'lemen all.' "

He laughed as he spoke, but when, just at that moment, a pan clattered in the galley, he jumped suddenly with an oath, and looked hard about the cabin.

Then Strokher confessed to a sense of distress also. He'd been having it since day before yesterday, it seemed.

"And I put it to you the glass is lovely," he said, "so it's no blow. I guess," he continued, "we're all a bit seedy and ship-sore."

And whether or not this talk worked upon my own nerves, or whether in very truth the Feel of the Sea had found me also, I do not know; but I do know that after dinner that night, just before going to bed, a queer sense of apprehension came upon me, and that when I had come to my stateroom, after my turn upon deck, I became furiously angry with nobody in particular, because I could not at once find the matches. But here was a difference. The other men had been merely vaguely uncomfortable.

I could put a name to my uneasiness. I felt that we were being watched.

.   .   .   .

It was a strange ship's company we made after that. I speak only of the Crows and myself. We carried a scant crew of stokers, and there was also a chief engineer. But we saw so little of him that he did not count. The Crows and I gloomed on the quarter-deck from dawn to dark, silent, irritable, working upon each other's nerves till the creak of a block would make a man jump like cold steel laid to his flesh. We quarreled over absolute nothings, glowered at each other for half a word, and each one of us, at different times, was at some pains to declare that never in the course of his career had he been associated with such a disagreeable trio of brutes. Yet we were always together, and sought each other's company with painful insistence.

Only once were we all agreed, and that was when the cook, a Chinaman, spoiled a certain batch of biscuits. Unanimously we fell foul of the creature with as much vociferation as fishwives till he fled the cabin in actual fear of mishandling, leaving us suddenly seized with noisy hilarity—for the first time in a week. Hardenberg proposed a round of drinks from our single remaining case of beer. We stood up and formed an Elk's chain and then drained our glasses to each other's health with profound seriousness.

That same evening, I remember, we all sat on the quarterdeck till late and—oddly enough—related each one his life's history up to date; and then went down to the cabin for a game of euchre before turning in.

We had left Strokher on the bridge—it was his watch—and had forgotten all about him in the interest of the game, when—I suppose it was about one in the morning—I heard him whistle long and shrill. I laid down my cards and said:

"Hark!"

In the silence that followed we heard at first only the muffled lope of our engines, the cadenced snorting of the exhaust, and the ticking of Hardenberg's big watch in his waistcoat that he had hung by the arm-hole to the back of his chair. Then from the bridge, above our deck, prolonged, intoned—a wailing cry in the night—came Strokher's voice:

"Sail oh-h-h."

And the cards fell from our hands, and, like men turned to stone, we sat looking at each other across the soiled red cloth for what seemed an immeasurably long minute.

Then stumbling and swearing, in a hysteria of hurry, we gained the deck.

There was a moon, very low and reddish, but no wind. The sea beyond the taffrail was as smooth as lava, and so still that the swells from the cutwater of the "Glarus" did not break as they rolled away from the bows.

I remember that I stood staring and blinking at the empty ocean —where the moonlight lay like a painted stripe reaching to the horizon—stupid and frowning, till Hardenberg, who had gone on ahead, cried:

"Not here—on the bridge!"

We joined Strokher, and as I came up the others were asking: "Where? Where?"

And there, before he had pointed, I saw—we all of us saw—And I heard Hardenberg's teeth come together like a spring trap, while Ally Bazan ducked as though to a blow, muttering:

"Gord 'a' mercy, what nyme do ye put to a ship like that?"

And after that no one spoke for a long minute, and we stood there, moveless black shadows, huddled together for the sake of the blessed elbow touch that means so incalculably much, looking off over our port quarter.

For the ship that we saw there—oh, she was not a half-mile distant—was unlike any ship known to present day construction.

She was short, and high-pooped, and her stern, which was turned a little toward us, we could see, was set with curious windows, not unlike a house. And on either side of this stern were two great iron cressets such as once were used to burn signal-fires in. She had three masts with mighty yards swung 'thwart ship, but bare of all sails save a few rotting streamers. Here and there about her a tangled mass of rigging drooped and sagged.

And there she lay, in the red eye of the setting moon, in that solitary ocean, shadowy, antique, forlorn, a thing the most abandoned, the most sinister I ever remember to have seen.

Then Strokher began to explain volubly and with many repetitions.

"A derelict, of course. I was asleep; yes, I was asleep. Gross neglect of duty. I say I was asleep—on watch. And we worked up to her. When I woke, why—you see, when I woke, there she was," he gave a weak little laugh, "and—and now, why, there she is, you see. I turned around and saw her sudden like—when I woke up, that is."

He laughed again, and as he laughed the engines far below our feet gave a sudden hiccough. Something crashed and struck the ship's sides till we lurched as we stood. There was a shriek of steam, a shout—and then silence.

The noise of the machinery ceased; the "Glarus" slid through the still water, moving only by her own decreasing momentum.

Hardenberg sang, "Stand by!" and called down the tube to the engine-room.

"What's up?"

I was standing close enough to him to hear the answer in a small, faint voice:

"Shaft gone, sir."

"Broke?"

"Yes, sir."

Hardenberg faced about.

"Come below. We must talk." I do not think any of us cast a glance at the Other Ship again. Certainly I kept my eyes away from her. But as we started down the companionway I laid my hand on Strokher's shoulder. The rest were ahead. I looked him straight between the eyes as I asked:

"Were you asleep? Is that why you saw her so suddenly?"

It is now five years since I asked the question. I am still waiting for Strokher's answer.

Well, our shaft was broken. That was flat. We went down into the engine-room and saw the jagged fracture that was the symbol of our broken hopes. And in the course of the next five minutes' conversation with the chief we found that, as we had not provided against such a contingency, there was to be no mending of it. We said nothing about the mishap coinciding with the appearance of the Other Ship. But I know we did not consider the break with any degree of surprise after a few moments.

We came up from the engine-room and sat down to the cabin table.

"Now what?" said Hardenberg, by way of beginning.

Nobody answered at first.

It was by now three in the morning. I recall it all perfectly. The ports opposite where I sat were open and I could see. The moon was all but full set. The dawn was coming up with a copper murkiness over the edge of the world. All the stars were yet out. The sea, for all the red moon and copper dawn, was gray, and there, less than half a mile away, still lay our consort. I could see her through the portholes with each slow careening of the "Glarus."

"I vote for the island," cried Ally Bazan, "shaft or no shaft. We rigs bit o' syle, y'know—" and thereat the discussion began.

For upward of two hours it raged, with loud words and shaken forefingers and great noisy bangings of the table, and how it would have ended I do not know, but at last—it was then maybe five in the morning—the lookout passed word down to the cabin:

"Will you come on deck, gentlemen?" It was the mate who spoke, and the man was shaken—I could see that—to the very vitals of him. We started and stared at one another, and I watched

little Ally Bazan go slowly white to the lips. And even then no
word of the ship, except as it might be this from Hardenberg:

"What is it? Good God Almighty, I'm no coward, but this
thing is getting one too many for me."

Then without further speech he went on deck.

The air was cool. The sun was not yet up. It was that strange,
queer mid-period between dark and dawn, when the night is even and
the day not yet come, just the gray that is neither light nor dark, the
dim dead blink as of the refracted light from extinct worlds.

We stood at the rail. We did not speak; we stood watching.
It was so still that the drip of steam from some loosened pipe far
below was plainly audible, and it sounded in that lifeless, silent
grayness like—God knows what—a death tick.

"You see," said the mate, speaking just above a whisper, "there's
no mistake about it. She is moving—this way."

"Oh, a current, of course," Strokher tried to say cheerfully,
"sets her toward us."

Would the morning never come?

Ally Bazan—his parents were Catholic—began to mutter to
himself.

Then Hardenberg spoke aloud.

"I particularly don't want—that—out—there—to cross our
bows. I don't want it to come to that. We must get some sails
on her."

"And I put it to you as man to man," said Strokher, "where
might be your wind?"

He was right. The "Glarus" floated in absolute calm. On all
that slab of ocean nothing but the Dead Ship.

She came on slowly; her bows, the high, clumsy bows pointed toward us, the water turning from her forefoot. She came on; she
was near at hand. We saw her plainly—saw the rotted planks, the
crumbling rigging, the rust-corroded metal-work, the broken rail,
the gaping deck, and I could imagine that the clean water broke
away from her sides in refluent wavelets as though in recoil from
a thing unclean. She made no sound. No single thing stirred
aboard the hulk of her—but she moved.

We were helpless. The "Glarus" could stir no boat in any direction; we were chained to the spot. Nobody had thought to put out
our lights, and they still burned on through the dawn, strangely
out of place in their red-and-green garishness, like maskers surprised by daylight.

And in the silence of that empty ocean, in that queer half-light between dawn and day, at six o'clock, silent as the settling of the dead to the bottomless bottom of the ocean, gray as fog, lonely, blind, soulless, voiceless, the Dead Ship crossed our bows.

I do not know how long after this the Ship disappeared, or what was the time of day when we at last pulled ourselves together. But we came to some sort of decision at last. This was to go on—under sail. We were too close to the island now to turn back for—for a broken shaft.

The afternoon was spent fitting on the sails to her, and when after nightfall the wind at length came up fresh and favorable, I believe we all felt heartened and a deal more hardy—until the last canvas went aloft, and Hardenberg took the wheel.

We had drifted a good deal since the morning, and the bows of the "Glarus" were pointed homeward, but as soon as the breeze blew strong enough to get steerageway Hardenberg put the wheel over and, as the booms swung across the deck, headed for the island again.

We had not gone on this course half an hour—no, not twenty minutes—before the wind shifted a whole quarter of the compass and took the "Glarus" square in the teeth, so that there was nothing for it but to tack. And then the strangest thing befell.

I will make allowance for the fact that there was no centre-board nor keel to speak of to the "Glarus." I will admit that the sails upon a nine-hundred-ton freighter are not calculated to speed her, nor steady her. I will even admit the possibility of a current that set from the island toward us. All this may be true, yet the "Glarus" should have advanced. We should have made a wake.

And instead of this, our stolid, steady, trusty old boat was—what shall I say?

I will say that no man may thoroughly understand a ship—after all. I will say that new ships are cranky and unsteady; that old and seasoned ships have their little crochets, their little fussinesses that their skippers must learn and humor if they are to get anything out of them; that even the best ships may sulk at times, shirk their work, grow unstable, perverse, and refuse to answer helm and handling. And I will say that some ships that for years have sailed blue water as soberly and as docilely as a street-car horse has plodded the treadmill of the 'tween-tracks, have been known to balk, as stubbornly and as conclusively as any old Bay

Billy that ever wore a bell. I know this has happened, because I have seen it. I saw, for instance, the "Glarus" do it.

Quite literally and truly we could do nothing with her. We will say, if you like, that that great jar and wrench when the shaft gave way shook her and crippled her. It is true, however, that whatever the cause may have been, we could not force her toward the island. Of course, we all said "current"; but why didn't the log-line trail?

For three days and three nights we tried it. And the "Glarus" heaved and plunged and shook herself just as you have seen a horse plunge and rear when his rider tries to force him at the steam-roller.

I tell you I could feel the fabric of her tremble and shudder from bow to stern-post, as though she were in a storm; I tell you she fell off from the wind, and broad-on drifted back from her course till the sensation of her shrinking was as plain as her own staring lights and a thing pitiful to see.

We roweled her, and we crowded sail upon her, and we coaxed and bullied and humored her, till the Three Crows, their fortune only a plain two days' sail ahead, raved and swore like insensate brutes, or shall we say like mahouts trying to drive their stricken elephant upon the tiger—and all to no purpose. "Damn the damned current and the damned luck and the damned shaft and all," Hardenberg would exclaim, as from the wheel he would catch the "Glarus" falling off. "Go on, you old hooker—you tub of junk! My God, you'd think she was scared!"

Perhaps the "Glarus" was scared, perhaps not; that point is debatable. But it was beyond doubt or debate that Hardenberg was scared.

A ship that will not obey is only one degree less terrible than a mutinous crew. And we were in a fair way to have both. The stokers, whom we had impressed into duty as A. B.'s, were of course superstitious and they knew how the "Glarus" was acting, and it was only a question of time before they got out of hand.

That was the end. We held a final conference in the cabin and decided that there was no help for it—we must turn back.

And back we accordingly turned, and at once the wind followed us, and the "current" helped us, and the water churned under the forefoot of the "Glarus," and the wake whitened under her stern, and the log-line ran out from the trail and strained back as the ship worked homeward.

We had never a mishap from the time we finally swung her about; and, considering the circumstances, the voyage back to San Francisco was propitious.

But an incident happened just after we had started back. We were perhaps some five miles on the homeward track. It was early evening and Strokher had the watch. At about seven o'clock he called me up on the bridge.

"See her?" he said.

And there, far behind us, in the shadow of the twilight, loomed the Other Ship again, desolate, lonely beyond words. We were leaving her rapidly astern. Strokher and I stood looking at her till she dwindled to a dot. Then Strokher said:

"She's on post again."

And when months afterward we limped into the Golden Gate and cast anchor off the "Front" our crew went ashore as soon as discharged; and in half a dozen hours the legend was in every sailors' boarding-house and in every seaman's dive, from Barbary Coast to Black Tom's.

It is still there, and that is why no pilot will take the "Glarus" out, no captain will navigate her, no stoker feed her fires, no sailor walk her decks. The "Glarus" is suspect. She will never smell blue water again, nor taste the trades. She has seen a Ghost.

THE GHOST IN THE CROSSTREES

I

CYRUS RYDER, the President of the South Pacific Exploitation Company, had at last got hold of a "proposition"—all Ryder's schemes were, in his vernacular, "propositions"—that was not only profitable beyond precedent or belief, but that also was, wonderful to say, more or less legitimate. He had got an "island." He had not discovered it. Ryder had not felt a deck under his shoes for twenty years other than the promenade deck of the ferryboat "San Rafael," that takes him home to Berkeley every evening after "business hours." He had not discovered it, but "Old Rosemary," captain of the barkentine "Scottish Chief" of Blyth, had done that very thing, and, dying before he was able to perfect the title, had made over his interest in it to his best friend and old comrade, Cyrus Ryder.

"Old Rosemary," I am told, first landed on the island—it is called Paa—in the later '60's. He established its location and took its latitude and longitude, but as minutes and degrees mean nothing to the lay reader, let it be said that the Island of Paa lies just below the equator, some 200 miles west of the Gilberts and 1,600 miles due east from Brisbane, in Australia. It is six miles long, three wide, and because of the prevailing winds and precipitous character of the coast can only be approached from the west during December and January.

"Old Rosemary" landed on the island, raised the American flag, had the crew witness the document by virtue of which he made himself the possessor, and then, returning to San Francisco, forwarded to the Secretary of State, at Washington, application for title. This was withheld till it could be shown that no other nation had a prior claim. While "Old Rosemary" was working out the proof, he died, and the whole matter was left in abeyance till Cyrus Ryder took it up. By then there was a new Secretary in Washington and times were changed, so that the Government of Ryder's native

land was not so averse toward acquiring Eastern possessions. The
Secretary of State wrote to Ryder to say that the application would
be granted upon furnishing a bond for $50,000; and you may be-
lieve that the bond was forthcoming.

For in the first report upon Paa, "Old Rosemary" had used the
magic word "guano." He averred, and his crew attested over their
sworn statements, that Paa was covered to an average depth of six
feet with the stuff, so that this last and biggest of "Cy" Ryder's
propositions was a vast slab of an extremely marketable product six
feet thick, three miles wide and six miles long.

But no sooner had the title been granted when there came a
dislocation in the proceedings that until then had been going forward so smoothly. Ryder called the Three Black Crows to him at
this juncture, one certain afternoon in the month of April. They
were his best agents. The plums that the "Company" had at its
disposal generally went to the trio, and if any man could "put
through" a dangerous and desperate piece of work, Strokher, Hardenberg, and Ally Bazan were those men.

Of late they had been unlucky, and the affair of the contraband
arms, which had ended in failure of cataclysmic proportions, yet
rankled in Ryder's memory, but he had no one else to whom he
could intrust the present proposition and he still believed Hardenberg to be the best boss on his list.

If Paa was to be fought for, Hardenberg, backed by Strokher
and Ally Bazan, was the man of all men for the job, for it looked as
though Ryder would not get the Island of Paa without a fight after
all, and nitrate beds were worth fighting for.

"You see, boys, it's this way," Ryder explained to the three as
they sat around the spavined table in the grimy back room of
Ryder's "office." "It's this way. There's a scoovy after Paa, I'm
told; he says he was there before 'Rosemary,' which is a lie, and
that his Gov'ment has given him title. He's got a kind of dough-
dish up Portland way and starts for Paa as soon as ever he kin fit
out. He's got no title, in course, but if he gits there afore we do
and takes possession, it'll take fifty years o' lawing an' injunctioning
to git him off. So hustle is the word for you from the word 'go.'
We got a good start o' the scoovy. He can't put to sea within a
week, while over yonder in Oakland Basin there's the 'Idaho Lass,'
as good a schooner, boys, as ever wore paint, all ready but to fit
her new sails on her. Ye kin do it in less than no time. The stores
will be goin' into her while ye're workin', and within the week I

expect to see the 'Idaho Lass' showing her heels to the Presidio. You see the point now, boys. If we beat the scoovy—his name is Petersen, and his boat is called the 'Elftruda'—we're to the wind'ard of a pretty pot o' money. If he gets away before you do—well, there's no telling; we prob'ly lose the island."

II

ABOUT ten days before the morning set for their departure I went over to the Oakland Basin to see how the Three Black Crows were getting on.

Hardenberg welcomed me as my boat bumped alongside, and extending a great tarry paw, hauled me over the rail. The schooner was a wilderness of confusion, with the sails covering, apparently, nine-tenths of the decks, the remaining tenth incumbered by spars, cordage, tangled rigging, chains, cables and the like, all helter-skeltered together in such a haze of entanglements that my heart misgave me as I looked on it. Surely order would not issue from this chaos in four days' time with only three men to speed the work.

But Hardenberg was reassuring, and little Ally Bazan, the colonial, told me they would "snatch her shipshape in the shorter end o' two days, if so be they must."

I stayed with the Three Crows all that day and shared their dinner with them on the quarterdeck when, wearied to death with the strain of wrestling with the slatting canvas and ponderous boom, they at last threw themselves upon the hamper of "cold snack" I had brought off with me and pledged the success of the venture in tin dippers full of Pilsener.

"And I'm thinking," said Ally Bazan, "as 'ow ye might as well turn in along o' us on board 'ere, instead o' hykin' back to town to-night. There's a fairish set o' currents up and daown 'ere about this time o' dye, and ye'd find it a stiff bit o' rowing."

"We'll sling a hammick for you on the quarterdeck, m'son," urged Hardenberg.

And so it happened that I passed my first night aboard the "Idaho Lass."

We turned in early. The Three Crows were very tired, and only Ally Bazan and I were left awake at the time when we saw the 8.30 ferryboat negotiating for her slip on the Oakland side. Then we also went to bed.

And now it becomes necessary, for a better understanding of what is to follow, to mention with some degree of particularization the places and manners in which my three friends elected to take their sleep, as well as the condition and berth of the schooner "Idaho Lass."

Hardenberg slept upon the quarterdeck, rolled up in an army blanket and a tarpaulin. Strokher turned in below in the cabin upon the fixed lounge by the dining-table, while Ally Bazan stretched himself in one of the bunks in the fo'c's'le.

As for the location of the schooner, she lay out in the stream, some three or four cables' length off the yards and docks of a ship-building concern. No other ship or boat of any description was anchored nearer than at least three hundred yards. She was a fine, roomy vessel, three-masted, about one hundred and fifty feet in length over all. She lay head up stream, and from where I lay by Hardenberg on the quarterdeck I could see her tops sharply outlined against the sky above the Golden Gate before I went to sleep.

I suppose it was very early in the morning—nearer two than three—when I awoke. Some movement on the part of Hardenberg—as I afterward found out—had aroused me. But I lay inert for a long minute trying to find out why I was not in my own bed, in my own home, and to account for the rushing, rippling sound of the tide eddies sucking and chuckling around the "Lass's" rudder-post.

Then I became aware that Hardenberg was awake. I lay in my hammock, facing the stern of the schooner, and as Hardenberg had made up his bed between me and the wheel he was directly in my line of vision when I opened my eyes, and I could see him without any other movement than that of raising the eyelids. Just now, as I drifted more and more into wakefulness, I grew proportionately puzzled and perplexed to account for a singularly strange demeanor and conduct on the part of my friend.

He was sitting up in his place, his knees drawn up under the blanket, one arm thrown around both, the hand of the other arm resting on the neck and supporting the weight of his body. He was broad awake. I could see the green shine of our riding lantern in his wide-opened eyes, and from time to time I could hear him muttering to himself, "What is it? What is it? What the devil is it, anyhow?" But it was not his attitude, nor the fact of his being so broad awake at the unseasonable hour, nor yet his unaccountable words, that puzzled me the most. It was the man's eyes and the direction in which they looked that startled me.

His gaze was directed not upon anything on the deck of the boat, nor upon the surface of the water near it, but upon something behind me and at a great height in the air. I was not long in getting myself broad awake.

III

I ROLLED out on the deck and crossed over to where Hardenberg sat huddled in his blankets.

"What the devil—" I began.

He jumped suddenly at the sound of my voice, then raised an arm and pointed toward the top of the foremast.

"D'ye see it?" he muttered. "Say, huh. D'ye see it? I thought I saw it last night, but I wasn't sure. But there's no mistake now. D'ye see it, Mr. Dixon?"

I looked where he pointed. The schooner was riding easily to anchor, the surface of the bay was calm, but overhead the high white sea-fog was rolling in. Against it the foremast stood out like the hand of an illuminated town clock, and not a detail of its rigging that was not as distinct as if etched against the sky.

And yet I saw nothing.

"Where?" I demanded, and again and again "where?"

"In the crosstrees," faintly whispered Hardenberg. "Ah, look there."

He was right. Something was stirring there, something that I had mistaken for the furled tops'l. At first it was but a formless bundle, but as Hardenberg spoke it stretched itself, it grew upright, it assumed an erect attitude, it took the outlines of a human being. From head to heel a casing housed it in, a casing that might have been anything at that hour of the night and in that strange place—a shroud, if you like, a winding-sheet—anything; and it is without shame that I confess to a creep of the most disagreeable sensation I have ever known as I stood at Hardenberg's side on that still, foggy night and watched the stirring of that nameless, formless shape standing gaunt and tall and grisly and wrapped in its winding-sheet upon the crosstrees of the foremast of the "Idaho Lass."

We watched and waited breathless for an instant. Then the

creature on the foremast laid a hand upon the lashings of the tops'l and undid them. Then it turned, slid to the deck by I know not what strange process, and, still hooded, still shrouded, still lapped about by its mummy-wrappings, seized a rope's end. In an instant the jib was set and stood on hard and billowing against the night wind. The tops'l followed. Then the figure moved forward and passed behind the companionway of the fo'c's'le.

We looked for it to appear upon the other side, but looked in vain. We saw it no more that night.

What Hardenberg and I told each other between the time of the disappearing and the hour of breakfast I am now ashamed to recall. But at last we agreed to say nothing to the others—for the time being. Just after breakfast, however, we two had a few words by the wheel on the quarterdeck. Ally Bazan and Strokher were forward.

"The proper thing to do," said I—it was a glorious, exhilarating morning, and the sunlight was flooding every angle and corner of the schooner—"the proper thing to do is to sleep on deck by the foremast to-night with our pistols handy and interview the—party if it walks again."

"Oh, yes," cried Hardenberg heartily. "Oh, yes; that's the proper thing. Of course it is. No manner o' doubt about that, Mr Dixon. Watch for the party—yes, with pistols. Of course it's the proper thing. But I know one man that ain't going to do no such thing."

"Well," I remember to have said reflectively, "well—I guess I know another."

But for all our resolutions to say nothing to the others about the night's occurrences, we forgot that the tops'l and jib were both set and both drawing.

"An' w'at might be the bloomin' notion o' setting the bloomin' kite and jib?" demanded Ally Bazan not half an hour after breakfast. Shamelessly, Hardenberg, at a loss for an answer, feigned an interest in the grummets of the lifeboat cover and left me to lie as best I might.

But it is not easy to explain why one should raise the sails of an anchored ship during the night, and Ally Bazan grew very suspicious. Strokher, too, had something to say, and in the end the whole matter came out.

Trust a sailor to give full value to anything savoring of the supernatural. Strokher promptly voted the ship a "queer old

"'MY CURSE IS ON HER WHO NEXT KISSES YOU'"

hooker anyhow, and about as seaworthy as a hen-coop." He held
forth at great length upon the subject.

"You mark my words, now," he said. "There's been some fishy
doin's in this 'ere vessel, and it's like somebody done to death crool
hard, an' 'e wants to git away from the smell o' land, just like them
as is killed on blue water. That's w'y 'e takes an' sets the sails
between dark an' dawn."

But Ally Bazan was thoroughly and wholly upset, so much so
that at first he could not speak. He went pale and paler while we
stood talking it over, and crossed himself—he was a Catholic—fur-
tively behind the water-butt.

"I ain't never 'a' been keen on ha'nts anyhow, Mr. Dixon," he
told me aggrievedly at dinner that evening. "I got no use for 'em.
I ain't never known any good to come o' anything with a ha'nt
tagged to it, an' we're makin' a ill beginnin' o' this island business,
Mr. Dixon—a blyme ill beginnin'. I mean to stye awyke to-night."

But if he was awake the little colonial was keeping close to his
bunk at the time when Strokher and Hardenberg woke me at about
three in the morning.

I rolled out and joined them on the quarterdeck and stood beside them watching. The same figure again towered, as before,
gray and ominous in the crosstrees. As before, it set the tops'l; as
before, it came down to the deck and raised the jib; as before, it
passed out of sight amid the confusion of the forward deck.

But this time we all ran toward where we last had seen it,
stumbling over the incumbered decks, jostling and tripping, but keeping wonderfully close together. It was not twenty seconds from
the time the creature had disappeared before we stood panting upon
the exact spot we had last seen it. We searched every corner of the
forward deck in vain. We looked over the side. The moon was
up. This night there was no fog. We could see for miles each
side of us, but never a trace of a boat was visible, and it was impossible that any swimmer could have escaped the merciless scrutiny
to which we subjected the waters of the bay in every direction.

Hardenberg and I dived down into the fo'c's'le. Ally Bazan was
sound asleep in his bunk and woke stammering, blinking, and bewildered by the lantern we carried.

"I sye," he cried, all at once scrambling up and clawing at our
arms. "D'd the bally ha'nt show up agyne?" And as we nodded he
went on more aggrievedly than ever—"Oh, I sye, y' know, I daon't
like this. I eyen't shipping in no bloomin' 'ooker wot carries a

ha'nt for supercargo. They waon't no good come o' this cruise—
no, they waon't. It's a sign, that's wot it is. I eyen't goin' to buck
again no signs—it eyen't human nature, no it eyen't. You mark
my words, 'Bud' Hardenberg, we clear this port with a ship wot
has a ha'nt an' we waon't never come back agyne, my hearty."

That night he berthed aft with us on the quarterdeck, but though
we stood watch and watch till well into the dawn, nothing stirred
about the foremast. So it was the next night, and so the night after
that. When three successive days had passed without any manifestation the keen edge of the business became a little blunted and
we declared that an end had been made.

Ally Bazan returned to his bunk in the fo'c's'le on the fourth
night, and the rest of us slept the hours through unconcernedly.

But in the morning there were the jib and tops'l set and drawing
as before.

IV

AFTER this we began experimenting—on Ally Bazan. We
bunked him forward and we bunked him aft, for some one had
pointed out that the "ha'nt" walked only at the times when the colonial slept in the fo'c's'le. We found this to be true. Let the little
fellow watch on the quarterdeck with us and the night passed without disturbance. As soon as he took up his quarters forward the
haunting recommenced. Furthermore, it began to appear that the
"ha'nt" carefully refrained from appearing to him. He of us all
had never seen the thing. He of us all was spared the chills and the
harrowings that laid hold upon the rest of us during these still
gray hours after midnight when we huddled on the deck of the
"Idaho Lass" and watched the sheeted apparition in the rigging; for
by now there was no more charging forward in attempts to run the
ghost down. We had passed that stage long since.

But so far from rejoicing in this immunity or drawing courage
therefrom, Ally Bazan filled the air with his fears and expostula-
tions. Just the fact that he was in some way differentiated from
the others—that he was singled out, if only for exemption—worked
upon him. And that he was unable to scale his terrors by actual
sight of their object excited them all the more.

And there issued from this a curious consequence. He, the very
one who had never seen the haunting, was also the very one to

unsettle what little common-sense yet remained to Hardenberg and Strokher. He never allowed the subject to be ignored—never lost an opportunity of referring to the doom that o'erhung the vessel. By the hour he poured into the ears of his friends lugubrious tales of ships, warned as this one was, that had cleared from port, never to be seen again. He recalled to their minds parallel incidents that they themselves had heard; he foretold the fate of the "Idaho Lass" when the land should lie behind and she should be alone in midocean with this horrid supercargo that took liberties with the rigging, and at last one particular morning, two days before that which was to witness the schooner's departure, he came out flatfooted to the effect that "Gaw-blyme him, he couldn't stand the gaff no longer, no, he couldn't, so help him; that if the owners were wishful for to put to sea" (doomed to some unnamable destruction) "he for one wa'n't fit to die, an' was going to quit that blessed day."

For the sake of appearances, Hardenberg and Strokher blustered and fumed, but I could hear the crack in Strokher's voice as plain as in a broken ship's bell. I was not surprised at what happened later in the day, when he told the others that he was a very sick man. A congenital stomach trouble, it seemed—or was it liver complaint—had found him out again. He had contracted it when a lad at Trincomalee, diving for pearls; it was acutely painful, it appeared. Why, gentlemen, even at that very moment, as he stood there talking—Hi, yi! O Lord!—talking, it was a-griping of him something uncommon, so it was. And no, it was no manner of use for him to think of going on this voyage; sorry he was, too, for he'd made up his mind, so he had, to find out just what was wrong with the foremast, etc.

And thereupon Hardenberg swore a great oath and threw down the capstan bar he held in his hand.

"Well, then," he cried wrathfully, "we might as well chuck up the whole business. No use going to sea with a sick man and a scared man."

"An' there's the first word o' sense," cried Ally Bazan, "I've heard this long day. 'Scared,' he says; aye, right ye are, me bully."

"It's Cy Rider's fault," the three declared after a two-hours' talk. "No business giving us a schooner with a ghost aboard. Scoovy or no scoovy, island or no island, guano or no guano, we don't go to sea in the haunted hooker called the 'Idaho Lass.'"

No more they did. On board the schooner they had faced the supernatural with some kind of courage born of the occasion.

Once on shore, and no money could hire, no power force them to go aboard a second time.

The affair ended in a grand wrangle in Cy Rider's back office, and just twenty-four hours later the bark "Elftruda," Captain Jens Petersen, cleared from Portland, bound for "a cruise to South Pacific ports—in ballast."

. . . .

Two years after this I took Ally Bazan with me on a duck-shooting excursion in the "Toolies" back of Sacramento, for he is a handy man about a camp and can row a boat as softly as a drifting cloud.

We went about in a cabin cat of some thirty feet over all, the rowboat towing astern. Sometimes we did not go ashore to camp, but slept aboard. On the second night of this expedient I woke in my blankets on the floor of the cabin to see the square of gray light that stood for the cabin door darkened by—it gave me the same old start—a sheeted figure. It was going up the two steps to the deck. Beyond question it had been in the cabin. I started up and followed it. I was too frightened not to—if you can see what I mean. By the time I had got the blankets off and had thrust my head above the level of the cabin hatch the figure was already in the bows, and, as a matter of course, hoisting the jib.

I thought of calling Ally Bazan, who slept by me on the cabin floor, but it seemed to me at the time that if I did not keep that figure in sight it would elude me again, and, besides, if I went back in the cabin I was afraid that I would bolt the door and remain under the bedclothes till morning. I was afraid to go on with the adventure, but I was much more afraid to go back.

So I crept forward over the deck of the sloop. The "ha'nt" had its back toward me, fumbling with the ends of the jib halyards. I could hear the creak of new ropes as it undid the knot, and the sound was certainly substantial and commonplace. I was so close by now that I could see every outline of the shape. It was precisely as it had appeared on the crosstrees of the "Idaho," only, seen without perspective, and brought down to the level of the eye, it lost its exaggerated height.

It had been kneeling upon the deck. Now, at last, it rose and turned about, the end of the halyards in its hand. The light of the earliest dawn fell squarely on the face and form, and I saw, if you please, Ally Bazan himself. His eyes were half shut, and through his open lips came the sound of his deep and regular breathing.

At breakfast the next morning I asked, "Ally Bazan, did you ever walk in your sleep?"

"Aye," he answered, "years ago, when I was by wye o' being a lad, I used allus to wrap the bloomin' sheets around me. An' crysy things I'd do the times. But the 'abit left me when I grew old enough to tyke me whiskey strite and have hair on me fyce."

I did not "explain away" the ghost in the crosstrees either to Ally Bazan or to the other two Black Crows. Furthermore, I do not now refer to the Island of Paa in the hearing of the trio. The claims and title of Norway to the island have long since been made good and conceded—even by the State Department at Washington —and I understand that Captain Petersen has made a very pretty fortune out of the affair.

THE RIDING OF FELIPE

I

FELIPE

As young Felipe Arillaga guided his pony out of the last intricacies of Pacheco Pass, he was thinking of Rubia Ytuerate and
of the scene he had had with her a few days before. He recon-
structed it now very vividly. Rubia had been royally angry, and
as she had stood before him, her arms folded and her teeth set,
he was forced to admit that she was as handsome a woman as
could be found through all California.

There had been a time, three months past, when Felipe found
no compulsion in the admission, for though betrothed to Buelna
Martiarena he had abruptly conceived a violent infatuation for
Rubia, and had remained a guest upon her rancho many weeks
longer than he had intended.

For three months he had forgotten Buelna entirely. At the end
of that time he had remembered her—had awakened to the fact
that his infatuation for Rubia *was* infatuation, and had resolved
to end the affair and go back to Buelna as soon as it was possible.

But Rubia was quick to notice the cooling of his passion. First
she fixed him with oblique suspicion from under her long lashes,
then avoided him, then kept him at her side for days together.
Then at last—his defection unmistakable—turned on him with
furious demands for the truth.

Felipe had snatched occasion with one hand and courage with
the other.

"Well," he had said, "well, it is not my fault. Yes, it is the
truth. It is played out."

He had not thought it necessary to speak of Buelna; but Rubia
divined the other woman.

"So you think you are to throw me aside like that. Ah, it is
played out, is it, Felipe Arillaga? You listen to me. Do not fancy

for one moment you are going back to an old love, or on to a new one. You listen to me," she had cried, her fist over her head. "I do not know who she is, but my curse is on her, Felipe Arillaga. My curse is on her who next kisses you. May that kiss be a blight to her. From that moment may evil cling to her, bad luck follow her; may she love and not be loved; may friends desert her, enemies beset her, her sisters shame her, her brothers disown her, and those whom she has loved abandon her. May her body waste as your love for me has wasted; may her heart be broken as your promises to me have been broken; may her joy be as fleeting as your vows, and her beauty grow as dim as your memory of me. I have said it."

"So be it," Felipe had retorted with vast nonchalance, and had flung out from her presence to saddle his pony and start back to Buelna.

But Felipe was superstitious. He half believed in curses, had seen two-headed calves born because of them, and sheep stampeded over cliffs for no other reason.

Now, as he drew out of Pacheco Pass and came down into the valley the idea of Rubia and her curse troubled him. At first, when yet three days' journey from Buelna, it had been easy to resolve to brave it out. But now he was already on the Rancho Martiarena (had been traveling over it for the last ten hours, in fact), and in a short time would be at the *hacienda of* Martiarena, uncle and guardian of Buelna. He would see Buelna, and she, believing always in his fidelity, would expect to kiss him.

"Well, this is to be thought about," murmured Felipe uneasily. He touched up the pony with one of his enormous spurs.

"Now I know what I will do," he thought. "I will go to San Juan Bautista and confess and be absolved, and will buy candles. Then afterward will go to Buelna."

He found the road that led to the Mission and turned into it, pushing forward at a canter. Then suddenly at a sharp turning reined up just in time to avoid colliding with a little cavalcade.

He uttered an exclamation under his breath.

At the head of the cavalcade rode old Martiarena himself, and behind him came a *peon* or two, then Manuela, the aged housekeeper and—after a fashion—duenna. Then at her side, on a saddle of red leather with silver bosses, which was cinched about the body of a very small white burro, Buelna herself.

She was just turned sixteen, and being of the best blood of the mother kingdom (the strain dating back to the Ostrogothic invasion), was fair. Her hair was blond, her eyes blue-gray, her eyebrows and lashes dark brown, and as he caught sight of her Felipe wondered how he ever could have believed the swarthy Rubia beautiful.

There was a jubilant meeting. Old Martiarena kissed both his cheeks, patting him on the back.

"Oh, ho!" he cried. "Once more back. We have just returned from the feast of the Santa Cruz at the Mission, and Buelna prayed for your safe return. Go to her, boy. She has waited long for this hour."

Felipe, his eyes upon those of his betrothed, advanced. She was looking at him and smiling. As he saw the unmistakable light in her blue eyes, the light he knew she had kept burning for him alone, Felipe could have abased himself to the very hoofs of her burro. Could it be possible he had ever forgotten her for such a one as Rubia—have been unfaithful to this dear girl for so much as the smallest fraction of a minute?

"You are welcome, Felipe," she said. "Oh, very, very welcome." She gave him her hand and turned her face to his. But it was her hand and not her face the young man kissed. Old Martiarena, who looked on, shook with laughter.

"Hoh! a timid lover this," he called. "We managed different when I was a lad. Her lips, Felipe. Must an old man teach a youngster gallantry?"

Buelna blushed and laughed, but yet did not withdraw her hand nor turn her face away. There was a delicate expectancy in her manner that she nevertheless contrived to make compatible with her native modesty. Felipe had been her acknowledged lover ever since the two were children.

"Well?" cried Martiarena as Felipe hesitated.

Even then, if Felipe could have collected his wits, he might have saved the situation for himself. But no time had been allowed him to think. Confusion seized upon him. All that was clear in his mind were the last words of Rubia. It seemed to him that between his lips he carried a poison deadly to Buelna above all others. Stupidly, brutally he precipitated the catastrophe.

"No," he exclaimed seriously, abruptly drawing his hand from Buelna's, "no. It may not be. I can not."

Martiarena stared. Then:

"Is this a jest, señor?" he demanded. "An ill-timed one, then."

"No," answered Felipe, "it is not a jest."

"But, Felipe," murmured Buelna. "But—why—I do not understand."

"I think I begin to," cried Martiarena. .

"Señor, you do not," protested Felipe. "It is not to be explained. I know what you believe. On my honor, I love Buelna."

"Your actions give you the lie, then, young man. Bah! Nonsense. What fool's play is all this? Kiss him, Buelna, and have done with it."

Felipe gnawed his nails.

"Believe me, oh, believe me, Señor Martiarena, it must not be."

"Then an explanation."

For a moment Felipe hesitated. But how could he tell them the truth—the truth that involved Rubia and his disloyalty, temporary though that was. They could neither understand nor forgive. Here, indeed, was an *impasse*. One thing only was to be said, and he said it. "I can give you no explanation," he murmured.

But Buelna suddenly interposed.

"Oh, please," she said, pushing by Felipe, "uncle, we have talked too long. Please let us go. There is only one explanation. Is it not enough already?"

"By God, it is not!" vociferated the old man, turning upon Felipe. "Tell me what it means. Tell me what this means."

"I can not."

"Then I will tell *you!*" shouted the old fellow in Felipe's face. "It means that you are a liar and a rascal. That you have played with Buelna, and that you have deceived me, who have trusted you as a father would have trusted a son. I forbid you to answer me. For the sake of what you were I spare you now. But this I will do. Off of my rancho!" he cried. "Off my rancho, and in the future pray your God, or the devil, to whom you are sold, to keep you far from me."

"You do not understand, you do not understand," pleaded Felipe, the tears starting to his eyes. "Oh, believe me, I speak the truth. I love your niece. I love Buelna. Oh, never so truly, never so devoutly as now. Let me speak to her; she will believe me."

But Buelna, weeping, had ridden on.

II

UNZAR

A FORTNIGHT passed. Soon a month had gone by. Felipe gloomed about his rancho, solitary, taciturn, riding the sheep-walks and cattle-ranges for days and nights together, refusing all intercourse with his friends. It seemed as if he had lost Buelna for good and all. At times, as the certainty of this defined itself more clearly, Felipe would fling his hat upon the ground, beat his breast, and then, prone upon his face, his head buried in his folded arms, would lie for hours motionless, while his pony nibbled the sparse alfalfa, and the jack-rabbits limping from the sage peered at him, their noses wrinkling.

But about a month after the meeting and parting with Buelna, word went through all the ranches that a hidedroger had cast anchor in Monterey Bay. At once an abrupt access of activity seized upon the rancheros. Rodéos were held, sheep slaughtered, and the great tallow-pits began to fill up.

Felipe was not behind his neighbors, and, his tallow once in hand, sent it down to Monterey, and himself rode down to see about disposing of it.

On his return he stopped at the wine shop of one Lopez Catala, on the road between Monterey and his rancho.

It was late afternoon when he reached it, and the wine shop was deserted. Outside, the California August lay withering and suffocating over all the land. The far hills were burned to dry, hay-like grass and brittle clods. The eucalyptus trees in front of the wine shop (the first trees Felipe had seen all that day) were coated with dust. The plains of sage-brush and the alkali flats shimmered and exhaled pallid mirages, glistening like inland seas. Over all blew the trade-wind; prolonged, insistent, harassing, swooping up the red dust of the road and the white powder of the alkali beds, and flinging it—white-and-red banners in a sky of burned-out blue—here and there about the landscape.

The wine shop, which was also an inn, was isolated, lonely, but it was comfortable, and Felipe decided to lay over there that night, then in the early morning reach his rancho by an easy stage.

He had his supper—an omelet, cheese, tortillas, and a glass of wine—and afterward sat outside on a bench smoking innumerable cigarettes and watching the sun set.

While he sat so a young man of about his own age rode up from the eastward with a great flourish, and, giving over his horse to the *muchacho,* entered the wine shop and ordered dinner and a room for the night. Afterward he came out and stood in front of the inn and watched the *muchacho* cleaning his horse.

Felipe, looking at him, saw that he was of his own age and about his own build—that is to say, twenty-eight or thirty, and tall and lean. But in other respects the difference was great. The stranger was flamboyantly dressed: skin-tight pantaloons, fastened all up and down the leg with round silver buttons; yellow boots with heels high as a girl's, set off with silver spurs; a very short coat faced with galloons of gold, and a very broad-brimmed and very high-crowned sombrero, on which the silver braid alone was worth the price of a good horse. Even for a Spanish-Mexican his face was dark. Swart it was, the cheeks hollow; a tiny, tight mustache with ends truculently pointed and erect helped out the belligerency of the tight-shut lips. The eyes were black as bitumen, and flashed continually under heavy brows.

"Perhaps," thought Felipe, "he is a *toreador* from Mexico."

The stranger followed his horse to the barn, but, returning in a few moments, stood before Felipe and said:

"Señor, I have taken the liberty to put my horse in the stall occupied by yours. Your beast the *muchacho* turned into the *corrale.* Mine is an animal of spirit, and in a *corrale* would fight with the other horses. I rely upon the señor's indulgence."

At ordinary times he would not have relied in vain. But Felipe's nerves were in a jangle these days, and his temper, since Buelna's dismissal of him, was bitter. His perception of offence was keen. He rose, his eyes upon the stranger's eyes.

"My horse is mine," he observed. "Only my friends permit themselves liberties with what is mine."

The other smiled scornfully and drew from his belt a little pouch of gold dust.

"What I take I pay for," he remarked, and, still smiling, tendered Felipe a few grains of the gold.

Felipe struck the outstretched palm.

"Am I a *peon?*" he vociferated.

"Probably," retorted the other.

"I *will* take pay for that word," cried Felipe, his face blazing, "but not in your money, señor."

"In that case I may give you more than you ask."

"No, by God, for I shall take all you have."

But the other checked his retort. A sudden change came over him.

"I ask the señor's pardon," he said, with grave earnestness, "for provoking him. You may not fight with me nor I with you. I speak the truth. I have made oath not to fight till I have killed one whom now I seek."

"Very well; I, too, spoke without reflection. You seek an enemy, then, señor?"

"My sister's, who is therefore mine. An enemy truly. Listen, you shall judge. I am absent from my home a year, and when I return, what do I find? My sister betrayed, deceived, flouted by a fellow, a nobody, whom she received a guest in her house, a fit return for kindness, for hospitality! Well, he answers to me for the dishonor."

"Wait. Stop!" interposed Felipe. "Your name, señor."

"Unzar Ytuerate, and my enemy is called Arillaga. Him I seek and—"

"Then you shall seek no further!" shouted Felipe. "It is to Rubia Ytuerate, your sister, whom I owe all my unhappiness, all my suffering. She has hurt not me only, but one—but— Mother of God, we waste words!" he cried. "Knife to knife, Unzar Ytuerate. I am Felipe Arillaga, and may God be thanked for the chance that brings this quarrel to my hand."

"You! You!" gasped Unzar. Fury choked him; his hands clutched and unclutched—now fists, now claws. His teeth grated sharply while a quivering sensation as of a chill crisped his flesh. "Then the sooner the better," he muttered between his set teeth, and the knives flashed in the hands of the two men so suddenly that the gleam of one seemed only the reflection of the other.

Unzar held out his left wrist.

"Are you willing?" he demanded, with a significant glance.

"And ready," returned the other, baring his forearm.

Catala, keeper of the inn, was called.

"Love of the Virgin, not here, señors. My house—the *alcalde*—"

"You have a strap there." Unzar pointed to a bridle hanging from a peg by the doorway. "No words; quick; do as you are told."

The two men held out their left arms till wrist touched wrist, and Catala, trembling and protesting, lashed them together with a strap.

"Tighter," commanded Felipe; "put all your strength to it."

The strap was drawn up to another hole.

"Now, Catala, stand back," commanded Unzar, "and count three slowly. At the word 'three,' Señor Arillaga, we begin. You understand?"

"I understand."

"Ready. . . . Count."

"One."

Felipe and Unzar each put his right hand grasping the knife behind his back as etiquette demanded.

"Two."

They strained back from each other, the full length of their left arms, till the nails grew bloodless.

"*Three!*" called Lopez Catala in a shaking voice.

III

RUBIA

When Felipe regained consciousness he found that he lay in an upper chamber of Catala's inn upon a bed. His shoulder, the right one, was bandaged, and so was his head. He felt no pain, only a little weak, but there was a comfortable sense of brandy at his lips, an arm supported his head, and the voice of Rubia Ytuerate spoke his name. He sat up on a sudden.

"Rubia, *you!*" he cried. "What is it? What happened? Oh, I remember, Unzar—we fought. Oh, my God, how we fought! But you— What brought you here?"

"Thank Heaven," she murmured, "you are better. You are not so badly wounded. As he fell he must have dragged you with him, and your head struck the threshold of the doorway."

"Is he badly hurt? Will he recover?"

"I hope so. But *you* are safe."

"But what brought you here?"

"Love," she cried; "my love for you. What I suffered after you had gone! Felipe, I have fought, too. Pride was strong at first, and it was pride that made me send Unzar after you. I told him what had happened. I hounded him to hunt you down. Then when he had gone my battle began. Ah, dearest, dearest, it all came back, our days together, the life we led, knowing no other word but love, thinking no thoughts that were not of each other. And love conquered. Unzar was not a week gone before I followed him— to call him back, to shield you, to save you from his fury. I came all but too late, and found you both half dead. My brother and my lover, your body across his, your blood mingling with his own. But not too late to love you back to life again. Your life is mine now, Felipe. I love you, I love you." She clasped her hands together and pressed them to her cheek. "Ah, if you knew," she cried; "if you could only look into my heart. Pride is nothing, good name is nothing; friends are nothing. Oh, it is a glory to give them all for love, to give up everything; to surrender, to submit, to cry to one's heart: 'Take me; I am as wax. Take me; conquer me; lead me wherever you will. All is well lost so only that love remains.' And I have heard all that has happened—this other one, the Señorita Buelna, how that she forbade you her lands. Let her go; she is not worthy of your love, cold, selfish—"

"Stop!" cried Felipe, "you shall say no more evil of her. It is enough."

"Felipe, you love her yet?"

"And always, always will."

"She who has cast you off; she who disdains you, who will not suffer you on her lands? And have *you* come to be so low, so base and mean as that?"

"I have sunk no lower than a woman who could follow after a lover who had grown manifestly cold."

"Ah," she answered sadly, "if I could so forget my pride as to follow you, do not think your reproaches can touch me now." Then suddenly she sank at the bedside and clasped his hand in both of hers. Her beautiful hair, unbound, tumbled about her shoulders; her eyes, swimming with tears, were turned up to his; her lips trembled with the intensity of her passion. In a voice low, husky, sweet as a dove's she addressed him. "Oh, dearest, come back to me; come back to me. Let me love you again. Don't you see my heart is breaking? There is only you in all the world for me. I was a proud woman once. See now what I have brought myself to. Don't let it all be in vain. If you fail me now, think how it will be for me afterward—to know that I—I, Rubia Ytuerate, have begged the love of a man and begged in vain. Do you think I could live knowing that?" Abruptly she lost control of herself. She caught him about the neck with both her arms. Almost incoherently her words rushed from her tight-shut teeth.

"Ah, I can *make* you love me. I can make you love me," she cried. "You shall come back to me. You are mine, and you can not help but come back."

"*Por Dios,* Rubia," he ejaculated, "remember yourself. You are out of your head."

"Come back to me; love me."

"No, no."

"Come back to me."

"No."

"You can not push me from you," she cried, for, one hand upon her shoulder, he had sought to disengage himself. "No, I shall not let you go. You shall not push me from you! Thrust me off and I will embrace you all the closer. Yes, *strike* me if you will, and I will kiss you."

And with the words she suddenly pressed her lips to his.

Abruptly Felipe freed himself. A new thought suddenly leaped to his brain.

"Let your own curse return upon you," he cried. "You yourself have freed me; you yourself have broken the barrier you raised between me and my betrothed. You cursed her whose lips should next touch mine, and you are poisoned with your own venom."

He sprang from off the bed, and, catching up his *serape*, flung it about his shoulders."

"Felipe," she cried, "Felipe, where are you going?"

"Back to Buelna," he shouted, and with the words rushed from the room. Her strength seemed suddenly to leave her. She sank lower to the floor, burying her face deep upon the pillows that yet retained the impress of him she loved so deeply, so recklessly.

Footsteps in the passage and a knocking at the door aroused her. A woman, one of the escort who had accompanied her, entered hurriedly.

"Señorita," cried this one, "your brother, the Señor Unzar, he is dying."

Rubia hurried to an adjoining room, where upon a mattress on the floor lay her brother.

"Put that woman out," he gasped as his glance met hers. "I never sent for her," he went on. "You are no longer sister of mine. It was you who drove me to this quarrel, and when I have vindicated you what do you do? Your brother you leave to be tended by hirelings, while all your thought and care are lavished on your paramour. Go back to him. I know how to die alone, but as you go remember that in dying I hated and disowned you."

He fell back upon the pillows, livid, dead.

Rubia started forward with a cry.

"It is you who have killed him," cried the woman who had summoned her. The rest of Rubia's escort, *vaqueros, peons,* and the old *alcalde* of her native village, stood about with bared heads.

"That is true. That is true," they murmured. The old *alcalde* stepped forward.

"Who dishonors my friend dishonors me," he said. "From this day, Señorita Ytuerate, you and I are strangers." He went out, and one by one, with sullen looks and hostile demeanor, Rubia's escort followed. Their manner was unmistakable; they were deserting her.

Rubia clasped her hands over her eyes.

"Madre de Dios, Madre de Dios," she moaned over and over again. Then in a low voice she repeated her own words: "May it be a blight to her. From that moment may evil cling to her, bad luck follow her; may she love and not be loved; may friends desert her, her sisters shame her, her brothers disown her—"

There was a clatter of a horse's hoofs in the courtyard.

"It is your lover," said her woman coldly from the doorway. "He is riding away from you."

"—and those," added Rubia, "whom she has loved abandon her."

IV

BUELNA

MEANWHILE Felipe, hatless, bloody, was galloping through the night, his pony's head turned toward the *hacienda* of Martiarena. The Rancho Martiarena lay between his own rancho and the inn where he had met Rubia, so that this distance was not great. He reached it in about an hour of vigorous spurring.

The place was dark, though it was as yet early in the night, and an ominous gloom seemed to hang about the house. Felipe, his heart sinking, pounded at the door, and at last aroused the aged superintendent, who was also a sort of *major-domo* in the house-hold, and who in Felipe's boyhood had often ridden him on his knee.

"Ah, it is you, Arillaga," he said very sadly, as the moonlight struck across Felipe's face. "I had hoped never to see you again."

"Buelna," demanded Felipe. "I have something to say to her, and to the *padron.*"

"Too late, señor."

"My God, dead?"

"As good as dead."

"Rafael, tell me all. I have come to set everything straight again. On my honor, I have been misjudged. Is Buelna well?"

"Listen. You know your own heart best, señor. When you left her our little lady was as one half dead; her heart died within her. Ah, she loved you, Arillaga, far more than you deserved. She dropped swiftly, and one night all but passed away. Then it was that she made a vow that if God spared her life she would become the bride of the church—would forever renounce the world. Well, she recovered, became almost well again, but not the same as before. She never will be that. So soon as she was able to obtain Mar-tiarena's consent she made all the preparations—signed away all her lands and possessions, and spent the days and nights in prayer and purifications. The Mother Superior of the Convent of Santa Teresa has been a guest at the *hacienda* this fortnight past. Only to-day the party—that is to say, Martiarena, the Mother Superior and Buelna—left for Santa Teresa, and at midnight of this very night Buelna takes the veil. You know your own heart, Señor Felipe. Go your way."

"But not *till* midnight!" cried Felipe.

"What? I do not understand."

"She will not take the veil till midnight."

"No, not till then."

"Rafael," cried Felipe, "ask me no questions now. Only *believe* me. I always have and always will love Buelna. I swear it. I can stop this yet; only once let me reach her in time. Trust me. Ah, for this once trust me, you who have known me since I was a lad."

He held out his hand. The other for a moment hesitated, then impulsively clasped it in his own.

"*Bueno,* I trust you then. Yet I warn you not to fool me twice."

"Good," returned Felipe. "And now *adios.* Unless I bring her back with me you'll never see me again."

"But, Felipe, lad, where away now?"

"To Santa Teresa."

"You are mad. Do you fancy you can reach it before midnight?" insisted the *major-domo*.

"I *will*, Rafael; I *will*."

"Then Heaven be with you."

But the old fellow's words were lost in a wild clatter of hoofs, as Felipe swung his pony around and drove home the spurs. Through the night came back a cry already faint:

"*Adios, adios.*"

"*Adios,* Felipe," murmured the old man as he stood bewildered in the doorway, "and your good angel speed you now."

When Felipe began his ride it was already a little after nine. Could he reach Santa Teresa before midnight? The question loomed grim before him, but he answered only with the spur. Pépe was hardy, and, as Felipe well knew, of indomitable pluck. But what a task now lay before the little animal! He might do it, but oh! it was a chance!

In a quarter of a mile Pépe had settled to his stride, the dogged, even gallop that Felipe knew so well, and at half-past ten swung through the main street of Piedras Blancas—silent, somnolent, dark.

"Steady, little Pépe," said Felipe; "steady, little one. Soh, soh. There."

The little horse flung back an ear, and Felipe could feel along the lines how he felt for the bit, trying to get a grip of it to ease the strain on his mouth.

The *De Profundis* bell was sounding from the church tower as Felipe galloped through San Anselmo, the next village, but by the time he raised the lights of Arcata it was black night in very earnest. He set his teeth. Terra Bella lay eight miles further ahead, and here from the town-hall clock that looked down upon the plaza he would be able to know the time.

"*Hoopa, Pépe; pronto!*" he shouted.

The pony responded gallantly. His head was low; his ears, in constant movement, twitched restlessly back and forth, now laid flat on his neck, now cocked to catch the rustle of the wind in the chaparral, the scurrying of a rabbit or ground-owl through the sage.

It grew darker, colder, the trade-wind lapsed away. Low in the sky upon the right a pale, dim belt foretold the rising of the moon. The incessant galloping of the pony was the only sound.

The convent toward which he rode was just outside the few scattered huts in the valley of the Rio Esparto that by charity had been invested with the name of Caliente. From Piedras Blancas to Caliente between twilight and midnight! What a riding! Could he do it? Would Pépe last under him?

"Steady, little one. Steady, Pépe."

Thus he spoke again and again, measuring the miles in his mind, husbanding the little fellow's strength.

Lights! Cart lanterns? No, Terra Bella. A great dog charged out at him from a 'dobe, filling the night with outcry; a hayrick loomed by like a ship careening through fog; there was a smell of chickens and farmyards. Then a paved street, an open square, a solitary pedestrian dodging just in time from under Pépe's hoofs. All flashed by. The open country again, unbroken darkness again, and solitude of the fields again. Terra Bella past.

But through the confusion Felipe retained one picture, that of the moon-faced clock with hands marking the hour of ten. On again with Pépe leaping from the touch of the spur. On again up the long, shallow slope that rose for miles to form the divide that overlooked the valley of the Esparto.

"Hold, there! Madman to ride thus. Mad or drunk. Only desperadoes gallop at night. Halt and speak!"

The pony had swerved barely in time, and behind him the Monterey stage lay all but ditched on the roadside, the driver fulminating oaths. But Felipe gave him but an instant's thought. 'Dobe huts once more abruptly ranged up on either side the roadway, staggering and dim under the night. Then a wine-shop noisy with carousing *peons* darted by. Pavements again. A shop-front or two. A pig snoring in the gutter, a dog howling in a yard, a cat lamenting on a rooftop. Then the smell of fields again. Then darkness again. Then the solitude of the open country. Cadenassa past.

But now the country road changed. The slope grew steeper; it was the last lift of land to the divide. The road was sown with stones and scored with ruts. Pépe began to blow; once he groaned. Perforce his speed diminished. The villages were no longer so thickly spread now. The crest of the divide was wild, desolate, forsaken. Felipe again and again searched the darkness for lights, but the night was black.

Then abruptly the moon rose. By that Felipe could guess the time. His heart sank, he halted, recinched the saddle, washed the pony's mouth with brandy from his flask, then mounted and spurred on.

Another half-hour went by. He could see that Pépe was in distress; his speed was by degrees slacking Would he last? Would he last? Would the minutes that raced at his side win in that hard race?

Houses again. Plastered fronts. All dark and gray. No soul stirring. Sightless windows stared out upon the emptiness. The plaza bared its desolation to the pitiless moonlight. Only from an unseen window a guitar hummed and tinkled. All vanished. Open country again. The solitude of the fields again; the moonlight sleeping on the vast sweep of the ranchos. Calpella past.

Felipe rose in his stirrups with a great shout. At Calpella he knew he had crossed the divide. The valley lay beneath him, and the moon was turning to silver the winding courses of the Rio Esparto, now in plain sight.

It was between Calpella and Proberta that Pépe stumbled first. Felipe pulled him up and ceased to urge him to his topmost speed. But five hundred yards further he stumbled again. The spume-flakes he tossed from the bit were bloody. His breath came in laboring gasps.

But by now Felipe could feel the rising valley-mists; he could hear the piping of the frogs in the marshes. The ground for miles had sloped downward. He was not far from the river, not far from Caliente, not far from the Convent of Santa Teresa and Buelna.

But the way to Caliente was roundabout, distant. If he should follow the road thither he would lose a long half-hour. By going directly across the country from where he now was, avoiding Proberta, he could save much distance and precious time. But in this case Pépe, exhausted, stumbling, weak, would have to swim the river. If he failed to do this, Felipe would probably drown. If he succeeded, Caliente and the convent would be close at hand.

For a moment Felipe hesitated, then suddenly made up his mind. He wheeled Pépe from the road, and calling upon his last remaining strength, struck off across the country.

The sound of the river at last came to his ears.

"Now, then, Pépe," he cried.

For the last time the little horse leaped to the sound of his voice. Still at a gallop, Felipe cut the cinches of the heavy saddle, shook his feet clear of the stirrups, and let it fall to the ground; his coat, belt

and boots followed. Bareback, with but the headstall and bridle
left upon the pony, he rode at the river.

Before he was ready for it Pépe's hoofs spashed on the banks.
Then the water swirled about his fetlocks; then it wet Felipe's bare
ankles. In another moment Felipe could tell by the pony's motion
that his feet had left the ground and that he was swimming in the
middle of the current.

He was carried down the stream more than one hundred yards.
Once Pépe's legs became entangled in a sunken root. Freed from
that, his hoofs caught in grasses and thick weeds. Felipe's knee
was cut against a rock; but at length the pony touched ground. He
rose out of the river trembling, gasping and dripping. Felipe put
him at the steep bank. He took it bravely, scrambled his way—almost on his knees—to the top, then stumbled badly and fell prone
upon the ground.

Felipe twisted from under him as he fell and regained his feet
unhurt. He ran to the brave little fellow's head.

"Up, up, my Pépe. Soh, soh."

Suddenly he paused, listening. Across the level fields there came
to his ears the sound of the bell of the convent of Santa Teresa
tolling for midnight.

.   .   .   .

Upon the first stroke of midnight the procession of nuns entered
the nave of the church. There were some thirty in the procession.
The first ranks swung censers; those in the rear carried lighted
candles. The Mother Superior and Buelna, the latter wearing a
white veil, walked together. The youngest nun followed these two,
carrying upon her outspread palms the black veil.

Arrived before the altar the procession divided into halves,
fifteen upon the east side of the chancel, fifteen upon the west. The
organ began to drone and murmur, the censers swung and smoked,
the candle-flames flared and attracted the bats that lived among the
rafters overhead. Buelna knelt before the Mother Superior. She
was pale and a little thin from fasting and the seclusion of the cells.
But, try as she would, she could not keep her thoughts upon the
solemn office in which she was so important a figure. Other days
came back to her. A little girl gay and free once more, she romped
through the hallways and kitchen of the old *hacienda* 'Martiarena
with her playmate, the young Felipe; a young schoolgirl, she rode
with him to the Mission to the instruction of the *padre;* a young
woman, she danced with him at the *fête* of All Saints at Monterey.

Why had it not been possible that her romance should run its appointed course to a happy end? That last time she had seen him how strangely he had deported himself. Untrue to her! Felipe! Her Felipe; her more than brother! How vividly she recalled the day. They were returning from the Mission, where she had prayed for his safe and speedy return. Long before she had seen him she heard the gallop of a horse's hoofs around the turn of the road. Yes, she remembered that—the gallop of a horse. Ah! how he rode—how vivid it was in her fancy. Almost she heard the rhythmic beat of the hoofs. They came nearer, nearer. Fast, furiously fast hoof-beats. How swift he rode. Gallop, gallop—nearer, on they came. They were close by. They swept swiftly nearer, nearer. What—what was this? No fancy. Nearer, nearer. No fancy this. Nearer, nearer. These—ah, Mother of God—are real hoof-beats. They are coming; they are at hand; they are at the door of the church; they are *here!*

She sprang up, facing around. The ceremony was interrupted. The frightened nuns were gathering about the Mother Superior. The organ ceased, and in the stillness that followed all could hear that furious gallop. On it came, up the hill, into the courtyard. Then a shout, hurried footsteps, the door swung in, and Felipe Arillaga, ragged, dripping, half fainting, hatless and stained with mud, sprang toward Buelna. Forgetting all else, she ran to meet him, and, clasped in each other's arms, they kissed one another upon the lips again and again.

The bells of Santa Teresa that Felipe had heard that night on the banks of the Esparto rang for a wedding the next day.

Two days after they tolled as passing bells. A beautiful woman had been found drowned in a river not far from the house of Lopez Catala, on the highroad to Monterey.

THE END